THE PENGUIN CLASSICS

FOUNDER EDITOR (1944–64): E. V. RIEU

ZOLA: LA BÊTE HUMAINE

ÉMILE ZOLA, born in Paris in 1840, was brought up at Aix-en-Provence in an atmosphere of struggling poverty after the death of his father in 1847. He was educated at the Collège Bourbon at Aix and then at the Lycée Saint-Louis in Paris. He was obliged to exist in poorly paid clerical jobs after failing his *baccalauréat* in 1859 but early in 1865 he decided to support himself by literature alone. Despite his scientific pretensions Zola was really an emotional writer with rare gifts for evoking vast crowd scenes and for giving life to such great symbols of modern civilization as factories and mines. When not overloaded with detail, his work has tragic grandeur, but he is also capable of a coarse, 'Cockney' type of humour. *L'Assommoir*, arguably his masterpiece, has both in full measure. From his earliest days Zola had contributed critical articles to various newspapers, but his first important novel, *Thérèse Raquin*, was published in 1867, and *Madeleine Férat* in the following year. That same year he began work on a series of novels intended to follow out scientifically the effects of heredity and environment on one family: *Les Rougon-Macquart*. The work contains twenty novels which appeared between 1871 and 1893, and is the chief monument of the French Naturalist Movement. On completion of this series he began a new cycle of novels, *Les Trois Villes: Lourdes, Rome, Paris* (1894–6–8), a violent attack on the Church of Rome, which led to another cycle, *Les Quatre Évangiles*. He died in 1902 while working on the fourth of these.

LEONARD TANCOCK has spent most of his life in or near London, exceptions being a year as a student in Paris, most of the 1939–45 war in Wales, and three periods in American universities as visiting professor. He is a Fellow of University College, London, and was formerly Reader in French at the university. Since preparing his first Penguin Classic in 1949 he has been intensely interested in problems of translation, which he believes is an art rather than a science. His numerous translations for the Penguin Classics include Zola's *Germinal*, *Thérèse Raquin*, *The Debacle* and *L'Assommoir*; Diderot's *The Nun*, *Rameau's Nephew* and *D'Alembert's Dream*; Maupassant's *Pierre and Jean*; Marivaux's *Up from the Country*; Constant's *Adolphe*; La Rochefoucauld's *Maxims*; Voltaire's *Letters on England*; and Madame de Sevigné's *Selected Letters*.

ÉMILE ZOLA

LA BÊTE HUMAINE

TRANSLATED
WITH AN INTRODUCTION BY
LEONARD TANCOCK

PENGUIN BOOKS

Penguin Books Ltd, Harmondsworth, Middlesex, England
Viking Penguin Inc., 40 West 23rd Street, New York, New York 10010, U.S.A.
Penguin Books Australia Ltd, Ringwood, Victoria, Australia
Penguin Books Canada Ltd, 2801 John Street, Markham, Ontario, Canada L3R 1B4
Penguin Books (N.Z.) Ltd, 182–190 Wairau Road, Auckland 10, New Zealand

—

This translation first published 1977
Reprinted 1978, 1980, 1981, 1982, 1984

—

—

Set, printed and bound in Great Britain by
Cox & Wyman Ltd, Reading
Set in Intertype Times

CONTENTS

Introduction   7
La Bête humaine   19

INTRODUCTION

La Bête humaine, the seventeenth of the twenty novels in the Rougon-Macquart cycle, the full title of which is *Les Rougon-Macquart. Histoire naturelle et sociale d'une famille sous le Second-Empire*, was written during 1889 and published in book form in March 1890, although it had been appearing in serial form during the winter. It is in some ways one of Zola's most violent and pessimistic novels, haunted by the theory he held at this stage of his career that 'love and death, possessing and killing, are the dark foundations of the human soul.' It is characteristic of the series as a whole that this sombre, frightening book should follow *Le Rêve*, Zola's nearest approach to the spiritual and other-worldly, which in its turn had followed the bestial *La Terre*. But this one lacks even the coarse high spirits that make Zola's epic of the soil a very distant ancestor of *Clochemerle*.

Yet in reality *La Bête humaine* is far more than a mere sex-and-murder thriller, though it certainly is that. It is a curious hybrid of two quite different themes. The first theme is also in a sense double, a study of homicide but also of the French judicial system, its corruption and inherent weakness; and the second is an interesting tale of the world of railways, the organization and running of a main line and the life of its employees. To discover how it came about that such a mixture became necessary in Zola's scheme, one must look back at the remote origins of the two themes which had been interesting him for some twenty years.

Already in his original plan of 1868 Zola had projected a novel on the murderer as a type of personality, an unbalanced person doomed by his heredity to have a criminal mentality and to be a homicidal maniac. Linked to this, of course, are such matters as environment, moral responsibility, emotional pressures, inextricable situations that can be settled only by death.

7

These things were to be the subject of a novel, just as coal-mining and labour troubles were to be that of *Germinal*, or farming and agrarian politics that of *La Terre*. At this early stage the hero, if such he could be called, was to be a son of Gervaise Macquart and her lover Lantier, the same Étienne (though the names were not yet settled) who was to be the hero of *Germinal*. Inevitably linked with the study of murder and the criminal psychopath must be that of the law and the functioning of justice, and this raised a general principle as important in the modern world of the late twentieth century as it was in France in Zola's time. It is this: how can truth, impartiality, justice, exist if the legal profession is in any way subject to pressure or even influence from vested interests, and above all from political parties or the government itself? And this peril is aggravated if the rewards of legal office are insufficient to put a judge beyond the reach of personal financial worry or ambition.

It has always been a weakness of the French system that magistrates and judges have been virtually ill-paid employees of the government, and thus the promotion or relegation of a magistrate has depended upon the government of the day. In such a system a judge or magistrate is exposed to all sorts of pressures, threats and bribes, and justice itself is subject to political interference and ideological distortion. We have seen it happen with appalling results in some European countries in the past fifty years, and in this respect the American system is not above criticism, at least in State legislatures, if not in Federal, for high legal and police officials can be appointed or dismissed by the reigning political party, and an electoral change can change the personnel of justice and even therefore reverse 'justice' itself. In Britain, quaint and cumbersome though our legal system may appear to some, law officers have so far been comparatively free from corruption and political interference, but today there are very ominous signs that this may not always be so. Zola's views on all this were not to crystallize until the mid 1880s, for reasons that will be seen later, but it is interesting that one of the main themes in this novel – a scandalous crime involving a person in a respected profession, the closing of ranks in that profession to protect the reputation of the victim and ward off political repercussions, and to that end the finding of

8

an innocent scapegoat and manipulation or suppression of evidence – is, with a few obvious differences, a prefiguration of the Dreyfus affair in which Zola was destined to play a spectacular part some ten years later.

But we also learn from letters, interviews and the testimony of friends that certainly from the late 1870s Zola projected a novel on railways and railwaymen. We know from Paul Alexis, his friend and first biographer, that by 1882 Zola was contemplating a novel on railway life, a great part of which would be set at or near some lonely level crossing, with the procession of the outer world rushing ceaselessly and heedlessly by. By 1884 both Louis Desprez and Edmond de Goncourt, reporting conversations with Zola about his projects for the remainder of the series, mention a novel on railways, with Étienne Lantier as the central figure, playing itself out in a setting of great termini, depots, smoke, steam and noise. Given Zola's meticulous concern with topographical accuracy and insistence wherever possible on examining the sites for himself, it is not surprising that he should choose the line he knew intimately and used frequently, the main Paris (Saint-Lazare)–Rouen–Normandy route; for, from 1878 onwards, he spent much of his time in the country house originally bought with money made by the huge success of *L'Assommoir* and later considerably enlarged from the proceeds of other successes. This house (now a Zola museum) is at Médan, a village on the left bank of the Seine between Poissy and Meulan, some twenty-five miles from Paris. Between Paris and Mantes there is a line following each bank of the river, but the one on the left, or west, bank runs between the bottom of Zola's garden and the river, and that is the one described in Chapter 8.

Well into the 1880s Zola still had in mind these two distinct novels, the one on crime and the law and the other on railway life, and he was taking notes on both subjects. He was much impressed by his reading in a French translation of the work of the Italian criminologist Cesare Lombroso (*L'Homme criminel*, 1887), whose theory that the criminal is psychologically a distinct and abnormal type tallied admirably with the basis of his own Rougon-Macquart work, which was that each one of us is formed and predestined by his own inherited traits, both physical and moral; our heredity is our doom. All this endorsed his idea that the criminal type he was to study must belong to the vitiated, alcoholic, 'tainted' branch of the family, the Macquarts, and this once again indicated a son of Gervaise.

It was at about this time that there occurred two sensational murders which served to crystallize Zola's vague ideas. In 1882 the wife of a chemist named Fenayron took an employee of her husband for a lover, the husband found out and forced his wife to help him lure the lover into an empty house and murder him. In January 1886 the Prefect of the Eure Department, M. Barrême, was murdered in the Cherbourg–Paris express, the murderer was never found, and of course all sorts of scandalous rumours were circulated and the story was pounced upon by the political parties in the way party politicians have of making party capital out of everything, the dirtier the better. Zola will write in his working notes for the novel: 'It would be the Fenayron case complicated by the Barrême one.' Here was his material for the murder of a highly-placed, politically protected person in revenge for a sordid sexual adventure in his past, and the efforts of a government-controlled legal profession to hush up the scandal by any means, fair or foul. Moreover, the Barrême case was to provide the link with the railway world which had now become necessary for another reason.

The sixteenth Rougon-Macquart novel, *Le Rêve*, appeared in 1888. That left only four to be done to complete the projected twenty, and of these four three were definitely planned: one on the world of high finance, centred on the Paris Bourse (*L'Argent*); one on the catastrophe of the Franco-Prussian war of 1870, which would complete the 'social' matter of the saga with the fall of the Second Empire (*La Débâcle*); and a final volume to account for the outstanding members of the families and thus conclude the 'natural' part of the subject (*Le Docteur Pascal*). And so there was room for only one more novel, and for years he had been turning two over in his mind. By November 1888 he had decided to solve the problem by fusing the two subjects into one novel. He wrote to his friend Van Santen

10

Kolff in that month: 'I shall probably place some terrible drama in a railway setting – a study of crime with a look at the magistracy...'

So far so good, but this decision at once brought its own problems. For many years he had intended to use a son of Gervaise Macquart, and Étienne was the only one available, since Gervaise's other son Claude (the two little boys of the opening of *L'Assommoir*) had before this become a half-crazy artistic genius and killed himself (*L'Œuvre*). But Étienne had worked out quite differently in *Germinal* and become, if not exactly admirable, at least a serious, stable and honest man. To make him an engine-driver and psychopathic murderer, with no reference to his earlier life and career, would be ridiculous not only psychologically but also chronologically. The action of *Germinal* had opened when Étienne was twenty-one, in 1867. To have the same man a fully fledged express-driver, after years of apprenticeship, at exactly the same time, would be ludicrous, since the action of the new novel must end with the outbreak of war in 1870. Yet Zola had to have his central figure cursed with the hereditary taint of his family, fighting against it as a man but doomed to succumb to it as a beast.

So nearly twenty years after his original plan Zola was obliged to get himself out of the muddle by inventing a third son of Gervaise and Lantier, born between Claude and Étienne, and modifying his famous genealogical tree accordingly. Not that this was the first afterthought of Zola, for in order to have a foundling girl for heroine of *Le Rêve* he had had to invent a child born mysteriously to Sidonie Rougon and suggest that the father was a priest. One little muddle remained, however, for we are told, on Jacques's first appearance in the novel, which must be in February 1869, that he was just twenty-six, whereas the genealogical tree says he was born in 1844. These chronological inconsistencies are not infrequent in Zola (e.g. variations in the age of old Bonnemort in the course of *Germinal*), which is strange in so conscientious an author.

The hybrid nature of this twin-subject novel means that unlike so many of his others, that play themselves out in one very limited environment which in itself is a 'character' in the novel, the action darts from place to place and from mood to mood, from sex to violence to the running of a railway, from lawyers' offices to the desolate countryside. The technique is that of the thriller, with a certain speciousness of construction, exploitation of suspense, holding back of climaxes and inevitable simplicity of characterization. In some elements of the plot, as well as in his use of the horrible and macabre, Zola harks back to the first successful novel he ever wrote, *Thérèse Raquin*. What better setting could be found for a thriller of this kind than the railway, especially in the late nineteenth century, when railways were the most modern form of rapid transport and railway stories played more or less the role of science fiction today? Accidents, sabotage, crimes and dramas were all to hand with material for Zola's speciality, powerful descriptive and 'atmospheric' passages – the bustle and confusion of stations, the eerie horror of tunnels, the engineman's battle on the footplate against wind, rain and snow. The vital links between the two subjects are the two principal women, Séverine and Flore, both victims of the murdered magistrate, the first directly and the second through her sister, both dependent upon the railway for their living, both rivals for the love of the same railwayman.

But the unity Zola thus imposes upon his two themes is unnecessarily complicated by his imposing over and above all this his 'scientific' interest in different types of killers. He strains one's credulity by making almost every important character a killer or potential killer – Grandmorin, Roubaud, Séverine, Jacques, Misard, Flore and even Pecqueux. Much of this complication comes from Zola's having had to invent a personal history for his hero Jacques Lantier, who has never been known to exist until now. As a child of seven, we learn, he was left at Plassans, in the south of France, when his mother Gervaise ran away to Paris at the age of twenty-two with her lover Lantier and the other two boys, and his parents never bothered about him again, which is not surprising, as within a few weeks of their departure they were involved in the long tragedy of *L'Assommoir*. Jacques was brought up by a relation on the Lantier side, whom he called Aunt Phasie. It was only because of the highly improbable remarriage of Phasie to the odious

Misard, a railway employee stationed at a section point on a lonely stretch of line in Normandy, that Jacques, now an engine-driver, again met Flore whom he had not seen since she was a little girl. Given all this it is simple to bring all the threads and themes together in this one wild piece of chalky, wooded hill-country and to work them together into a tragic dénouement.

Thanks to these manœuvrings, Zola can let the reader watch several quite different types of murder: the man who kills in a blind rage of sexual jealousy, the cold, slow poisoner after his victim's money, the psychopath whose decent, reasonable side struggles in vain against his hereditary predisposition, and various sub-species such as the woman maddened by passion or jealousy or the man with a grievance turned into a brute by alcohol. Of course some of the apparent speciousness is less improbable when it is remembered that in any occupation or trade people inevitably live and work together in enforced propinquity.

It is not necessarily an adverse criticism of this novel to say that the characterization is simple. To begin with, subtle analysis of character is not one of Zola's interests or objects. On the contrary, he is at pains to show that in the modern world the mass, the crowd, is more significant than the individual, and that herd instincts and what is now called mass-psychology are depriving modern man of the means or even the will to think and act for himself. It is a fact of modern civilization, delightful or disastrous according to your political views. Zola had neither the wish nor the equipment to be a Stendhal or a Proust, but he can tell a story and can set it in unforgettable scenes and atmospheres, with an artist's eye for light, shade and colour. Moreover, his subject would be weakened and dissipated by too much analysis of character and motives. Such analysis as there is consists of the agonizing efforts of poor, trapped people to understand themselves.

Yet the main people in the tale are anything but puppets and lay figures. Zola is too sensible – and French – to suppose that there could exist unsuspected and inactive for a long time an entirely simple psychopathic murderer. Dracula is not a human being. It is true that Jack the Ripper existed in real life at about the time when Zola was writing his novel, but his identity was never discovered, so he proves nothing. Jacques is no simple maniac, but a tragic figure pursued by destiny, aware of his own fatal flaw of character, who struggles against it but is ultimately overtaken by his doom. Séverine is a little more complicated, but a recognizable Zola type, related to Catherine of *Germinal* or Françoise of *La Terre*, the girl brutally abused by the lust of men but still psychologically virgin until aroused by the one man she can love and who makes her blossom into full womanhood. Perverted as a girl by the elderly and disgusting Grandmorin and then married off by him to a man with the sexual delicacy of a bull, her very candour and single-minded devotion to her lover turn her into a Lady Macbeth urging him on to murder.

The others are simpler: Roubaud, the brutal, insensitive husband who, however, after murdering out of jealousy deteriorates into a kind of truculent apathy, Misard the obsessive miser and slow poisoner, Flore the woman scorned and seeking her revenge. But Cabuche has a long literary pedigree. He is typecast as the good, simple-minded victim, capable of dog-like devotion, turned by love into a shy, adoring giant. Not only is he the stock underdog of all romantic literature of the nineteenth century, the innocent working man victimized by society or those with more brains and fewer scruples – Victor Hugo's Jean Valjean is the archetype, and there are the countless heroes of serial novels such as those of Eugène Sue – but his ancestry goes back to Mauprat, George Sand's wild man of the woods and to the noble savage of the eighteenth century and the fountainhead of all such over-simplification into Right and Left, Them and Us, Jean-Jacques Rousseau.

But if some of these can be called types rather than fully drawn characters, the two members of the legal profession are far more interesting and delineated with considerable subtlety. Their relationship illustrates the danger to truth and justice of the system whereby the direction of a local examining magistrate's interrogations, and the shape of the case he prepares, can be manipulated by a highly-placed official in the so-called Ministry of Justice. Impartial justice is not possible when its conclusions are dictated by politicians for their own ends; the law is a farce if government departments can use it, bend it or ignore it as they like, as can be seen today in many if not most parts of the world. So M. Denizet's career is in the hands of M. Camy-Lamotte, whose cynicism is total and whose allegiance is to the party in power. But these two men are not mere examples of the iniquity of politically inspired legal procedure; they are both real men with individual characters. M. Denizet has in addition the besetting French tendency to construct elaborate and subtle edifices of pure theory upon the flimsiest foundations of intuition, prejudice or circumstantial evidence and then to defend them tenaciously out of intellectual vanity. He has built up a case against Cabuche because the latter is a rough, churlish type who has once before been convicted for violence and so must be guilty. He has made up his mind and so does not want to be disturbed by facts. Moreover, he fancies himself as a master psychologist, a man gifted with almost hypnotic power to force the truth out of anybody. Given his ambition and vanity he is as wax in the accomplished hands of M. Camy-Lamotte, representing political pressure, and M. Camy-Lamotte deliberately destroys vital evidence and condones the iniquitous conviction of an innocent man because (a) Séverine is a pretty woman, (b) Grandmorin was a friend of his and (c) political expediency requires it. The chapters in which these men appear are the subtlest in the book.

The descriptive art of this novel speaks for itself from the very opening scene, a view over the great station on a sunny but hazy winter afternoon, which illustrates as well as any other Zola's close affinity with the Impressionists, whose champion and personal friend he was. It immediately suggests Monet's celebrated paintings of the same station, and Monet also did one of a train in snow and another of the Pont de l'Europe, which plays quite a part in this story. Throughout there are masterly descriptions in the Impressionist style, that is to say without sharp outlines and shapes but with wonderful effects of light and shade, beams of light piercing the shadows, flickering lamps, often full of emotional or moral symbolism. All Zola's novels have symbols – things, buildings or scenes which seem to have a life of their own and exert a powerful influence, often malignant, upon powerless human beings. No symbol in Zola is more striking, more sinister or more fraught with prophetic meaning for our world today than the scene in the closing pages. A runaway troop train, without driver or fireman, goes careering on to certain disaster. The men in control, having abdicated their humanity and become beasts, have allowed the machine to take over and hurtle to destruction while the rest of the human cattle, concerned only to keep themselves from thinking, yell pop songs to pass the time.

A topographical note may be of interest. Every scene in this story is authentic except, obviously, the actual level crossing and house at La Croix-de-Maufras, and even these can be placed within a mile or two. All the places at the Paris end of the line really existed, and most can be seen today in the course of a fairly short walk. But the line immediately beyond the end of the platforms of the Gare Saint-Lazare has been changed in one important respect. After a few yards, then as now, the line ran under a huge iron bridge which formed, above the tracks themselves, a crossing of six roads each named after some great European city, as indeed are all the streets in the surrounding neighbourhood, which is known as the Quartier de l'Europe, and the bridge, which features in this novel, is the Europe bridge. North of the bridge the line narrowed and went into three tunnels, the Batignolles tunnels. The general layout was much like that just outside King's Cross Station, London, and the resulting bottleneck caused similar traffic problems and delays, but far worse in Paris because Saint-Lazare has always handled a dense suburban and commuter traffic. The situation became increasingly difficult over the years, and a project for widening the line was scheduled for 1914 but had to be shelved because of the war. Then in 1921 there was an appalling accident when trains collided in the tunnel and caught fire. It was then decided to demolish the Batignolles tunnels and open the line out into a deep cutting. I well remember seeing the huge job of demolition in progress when as a youth I made my first journey to Paris in 1923 via Newhaven–Dieppe. Since then the line out of Saint-Lazare has resembled that north of Liverpool, Lime Street, a long cutting lined with masonry.

A note on this translation. Technical vocabulary of a past age always places the translator in the same dilemma. He has to choose between being accurate, and therefore incomprehensible and boring to many modern readers, or being clearly understood but approximate or even slightly inaccurate and incurring the scorn of those who happen to know. But at the same time he has to try to reproduce the effect that the original text may have had upon its original readers, and it may have struck them as technical and boring, too. No doubt some of Balzac and Zola did. Fortunately much of the vocabulary of railways and steam locomotives is fairly self-explanatory. But one little example may help some readers who have no idea how the controls of a steam locomotive work. Jacques the driver, we are told, is constantly turning the reversing-wheel (*le volant de changement de marche*) while the engine is running at full speed ahead. With car-driving in mind some may well ask why any manipulation of the reversing-gear while travelling ahead does not wreck the machine. In very simple language, the wheel in the driver's cab adjusts the cut-off of steam to one end of the cylinder or the other, and thus the effort the engine puts out and the speed. Only when the reversing-wheel is turned through many revolutions does the admission of steam so to speak change ends and reverse the direction of travel. Adjustments of cut-off by slight turns of the wheel give exactly the same kind of control over effort and speed that the car-driver's foot has through the accelerator pedal.

The text used for this translation has been that in volume 6 of the *Œuvres complètes* of Émile Zola published under the general editorship of Henri Mitterand, Paris, Cercle du Livre Précieux, Fasquelle, 1967. The text in the paperback Livre de Poche edition is corrupt, with some grotesque misprints. For a critical appraisal of Zola, English-speaking readers are referred to F. W. J. Hemmings, *Émile Zola*, Oxford, Clarendon Press, 1966.

I am deeply grateful to my wife, not only for her unfailing help with the drudgery, but for criticism and advice often unpalatable but always salutary.

L.W.T.

1

ROUBAUD came into the room and put the pound loaf, pâté and bottle of white wine on the table. But that morning Ma Victoire, before going down to her job, must have banked up the fire in the stove with so much slack that the heat was stifling. So the deputy stationmaster opened the window and leaned out.

It was the last house on the right along the Impasse d'Amsterdam, a tall building used by the Western Railway Company as lodgings for some of its employees. The fifth-floor window, at the corner of the mansard roof, looked over the station, a wide trench cutting through the Europe district like a sudden broadening out of the view, an effect made the more striking that afternoon by a grey mid-February sky, a misty, warm greyness through which the sun was filtering.

Opposite, in this vapoury sunshine, the buildings in the rue de Rome seemed hazy, as though fading into air. To the left yawned the huge roofs spanning the station with their sooty glass; the eye could see under the enormous main-line span, which was separated from the smaller ones, those of the Argenteuil, Versailles and Circle lines, by the buildings of the foot-warmer depot and the mails. To the right the Europe bridge straddled the cutting with its star of girders, and the lines could be seen emerging beyond and going on as far as the Batignolles tunnel. And right below the window, filling the huge space, the three double lines from under the bridge fanned out into innumerable branches of steel and disappeared under the station roofs. In front of the arches the three pointsmen's posts looked like bare little gardens. Amid the confusion of carriages and engines crowding the lines, one big red signal shone through the thin daylight.

For a moment Roubaud looked at the scene with interest, comparing it with his own station at Le Havre. Each time he came like this for a day in Paris and stayed at Ma Victoire's, the job caught hold of him again. Below the roof over the main lines the arrival of a train from Mantes was causing a bustle on the platforms, and he watched the shunting engine, a little six-coupled tank with small wheels, as it began to take out the train, busy and fussy, pulling the carriages out and then backing them into the sidings. Another engine, a powerful four-coupled express, with big wheels for high speed, stood alone, its chimney sending up thick black smoke slow and straight in the still air. But then his whole attention was caught by the 3.25 Caen train, already full of passengers and waiting for its engine. He could not see that this was already standing beyond the Europe bridge, but could only hear it asking for the road with sharp little whistles like someone getting impatient. An order was shouted and the engine acknowledged with a short whistle that it had understood. Before it started there was a silence, then the steam-cocks were opened and the steam hissed along the ground in a deafening jet. Then he saw the white cloud billowing out from under the bridge, whirling like downy snow and flying through the iron lattice-work. A large area was turned into whiteness, while the lingering smoke from the other engine spread its black veil. Somewhere behind were long faint blasts on a horn, shouted orders and the clatter of turntables. A gap appeared and Roubaud made out in the background a Versailles train and one from Auteuil passing each other in opposite directions.

As he was about to leave the window, a voice calling his name made him lean out. He saw on the balcony of the fourth floor below him a young man of about thirty, Henri Dauvergne, a guard who lived there with his father, a deputy stationmaster on the main line side, and his two sisters, Claire and Sophie, charming blondes of eighteen and twenty who, on the six thousand francs from the two men, kept house in a continual burst of gaiety. He could hear the elder one laughing while the younger one was singing, her warblings rivalled by a cage of song-birds.

'Hallo, M. Roubaud, you in Paris? Oh yes, about your trouble with the Sub-Prefect!'

Leaning out once more, the deputy stationmaster explained that he had had to leave Le Havre that morning by the 6.40

express. He was summoned to Paris by an order from the traffic manager, and he had been severely hauled over the coals. He was lucky not to have lost his job.

'And Mme Roubaud?'

She had wanted to come with him to do some shopping. Her husband was expecting her now in the room that Ma Victoire gave them the key of whenever they came up, and in which they used to enjoy a quiet meal on their own while the good woman was occupied down there at her job of lavatory attendant. That day they had had a snack at Mantes so as to get their jobs out of the way first. But it was now gone three and he was dying of hunger.

Wanting to be pleasant, Henri asked another question:

'Are you staying the night in Paris?'

Oh no, they were both going back to Le Havre that evening by the 6.30 express. Some holiday this! They put you to all this trouble just to give you a telling-off, then straight back home!

The two employees gazed at each other for a moment, shaking their heads. But now they could not hear themselves speak, for a piano had burst forth madly into deafening noise. The two sisters must be banging away on it together, laughing louder and gingering up the song-birds. So the young man, catching the laughter as well, nodded and went back indoors, leaving Roubaud alone for a minute, looking down on the balcony from which all this youthful jollity was coming. Then he raised his eyes and saw the engine, which had shut off its steam-cocks and which the pointsman was sending down to the Caen train. The last flakes of white steam melted away into the thick clouds of black smoke dirtying the sky. Then he went inside too.

Roubaud made a despairing gesture at the cuckoo clock, which now said twenty past three. What the devil could be making Séverine so late? Once she got into a shop she never came out any more. To take his mind off the hunger pains in his stomach he thought he would lay the table. He knew this big room with two windows very well: it was bedroom, dining-room and kitchen all in one, with walnut furniture, bed with red cotton hangings, sideboard-cum-dresser, round table and Norman wardrobe. He took napkins, plates, knives and forks and two glasses out of the sideboard. Everything was spotlessly

21

clean, and he enjoyed these household jobs as though he were playing at dolls' tea-parties, delighted at the whiteness of the linen, very much in love with his wife, laughing to himself at the good old laugh she would burst into when she opened the door. But when he had put the pâté on a plate, with the bottle of wine on one side, he got puzzled and looked about him. Then he quickly took out of his pockets two little packages he had forgotten, a small tin of sardines and some Gruyère cheese.

It struck the half hour. Roubaud paced up and down the room, turning towards the staircase at the slightest sound. During this idle waiting about, finding himself in front of the mirror he stopped and looked at himself. He was showing no sign of age and, although he was nearly forty, the fiery red of his curly hair had not yet faded. His full beard was thick too and as fair as sunshine. Of medium height but extraordinarily vigorous, he liked the look of himself and was pleased with his rather flat head, low forehead, thick neck, round and fresh-coloured face in which shone a pair of big, keen eyes. His eyebrows met across his forehead, casting over it a shadow of jealousy. As he had married a woman fifteen years his junior he found reassurance in these frequent glances into the mirror.

There was a sound of footsteps, and Roubaud rushed and half opened the door, but it was one of the women on the station bookstall coming home to her room next door. So he went in again and had a look at a shell-covered box on the sideboard. He knew this box of old, for it was a present from Séverine to Ma Victoire, her foster-mother. This little trinket was all that was needed to remind him of the whole story of his marriage. Nearly three years already. He was a southerner, born in Plassans, the son of a carter, had come out of his national service with a sergeant's stripes, worked for a long time as a porter at Mantes station, then been promoted to head porter at Barentin, and that was where he had met his dear wife when she came from Doinville to catch the train with Mlle Berthe, daughter of President Grandmorin. Séverine Aubry was nothing more than the youngest child of a gardener who had died in the Grandmorins' employ, but the President, who was her godfather and guardian, had so spoiled her, making her his own daughter's companion, sending them both to the same boarding-school in Rouen, and she herself was so much a natural lady, that for a long while Roubaud had been content to worship her from afar, with the passion of a once uncouth workman for a delicate jewel that he knew was valuable. That was the only romance in his existence. He would have married her without a penny for the joy of having her, and when at last he plucked up his courage the reality had surpassed his dreams, for over and above Séverine and a dowry of ten thousand francs, the President, now in retirement and a member of the board of directors of the Western Railway Company, had taken him under his wing. Immediately after his marriage he had been promoted to deputy stationmaster at Le Havre. Of course he had been helped by reports that he was a good employee, reliable at his job, punctual, honest if not over-intelligent, which might explain the immediate acceptance of his proposal and the speed of his advancement. He preferred to think he owed it all to his wife. He worshipped her.

Having opened the tin of sardines, Roubaud got really impatient. They were to meet at three. Where could she be? Surely she couldn't tell him that it took the whole day to buy a pair of boots and half a dozen chemises. As he went past the mirror again, he noticed his beetling eyebrows and the hard frown on his forehead. He never had any suspicions at Le Havre, but in Paris he thought of all kinds of dangers, deceptions and misdeeds. The blood rushed up into his head and his fists, the fists of an ex-labourer, clenched themselves as they used to when he pushed trucks along. He became once again the brute unaware of his own strength, capable of pulverizing her in a fit of blind rage.

Séverine pushed open the door and came in all young and gay.

'Here I am ... I say, you must have thought I'd got lost.'

In the radiance of her five and twenty years she looked tall, slender and very lithe, yet well covered and small boned. She did not look pretty at first glance, with her long face and large mouth shining with wonderful teeth. But as you looked at her, she charmed you with the magic and strangeness of her big blue eyes beneath a mass of thick, black hair.

As her husband made no answer but went on examining her

with that worried and doubtful look she knew so well, she went on:

'Oh, I haven't half been running! You see, there wasn't a bus anywhere to be found. So as I didn't want to spend the money for a cab I just ran . . . Look how hot I am!'

'Come on,' he said angrily, 'you're not going to make me believe you've come just from the Bon Marché.'

All of a sudden, like a lovable child, she threw herself on his neck and put a pretty little plump hand over his mouth.

'Naughty, naughty, stop it! You know I love you.'

Her whole person gave out so much sincerity, and he felt she was still so candid and straightforward that he hugged her wildly. His suspicions always ended like this. She let herself go, loving to be petted. He smothered her with kisses which she did not return, and that was what made him vaguely uneasy – she was a big, passive child with a filial affection in which no passion was ever aroused.

'Well then, you must have cleaned out the Bon Marché.'

'Oh yes, I'll tell you all about it. But let's have some food first. Oh, I'm starving! By the way, I've got a little present for you. Say: "My little present, please." '

She laughed close to his face. She had her right hand deep in her pocket, holding something she wouldn't bring out.

'Say at once: "My little present, please." '

He laughed as well, like a good fellow, then made up his mind.

'My little present, please.'

It was a knife she had bought him to replace one he had lost and had been moaning about for a fortnight. He went into raptures and thought his lovely new knife was superb, with its ivory handle and gleaming blade. He would use it at once. She was delighted at his joy and jokingly made him give her a sou so as not to sever their friendship.

'Come on, let's have something to eat. No, no, please don't shut it yet, I'm so hot.'

She had joined him at the window, and stayed there a few seconds, leaning against his shoulder and looking down on the huge expanse of the station. The smoke had momentarily cleared, and the copper disc of the sun was setting in the haze behind the buildings in the rue de Rome. Down below a shunting engine was backing in the Mantes train, already made up and due out at 4.25. It pushed it up the platform under the roof and was uncoupled. On the far side the banging of buffers in the Circle Line station showed that some extra carriages were being put on unexpectedly. And alone in the middle of the lines, with its driver and fireman black with the dirt of the journey, stood the heavy engine of a slow train, looking weary and breathless, with only a thin wisp of steam rising from a valve. It was waiting for a clear road back to the Batignolles depot. A red signal vanished with a clack. The engine moved off.

'Aren't those Dauvergne girls having a time!' said Roubaud, coming away from the window. 'Just listen to them banging away on their piano! I saw Henri just now and he asked to be remembered to you.'

'Come on, let's start!' called Séverine.

She attacked the sardines and ate ravenously. Oh what a long time since the roll at Mantes! Coming to Paris always went to her head. She was all excited with the joy of being foot-loose on the pavements, and was still thrilled with her purchases at the Bon Marché. Every spring she spent the whole winter's savings at one go, preferring to buy everything there and saying that it saved enough to pay for the journey. And so she prattled on, but without losing a mouthful of food. In the end, a bit shame-faced and red, she let out the total sum she had spent, over three hundred francs.

'Gosh!' said Roubaud, staggered. 'You do dress well, don't you, for a deputy stationmaster's wife! But all you had to get was half a dozen chemises and a pair of boots.'

'Oh but, my dear, such wonderful bargains! A silk with gorgeous stripes! A hat with such style, a dream! Ready-made petticoats with embroidered flounces! And all for next to nothing. I would have paid twice as much in Le Havre . . . They're going to send them, and you'll see!'

He had decided to see the joke, for she was so pretty with her delight and her look of supplicating embarrassment. And besides, this improvised picnic was so charming, in this room they had all to themselves, much nicer than a restaurant. She usually drank just water, but now she let herself go and emptied her glass of white wine without noticing. The tin of sardines was empty and they started on the pàté with the grand new knife, which was a triumphant success, it cut so well.

'And now what about you and this business of yours?' she asked. 'You make me go on chattering and don't tell me how it went off, the business about the Sub-Prefect.'

So he told her the whole story of how the traffic manager had received him. Oh, a proper dressing-down! He had stood up for himself and told him the real truth, how that la-did-da Sub-Prefect had insisted on taking his dog into a first-class carriage when there was a second-class one reserved for huntsmen and their hounds, and how it had ended in a set-to and the words that had been exchanged. Anyway, the Manager had approved of his having tried to have the regulations enforced, but the terrible thing was the words he had owned up to himself: 'You won't always be the masters!' He was suspected of republicanism. The debates that had just marked the opening of the 1869 session, and the vague fear about the forthcoming general election, made the government sensitive. And he would certainly have been transferred had it not been for a strong recommendation from President Grandmorin. And even then he had had to sign a letter of apology which the latter had written and advised him to send.

Séverine cut him short.

'Now wasn't I right to send him a note and call on him with you this morning before you went to have your wigging. I was sure he would see us through.'

'Yes, he's very fond of you,' Roubaud went on, 'and he has quite a pull with the Company. So you see what a lot of good it is being a good employee. Mind you, they didn't spare the praise: not much initiative, but good behaviour, obedience, courage – the lot, in fact! Well, my love, if you hadn't been my wife and Grandmorin hadn't pleaded my cause out of friendship for you, I'd have been out on my ear, sent to do penance in some out of the way station.'

She gazed into space and murmured, as if to herself:

'Oh certainly he does have a pull!'

There was silence, and she sat there with staring eyes gazing into the distance, not touching her food. Perhaps she was re-

26

calling the days of her childhood at the château of Doinville, four leagues from Rouen. She had never known her mother. When her father, Aubry the gardener, died she was just twelve, and then the President, already a widower, had kept her with his own daughter Berthe, under the supervision of his sister, Mme Bonnehon, who had married an industrialist but was also widowed, and now owned the château. Berthe, two years older, had married six months after Séverine, her husband being M. de Lachesnaye, a judge in the Rouen Law Courts, a bloodless, pale little man. Until a year ago the President was still at the head of this court, which was in his own province, and then he had retired at the end of a distinguished career. Born in 1804, a deputy public prosecutor at Digne after the revolution of 1830, then at Fontainebleau, then Paris, then prosecutor at Troyes, advocate-general at Rennes and finally first president at Rouen. Worth several millions, he had been a county councillor since 1855 and made a Commander of the Legion of Honour on the very day of his retirement. And as far back as she could remember, she saw him just as he still was, sturdy and thickset, with hair cut short and prematurely white – the golden white- ness of once blond hair – and his square face, framed by a close- cut beard, no moustache, looked severe because of the hard blue eyes and strong nose. He had an abrupt way of talking, and spread fear and trembling all round.

Roubaud had to raise his voice and say twice:

'Well, what are you dreaming about?'

She jumped and a little shiver ran through her as though she were startled and frightened.

'Oh, nothing.'

'You've stopped eating, aren't you hungry any more?'

'Oh yes I am . . . You watch.'

She emptied her glass of wine and finished the slice of pâté on her plate. But then there was a scare: they had eaten all the loaf and there wasn't a mouthful left to go with the cheese. There were exclamations and then laughter as they turned every- thing upside down and dug out a heel of stale bread at the back of Ma Victoire's sideboard. Although the window was open it was still hot and Séverine was not exactly getting any cooler, what with the stove behind her and this improvised meal and the chatter. She was getting more and more flushed and excited. The thought of Ma Victoire brought Roubaud back to Grandmorin – she was another one who owed him a packet. She had been seduced as a girl, and after losing her own child had been wet-nurse to Séverine, who had just cost her own mother's life, then later she had married a fireman on the line and had just made ends meet in Paris thanks to a bit of dressmaking, because her husband blew everything. At that stage, through a chance meeting with her foster-child, she had picked up the old threads again and so become another protégée of the President. Recently he had found her a job in the Sanitary Department as attendant in the first-class ladies' lavatory, a really good thing. The Company only paid her a hundred francs a year, but she made nearly fourteen hundred on tips, apart from free lodging with even heating thrown in. Altogether a very pleasant situation. Roubaud calculated that if Pecqueux, the husband, had brought home his fireman's pay, two thousand eight hundred counting bonuses, instead of blowing it up and down the line, the couple would have netted over four thousand, double what he himself got as deputy stationmaster at Le Havre.

'Of course,' he concluded, 'not every woman would want to be a lavatory attendant. But a job's a job.'

By now they had taken the edge off their hunger and were only picking at the food and cutting the cheese into tiny bits to make the banquet last. And their conversation languished as well.

'Oh, by the way,' he said, 'I forgot to ask you ... Why did you turn down the President's invitation to spend a day or two at Doinville?'

In this moment of well-being after a meal his mind had gone back to their visit that morning to the mansion in the rue du Rocher, and he saw himself again in the big, plainly furnished study, hearing the President tell them that he was leaving for Doinville next day. Then, as if on a sudden impulse, he had offered to go with them on the 6.30 that evening and take his goddaughter on to his sister, who had been wanting to see her for a long time. But Roubaud's wife had alleged all sorts of reasons which prevented, she said.

28

'You know,' Roubaud went on, 'I couldn't see anything against that little trip. You could have stayed there until Thursday and I would have managed all right. In our position we can do with their help, can't we? It's not a very good idea to turn down their kind attentions, especially as your refusal looked as if it really upset him. That's why I went on urging you to accept until you tugged at my coat. Then I said the same as you, but I don't know why. Now why didn't you want to?'

Séverine's eyes avoided his and she made a gesture of impatience.

'And leave you all alone?'

'That's no reason. Since we have been married you have been twice in three years and spent a week at Doinville. There's no reason why you shouldn't go a third time.'

Her embarrassment increased and she turned her head away.

'Anyway, I wasn't keen. You aren't going to force me to do things I dislike, are you?'

Roubaud opened his arms as if to declare that he was not going to force her to do anything. Yet he went on:

'Look, you're hiding something. Was Mme Bonnehon nasty to you last time?'

Oh no, Mme Bonnehon had always been most welcoming. She was so nice, tall, with a full figure, lovely fair hair and still beautiful for all her fifty-five years! Since she had been a widow, and even while her husband was alive, it was said that her heart had often been involved. They worshipped her at Doinville, and she made the château a delightful place to which all Rouen society flocked, especially the legal profession. It was in legal circles that Mme Bonnehon had had many gentlemen friends.

'Well then, own up, it must be the Lachesnayes who've turned a cold shoulder.'

It was true that since her marriage to M. de Lachesnaye Berthe no longer meant to her what she had been before. Poor Berthe, she was hardly improving, she was so ordinary-looking, what with her red nose and all! The ladies of Rouen greatly praised her distinction. And besides, a husband like hers, ugly, hard, tight-fisted, seemed designed if anything to infect his wife and make her ill-natured. But not at all, Berthe had been very civil to her old friend, who could not put her finger on anything to reproach her with.

'Perhaps it's the President you don't like, then?'

Séverine, who until that moment had been answering slowly in an expressionless voice, became impatient again.

'Him? What a funny idea!'

She went on talking in nervous little phrases. It was a job even to see him. He had reserved for himself a little cottage in the park with a door opening on to a deserted lane. He came and went without anybody's knowledge, and not even his sister ever knew exactly on which day he arrived. He took a carriage at Barentin and had himself driven to Doinville in the dark, and lived for days on end in his cottage without anybody knowing. Oh, he wasn't the one who bothered you there.

'I only mention it because you've said a score of times that he scared you stiff when you were a kid.'

'Scared me stiff! You are exaggerating as usual. Of course he wasn't very jovial. He stared so hard at you with his bulging eyes that you dropped your own eyes at once. I have known people lose their nerve and be at a loss for a single word they were so cowed by his reputation for being severe and straight-laced. But he was never grumpy with me and I always felt he had a soft spot for me.'

Once again her voice trailed off and her eyes looked far away.

'It all comes back ... When I was a kid, playing with other girls under the trees, if he came into sight they all hid, even his own daughter Berthe, who was always afraid she had done something wrong. But I calmly waited for him. As he came by and saw me standing there grinning, with my face looking up at him, he would give me a little pat on the cheek. Later on, when we were sixteen and Berthe wanted some favour out of him, I was always the one she got to ask him. I spoke without lowering my eyes, and I felt his boring right into me. But I didn't care, for I was so sure he would grant anything I wanted. Oh yes, it's all coming back. There isn't a single corner in the park, not one passage or room in the château that I can't visualize if I shut my eyes.'

She fell silent with her eyes shut, and a quiver seemed to pass over her hot, flushed face at the recollection of things past, things she left unsaid. She remained like that for a moment, with a little quiver of the lips, like an involuntary twitch, painfully distorting a corner of her mouth.

'He certainly has been very good to you,' went on Roubaud when he had lit his pipe. 'Not only did he bring you up like a young lady, but he looked after your bit of money very well and added to it when we were married. To say nothing of the fact that he is going to leave you something – he has said as much in front of me.'

'Oh yes,' she murmured, 'that house at La Croix-de-Maufras with the land cut in two by the railway. We sometimes used to go there for a week ... Oh, I'm not really counting on it, the Lachesnayes must be working on him to leave me nothing. And besides, I'd rather have nothing, nothing!'

She pronounced the last words in such a vehement tone that he was amazed, took his pipe out of his mouth and stared at her round-eyed.

'Aren't you funny! They say he is worth millions, and what harm could there be in mentioning his goddaughter in his will? Nobody would be surprised, and it would be a very good arrangement for us!"

Then a thought came into his mind that made him laugh.

'You aren't by any chance afraid they'll think you're his daughter? You know that for all his cold manner there are some pretty hot stories whispered about him. It seems that when his wife was still alive all the maids had to go through it. Anyway, he's a randy old devil who even now is good for a roll in the hay. Good Lord, what the hell? Suppose you really were his daughter?'

Séverine leaped to her feet, furious, her face ablaze, with a wild, scared look in her blue eyes, under the thick mass of black hair.

'His daughter! his daughter! I won't have you making jokes like that, d'you hear? Do I look like him? That's quite enough, let's change the subject. I don't want to go to Doinville because I don't, because I'd rather go home to Le Havre with you.'

He nodded and calmed her with a gesture. All right, all right, no need to let it get her down. He smiled, he had never seen her so worked up. That white wine perhaps? In his desire to be forgiven he took up the knife again, going into fresh raptures about it and carefully wiping it, and to show that it was as sharp as a razor he trimmed his nails with it.

'It's already a quarter past four,' murmured Séverine, standing by the clock. 'I've still a few more errands to do ... We must be thinking about our train.'

But as if to regain her composure before tidying the room, she went back and leaned out of the window. So he put down the knife and his pipe, went up to her and standing behind her gently put his arms round her. He held her like that, put his chin on her shoulder and leaned his head against hers. Neither of them made any further movement, but just stood there watching.

Down below them the little shunting engines were continually coming and going, hardly making a sound as they moved about like busy, efficient housewives, with noiseless wheels and muted whistles. One went by and disappeared under the Europe bridge, hauling the carriages of a train from Trouville for reassembling in the sidings. Away beyond the bridge it slid past an engine that had come in light from the sheds, as though taking a walk on its own, its brass and steel all gleaming fresh and perked up for the journey. It had stopped and with two sharp whistles asked the pointsman for the road, and almost at once he sent it down to its train standing ready at a platform under the great roof-span of the main line station. It was the 4.25 for Dieppe. A stream of passengers was hurrying along, truckloads of luggage could be heard rumbling and men were putting foot-warmers into the carriages. The engine and tender struck the van at the head of the train with a soft clang, and they saw the foreman himself tighten up the screw of the coupling. Above the Batignolles the sky had darkened, and an ashen haze blurred the buildings and seemed to be settling over the spreading fan of lines. All the time in this fading light on the far side the suburban and Circle Line arrivals and departures kept on passing each other. Beyond the dark mass of the great station roofs ragged clouds of ruddy steam went up into the black Paris sky.

'No, no, leave me alone,' Séverine murmured.

32

Without saying anything he had gradually tightened his arms round her in a close embrace, his passions roused by the warmth of the young body he was enfolding. She intoxicated him with her scent, and her efforts to free herself by wriggling her buttocks only worked his desire up into a frenzy. He pulled her away from the window, pushing it to with his elbow. His lips crushed hers as he carried her towards the bed.

'No, no, this isn't our own home. Not in this room, please!'

She was feeling worked up herself, slightly fuddled with food and wine and still excited after rushing about in Paris. This overheated room, the table with the remains of the meal, the day trip that had unexpectedly turned into a private lunch-party, it all quickened her blood and made her flesh tingle. And yet she refused, resisted, with her back to the bedstead in a desperate revolt that she could not have explained to herself.

'No, no, I don't want to!'

He was flushed and trying to control his big, rough hands. He was quivering and could have crushed her to death.

'Don't be so silly! How will anybody know? We can put the bed to rights.'

At home in Le Havre she usually abandoned herself with amiable docility after their lunch when he was on night duty. It didn't seem to give her much pleasure, but she showed a willing passivity and affectionate consent to his pleasure. What was driving him mad at this moment was that he could tell that she was now as he had never felt her before – ardent, quivering with sensual passion. The blackness of her hair deepened the calm blue of her eyes, her wide mouth was blood-red in the soft oval of her face. This was a woman he did not know. Why was she holding back?

'Tell me, why not? We've got time!'

Then in indescribable anguish, as though lost in a debate she could not clearly understand, or as if she did not even understand herself either, she uttered a cry of real pain which made him stop.

'No, no, I beg of you, leave me alone. I don't know why, but just at this moment the very idea of it makes me feel sick ... It would be wrong.'

They had both sunk down on the edge of the bed. He rubbed

his hand over his face as though he were trying to wipe off the burning flush. Seeing he was sensible again, she leaned over and gave him a nice big kiss on the cheek to show him that she loved him just the same. For a minute they stayed there like that without a word, recovering. He had taken her left hand and was playing with an old gold ring, a gold serpent with a little ruby head, which she wore on the same finger as her wedding ring. She had always worn it there ever since he had known her.

'My little serpent,' she said, unthinking, in a dreamy voice, assuming that he was looking at the ring and feeling an irresistible urge to talk. 'He gave me it at La Croix-de-Maufras for my sixteenth birthday.'

Roubaud looked up, startled.

'Who? The President?'

As her husband's eyes looked into hers she woke up with a jerk. She felt a chill numb her cheeks. She tried to answer but found nothing to say, stifled by the sort of paralysis that had come over her.

'But,' he went on, 'you've always told me your mother left you that ring.'

Even at that moment she could still have taken the words back. She only needed to laugh and pretend she had been absent-minded. But she stuck to it in spite of herself, not knowing what she was doing.

'No, never, darling. I never said Mother had left me that ring.'

That made Roubaud look closely at her, and he went pale too.

'What! You never said that? You've told me twenty times! There's no harm in the President giving you a ring. He's given you lots of other things. But why keep it from me? Why tell a lie and talk about your mother?'

'I never mentioned my mother, dear, you're mistaken.'

It was crazy to stick to it like this. She realized she was destroying herself and that he could read her like a book; she would have liked to pull herself up and take back what she had said, but it was too late now, and she felt that her face was completely changing its expression, and that an admission was coming out of her whole person, do what she might. The numb-

34

ness of her cheeks had spread all over her face and her lips were drawn in a nervous twitch. And now he was terrifying and had suddenly reddened again as if he was going to burst a blood-vessel. He seized her wrists and looked right into her so as to read in her horrified eyes what she was not saying aloud.

'Oh Christ!' he muttered. 'Christ Almighty!'

In an attack of terror she ducked her face to shield it under her arm, thinking he was about to strike her. A wretched little insignificant fact, her forgetting a fib about that ring, had supplied clear evidence in only a few words of conversation. One minute had been enough. He threw her across the bed and rained blow after blow on her, anywhere. In three years he had never laid a finger on her and now he was murdering her, blind, furious, carried away like a brute – the man with big fists who formerly pushed trucks about.

'Bloody bitch, he's had you! ... he's had you ... he's had you!'

He worked himself up with these repetitions, and each time he said the words he brought down his fists as if to drive them into her body.

'An old man's leavings! Christ, what a whore! He's had you ... he's had you!'

He was in such a rage that his voice gave out, died into a wheeze and wouldn't make another sound. Only then did he hear her, as she cringed beneath the blows, saying no over and over again. She could not find any other defence except denial, to stop him from killing her. This repeated persistence in a lie drove him right out of his mind.

'Own up, you've been with him.'

'No, no!'

He seized her again and held her up in his arms to prevent her falling face downwards on the bed like a poor creature trying to hide. He forced her to look him in the eyes.

'Own up, you've been with him.'

But she slipped out of his grasp and tried to run for the door. With one bound he was on her again, fist in the air, and with a furious blow he knocked her down near the table. He threw himself down by her side and seized her hair to keep her on the floor. For a moment they stayed like that on the floor, face to face, without moving. In the awful silence there came up the singing and laughter of the Dauvergne girls, whose piano was going like mad. Fortunately it was below and deadened the noise of the struggle. Claire was singing little girls' songs and Sophie was banging out the accompaniment for all she was worth.

She had not the courage to go on denying, and said nothing.

'Admit that you've been with him, or I'll bloody well slit you open!'

And indeed he might have killed her, she could read it clearly in his eyes. As she had fallen she had seen the open knife on the table, and now she saw again the gleam of the blade and thought he was reaching out for it. She was overcome by cowardice, a desire to let herself and everything else go, to get it over with.

'All right, yes, it's true, now let me go.'

There was an appalling scene. The admission that he had demanded with such violence hit him right in the face like something impossible, against nature. Never, it now seemed, could he have envisaged such an abomination. He seized her head and banged it against a leg of the table. She fought, and he dragged her across the floor by the hair, knocking chairs out of the way. Each time she tried to get up he felled her to the floor with his fist. And he was gasping through clenched teeth, in savage, mindless fury. The table was pushed away and almost knocked the stove over. There was blood and hair sticking on one corner of the sideboard. When they recovered their breath, still gasping with the horror of it all, exhausted with hitting and being hit, they found themselves back by the bed, she still cowering on the ground and he crouching and still holding her by the shoulders. There they stayed puffing, while downstairs the music went on, with peals of laughter, very loud and very young.

Roubaud jerked Séverine up and propped her against the bedstead. Then at last, still kneeling and holding her down, he managed to speak. He no longer beat her but tortured her with questions in an insatiable desire to know.

36

'So you've done it with him, you whore! Go on, say it again, you've slept with that old man. And how old were you, eh? Quite a child, quite a child, were you?'

She suddenly burst into tears and could not speak for sobbing.

'Bloody hell! Are you going to tell me? So you were under ten, I suppose, when you were giving that old sod his fun! That's why he brought you up all ladylike, for his disgusting tricks! Go on, say so, or I'll bloody well start again.'

She went on crying and couldn't say a word, and he raised his fist and dazed her with another blow. Three times, being unable to get any more out of her, he punched her and repeated his question.

'How old? Tell me, how old? Go on, you bitch, tell me!'

Why go on struggling? Her whole being seemed to be collapsing beneath her. He could have clawed her heart out with his clumsy, workman's fingers. The questions went on and she told him everything, so cowed by shame and fear that her whispered words could scarcely be heard. Tormented by his atrocious jealousy and maddened by the pain with which these visions tore him, he never could learn enough, but forced her to go over and over the details and give the exact facts. With his ear close to the poor creature's lips, he suffered agonies from this confession, but kept his fist raised in a continual threat to hit her again if she stopped.

Once again all the past at Doinville, her childhood and early youth, was gone over. Was it in the clumps of trees in the great park? Or was it in some hidden corner in a corridor in the château? So the President already had his eye on her when he kept her after the death of his gardener and brought her up with his own daughter? To be sure it must have begun in those days when the other little girls ran away if he appeared in the middle of their games, whilst she, smiling away with her nose in the air, waited for him to come by and give her a little tap on the cheek. And then later, if she plucked up courage to talk to him and got anything out of him, wasn't it because she felt she was mistress of the situation while he, so respectable and so forbidding with everyone else, was winning her over with the

37

favours with which he seduced servant-girls? Oh what a disgusting thing, this old boy making this little girl kiss him like a grandfather as he watched her grow, pawing her over, trying her out a bit more hour by hour, too impatient to wait until she was ripe!

Roubaud was gasping for breath.

'Well, how old were you? Tell me again, how old?'

'Sixteen and a half.'

'Liar!'

Why on earth should she lie? She shrugged her shoulders with infinite hopelessness and weariness.

'And where did it happen the first time?'

'At La Croix-de-Maufras.'

He hesitated a moment, his lips quivered and there was a tawny glint in his eyes.

'And I insist on your telling me, what did he do to you?'

She said nothing. Then, as he was raising his fist:

'You'll never believe me.'

'Tell me all the same . . . He couldn't do anything, was that it?'

She nodded in reply. That was it. Then he turned the scene over and over, wanted to know every possible thing about it, descended to crude words and disgusting questions. She kept her teeth clenched and said yes or no by signs. Perhaps it might have given them both relief if she had gone into it all. But he was more and more hurt by these details which she thought were an attenuation. Normal, complete intercourse would have haunted him with a less torturing vision, but this unnatural vice made everything stink, thrust the poisoned knives of jealousy deep into his flesh and twisted them round. It was all over for him and he would never live again without conjuring up the loathsome picture.

He was rent by a sob.

'Oh God, oh God, it can't be! No, no, it's too much, it can't be!'

Then he suddenly shook her.

'But why did you marry me, you filthy bitch? Don't you realize it's vile to have tricked me like that? There are women criminals in prison who haven't got as much on their con-

38

sciences. So you despised me and you didn't love me? Well, why did you marry me?'

She waved her hand vaguely. How could she really tell now? By marrying him she found happiness, hoping to have done with the other man. There are so many things you might not want to do but do all the same because they really are the most sensible thing to do. No, she didn't love him. But what she avoided telling him was that, but for this business, she would never have consented to be his wife.

'It was him, I suppose, he wanted to fix you up and so he found a poor mutt. Was that it, he wanted to get you settled so it could go on? And you have gone on, haven't you, on both your trips there? That was what he had you there for?'

She nodded again.

'And that was what he has invited you for again this time? And these filthy things would have gone on for ever. And if I don't strangle you now it'll start up again!'

His hands were moving uncontrollably to take her by the throat. But this time she answered back.

'Look here, you're not being fair. Wasn't I the one who refused to go there? You were for making me go and I had to get angry, you remember. You see perfectly well I didn't want to go. It was all over. Never, never again would I have agreed.'

He realized she was telling the truth, but it didn't make him feel any better. The dreadful pain, like a knife sticking into his breast, and for which there could be no remedy, was the fact of what had happened between her and this man. The horrible suffering came solely from his powerlessness to undo that fact. Still without letting go of her he looked closely into her face, he seemed to be fascinated and held there as if he were trying to trace in the blood of her tiny blue veins everything she had admitted. As though beset by hallucinations he murmured:

'At La Croix-de-Maufras, in the red room ... I know it, the window looks out on to the railway and the bed is on the opposite wall. It was there, in that room ... I can see why he talks about leaving you the house. You've earned it. He might well look after your savings for you and give you a dowry, it was a good bargain. A judge, a man worth millions, so respected, so learned, so highly placed! It makes your head spin, it really does ... And suppose he were your father?'

With a great effort Séverine got to her feet, having pushed him away with extraordinary strength considering how weak she was, poor battered creature. She protested violently.

'No, no! Not that! Anything else you like, beat me, kill me, but don't say that. It's a lie!'

Roubaud had kept hold of one of her hands.

'How can you know anything about it? It's because you have suspicions yourself that it upsets you so.'

As she pulled away her hand he felt the ring, the little gold snake with the ruby head. He tore it off and crushed it on the floor with his heel, in a renewed fit of rage. Then he strode up and down the room in silent bewilderment. She had sunk down on the edge of the bed, looking at him with her big, staring eyes. The terrible silence went on.

Roubaud's fury did not abate. As soon as it seemed to calm down a little it came back again at once, like drunkenness, in great, successive waves carrying him away on their swell. He was now quite beside himself, hitting out at the air, carried hither and thither by each squall of the storm of violence lashing him, reduced now to the single need to appease the roaring beast within him. It was a physical, imperious need, like a hunger for vengeance twisting his guts which would give him no respite as long as he had not satisfied it.

Still walking up and down he banged his temples with his two fists and cried out in anguish:

'What am I going to do?'

Since he had not killed this woman at once, he would not kill her now. He was exasperated by his own cowardice in letting her live, for cowardice it was, since he hadn't throttled her because he still loved her whore's body. Well then, as he couldn't keep her like this, was he going to turn her out, throw her into the street and never see her again? He was overcome by a fresh wave of pain, submerged by a hateful feeling of nausea as he realized he would not even do that. What then? The only thing left was to accept this abomination and take this woman back to Le Havre and resume the humdrum life with her as though nothing had happened. No, no, sooner death! Death for them both, now! He was carried away by such agony of mind that he shouted louder still, like a madman:

'What am I going to do?'

Séverine was still sitting on the bed, following him with her wide eyes. With the calm, comradely affection that she had felt for him she was already deeply concerned by the immense distress she could see he felt. The curses and blows she could have excused if this insane rage had not surprised her so much, an amazement she still could not get over. This passive and docile woman, who as a young girl had lent herself to the desires of an old man and later had accepted her marriage solely because she wanted to regularize her life, simply could not comprehend such an outburst of jealousy over some misconduct long past and that she repented of. She had no vice in her, her flesh had scarcely yet been aroused, and being only half able to grasp the real values of things, still virginal despite everything, she watched her husband going up and down and turning in fury just as she might have watched a wolf or some creature of another species. What had got into him? So many men would not have been angered. What terrified her was to sense that the animal whose existence she had suspected for three years from its scarcely audible growlings, was now unleashed, savage, ready to bite. What could she say to prevent his doing something desperate?

With each turn he came back to the bed in front of her. She waited for him to come and then ventured to speak:

'Listen, dear.'

But he didn't hear, and was off to the other end of the room like a straw before a gale.

'What am I going to do? What am I going to do?'

Finally she seized him by the wrist and stopped him for a minute.

'Look, dear, as I was the one who wouldn't go ... I would never have gone there again, never, never! You're the one I love.'

She tried to cajole him, drawing him to her and raising her lips for a kiss. But as he fell down beside her he pushed her away with a movement of horror.

'Oh, you bitch, so now you want to ... Just now you

41

wouldn't, you didn't want me. And now you would like to again so as to get me back, is that it? When you've got a man that way you can hold him tight ... But it'd burn me up to go with you now, yes, I can feel that it would burn me up like a poison.'

He shivered. The thought of possessing her, the vision of their two bodies falling on the bed, had gone through him like a flame. In the troubled darkness of his flesh, in his desire that had been sullied and was bleeding, there suddenly rose up the necessity of death.

'So that it doesn't kill me to go with you, I've first got to kill the other man ... Yes, I've got to kill him, kill him!'

His voice rose higher, repeating that word as he stood up, feeling himself grown in stature as though the word had made up his mind for him and given him peace. He said no more, but walked slowly over to the table and looked at the knife with its open, gleaming blade. He mechanically closed it and put it into his pocket. And with his arms dangling and his gaze lost in the distance he stood there, thinking. Difficulties furrowed his brow with two deep lines. To try and find a solution he went over and opened the window and planted himself there with his face in the cool, twilight air. Behind him his wife had risen to her feet, seized with fear again and, not daring to question him, yet trying to guess what was going on in that hard head, she stood waiting too, facing the broad sky.

As night was drawing in, the distant buildings stood out black and the vast trench of the station was filling with a purplish haze. Especially in the Batignolles direction the deep cutting seemed misty with particles of ash into which the girders of the Europe bridge were beginning to merge. Towards Paris the last glimmer of daylight still lightened the glass of the great station roof, while underneath it the darkness gathered in clouds. Little stars twinkled, the gas lights were being lit along the platforms. There was one big white light, the headlamp of the Dieppe train which was crammed with passengers, the doors already closed, waiting for the traffic manager's order to depart. There was some hitch, the road was closed by the pointsman's red light while a little engine came to pick up some coaches left on the line through a mistake in shunting. In the deepening shadows trains were continually on the move over the inextricable net-

42

work of lines between rows of stationary carriages waiting on sidings. One left for Argenteuil, another for Saint-Germain; one came in from Cherbourg, a very long one. Signals changed busily, with whistles and blowing horns, and in all directions red, green, amber or white lights came on. It looked a complete muddle in this dismal twilight, as if everything was going to smash into everything else, but they all got through, brushed past each other and emerged with the same gentle crawling motion, difficult to see in the dusk. The pointsman's red light disappeared, the Dieppe train whistled and began to move. A few spots of rain drifted down from the colourless sky. It would be a very wet night.

When Roubaud turned round, his face looked mulish and obstinate as though clouded over by the oncoming night. He had made up his mind, his plan was settled. In the fading light he looked at the clock and said out loud:

'Twenty past five.'

It surprised him; one hour, barely an hour for so many things to happen. He could have believed they had both been tearing each other to pieces for weeks on end.

'Twenty past five, we've got time.'

Séverine dared not ask him anything, but her worried eyes had not stopped following him. She saw him ferreting about in the cupboard, taking out some paper, a small bottle of ink and a pen.

'Look, you're going to write a letter.'

'Who to?'

'Him. Sit down.'

As she instinctively recoiled from the chair, not yet knowing what he was going to make her do, he pulled her back and sat her down at the table with such force that she stayed there.

'Write this: "Leave this evening on the 6.30 express and don't let anybody see you before Rouen." '

She held the pen, but her hand was shaking and her panic increased with the vista of the unknown that these two simple lines opened out in front of her. So she found the courage to look up imploringly.

'My dear, what are you going to do? Do please explain.'

He repeated, loud and inexorable:

43

'Write, write.'

Then, looking her straight in the eyes, with no anger or harsh words, but with a determination that she felt crushed her beneath its weight:

'What am I going to do? You'll see all right. And understand this, what I am going to do I mean you to do with me ... In that way we shall stay together and there'll be something binding between us.'

He frightened her and she drew back again.

'No, no, I want to know ... I shan't write anything until I know.'

Then without another word he took her hand, a frail little child's hand, and squeezed it to breaking-point in an iron grip with the continuous pressure of a vice. It was his will entering into her very flesh with the pain. She screamed, and everything in her broke down and was his. The ignorant girl she had remained could do nothing but obey. Instrument of love, instrument of death.

'Write, write.'

She wrote painfully, with her poor hurt hand.

'That's right, now you're behaving nicely,' he said when he had the letter. 'Now just tidy up here a bit and get everything ready. I'll come back for you.'

He was perfectly collected. He redid the knot of his tie in front of the mirror, put on his hat and went off. She heard him double-lock the door and take out the key. It was getting darker and darker. She remained seated for a minute, listening intently to all the sounds outside. In the room of the next-door neighbour, the newsvendor, there was a soft, continuous moan, no doubt a little dog left there. In the Dauvergnes' down below the piano had stopped. Now there was a cheerful noise of pots and pans, the two young housewives were busying themselves in their kitchen, Claire seeing to some stewed lamb, Sophie cleaning the salad. Exhausted, she listened to their laughter in the horrible distress of this oncoming night.

By a quarter past six the engine of the Le Havre train emerged from under the Europe bridge, was switched on to its train and coupled. Because of extra traffic it had not been possible to put this train under the main-line roof. It was waiting in

44

the open air at the platform extension which ran out like a long jetty under a pitch-black sky and on which the few gas-jets along the platform did no more than string a line of smoky stars. A downpour of rain had just stopped, but it had left behind a damp, icy air spreading a mist through this vast open space as far as the little dim lights in the windows of the rue de Rome. It was immense, dreary, drenched with rain, pierced here and there by a blood-red light, vaguely peopled by opaque masses, isolated engines or carriages, bits of trains slumbering on side lines; and out of the depths of this sea of darkness came noises, the breathing of giants feverishly gasping, whistle-blasts like piercing shrieks of women being violated, distant horns sounding dismally amid the roar of the neighbouring streets. Somebody shouted orders for an extra carriage to be put on. The express engine stood motionless, letting off from its safety valve a great jet of steam up into all this blackness, and there it flaked off in little wisps, bedewing with white tears the limitless funereal hangings of the heavens.

At twenty past six Roubaud and Séverine appeared. She had just given back the key to Ma Victoire on her way past the lavatories next to the waiting-rooms, and he was pushing her on like a typical husband in a hurry whose wife has kept him waiting, the man impatient and brusque, with his hat on the back of his head, the woman holding her veil to her face, stumbling as if collapsing with fatigue. A stream of passengers was moving up the platform, and they joined them, walked along the line of coaches looking for an empty first-class compartment. The platform was in a bustle, porters were pushing barrows of luggage to the front van, an overseer was trying to find room for a large family. The deputy traffic manager was casting an eye on the couplings with his signal lamp to check whether they were properly screwed up. Roubaud at last found an empty compartment into which he was about to help Séverine up when he was spotted by the stationmaster, M. Vandorpe, who was passing along with his deputy for the main lines, M. Dauvergne, both with hands behind their backs, watching the operation of adding the extra coach. There were greetings and they had to stop and chat.

First it was that business with the Sub-Prefect, which had

45

passed off to everybody's satisfaction. Then there was the matter of a mishap that morning at Le Havre which they had heard of by telegraph: an engine, Lison, which worked the 6.30 express on Thursdays and Saturdays, had broken a coupling-rod just as the train was entering the station, and because of the repair job the driver, Jacques Lantier, who hailed from the same part of the world as Roubaud, and his fireman, Pecqueux, Ma Victoire's good man, would be held up there for two days. Séverine stood waiting by the door of the compartment without climbing in, while her husband put on a great show of matey-ness, shouting and laughing. But there was a jolt and the train went back several metres as the engine backed the leading car-riages on to the one they were adding, No. 293, in order to provide a reserved coupé. The younger Dauvergne, Henri, who was going on the train as guard, recognized Séverine through her veil and saved her from being struck by the open door by pulling her aside with a quick movement, then, apologizing most amiably, he explained that the coupé was for one of the directors of the Company, who had requested it only half an hour before departure time. She giggled nervously for no reason, and he hurried on to his job, feeling delighted because he had often told himself that she would make a very pleasant mistress.

The clock said six twenty-seven. Three more minutes. Sud-denly Roubaud, who was keeping an eye on the doors of the waiting-rooms all through the talk with the stationmaster, left him to return to Séverine. But the carriage had moved and they had to walk several steps to get to the empty compartment, and turning his back he hurried his wife in, helping her up with a deft movement of his arm while she, docile yet anxious, instinc-tively looked behind so as to know. There was one last-minute passenger coming along, carrying nothing but a rug, and the upturned collar of his big blue greatcoat came so high, and the brim of his felt hat so low over his eyes, that the only part of his face which could be made out in the flickering gaslight was a bit of white beard. All the same, M. Vandorpe and M. Dauvergne had stepped forward in spite of the traveller's obvious desire not to be seen. They walked behind him and he nodded at them

46

only when he was three carriages further on, by the reserved compartment into which he hastily climbed. It was him. Séverine dropped on to her seat all of a tremble. Her husband crushed her arm in a tight squeeze, like a final act of possession, exultant now that he was sure of pulling it off.

In a minute the half-hour would strike. A newsvendor was still doggedly offering evening papers, and passengers were still dawdling on the platform, finishing a cigarette. But they all got in when overseers could be heard slamming the doors, working from both ends. And then Roubaud, who had had the unpleasant surprise of seeing in the compartment he thought was empty a black, still, silent form occupying a corner, presumably a woman in mourning, could not hold back an exclamation of real annoyance when the door opened again and a porter bundled in a couple, a fat man and a fat woman, who flopped down breathless. The train was about to move. The fine drizzle had begun again, filling the huge, dark space through which trains were continually passing, but all that could be seen of them was the square glass lights, rows of little moving windows. Green lights had appeared, and some lamps were dancing about at ground level. That was all, nothing but an immense blackness in which the only thing to be made out was the roof over the main-line platforms showing dim in the gaslight. Everything else was lost in shadows, and even the noises were dying down, except the roar of the engine as it opened its steam-cocks and emitted whirling masses of white vapour. A cloud went up and spread like a ghostly shroud, streaked with black smoke from some unknown source. The sky was obscured again, and a cloud of soot moved off over the blazing furnace of the night life of Paris.

Then the assistant stationmaster raised his lamp for the driver to ask for the road. There were two whistle-blasts and the red light by the pointsman's post gave way to a white one. Standing at the door of the van the guard waited for the order to depart, which he passed on. The driver whistled once again, a long blast, opened the regulator and the engine began to move. They were off. At first the motion was imperceptible, then the train moved off under the Europe bridge and into the Batignolles tunnel. Nothing could be seen of it except the three rear lamps, the red triangle, blood-red like open wounds. It could be followed for a few more seconds in the eerie blackness of the night. Then it sped away and nothing now could halt this train hurtling full speed ahead. It vanished.

2

THE house at La Croix-de-Maufras, in a garden cut in two by the railway, stands obliquely so near the line that it is shaken by every passing train, and a single train journey is enough to stamp it on your memory; everybody passing the place at full speed knows it is here, but knows nothing about it, for it is always shut up, abandoned like a ship in distress, with its grey shutters going green in the lashing rains from the west. It is a wilderness, and the house seems to emphasize still more the solitude of this remote spot, cut off by a league in all directions from any living soul.

The level-crossing keeper's house stands there isolated, by the bend in the road which crosses the line and goes to Doinville five kilometres away. Squat, with cracked walls and tiled roof decayed with moss, it crouches there like an abandoned pauper in the middle of the garden – a garden planted with vegetables, surrounded by a green hedge – in which stands a big well, as high as the house. The level crossing is just midway between Malaunay and Barentin stations, four kilometres from each. It is very little used, in any case, and the old, half-decayed gate is hardly opened except for the drays from the Bécourt quarries half a league away in the forest. A more remote spot could scarcely be imagined, or more cut off from human beings, for the long tunnel on the Malaunay side cuts off all communication, and the only way to Barentin is a neglected path alongside the railway. So visitors are few and far between.

On this particular evening, at dusk on a grey and very muggy day, a traveller who had got off a train from Le Havre at Barentin was striding along the path to La Croix-de-Maufras. The country is a continual series of hills and valleys, a sort of rough sea of land, which the railway traverses alternately on embankments or through cuttings. On both sides of the line these continual ups and downs of the terrain make routes doubly difficult, which accentuates the sensation of deep loneliness. The barren, whitish earth is uncultivated, trees crown the hills with little copses, and willow-shaded streams run down the narrow valleys. Other chalky mounds are absolutely bare and the hills succeed each other, sterile and silent in the deathly solitude. The walker, a strong young fellow, quickened his step as if to get away from the dreariness of the still twilight in this desolate country.

In the garden of the level-crossing keeper, a girl was drawing water from the well, a tall girl of eighteen, fair and well built, with a strong mouth, big greenish eyes and low forehead under a thick head of hair. She was far from pretty, with solid hips and the muscular arms of a young man. As soon as she saw the man walking along the path she put down the pail and ran and stood at the gate in the hedge.

'Well, it's Jacques!' she exclaimed.

He looked up. He was just twenty-six, tall also, very dark, a good-looking fellow with a round face and regular features, a little spoilt by an over-prominent jaw. His thick hair was curly, like his moustache, which was so thick and black that it emphasized the pallor of his skin. From the look of his delicate complexion and well-shaved face you might have taken him for a city gentleman, had you not seen elsewhere the indelible imprint of his job, the oil already staining his mechanic's hands.

'Hallo, Flore,' was all he said.

But his eyes, which were big and black, flecked with gold, seemed to have veiled themselves with a reddish mist which turned them pale. His lids fluttered and his eyes looked away in sudden embarrassment, even discomfort to the point of pain. His whole body had instinctively recoiled.

Standing quite still and looking straight at him, she had noticed the involuntary shudder he tried to overcome every time he came near a woman. It seemed to make her thoughtful and sad. Then, as he tried to cover his embarrassment by asking her if her mother was at home, although he knew she was ill and unable to go out, she merely nodded and stood aside so that he could go in without touching her, and saying no more walked back to the well, upright and proud.

Jacques went quickly across the little garden and into the house. There, in the middle of the first room, a huge kitchen where they lived and had their meals, was Aunt Phasie, as he had called her since childhood, sitting alone by the table on a wicker chair with an old shawl over her legs. She was a cousin of his father's, a Lantier, who had been his godmother and had taken him into her own home when he was six, at the time when his father and mother had run off to Paris and disappeared.* He had stayed at Plassans, where in due course he had been to the technical school. He had remained deeply grateful to her, saying that he owed it to her that he had made his way in life. When he had become an express-driver on the Western Railway after two years of service on the Paris–Orléans, he found that his foster-mother had remarried – a level-crossing keeper of the name of Misard – and was exiled with the two girls of her first marriage in this outlandish spot called La Croix-de-Maufras. Today, although she was barely forty-five, his fine Aunt Phasie, formerly so tall and buxom, looked more like sixty, shrunk and sallow and shaken by constant spasms.

She exclaimed with delight:

'What! It's you, Jacques? Oh my dear boy, what a surprise!'

He kissed her on both cheeks and explained that he had suddenly got two days of enforced holiday. That morning, as they were arriving at Le Havre, his engine Lison had broken her coupling-rod, and as the repair could not be done in under twenty-four hours he would not go on duty again until the following night on the 6.40 express. So he thought he'd like to come and see her. He would stay the night and not leave Barentin until the 7.26 in the morning. He held her poor, useless hands in his and told her how her last letter had worried him.

'Oh yes, my dear boy, I'm no good at all now, no good at all. How nice of you to guess how much I wanted to see you! But I know how taken up you are, and didn't dare ask you to come. Anyhow, here you are, and I'm so worried, so sick at heart!'

She paused to look anxiously out of the window. In the failing light, on the opposite side of the line, her husband Misard could be seen in a block-section post, one of those wooden huts every five or six kilometres, connected by telegraph to check the correct running of trains. As his wife, and later Flore, had re-

---

* Gervaise Macquart and Auguste Lantier (*L'Assommoir*).

sponsibility for the level-crossing gate Misard had been given a watchman's job.

As though her husband could hear her, she lowered her voice and shuddered.

'I feel sure he's poisoning me!'

This burst of confidence made Jacques start in surprise, and as his eyes also turned to the window they once again clouded over with this peculiar reddish mist which lightened their intense blackness with golden flecks.

'Oh, Aunt Phasie, what an idea!' he murmured. 'He looks so meek and mild.'

A train for Le Havre had just passed and Misard had come out of his hut to close the section behind it. While he was pulling up the lever, setting the signal at red, Jacques had a look at him. A seedy little man with scanty hair and beard of a nondescript hue and a lined misery of a face. And he was silent, self-effacing, never got angry and was obsequiously polite to his superiors. But by now he had gone back into the hut to enter the time of the train in his time-book and push the two electric buttons, one to give the road clear to the previous post and one to offer the train to the following one.

'Oh, you don't know him!' Aunt Phasie went on. 'I tell you he's going to try to make me swallow some muck or other ... To think that I used to be so big that I could have eaten him up, that pygmy of a man, that whippersnapper, and now he's eating me!'

She was working herself up with festering hatred and fear and was now enjoying having someone to listen to her. What on earth could have possessed her to marry again, and such a miserable little sneak, and penniless and miserly into the bargain, and she five years older and with two girls, one six and the other eight? It was now nearly ten years since she had done this clever trick, and not a single hour had gone by when she hadn't regretted it. A life of poverty, exile in this frozen hole up in the north where she shivered all the time, boredom enough to kill you, with never a soul to talk to, not even a neighbour. He had been a platelayer, but was now earning 1200 francs as a watchman; she at the beginning had had 50 francs for the level crossing that Flore now looked after, and that was the present and the future, with no other hope – the certainty of living on and kicking the bucket in this hole a thousand leagues from a living soul. What she omitted to mention were the consolations she had still had before she fell ill, when her husband worked on the ballast and she stayed there alone looking after the crossing with her daughters. For in those days she enjoyed such a reputation for her attractions up and down the line from Rouen to Le Havre that the permanent-way inspectors all used to visit her when they passed; and there had even been rivalries, with foremen platelayers from another gang always doing their rounds and extra vigilant with their supervision. The husband gave no trouble, always smarmy with everybody, gliding through doors, coming and going without ever seeing anything. But those pastimes were no more, and there she stayed for weeks and months on end in this chair, in this loneliness, feeling her body dying a little more hour by hour.

'I tell you,' she repeated by way of conclusion, 'he's after me and he'll get me, little misery though he is.'

The sudden ringing of a bell made her cast the same anxious glance outside. It was the previous box offering Misard an up train, and the needle of the section indicator in front of the window had gone over in the direction the train was going. He stopped the bell and came out to warn of the train's approach by two horn blasts. At this point Flore came and pushed the gate to, then stood there holding her flag upright in its leather case. The train, an express, could be heard approaching with a growing roar though it was hidden by a curve. It passed like a thunderbolt, shaking the little house and threatening to carry it away in a hurricane. Already Flore was going back to her vegetables while Misard, having closed the up line behind the train, was going to open the down by lowering the lever to block out the red signal, for a fresh ringing, with the other needle rising, had warned him that the train that had passed five minutes before had now left the next section. He went in, warned the two boxes, entered the time and then waited. Always the same job for twelve hours, living there and eating there without reading three lines of a newspaper and without appearing to have a single thought in that twisted mind of his.

Jacques, who used to tease his foster-mother about the

ravages she inflicted among the permanent-way inspectors, could not help smiling as he said:

'Perhaps he is jealous.'

But Phasie shrugged her shoulders pityingly, while at the same time a laugh came unbidden into her poor, tired eyes.

'Oh, my boy, what are you talking about? Jealous, him! He never cared a damn so long as it didn't cost him anything!'

Then her panic came back.

'No, no, he was never particularly interested in that side of things. He's only keen on money. What has caused trouble between us, you see, is that I wouldn't hand over the thousand francs I inherited from Dad last year. So, just as he threatened, it has brought me bad luck and I have got ill. And the illness has never given over since then, yes, since just then.'

The young man understood, but as he thought it was all just the black thoughts of a sick woman he tried to talk her out of it once again. But she stuck to it, shaking her head like someone who is quite convinced. So in the end he said:

'All right then, nothing is simpler if you want it to end. Just give him your thousand francs.'

With a superhuman effort she rose to her feet, her old self again, and she shouted furiously:

'My thousand francs? Never! I'd rather peg out! Oh, it's hidden, properly hidden all right! You could turn the house-inside out and I defy you to find it. And he has pretty well turned it inside out, too, the old twister. I've heard him at night tapping on all the walls. Hunt! Hunt! If only for the pleasure of watching his nose poking about, I'd find patience . . . We shall see who'll give over first, him or me. I'm on my guard and now I don't swallow anything he's touched. And if I did peg out, well, he still wouldn't get those thousand francs. I'd rather leave them to the earth.'

She fell back on to the chair, exhausted and shaken by a second blast on the horn. It was Misard at the door of his hut, this time signalling a down train for Le Havre. In spite of her withdrawal into an obstinate determination not to give up her legacy, she lived in a secret, growing fear of him, the fear that a colossus feels for the insect that is devouring it. The train that had been signalled, the slow, leaving Paris at 12.45 p.m., could be heard coming a long way off with a dull roar. Then it emerged from the tunnel with a sudden loud beat echoing through the countryside, and passed with its thunderous wheels and the mass of its coaches, invincible, powerful as a hurricane.

Jacques had looked up through the window at the moving line of little square windows in which could be seen profiles of passengers. Wanting to dispel Phasie's black thoughts, he said jokingly:

'Mum, you grumble about never seeing even a cat in this hole. But look at all those people!'

At first she failed to understand, and said in surprise:

'People, where? Oh yes, those people going by. A fat lot of good! I don't know them from Adam, and can't talk to them!'

He went on laughing.

'But you know me very well, and often see me going past.'

'You, yes, that's very true, I know you and I know the time of your train, and I look out for you on your engine. Only you go so fast, so very fast! Yesterday you waved your hand like this. I can't even answer . . . No, no, that's no way to see people.'

Yet this idea of the tide of people that the up and down trains bore along past her every day in the deep silence of her solitude left her pensive, looking at the line as night was falling. When she was fit and well and able to get about, standing at the barrier with her flag in her hand, she never used to think about these things. But vague dreams, hardly formulated, had befuddled her brain since she had been sitting for whole days in this chair with nothing to think about except her private struggle with her man. It seemed funny being buried in this wilderness, without a soul to confide in, when day and night, all the time, so many men and women were rushing past in the thunder of trains shaking the house, and then tearing away at full speed. It was a fact that all the world went by, not only French people but foreigners too, people from the most distant lands, since nowadays nobody could stay at home and all the nations, it was said, would soon be only one. That was progress, all brothers together, all going along to some Better Land! She tried to count them roughly, at so many per carriage, but there were too many and she couldn't keep up. Often she thought she recognized faces: there was a gentleman with a fair beard, English perhaps, who went to Paris every week, and the little dark lady who travelled regularly on Wednesdays and Saturdays. But they went by in a flash and she was never quite sure she really had seen them; all the faces got blurred and merged one into another, indistinguishable. The torrent rushed on, leaving nothing behind. What depressed her so much was the feeling that, behind this non-stop movement and all the comfort and money going by, the breathless crowd had no idea she was there, in danger of death. So if her man finished her off one night, the trains would go on passing each other near her dead body without even suspecting the crime in this lonely house.

Phasie had kept her eyes on the window and she expressed in a word what she felt too vaguely to explain at length.

'Oh, it's a wonderful invention, you can't deny it ... People travel fast and know more ... But wild beasts are still wild beasts, and however much they go on inventing still better machines, there will be wild beasts underneath just the same.'

Jacques nodded again to show he thought so too. He had been watching Flore for a minute as she opened the barrier again for a dray from the quarry carrying two huge blocks of stone. The road was used only by the Bécourt quarries, and so at night the gate was padlocked, and it was very seldom that the girl had to get out of bed. Seeing her exchanging a friendly word with the driver, a small dark fellow, he exclaimed:

'Oh, is Cabuche ill then? His cousin Louis is driving the horses ... Poor Cabuche, do you often see him, Mum?'

She said nothing, but raised her arms and sighed. There had been a dreadful business the previous autumn, which had done nothing to restore her health. Her daughter Louisette, the younger one, who had a job as maid with Mme Bonnehon at Doinville, had run away one night in terror, and badly knocked about, to die in the hut where her sweetheart Cabuche lived in the depths of the forest. Tales had spread accusing President Grandmorin of using violence on her, but people were afraid of voicing them aloud. The mother herself, though she knew what it was all about, didn't like dwelling on the subject. However, she did say eventually:

'No, he never comes now, he's turned into a real lone wolf. Poor Louisette, she was so dainty, so white, so sweet! She really

56

loved me and would have looked after me. But Flore, well, I'm not complaining, but there is something a bit cracked about her, there really is. She always goes her own way, disappears for hours on end, and so proud with it, and so violent! It's all sad, very sad.'

As he listened, Jacques went on watching the dray which was now crossing the line. But the wheels caught in the rails and the driver had to crack his whip while Flore shouted as well, to get the horses moving.

'Golly!' he exclaimed. 'It wouldn't do for a train to come ... there wouldn't half be a mess!'

'Oh, no fear of that,' said Aunt Phasie. 'Flore is funny sometimes, but she knows her job all right and keeps her eyes open. Thank God, we've had no accidents for five years. A man was cut in pieces once. So far we've only had one cow, but that nearly derailed a train. Poor beast, they found the body here and the head near the tunnel ... With Flore you can sleep in peace.'

The dray had got across and they could hear the heavy jolts of the wheels in deep ruts. Then she came back to her constant preoccupation with health, other people's as well as her own.

'And yourself? Are you quite all right now? You remember back home the things you suffered from that the doctor couldn't make out at all?'

His eyes flickered with misgiving.

'Oh, I'm fine, Mum.'

'You really are? It's all gone, that pain you used to get in the head, behind the ears, and those sudden temperatures and fits of depression that made you hide away like an animal in its den?'

As she was speaking he got more and more uncomfortable and so upset that he cut her short:

'I tell you, I'm quite fit. No trouble left, nothing at all.'

'Ah, that's better, dear. It's not as though your being ill would cure me. And besides, you ought to be well at your age, there's nothing like good health. It really is nice of you to find time to come and see me when you might have gone and enjoyed yourself somewhere else. You will have supper with us, won't you? And you can sleep upstairs in the loft, next to Flore's room.'

But once again she was interrupted by a blast on the horn. It was quite dark now, and turning to the window they could just make out Misard talking to another man. It had just struck six and he was handing over to the night man replacing him. He was going to be free now, after his twelve hours in that hut with no furniture except a little table under the instrument panel, a seat, and a stove that made the place so hot that he was obliged to keep the door open almost all the time.

'Oh, here he is, he's coming in,' murmured Phasie, her fear returning.

The train now due, a very heavy one, was approaching with an increasing roar, and the young man had to lean over for the sick woman to hear him. He was very moved by the wretched state he could see her getting into, and he said, to cheer her up:

'Look here, Mum, if he really has evil intentions perhaps it would stop him if he knew he'd got me to deal with as well ... It might be a good idea to entrust your thousand francs to me.'

This brought a final reaction:

'My thousand francs! No, not to you any more than to him! I tell you, I'd rather die!'

At that moment the train passed like a fierce storm sweeping all before it. The house shook in a squall of wind. This train, for Le Havre, was very full because there were festivities the following day, Sunday, for the launching of a ship. In spite of the speed they had caught a glimpse through the lighted windows of crammed compartments, rows of heads close-packed, each in profile. Row followed row and disappeared. What a lot of people! The crowd again, the endless crowd amid the roar of trains, whistling of engines, buzzing of telegraphs and ringing of bells. It was like a huge body, a gigantic creature lying across the land, with its head in Paris and joints all along the line, limbs spreading out into branch lines, feet and hands at Le Havre and other terminal towns. On and on it went, soulless and triumphant, on to the future with a mathematical straightness and deliberate ignorance of the rest of human life on either side, unseen but always tenaciously alive – eternal passion and eternal crime.

Flore was the first in. She lit the light, a little paraffin lamp with no shade, and laid the table. Not a word was exchanged, and she hardly looked at Jacques, who was looking away as he

stood by the window. Some cabbage soup was keeping hot on
the stove. She was serving it when Misard too came in. He
showed no surprise at seeing the young man there. Perhaps he
had seen him come, but he didn't ask any questions, wasn't
interested. A handshake, three short words, nothing else.
Jacques had to volunteer once more the story of the broken
coupling-rod and the idea of coming to see his foster-mother
and staying the night. Misard merely nodded gently, as though
he thought that was all right, and they sat down to a leisurely
meal, at first in silence. Phasie, who had never taken her eyes off
the saucepan in which the soup had been bubbling all day,
accepted a plateful. But when her husband got up to give her
the iron-water that Flore had forgotten – a carafe in which
some nails were left to steep – she didn't touch it. But he, meek,
sickly, with a nasty little cough, didn't seem to notice the
anxious look with which she followed his every movement. As
she asked for some salt because there was none left on the table,
he said she would be sorry she had so much of it because that
was what made her ill; he then got up to get some and brought a
little back in a spoon, which she took without any hesitation,
for, she used to say, salt purifies everything. Then they talked
about how very warm the weather had been for some days, and
about a derailment at Maromme. Jacques was coming to think
that his foster-mother suffered from nightmares in the daytime,
for he could not spot anything amiss in this obliging little man
with the dreamy eyes. They sat on for over an hour. Twice
Flore disappeared for a minute or two when the horn sounded
its signal. The trains passed, shaking the glasses on the table, but
none of them even noticed.

Another horn signal was heard and this time Flore, who had
cleared the table, did not reappear. She left her mother and the
two men at the table with a bottle of apple brandy in front of
them. The three stayed there another half-hour, then Misard,
whose darting eyes had settled in a corner of the room, picked
up his cap and went out with a simple good night. He poached
in the little streams round about, where there were superb eels,
and he never went to bed without having been to look at his
ground lines.

As soon as he had gone Phasie looked hard at her foster-son.

'Well, what do you think? Did you see him ferreting about with his eyes in that corner? He has taken it into his head that I have hidden my nest-egg behind the butter-crock. Oh, I know him, and I bet he'll move that pot tonight to find out.'

But she began breaking out into a sweat, and her limbs started to shake.

'Look, it's coming on again! He must have drugged me, I've got a bitter taste in my mouth as if I had swallowed a lot of old pennies! And yet I had nothing from his hand, God knows! It's enough to make you go and drown yourself. Tonight I'm worn right out, and I'd better go to bed. So good-bye, dear, because if you go on the 7.26 it will be too early for me. And do come back, won't you? And let's hope I shall still be here.'

He had to help her back into the other room, where she lay down and went to sleep, exhausted. Left alone, he hesitated and wondered whether he ought not to go up himself and stretch out on the hay in the loft. But it was only ten to eight and he had plenty of time for sleep. So he too went out, leaving the little paraffin lamp burning in the empty, slumbering house, shaken from time to time by the sudden thunder of a train.

Jacques was surprised how warm it was outside. Perhaps it was going to rain again. A uniform, milky cloud had spread all over the sky, and the full moon, behind but invisible, lit the whole vault of heaven with a pinky glow. So he could make out the countryside quite clearly, for the land round him, hills and trees, stood out black in this uniform, dismal light, as soft as a night-light. He went round the little kitchen garden. Then he thought he would take a walk in the Doinville direction as the road was not so steep that way. But then his attention was caught by the lonely house standing obliquely along the line on the other side, so he crossed the railway through the wicket gate because the main barrier was already shut for the night. He knew this house very well by sight through having looked at it on every trip he made in his shaking and roaring engine. For some reason it haunted him with a vague sensation that it had something to do with his own life. He felt it every time, first a sort of fear that he might not see it there this time, and then a kind of uneasiness when he found it was still there. He had never seen the doors or windows open. All he had been told about it was that it belonged to President Grandmorin, and that evening he was seized with an irresistible desire to have a look round it and find out a little more.

For a long time Jacques remained standing on the road opposite the railings. He stepped back, stood on tiptoe, trying to find out. In cutting through the grounds the railway had in any case left only a small walled garden in front of the main steps, while in the rear stretched quite a large piece of land with just a hedge round it. The house looked lugubriously dreary in its neglect, in the reddish glow of this cloudy night, and he was about to go off with a slight shudder when he noticed a gap in the hedge. The thought that it would be cowardly not to do so made him go through the gap. His heart beat faster. Then suddenly, as he was going past a little tumbledown greenhouse, the sight of a shadow crouching by the door pulled him up sharp.

'What, you?' he cried in astonishment, recognizing Flore. 'Whatever are you doing here?'

She also had jumped in surprise, but then she said calmly:

'You can see. I'm pinching bits of cord. They've left a lot of them here that are just rotting away and no use to anyone. So as I'm always wanting cord I've come to get some.'

And indeed she was squatting on the ground with a pair of big scissors in one hand, untangling bits of cord and cutting through knots if they wouldn't untie.

'Doesn't the owner ever come over now?' he asked.

She began to laugh.

'Oh, since the Louisette business there's no danger of the President risking the end of his nose at La Croix-de-Maufras. Oh no, I can take his cord.'

He said nothing for a moment, looking concerned at the memory of the tragic story that she had revived.

'And what about you, do you believe Louisette's story, that he tried to get her and she hurt herself while struggling?'

She stopped laughing and exclaimed in a burst of violence:

'Louisette never told lies, nor did Cabuche. Cabuche is my friend.'

'And lover now, perhaps?'

'What, him? Well, you'd have to be a fine old slattern! No, no, he's a friend. I've got no lovers and I don't want any.'

61

She held up her powerful head, with its thick mop of curly fair hair coming down low on her forehead, and from all her strong, catlike being there emanated a savage will-power. Already she was becoming quite a legend in those parts. Stories went round about disasters she had prevented: a cart pulled out of the way with one heave just as a train was coming; a runaway goods truck coming down the Barentin incline stopped as it was tearing like a wild beast straight at an express. And these astonishing feats of strength made men desire her, especially because at first they thought she was easy to get, as she always went wandering in the fields as soon as she finished work, looking for lonely spots, lying in hollows silent and motionless, just gazing up into the sky. But the first men to venture had not wanted to try that game again. As she was given to bathing naked in a stream near by for hours on end, some lads of her own age had organized parties to watch her, and she had seized one of them, without even bothering to put her vest on, and had settled his hash so well that nobody spied on her again. And finally there was the tale of her encounter with a signalman on the junction for Dieppe, at the far end of the tunnel, a certain Ozil, a man of thirty and a very decent fellow whom she had appeared to encourage for a little while. But when one evening, thinking she was in the mood, he had tried to take her, she had half killed him with a cudgel. She was a virgin warrior, scorning the male, which convinced people in the end that she certainly must be a bit wrong in the head.

Hearing her declare that she didn't want any lovers, Jacques went on teasing:

'So it's all off, the wedding with Ozil? I had heard tell that you went off through the tunnel every day to see him.'

She shrugged her shoulders.

'Wedding! What, me! No, I like the tunnel. Two and a half kilometres to run in the dark, with the thought that you might be cut to bits by a train if you don't keep your eyes skinned. You should just hear the din the trains make in there! No, Ozil got on my nerves, he isn't the one I want.'

'You want somebody else, then?'

'Oh, I don't know . . . Oh no, I don't think so.'

She started laughing again, and feeling a bit awkward she

62

went back to one of the knots that she couldn't manage. Then, without looking up, as though quite absorbed by her task:

'And what about yourself? No girl-friend?'

It was his turn to be serious. His eyes turned away and looked vaguely into the night. He snapped back:

'No!'

'So there it is,' she went on, 'I've been told that you can't stand women. In any case I've known you a long time and you never would say anything nice to us women. Why?'

He said nothing, and she decided to give up the knot and look straight at him.

'Are you only in love with your engine? It's quite a joke, you know. They make out that you are for ever polishing her, making her shine as if you had no endearments for anybody but her . . . I'm telling you this because I'm your friend.'

It was his turn to look at her, in the dim light of the overcast sky. He remembered what she was like when she was quite a little girl, already violent and headstrong, but jumping up to kiss him as soon as he came in, full of a wild, girlish passion. And later, though he often lost sight of her, he had each time found her grown bigger but greeting him with the same leap into his arms, and disturbing him more and more with the flame of her big light-blue eyes. Now she was a magnificent and most desirable woman, and no doubt her love for him went back for a very long time, in fact to her early childhood. His heart began to pound, and he suddenly felt that he was the one she was waiting for, and with the blood being pumped into his head there rose a terrible disquiet. In his mounting anguish his first impulse was to get away. Desire had always gone to his head and made him see red.

'What are you standing up for?' she said. 'Why not sit down?'

He still hesitated, but then his legs suddenly went very tired, he was overcome by the urge to make one more attempt at lovemaking, and fell down beside her on the heap of cords. He could not speak, his throat had gone dry. Now it was she, the proud, the taciturn one, who was chattering away breathlessly, merrily, making herself quite giddy.

'You know, Mother made a great mistake marrying Misard. It'll do her no good . . . I can't be bothered about it myself.

because it's quite enough to think about your own troubles, isn't it? And besides, Mother packs me off to bed as soon as I try to put a spoke in ... So let her get out of it herself! I live outdoors and think about things for later on ... Do you know, I saw you go past this morning on your engine from over there in those bushes where I was sitting. But you never look. And I'll tell you the things I think about, but not now, sometime later when we really are friends.'

She had dropped her scissors and he, still not saying a word, had taken both her hands, which she left in his, overjoyed. But when he raised them to his burning lips, she recoiled like a frightened virgin. The Amazon revived, jibbing, embattled at the first approach of the male.

'No, no, leave me alone! I don't want to! Just stay like that, and let's talk ... That's all you men think of. Oh, if I were to tell you what Louisette told me on the day she died at Cabuche's! As it was, I already knew a thing or two about the President because I'd seen some goings-on when he brought young girls here ... There's one nobody suspects, he's married her off ...'

He wasn't listening or even hearing. He seized her in a brutal embrace and crushed her mouth under his. She uttered a little cry, more like a moan, so deep and so tender that it clearly revealed her long concealed love for him. Yet she went on struggling and refusing to yield, instinctively fighting back. She longed for him yet fought against him, needing to be conquered. Without a word, breast to breast, they both were breathing hard as each tried to hurl the other backwards. For a moment she seemed to be the stronger and might well have got him down, for he was tiring so quickly, had he not seized her by the throat. Her bodice was torn off and her breasts stood forth hard and swollen from the battle, milk-white in the pale night. Then she suddenly collapsed on her back, ready to give herself, defeated.

But then, gasping for breath, instead of taking her he stopped and looked at her. Some madness seemed to be taking possession of him, some ferocity making him cast his eyes round for a weapon, a stone, anything to kill her with. He caught sight of the scissors gleaming in the heap of cord, and in a flash he picked them up and would have plunged them into the naked chest between the rose-tipped white breasts. But a sudden chill sobered him, and he threw down the scissors and ran madly away while she, lying with her eyes closed, thought that now she was the one to be turned down because she had resisted.

Jacques ran off into the gloomy night. He ran at full speed up a path to the top of a hill and down into a narrow coomb. Pebbles dislodged by his feet startled him and he turned left and darted into a thicket, hooked round to the right again and that brought him back to the bare hilltop. Then he tore down the slope and bumped into the fence of the railway. A train was approaching with a roar and a fiery light; at first he did not understand and was terrified. Oh yes, the world passing by, the continual tide of men, while he was here suffering agonies! He set off again, climbed a slope and came down yet again. Now he kept coming upon the line, either in deep cuttings like yawning chasms or on embankments that shut out the horizon like huge barricades. This empty country with its ranges of hills was like a maze with no way out, in which his madness went round and round in the dismal abandon of the wilderness. He had been tramping up hill and down dale for many a long minute when he saw a round opening in front of him, the black mouth of the tunnel. An up train was disappearing into it, roaring and whistling, and after it had vanished, swallowed up in the earth, it left the ground shaking and trembling for a long time.

His legs would carry him no more and he fell down beside the line and burst into convulsive sobs, lying full-length on his belly, burying his face in the grass. Oh God, so this horrible affliction he thought he was cured of had come back again, had it? He had really tried to kill this girl! Kill a woman, kill a woman, that had buzzed through his ears since his earliest adolescence with the increasing, all-powerful fever of desire. As others, awakening into puberty, dream of possessing a woman, so he was maddened by the vision of killing one. For it was no use lying to himself, he had taken up those scissors to plunge them into her flesh as soon as he had seen that flesh, that warm and white breast. And it was not because she was resisting him, oh no, it was for the enjoyment of it, because he wanted to and wanted to so badly that if he were not clinging to the grass he would even now rush back there and slit her open. And her! Oh God, Flore, whom he had seen grow up, this wayward child

65

who, he had just realized, loved him so deeply. His twisting fingers dug into the earth and the sobs lacerated his throat with gasps of dreadful despair.

Nevertheless he forced himself to calm down and try to understand. What was there so different about him, compared with others? Already down in Plassans as a youngster he had tried to understand himself. It was true that his mother Gervaise had had him when she was very young, fifteen and a half, but he was her second, and she was well under fourteen when she had had her first, Claude. But neither of his two brothers, Claude or Étienne, who was born later, seemed to suffer because their mother was such a child and their father only a kid as well – the handsome Lantier, whose worthless character was to cost Gervaise so many tears. Maybe each of his brothers also had his own trouble that he wouldn't admit, especially the elder one who wore himself out trying to be a painter so furiously that he was said to be half insane with his genius. The family was really not quite normal, and many of them had some flaw. At certain times he could clearly feel this hereditary taint, not that his health was bad, for it was only nervousness and shame about his attacks that had made him lose weight in his early days. But there were sudden attacks of instability in his being, like cracks or holes through which his personality seemed to leak away, amid a sort of thick vapour that deformed everything. At such times he lost all control of himself and just obeyed his muscles, the wild beast inside him. Yet he did not drink, not even allowing himself a single tot of spirits, having seen that the least drop of alcohol drove him out of his mind. He was coming to think that he was paying for others, fathers, grandfathers who had drunk, generations of drunkards, that he had their blood, tainted with a slow poison and a bestiality that dragged him back to the woman-devouring savages in the forests.*

Jacques lifted himself on to one elbow, thinking, looking at

* This paragraph, necessary because Zola invented Jacques as an afterthought (see Introduction), stretches probability to breaking-point. There is no evidence that Jacques ever saw his brothers again after childhood. In reality Claude was almost insane and finally hanged himself (*L'Œuvre*) and Étienne could only control his fits of murderous fury by almost total abstinence from alcohol (*Germinal*).

the black entrance of the tunnel, and fresh sobs seemed to run all up his back and he sank down again, rolling his head on the ground and crying out in his distress. That girl, that girl, he had tried to kill her! The pain kept coming back, acute and dreadful, as though the scissors had pierced his own flesh. No amount of reasoning would calm him; he had wanted to kill her and he would kill her now if she were still there with her clothes open and her breasts bare. He well remembered the first time this evil thing had come over him, when he was barely sixteen and was playing about with a girl, the young daughter of some relation and two years younger. She had fallen down and he had seen her legs and simply gone for her. The following year, he remembered, he had sharpened a knife in order to thrust it into the neck of another girl, a little blonde he used to see passing his door every morning. That one had a very plump, pink neck, and he had already decided on the place, a brown mark below one ear. And then there had been others, and yet others, a nightmare procession of women he had just been near when he had his sudden lust for murder, women he barely touched as he passed them in the street, women chance meetings placed by his side. There was one in particular, a young married woman sitting next to him in the theatre and laughing very loud, whom he had to rush away from in the middle of a performance for fear of ripping her open. He did not even know who they were, so what cause for mad rage could he have against them? For each time it was a sudden fit of blind fury, an insatiable urge to avenge some age-old offences he could not clearly remember. Did it come from the remote past, some malady with which women had infected his race, the resentment passed down from male to male since the first betrayal in the depths of some cave? For in these fits he also felt that it was necessary to fight to conquer the female and subdue her, that there existed a perverted need to throw her dead body over his shoulder, like a prize snatched away from the others for ever. His skull felt like bursting under the strain and he could find no answer to his questionings, thinking himself too ignorant, with too dull a brain in this anguish of a man forced into acts in which his will counted for nought and the cause of which within himself had vanished.

Once again a train flashed by in a blaze of light, to be swallowed up with a thunderous roar that died away in the depths of the tunnel, and just as though that nameless crowd, oblivious and hurrying on, could have heard what he said, he got to his feet, choked back his tears and put on an unconcerned look. How many times, after one of his attacks, had he jumped like a guilty thing at the slightest sound! Only on his engine did he live calm, happy, and away from the world. When she bore him along with the clatter of her wheels, at full speed, when he had his hand on the regulator and was wholly taken up with keeping an eye on the road, looking out for signals, he stopped thinking and took great gulps of the pure, fresh air that always blew like a hurricane. That was why he was so in love with his engine, like a comforting mistress from whom he expected only happiness. When he left the technical school, although he was extremely intelligent, he had chosen the trade of engine-driver for the sake of the solitude and oblivion he found in it, quite without ambition but reaching the position of first-class driver in four years. He was already earning 2800 francs with bonuses for firing and oiling which brought him up to over 4000, but he had no further aspirations. He saw his mates in the third or even second grades. the ones the Company was training, the cleaners taken on to be instructed, he saw nearly all of them marrying work-girls, colourless women you noticed only occasionally at departure time, when they brought their little lunch baskets; whilst the more ambitious colleagues, especially the ones from a technical school, waited until they were heads of depots before marrying, in the hope of finding a classy woman, a real lady who always wore a hat. But he ran away from women, so what did it matter? He would never marry, he had no future except to drive alone, drive on and on and never stop. Which was why all his superiors cited him as an outstanding driver, never drinking, never after the women, and he was only chipped by his loose-living mates about overdoing his good behaviour, while others had vague misgivings when he fell into his gloomy fits and was silent, with vacant eyes and ashen face. In his little room in the rue Cardinet, from which he could see the Batignolles sheds, his engine's home depot, how many hours he remembered spending, in fact all his hours off, shut up like a monk in his cell, using up the overflow of his desires lying on his stomach!

Jacques tried to force himself to his feet. What was he doing there in the grass on a warm, foggy winter night? The country-side was veiled in shadows, the only light came from the sky, with its thin cloud like an immense dome of frosted glass which the moon behind lit up with a pale yellow glow, and the black horizon slept with the stillness of death. Come on, it must be getting on for nine, and the best thing to do would be to go in and get to bed! But in his numbed state he saw himself back at the Misards' going upstairs to the loft and lying down on the hay next to Flore's room, with nothing but a matchboard par-tition between. She would be there and he would hear her breathing; he even knew that she never shut her door, so he could go in to her. His shuddering horror came on again, and the vision he conjured up of this girl naked with her limbs undefended and warm from bed shook him again with sobs that threw him back on to the ground. He had wanted to kill her, kill her, oh God! He gasped in agony as he thought that he would go and kill her in her bed, now, if he went back there. Nor would it matter if he had no weapon, it would avail him nothing to hold his head in his arms and try to forget – he realized that the male in him, independent of his own will, would push open the door and strangle that girl, lashed on by the instinct for rape and the urge to avenge the age-old outrage. No, no, better to spend the night tramping round in the country than go back there! He leapt up in one bound and began to run.

Then for another half hour he rushed on through the black fields as though hunted by the unleashed pack of his terrors. He ran up hills and down into narrow dales. Two streams crossed his path; he forded them and was soaked to the middle. A thicket was in his way and this exasperated him, for his one thought was to go in a straight line, further and further, and still further, to get away, away from his other self, this savage beast he could feel inside him. But he was taking it with him and it was running just as fast. For seven months he had thought he had got rid of it and had been getting back into normal life, and now it was all starting again, he would have to struggle again to prevent this beast from leaping on to the first woman he happened to pass near. Yet the deep silence and total solitude did calm him a little and made him dream of a life as silent and lonely as this desolate countryside in which he could walk on for ever without meeting a soul. But he must have been bearing round without realizing it, for he came back and hit the railway line on the opposite side, having described a big semicircle among the brakes and briars and ups and downs above the tunnel. He recoiled, frightened and irritated at coming back to the land of the living. Then, having tried to cut behind a little hill, he lost himself, but turned up by the railway fence just at the end of the tunnel and opposite the meadow where he had been sobbing not long before. He was standing still, beaten, when the roar of a train emerging from the bowels of the earth, distant at first, but increasing every second, rooted him to the spot. It was the Le Havre express, the 6.30 from Paris which passed that spot at 9.25, a train he himself drove every other day.

First Jacques saw the mouth of the tunnel light up, like the door of a furnace full of blazing wood. Then, bringing the din with it, the engine poured forth with its dazzling round eye, its headlamp blazing a gap through the landscape and lighting the rails far ahead with a double line of flame. But that was but a flash – the whole line of carriages followed, the little square windows, blindingly light, making a procession of crowded compartments tear by at such a dizzying speed that the eye was not sure whether it had really caught the fleeting visions. And in that precise quarter-second Jacques quite distinctly saw through the window of a brilliantly lit coupé a man holding another man down on the seat and plunging a knife into his throat, while a dark mass, probably a third person, possibly some luggage that had fallen from above, weighed down hard on the kicking legs of the man being murdered. Already the train had gone and was disappearing towards La Croix-de-Maufras, showing no more of itself in the darkness than the three rear lamps, the red triangle.

Rooted to the spot, he watched the receding train as its roar died away in the great dead peace of the country. Had he seen

70

aright? He hesitated now, not daring to admit the reality of this vision that had appeared and disappeared in a flash. Not one feature of the two actors in the drama had remained clear in his mind. The dark mass might after all have been a travelling-rug that had fallen across the victim's body. And yet at first he thought he had glimpsed a delicate, pale profile beneath a thick mass of hair. But everything ran together and evaporated like a dream. Momentarily that profile came back, then it vanished for good. It was presumably just something he had imagined. It all struck him as so horrible and extraordinary that in the end he persuaded himself it was a hallucination, born of the dreadful nerve-storm he had just been through himself.

Jacques went on walking for nearly another hour, and his head was fuddled with conflicting thoughts. He now felt worn out, a reaction had set in, a chill within him had carried away his fever. Without meaning to, he ended by making for La Croix-de-Maufras again. But when he found himself at the level crossing house he told himself that he would not go in, but sleep in the little lean-to attached to one of the gable-ends. But a ray of light was coming under the door and he pushed it open without thinking. On the threshold he was arrested by an unexpected sight.

In the corner Misard had moved the butter-crock and on all fours, with a lantern standing beside him, he was sounding the wall with light taps of his fist. He was searching. The sound of the door made him sit up. Not that he was in the least put out, and he simply said quite naturally:

'It's some matches that have fallen down here.'

Having replaced the butter-crock, he added:

'I came in to get my lamp because just now on my way back I saw somebody stretched out on the line . . . I think he must be dead.'

At first Jacques was struck by the thought that he was catching Misard in the act of hunting for Aunt Phasie's secret hoard, and that turned his scepticism about the latter's allegations into sudden certainty. But then he was so violently stirred by this news of the discovery of a body that it drove out of his mind the other drama that was playing itself out in this little lonely

71

house. The scene in the coupé, the fleeting glimpse of one man murdering another, came back in the same flash of enlightenment.

'A man on the line, where?' he asked in horror.

Misard was going to describe how he was bringing home two eels he had taken off his ground-lines, and that he had just rushed all the way home to hide them. But why tell this chap all that? He just made a vague gesture and replied:

'That way, looked about five hundred metres ... must see properly so as to know.'

Just then Jacques heard a soft thump over his head. He was in such a nervy state that he jumped.

'It's nothing,' said Misard, 'only Flore moving about.'

Jacques did indeed recognize the sound of bare feet on the floor. She must have been waiting up for him and was going to listen at her open door.

'I'll come with you,' he said. 'You're sure he's dead?'

'Well, that's what it looked like to me. With the lamp we'll see properly.'

'But what do you make of it? An accident, I suppose?'

'May be. Some bloke got himself run over or perhaps a passenger who jumped out of a carriage.'

Jacques shuddered.

'Come on, quick!'

He had never been possessed with such a desperate need to know. Outside, while his companion, completely unmoved, walked along the line swinging his lamp, and its circle of light travelled along the rails, he ran on ahead chafing at this slowness. It was like physical desire, the inner fire that speeds the pace of lovers to their meeting place. He was afraid of what was waiting for him along there, yet he was rushing to it as fast as his muscles and legs could take him. When he reached the spot and nearly stumbled into a black mass stretched out by the down line he stopped, rooted there, and a shiver ran from his heels up to his neck. His frustration at not seeing anything clearly turned into cursing the other man for dawdling more than thirty paces behind.

'For God's sake, get a move on! If he were still alive we could help him!'

Misard dawdled on phlegmatically. Then, having looked over the body with his lantern:

'Don't you believe it! He's handed in his chips!'

The man, probably falling out of a carriage, had landed on his front with his face to the ground, fifty centimetres at the most from the rails. All that could be seen of his head was a thick cap of white hair. The legs were wide apart. The right arm lay as though it had been torn out, but the left was twisted under the body. He was very well dressed, with a big blue overcoat, smart boots and an expensive shirt. The body showed no sign of having been run over, but much blood had come from the throat and stained his collar.

'Some gent who's been polished off,' Misard went on calmly, after studying the situation for a few seconds.

Then turning to Jacques, who stood there gaping:

'Mustn't touch, it's forbidden ... You stay here on guard while I run to Barentin and report to the stationmaster.'

He raised his lamp to a kilometre post.

'Good! Just at post 153.'

Leaving his lamp on the ground by the body, he took himself off at his dragging pace.

Left alone, Jacques stood motionless, still looking at that inert lump of flesh, indistinct in the dim lamplight at ground level. Inside him the excitement that had made him hurry along and the horrible fascination that kept him there, all culminated in this intense thought, pervading his whole being like a ferment: that other man, the one he had seen with the knife in his hand, he had dared! He had followed out his desire to the end and had killed! Oh, not to be a coward, to find fulfilment at last and plunge the knife right in! The desire had tortured him for ten years. In his agitation there was an element of contempt for himself and admiration for the other man and above all an urge to have a look, an irresistible craving to feast his eyes on this human lump, the broken doll, the limp rag that a stab with a knife had made of a living soul. What he had merely dreamed about the other man had done, and there it was. If he were to kill, there it would be, on the ground. His heart was beating furiously and his itch for murder intensified like a physical lust at the sight of this pathetic corpse. He took a step nearer, like a nervous child coming to terms with his fear. Yes, he would dare! He himself would dare, too!

But a roar behind him made him jump to one side. A train was coming that he had not heard in his deep contemplation. He was nearly run over, and only the hot breath, the formidable blast of the engine had warned him just in time. The train passed in its hurricane of noise, smoke, and flame. Still crowds of people; the stream of passengers was still pouring towards Le Havre for tomorrow's holiday. A child was squashing its nose against the glass, staring at the black countryside, profiles of men caught the eye, and a young woman let down a window and threw out a piece of paper soiled with butter and sugar. Already the happy trainload was far away, heedless of the corpse its wheels had almost touched. The corpse lay there on its face, dimly lit by the lamp in the dreary peace of the night.

Then Jacques was seized by desire to see the wound while he was alone. Only one misgiving held him back, the thought that if he meddled with the head it might be noticed. He had reckoned that Misard could not be back with the stationmaster in under three quarters of an hour. And he was letting the minutes slip by, thinking about Misard, this puny little man, so slow and stolid, but who also dared, killing as coolly as you please, with doses of drugs. So killing was quite easy, then? Everybody did it. He went nearer. The idea of seeing the wound stung him so sharply that it set his flesh burning. Just to see how it was done and how much blood had come out and what the red hole was like! If he was careful how he put the head back nobody would know. But underlying his hesitation there was another kind of fear he would not admit, the fear of blood itself. In him, always and in every case, terror awoke with desire. Still another quarter of an hour on his own, and he was on the point of making up his mind, when a little sound beside him made him jump.

Flore was standing there, looking too. She loved accidents: any mention of an animal run over, a man cut in pieces by a train, was bound to make her rush to the spot. She had put her clothes on again and she wanted to see the dead man. After the first glance she had no hesitation, but stooped and held up the lantern with one hand and turned over the head with the other.

74

'Mind what you're doing, it's not allowed,' whispered Jacques.

She merely shrugged her shoulders. Now the head could be seen in the yellow glimmer, an old man's head with a prominent nose; and the blue eyes of someone formerly fair were wide open. Below the chin gaped the horrible wound, a deep gash that had cut into the neck, and the wound was ragged as though the knife had been turned round as it dug in. Blood had soaked all the right side of the chest. In the buttonhole on his left lapel the rosette of Commander of the Legion of Honour looked like an isolated red clot.

Flore had uttered a little exclamation of surprise.

'Good Lord! It's the old chap!'

Jacques bent forward with her to see better, so close that his hair touched hers, and he gasped and sated himself with the sight. Without thinking he repeated after her:

'The old chap . . . the old chap?'

'Yes, old Grandmorin . . . the President.'

For another moment she went on examining that bloodless face with the twisted mouth, those eyes staring in terror. Then she dropped the head, which was beginning to go rigid in death, and it fell to the ground, closing up the gash.

'No more fun with the girls!' she went on softly. 'This is to do with one, I'll be bound. Oh, poor Louisette! Oh, the swine, and a good job too!'

There was a long silence. Flore set down the lantern and waited, casting sidelong glances at Jacques while he, separated from her by the corpse, had still not moved, lost, wholly possessed by what he had seen. It must have been nearly eleven. After the scene that evening, she felt shy of being the first to speak. But then voices could be heard, it was Misard bringing back the stationmaster and, not wanting to be seen, she made up her mind.

'Aren't you coming back for the night?'

He shuddered, and for a minute seemed to be debating. Then he said, in a desperate effort to back out:

'No, no!'

She gave no sign, but the way her strong arms hung limp expressed great disappointment. As if to beg forgiveness for her

75

resistance earlier, she was very humble, and said once again:
'So you aren't coming back, and I shan't see you again?'
'No, no!'

The voices came nearer, and without trying to shake hands, since he seemed to be keeping the corpse between them purposely, without even calling out the familiar cheerio of their childhood friendship, she went away into the darkness, breathing heavily, as though fighting back her tears.

A moment later the stationmaster was there with Misard and two gangers. He corroborated the identity: yes, it was certainly President Grandmorin, whom he knew from seeing him come off the train each time he went to see his sister, Mme Bonnehon, at Doinville. The body could stay where it had fallen, but he did have it covered with a coat brought by one of his men. Another railwayman had gone off on the 11.00 p.m. train from Barentin to report to the Public Prosecutor at Rouen. But the latter could hardly be expected before five or six in the morning, because he would have to bring with him an examining magistrate, the coroner's officer and a doctor. So the stationmaster arranged for the body to be guarded, and all night they would relieve each other so that one man would always be there watching with the lantern.

Before he could make up his mind to go and lie down in some shed at Barentin station, which he was not due to leave until 7.20,* Jacques still stayed there motionless and obsessed. Then the thought of the expected examining magistrate struck fear into him as though he felt in some way involved as an accomplice. Should he say what he had seen as the express passed? At first he resolved to tell all, as in any case he had nothing to fear. Nor was there any doubt as to where his duty lay. But then he wondered what was the point, he could not give them a single definite fact nor dare to vouch for any precise detail about the murderer. It would be silly to get mixed up in it, waste his time and get all worked up and with no advantage to anybody. So finally he walked away, but turned round twice to look at the black mound the body made on the ground in the yellow circle of lamplight. A keener chill came down from the misty sky on

* Zola's own discrepancy. Given as 7.26 on pp. 51 and 60.

to this desolate wilderness with its barren hills. More trains had passed, and another, a very long one, heading for Paris. As they all passed each other and in their inexorable mechanical power tore ahead to their distant goals in the future, they almost touched unwittingly the half-severed head of this man whom another man had slaughtered.

3

ON the following day, Sunday, all the bells in Le Havre had just
struck five in the morning when Roubaud came down into the
station to go on duty. It was still quite dark, but the wind
blowing off the sea had freshened and was dispersing the mists
covering the hills from Sainte-Adresse to the fort of Tourne-
ville, while westward over the open sea there was a clear patch
of sky in which the last stars were twinkling. Under the station
roof the gas-lamps were still burning palely in the damp cold
of this early hour, and the first train for Montivilliers was
being made up by shunters under the night deputy. The waiting-
room doors were not yet open and the platforms stretched on
deserted in the sluggish reawakening of the station.

As he was leaving his own quarters above the waiting-rooms
Roubaud had run into the cashier's wife, Mme Lebleu, standing
in the middle of the central passage on to which the employees'
quarters opened. For weeks this lady had been getting up in the
middle of the night to spy on Mlle Guichon, who worked in the
office and whom she suspected of carrying on with the stationmaster, M. Dabadie. Not that she had ever come across the
slightest thing, not a shadow or breath. And that morning,
once again, she had dodged quickly indoors with nothing to
take back with her beyond astonishment at having glimpsed
inside the Roubauds', during the three seconds it had taken the
husband to open and shut the door, the wife, the winsome
Séverine, standing in the dining-room already dressed, hair
done, shoes on; for usually she lazed in bed until nine. So Mme
Lebleu had woken her husband up to acquaint him with this
extraordinary fact. The night before they had stayed up until
the arrival of the express from Paris at five past eleven, dying to
know the upshot of the business about the Sub-Prefect. But
they had not managed to gather anything from the attitude of
the Roubauds, who had come home with their everyday expressions, and in vain had they strained their ears until midnight

– no sound came from their neighbours, who must have gone off at once into deep slumber. For certain their journey couldn't have turned out well, otherwise Séverine would never have got up at such an hour. The cashier having asked what sort of a face she had, his wife had done her best to describe it: very stiff, very pale, with her big blue eyes looking so light beneath her black hair, and never the slightest movement, just like a sleepwalker. Ah well, they would find out later in the day what it was all about.

Down below Roubaud found his colleague Moulin who had done the night turn. He took over from him and Moulin stayed on a few minutes, walking up and down and talking, putting him in the picture about little things that had happened since the day before. Some marauders had been caught in the act of breaking into the left-luggage office, three gangers had been told off for bad behaviour, a drawbar had broken while they were making up the Montivilliers train. Roubaud listened in silence with a calm expression, but he looked a bit pale, no doubt because he was still tired, as the circles under his eyes showed too. But when his colleague had finished talking Roubaud still seemed to be waiting for something else, as though expecting other things to have happened. But that was really all, and he looked down at the ground for a moment.

Having walked the length of the platform the two men had reached the end of the covered station, at a point where there was a shed on the right in which were parked the carriages in current service which arrived one day and were used to make up the train departing on the next. As he looked up his eye was caught by a first-class carriage with a coupé compartment. Its number, 293, happened to show up in the flickering light of a gas-lamp just as Moulin said:

'Oh, that reminds me . . .'

Roubaud's pale face flushed and he could not repress a slight start.

'That reminds me. That carriage mustn't go out, so don't put it on the 6.40 express this morning.'

There was a pause before Roubaud answered in a natural-sounding voice:

'Oh, why not?'

'Because a coupé has been reserved for this evening's express. We don't know whether another one will come in during the day, so we'd better hang on to this one.'

Roubaud went on looking closely at him, then answered:

'Yes, of course.'

But he had something else on his mind, and suddenly burst out:

'It's disgusting! Just look how those buggers do their cleaning! That carriage looks as though it's got a week's dust on it.'

'Oh well,' went on Moulin, 'when trains get in after eleven there's no risk of the chaps giving them a flick with a duster ... It's something if they consent to look through them. The other day they overlooked a passenger fast asleep on a seat, and he didn't wake up till next morning!'

Then stifling a yawn he said he was going up to bed. As he was going off a sudden thought brought him back.

'Oh, by the way, that fuss of yours with the Sub-Prefect is all over, isn't it?'

'Oh yes, a very successful trip. I'm quite happy.'

'Right, that's fine. And don't forget that No. 293 doesn't go.'

When Roubaud was left alone on the platform he went slowly back towards the Montivilliers train standing ready. The doors of the waiting-rooms had been opened and some passengers were appearing – a few men off hunting with their dogs, two or three shopkeepers and their families taking advantage of a Sunday, not many people really. But when that train had gone, the first of the day, he had no time to waste, having at once to see the 5.45 made up, a stopping train for Rouen and Paris. At that early hour there were not many staff on duty, and the deputy stationmaster's job was complicated by all sorts of responsibilities. Having given an eye to the marshalling of the vehicles, taken one by one from the shed, put on a transporter and then pushed under the station roof by a gang of men, he then had to hurry to the booking-hall and give an eye to the sale of tickets and registering of luggage. A dispute broke out between some soldiers and a railwayman in which he had to intervene. For another half-hour, what with freezing draughts, shivering passengers, and eyes heavy with sleep, and his own irritability through fussing about in the dark, he never had a moment to think of himself. Then, when the departure of the slow train had cleared the station, he hurried off to the points-man's box to make sure that everything was all right in that quarter because another train was due in, the semi-fast from Paris which was running late. Back he went to see the people off that, and waited until the stream of passengers had given up their tickets and piled into the hotel buses, which in those days came in and stood under the roof with only a low fence between them and the line. And it was only then that he had a minute to breathe in the now deserted and silent station.

It struck six. Roubaud went out from the covered station and outside in the open looked up, took a breath and saw that day was breaking at last. The wind from the sea had blown away the last of the mist, and it was the bright morning of a lovely day. He looked northwards at the heights of Ingouville and along as far as the trees in the cemetery, standing out purple as the sky grew lighter; then, turning south and west, he noticed over the sea the last group of thin white clouds sailing slowly along in a flotilla, while the whole eastern sky, the immense gap of the Seine estuary, was beginning to catch fire with the imminent rising of the sun. He automatically took off his silver-braided cap as if to cool his brow in the keen, pure air. This familiar horizon, the great flat expanse of the station dependencies, goods arrival side on the left, then the engine-sheds, and then dispatch on the right, a veritable town, all seemed to settle and restore him to the calm of of the daily routine, always the same. Above the wall of the rue Charles-Lafitte the factory chimneys were smoking away, and there were the huge stacks of coal in the depots alongside the Vauban dock. And a noise of activity was already rising from the other docks. Whistles from freight trains, the reawakening of life and the smell of the sea borne on the wind, all these things made him think of the day's festivities, the ship about to be launched round which the crowds would be milling.

As Roubaud was making his way back to the covered part of the station he found the men beginning to make up the 6.40 train, and thought they were putting coach 293 on to the trans-porter. All the calming effect of the fresh morning vanished in a sudden outburst of temper.

'No, blast you! Not that one! Leave it alone, it isn't going until tonight.'

The foreman of the gang pointed out that they were only shifting the coach so as to get another that was behind it. But he did not hear, for his quite unreasonable rage had made him deaf.

'You clumsy lot of buggers, you've been told not to touch it!'

When at last he saw the point he was still furious, but switched to the inconvenience of the station, in which you couldn't even turn a carriage round. And indeed that station, one of the earliest to be built on the line, was inadequate and quite unworthy of Le Havre, what with its old timber carriage-sheds, station roof of wood and zinc with small skylights, and bare, dreary buildings with cracks everywhere.

'It's a disgrace, and I don't know why the Company hasn't knocked the whole lot down before now!'

The men stared at him in surprise at the open way he was talking, because he was usually such a stickler for discipline. He noticed it and suddenly stopped, then stiffly and in silence he watched the rest of the job. His low forehead was furrowed with annoyance and his round and florid face, with its stiff red beard, took on a look of great tension from the effort of will.

From then onwards Roubaud maintained all his presence of mind. He saw to the express and checked every detail. Some couplings looked badly done, and he insisted on their being tightened under his eye. A mother and her two daughters, friends of his wife's, wanted him to find a Ladies Only compartment. Then, having checked that everything was in order with the train, he blew the whistle for departure and for a long time watched it moving away with the keen glance of a man for whom a moment of absentmindedness might cost human lives. But then he had at once to cross the line to see in a train from Rouen that was approaching. It happened that there was a Post Office employee on it with whom he regularly passed the time of day. It was a short, quarter-of-an-hour breather in his very busy morning, as no pressing job needed his attention. So that morning as usual he rolled a cigarette and had a lively chat. It was lighter now and the gas-lamps under the station roof had just been put out. The roof was so poorly glazed that there was still a grey gloom under it, but the vast expanse of sky on to which it opened at the end was already ablaze with fiery rays, and the whole horizon was turning pink, with the details crystal clear in the pure air of a peaceful winter morning.

At eight o'clock M. Dabadie, the stationmaster, usually came down and the deputy went to report. He was a handsome man, very dark and smartly dressed, looking like an important businessman entirely taken up with his affairs. As a matter of fact he was not very interested in the passenger station, but concentrated above all on the dock traffic and the enormous trans-shipment of cargo and its continuous movement to and fro between the big commercial concerns in Le Havre and places all over the world. This morning he was late, and twice already Roubaud had opened his office door and not found him. His mail on the desk was not even opened. The deputy stationmaster's eye had lighted on a telegram among the letters, and as though rooted there by some fascination he had stayed at the door, turning round in spite of himself and glancing at the desk.

At last, at ten past eight, M. Dabadie appeared. Roubaud sat down and said nothing so as to let him open the telegram. But his boss was in no hurry and anxious to be pleasant with his subordinate, whom he liked.

'And it all went off all right in Paris, of course?'

'Yes, sir, thank you.'

At last he opened the wire, but still did not read it, smiling at the other man, whose voice had gone very soft because of the extreme effort he was making to master a nervous twitch which made his chin quiver.

'We are very glad to keep you here.'

'And I'm very glad to stay with you, sir.'

Then M. Dabadie made up his mind to read the telegram, and Roubaud watched him, a slight sweat breaking out on his face. But the emotion he was expecting did not come and his chief calmly finished reading the telegram and threw it down on his desk. No doubt it was some straightforward service matter. And he went straight on opening his correspondence while, as every morning, his deputy made his usual verbal report on happenings of the night and early morning. But this morning Roubaud lost the thread and had to cast about before remembering what his colleague had told him about the marauders discovered in the left luggage. A few more words were exchanged and the boss was waving him away when the two deputies, one of the docks and the other of goods traffic, came in also to report. They brought another telegram that one of the men had given them on the platform.

'You can go,' said M. Dabadie, seeing Roubaud hesitate at the door.

But he still waited there with round, staring eyes, and did not go until the little bit of paper had fallen on to the desk, thrown down with the same unconcern. He wandered about in the station for a minute or two, puzzled and abstracted. The clock said 8.35 and he had no train to see out before the 9.50 slow. Usually he took advantage of this hour's lull and did the rounds of the station. He walked about for several minutes without knowing where his feet were taking him. Then as he glanced up and found himself once again opposite coach 293 he suddenly wheeled round and went off towards the engine-sheds although there was nothing he had to attend to over there. By now the sun was coming up over the horizon and a golden dust looked like fine rain in the pale sky. But he no longer enjoyed the lovely morning, he quickened his steps, looking very busy and trying to overcome his obsession with this suspense.

Suddenly a voice stopped him.

'Morning, Monsieur Roubaud, did you see my wife?'

It was Pecqueux the fireman, a tall fellow of forty-three, thin but with big bones and a face burnt brown by fire and smoke. His grey eyes beneath a low brow and his big mouth and prominent jaw were laughing – the continual laughter of a gay dog.

'Oh, it's you!' said Roubaud, stopping in surprise. 'Oh yes, the mishap to the engine, I forgot . . . So you aren't going back until tonight? Twenty-four hours off, that's a bit of all right, isn't it?'

'You bet it is,' echoed the other, still tight after a binge the night before.

Native of a village near Rouen, he had begun with the Company very young as a fitter's mate. Then at thirty, having had enough of the workshop, he had decided to be a fireman with a view to becoming a driver, and at that stage he had married Victoire, who came from the same village. But the years had gone by and he was still a fireman, and now he would never rise to driver, for he was a loose liver, feckless, given to drink and women. He would have been sacked twenty times over had he not been protected by President Grandmorin and had people not got used to his vices, which he made up for by his good humour and long experience at his job. He only became dangerous when he was drunk, and then he turned into a real brute, capable of any foul deed.

'Did you see my wife?' he repeated with a broad grin.

'Yes, of course we saw her. We even had our lunch in your room ... Oh, you've got a good wife there, Pecqueux, and it's wrong of you to play her up.'

He grinned more broadly still.

'Oh, come off it! Why, she's the one who wants me to have a good time.'

It was true. Victoire, two years older than him, had grown enormously fat and difficult to do anything with, and she slipped five-franc pieces into his pockets so that he could get his fun elsewhere. She had never been particularly hurt by his infidelities and the continual whoring his nature demanded, and now their existence had been regularized: he had two women, one at each end of the line, his wife in Paris for the nights he spent there and the other at Le Havre for the time off there between trains. Victoire, who was herself very economical and lived very frugally, who knew everything and treated him like a mother, often used to say that she didn't want him to look a disgrace to the other one, so she even looked over his under-clothes before each trip, for she would have been very upset if the other one had accused her of not looking after their man properly.

'All the same,' went on Roubaud, 'it's not very nice. My wife, who adores her foster-mother, wants to tell you off.'

But he stopped short as he saw a tall, lean woman, Philomène Sauvagnat, coming out of the shed near where they were standing. She was the sister of the depot foreman, the extra wife Pecqueux had had at Le Havre for the past year. They must both have been talking in the shed when he had come out to greet Roubaud. Still young-looking for her thirty-two years, tall, angular, flat chested, her flesh consumed by continual desire, she had the long head and burning eyes of a stringy, neighing steed. They said she drank. All the men at the station had trailed through her bedroom in the little house her brother occupied near the engine-sheds, which she allowed to get into a very dirty state. Her brother, from Auvergne, was a pig-headed man, a strict disciplinarian and well thought of by his superiors, and he had had the greatest trouble because of her, to the point of being threatened with the sack; and if they now put up with her because of him, he insisted on keeping her only because of family feeling. But that did not prevent his belabouring her so brutally that he left her half dead on the floor every time he found her with a man. It had been a real match between her and Pecqueux; she was fully satisfied at last by the great rollicking oaf, while he, enjoying the change from his over-fat wife, was delighted with this over-thin one and often used to say that he never need look elsewhere again. Only Séverine, feeling she owed it to Victoire, had broken off relations with Philomène whom she had already been avoiding as much as she could out of natural pride, and she had now given up nodding to her.

'Well,' Philomène said insolently, 'see you later, Pecqueux. I'm off, as M. Roubaud is going to preach morality to you on his wife's behalf.'

Being an amiable sort of chap he just went on laughing.

'Don't go, he's only joking.'

'No, no, I've got to take a couple of my eggs I've promised to Mme Lebleu.'

She had dropped that name on purpose, being well aware of the rivalry between the cashier's wife and the deputy station-master's, and affecting to be on excellent terms with the one so as to infuriate the other. But she did stay all the same, being suddenly interested when she heard the fireman asking about the business with the Sub-Prefect.

'It's all sorted out and you're pleased, I suppose, Monsieur Roubaud?'

'Very pleased.'

Pecqueux screwed up his eyes in a knowing way.

'Oh, there was no need for you to worry, because when you've got a bigwig in your pocket ... Well, you know what I mean. My wife's got a lot to thank him for, too.'

Roubaud cut short this allusion to President Grandmorin by repeating sharply:

'So you're not off again till this evening?'

'That's right, Lison is nearly repaired, they're just finishing adjusting the coupling-rod. And I'm waiting for my driver, who's gone off to take an airing. You know Jacques Lantier, don't you? He comes from your part of the world.'

Roubaud didn't answer for a moment, he was somewhere else, his mind wandering. Then he woke up with a jerk.

'What, Jacques Lantier, the driver? Of course I know him. Oh, you know, just hallo and good-bye. We first met here because he's younger than me and I'd never seen him down there in Plassans ... Last autumn he did a little job for my wife, going to see some cousins of hers in Dieppe ... He's a capable fellow, they say.'

He was talking for the sake of talking, and talking a lot. Then he suddenly took himself off.

'Well, be seeing you, Pecqueux ... I must have a look round over there.'

Only then did Philomène go, with her long, loping stride, while Pecqueux, standing there with his hands in his pockets laughing for joy at having nothing to do on this lovely morning, was astonished to see the deputy stationmaster quickly coming back after just rushing round the shed. His look round hadn't taken very long. Now who might he have come to spy on?

As Roubaud went back under the station roof it was just before nine. He walked straight through to the parcels office at the other end, looked round without apparently finding what he wanted, then came back with the same hurried step. He looked anxiously at the different departments, one after the other. At that time of day the station was quite deserted, and he moved about alone, looking as though this peacefulness was getting more and more on his nerves, like a man tormented by the threat of catastrophe and finally longing for it to come. His self-control was at an end and he could not keep still, nor could he now keep his eyes off the clock. Nine, five past nine. Normally he did not go up home again for his lunch until ten, after the departure of the 9.50. Yet now he suddenly went upstairs as he thought of Séverine, who must be on tenterhooks as well.

At that exact moment Mme Lebleu was opening her door in the passage to Philomène who was paying a neighbourly call, her hair all over the place and bearing two eggs. They stood there waiting and Roubaud had to get into his own flat with their eyes glued on him. He had his key ready and took no time at all. But all the same, in the quick opening and shutting of the door, they caught sight of the pale profile of Séverine sitting on a chair in the dining-room with idle hands, motionless. Pulling Philomène in with her and shutting her door as well, Mme Lebleu explained that she had already seen her looking like that early in the morning – it must be the business with the Sub-Prefect that was turning out badly. But no, Philomène explained that she had rushed over because she had news, and repeated what she had just heard the deputy stationmaster say himself. Thereupon the two women got carried away into conjecture. It was always the same every time they met, gossip without end.

'They've had a good ticking off, my dear, believe you me! They're in a tight corner, and that's a fact!'

'Ah, my dear friend, if only we could see the back of them!'

The increasingly venomous rivalry between the Lebleus and the Roubauds had its origin in a simple matter of accommodation. The whole of the first floor, above the waiting-rooms, was given over to housing employees, and the central passage, a real hotel corridor, painted cream and lit from above, divided the floor in two, with lines of brown doors on either side. The only thing was that the flats on the right had windows overlooking the station yard, planted with old elms above which opened out the wonderful view of the Ingouville hills; while those to the left had low, arched windows which looked straight out at the station roof, the steep pitch of which, with its ridge of zinc and dirty glass skylights, shut out the horizon. Nothing was more cheerful than the one side, with the continual bustle of the station yard, the green trees and distant views of the country, while you could die of boredom on the other side, in which you

88

could hardly see, and the bit of sky was walled round like a prison. On the front lived the stationmaster, the other deputy stationmaster, Moulin, and the Lebleus; on the back the Roubauds and Mlle Guichon the clerk, and there were three rooms kept for visiting inspectors. Now it was an established fact that the two deputy stationmasters had always lived next door to each other. The fact that the Lebleus were there was due to the kindness of Roubaud's predecessor, the former deputy, who, as he was a widower with no children, had wanted to be pleasant to the Lebleus and had given them his flat. But shouldn't this accommodation have reverted to the Roubauds? Was it fair to relegate them to the rear when they had the right to be in the front? So long as the two households had lived together peacefully Sèverine had yielded to her neighbour, who was twenty years her senior and moreover in poor health and so fat that she was always short of breath. And war had only been declared since Philomène had made mischief between the two women with her abominable scandal-mongering.

'You know,' she went on, 'they are quite capable of taking advantage of their trip to Paris to demand that you should be turned out . . . I've been told that they sent the Managing Director a long letter setting out their claim.'

Mme Lebleu choked with rage.

'The wretches! And I'm quite sure they're scheming to get that clerk woman on their side and she's hardly even nodded to me for a fortnight . . . And that's another nice business, too! So I'm keeping my eye on her.'

She lowered her voice to assert that every night Mlle Guichon went and slept with the stationmaster, she was sure. Their two doors were facing each other. It was M. Dabadie, a widower with a daughter always away at school, who had brought her here, a thirty-year-old blonde and already faded, silent and skinny, who glided about like a snake. She must have been some sort of schoolmarm. You couldn't possibly catch her by surprise, so noiselessly did she slip through the narrowest cracks. In herself she was of no importance. But if she slept with the stationmaster her importance was decisive, and victory depended upon having a hold over her by knowing her secret.

'Oh I shall find out in the end,' went on Mme Lebleu. 'I don't mean to let them down me . . . Here we are and here we stay. Decent people are on our side, aren't they dear?'

The fact was that the whole station was passionately involved in this war of the two flats. The passage in particular was in a ferment. Only the other deputy, Moulin, took no part, satisfied to be on the front, married to a timid, frail little woman whom nobody ever saw and who gave him a child every twenty months.

'Anyhow,' concluded Philomène, 'even if they are in a spot of bother, this isn't what's going to bring them down . . . So mind how you go, because they know people with a long arm.'

She was still holding her two eggs, and now she presented them, this morning's eggs that she had just taken from under her hens. The old girl fell over herself with thanks.

'Oh, how nice of you. You do spoil me . . . Come and see me more often. You know my husband is always in his office, and I get so bored stuck here because of my bad legs! Whatever should I do if those beastly people did me out of my view?'

Then as she was seeing her out and opening the front door she put her finger on her lips.

'Sh! Listen.'

They both stood there in the passage for a full five minutes, motionless, holding their breath. Heads well forward they strained their ears towards the Roubauds' room. But not a sound came forth, a deathly silence reigned. And for fear of being caught they eventually separated with a final nod to each other, without a word. The one tiptoed away and the other closed her door so quietly that the latch made no sound as it slipped into place.

At twenty past nine Roubaud was down in the station again, giving an eye to the make-up of the 9.50 slow, and for all his self-control he was gesticulating more, walking up and down and constantly looking round to scan the platform from end to end. Nothing happened, and his hands were beginning to shake.

Then all of a sudden, as he was once more looking back to cast his eye over the station, he heard quite near him the voice of one of the telegraph operators saying breathlessly:

'Monsieur Roubaud, you wouldn't know where the station-master and the superintendent are, would you? I've got telegrams for them and have been running round for ten minutes.'

He turned round, and his whole being was frozen so stiff that not a muscle moved in his face. His eyes fell on the two telegrams the man was holding. This time the latter's emotion left no doubt. This at last was it.

'Monsieur Dabadie went along that way just now,' he calmly answered.

Never had he felt so cool and clear-headed, with his whole being taut, on the defensive. Now he was sure of himself.

'Look,' he said, 'here he is now.'

The stationmaster was indeed returning from the parcels office. As soon as he had read the telegram he exclaimed:

'There has been a murder on the line ... This is from the inspector at Rouen.'

'What?' asked Roubaud. 'One of our staff murdered?'

'No, no, a passenger in a coupé ... The body was thrown out just after the exit from the Malaunay tunnel, at post 153. The victim is one of our directors, President Grandmorin.'

It was the deputy's turn to exclaim.

'The President! Oh, my poor wife will be upset!'

The exclamation was so natural and so concerned that M. Dabadie paused a moment.

'That's true, you knew him, such a good man, wasn't he?'

Then he turned to the other telegram, addressed to the superintendent of railway police.

'This must be from the examining magistrate, no doubt some formality ... And it's only twenty-five past nine. M. Cauche isn't here, of course ... Somebody must run over to the Café du Commerce on the Cours Napoléon. That's where he'll be, for certain.'

M. Cauche came five minutes later, fetched by one of the porters. An ex-officer, considering this job as retirement, he never showed himself at the station before ten, strolled about a bit and then went back to the café. This sensation had landed on him between two games of piquet, and had amazed him at first because the things that usually passed through his hands were pretty trivial. But the telegram did indeed come from the examining magistrate in Rouen, and if it only reached him twelve hours after the discovery of the body that was because the magistrate had first telegraphed Paris and the stationmaster there to ascertain in what circumstances the victim had left, and only after that, with the information about the number of the train and of the carriage, had he sent the superintendent instructions to examine the coupé in the carriage 293 if it was still at Le Havre. All of a sudden M. Cauche's display of bad temper at having been, no doubt, so pointlessly inconvenienced disappeared, and an attitude of extreme importance befitting the exceptional gravity of the affair was substituted.

'But' he said, suddenly afraid that the inquiry might slip out of his grasp, 'that carriage can't still be there, it must have gone off this morning.'

Roubaud reassured him in his calm manner.

'Oh no, it hasn't, begging your pardon . . . There was a coupé reserved for this evening, and so the carriage is over there in the shed.'

He led the way, with the superintendent and the stationmaster after him. But the news must have spread, for workmen were stealing away from their jobs and following as well, while clerical staff appeared at the doors of the various offices and eventually drew near one by one. Soon there was quite a gathering.

As they reached the carriage M. Dabadie thought aloud:

'But the usual inspection was done last night. If there had been any traces they would have been put down in the report.'

'We shall soon see,' said M. Cauche.

He opened the door and climbed into the compartment. But he recoiled at once, forgetting his dignity in a towering rage and swearing:

'Bloody hell! It looks as though someone has bled a pig!'

A murmur of horror ran through the crowd, necks were craned. M. Dabadie was one of the first to want to have a look, and he got up on the step, while behind him Roubaud also craned his neck, to be like everybody else.

Inside the coupé nothing was out of place. The windows were still shut and everything looked in order. But a horrible stench came through the open door and a dark pool of blood had congealed in the middle of the upholstery, and the pool was so deep and wide that a trickle had flowed down as though from a

92

spring and spread over the carpet, and clots were sticking to the material. Nothing else except this revolting blood.

M. Dabadie flew in into a rage.

'Where are the men who did the inspection last night? Bring them here!'

They happened to be there and came forward, mumbling excuses: how can you tell at night? And besides, they ran their hands over everything. They swore they had not felt anything last night.

Meanwhile M. Cauche, still standing inside the compartment, was making notes in pencil for his report. He called over Roubaud, who was a crony of his, for they sometimes smoked a cigarette together when they were strolling along the quayside off duty.

'Monsieur Roubaud, come up here and help me, will you?'

When Roubaud had stepped over the blood on the carpet so as not to tread in it:

'Look under the other cushion and see if anything has slipped down there.'

'No, nothing there.'

But his attention was caught by a stain on the padded back of the seat and he pointed it out to the superintendent. Wasn't it a bloodstained fingerprint? No, they finally agreed that it was only a splash. The crowd of onlookers had drawn near to watch the examination, smelling out a crime and pushing behind the stationmaster who, being a squeamish sort of man, could not bear to go beyond the step.

Suddenly a thought occurred to him:

'By the way, Monsieur Roubaud, you were on the train. You did come back on the night express, didn't you? Perhaps you could give us some information.'

'Oh yes, of course,' exclaimed the superintendent. 'Did you notice anything?'

For three or four seconds Roubaud made no sound. At that moment he was stooping to examine the carpet. But he straightened up almost at once and answered in his usual, slightly gruff voice:

'Certainly, certainly I'll tell you ... My wife was with me,

93

and if what I know has to go down in the report I'd rather she came down and checked my recollections with hers.'

This seemed very reasonable to M. Cauche, and Pecqueux, who had just turned up, offered to go and fetch Mme Roubaud. He strode off and there was a moment of waiting. Philomène, who had come with Pecqueux, followed him with her eyes, vexed that he should offer to take on this job. But having caught sight of Mme Lebleu, hurrying along as fast as her poor swollen legs would carry her, she rushed to help her, and the two women threw up their hands to heaven and uttered exclamations, thrilled at the discovery of such an abominable crime. Although absolutely nothing was yet known, various versions were already circulating round them, accompanied by startled looks and gestures. Dominating the hubbub of voices Philomène herself, with no authority for the fact, stated on her word of honour that Mme Roubaud had seen the murderer. A silence fell when Pecqueux reappeared, bringing the lady in question.

'Just look at her!' hissed Mme Lebleu. 'Would you ever say she was a deputy's wife? Giving herself airs like a princess! This morning before it was light she was like that already, hair all done and corset on as though she was going out visiting!'

Séverine came along with dainty steps. There was quite a long stretch of platform to walk beneath the scrutiny of the on-lookers, and she did not shrink, but just held her handkerchief to her eyes because of the great shock of grief she had just had on learning the name of the victim. Clad in a black woollen dress and very elegant, she seemed to be in mourning for her benefactor. Her heavy dark hair gleamed in the sunlight, for she had not even taken the time to cover her head despite the cold. Her soft blue eyes, full of anguish and suffused with tears, made her look very touching.

'She might well cry,' whispered Philomène, 'They're up the spout now their God Almighty has been killed.'

When Séverine had reached the middle of the crowd in front of the open door of the coupé M. Cauche and Roubaud came out and at once the latter began to say what he knew.

'Yesterday morning as soon as we got to Paris we went to see M. Grandmorin, isn't that so, dear? It would be a quarter past eleven, wouldn't it?'

94

He looked hard at her and she repeated in a docile voice:

'Yes, a quarter past eleven.'

But then she caught sight of the cushion black with blood, and she had a choking fit and broke into violent sobs. The stationmaster was deeply moved and considerately broke in:

'Madame, if you can't bear this sight ... We do understand your grief.'

'Oh, only a word or two,' chimed in the superintendent, 'and then we'll get someone to take Madame home.'

Roubaud hurried on:

'And then, after we had talked about this and that, M. Grandmorin told us he was leaving the following day for Doinville, to stay with his sister ... I can still see him sitting there at his desk. I was here, my wife was there ... That's so, isn't it, my dear? He did say he was going the next day?'

'Yes, the next day.'

M. Cauche, still taking down rapid notes in pencil, glanced up.

'The next day? But surely he left that evening?'

'Just a minute,' countered Roubaud. 'When he heard that we were going back that evening he even thought for a moment that he would take the express with us if my wife would like to go with him to Doinville and stay a few days with his sister as she has done before. But my wife, who had a lot of things to do here, declined. That's right, you declined, didn't you?'

'Yes, I declined.'

'So that was that, he was very nice about it. He looked into my affairs and then saw us to the door of his office, didn't he, dear?'

'Yes, to the door.'

'We left in the evening. Before going into our compartment I had a word with M. Vandorpe, the stationmaster. And I didn't see anything at all. I was very put out because I thought we were on our own, and there was a woman I hadn't noticed sitting in a corner seat, and then even more because two other people, a married couple, got in at the last moment. Nothing out of the way as far as Rouen either; I didn't see anything. So as we got out at Rouen to stretch our legs, imagine our surprise when we saw M. Grandmorin standing by the door of a coupé three or four carriages along from ours. "Oh, President," I said, "so you did leave? Well, we hardly thought we should be travelling with you!" And he explained that he had had a wire . . . The whistle blew and we ran back to our own compartment in which, by the way, there was nobody, as all our fellow travellers had got out at Rouen, which didn't upset us at all. So there it is, that's all, isn't it, my dear?'

'Yes, that's all.'

This story, simple as it was, had made a deep impression on the audience. They were all gaping, trying to understand. The superintendent stopped writing and voiced the general surprise:

'And you are sure that there was nobody in the coupé with M. Grandmorin?'

'Oh yes, quite sure of that.'

A thrill ran round. The mystery that faced them breathed fear like a little cold draught which everyone felt blowing down the back of his neck. If the passenger was alone, by whom could he have been murdered and thrown out of the compartment, three leagues from there, before any other stop of the train?

In the silence could be heard the malevolent voice of Philomène:

'It's funny all the same!'

Feeling she was staring at him, Roubaud stared back and nodded, as much as to say that he thought it was funny too. He noticed next to her Pecqueux and Mme Lebleu, also nodding. Everybody's eyes were now upon him, they were expecting something more, searching his person for some forgotten detail which might throw some light on the affair. There was no accusation in these desperately searching looks, but still he thought he could detect the dawn of a suspicion, a doubt that the tiniest thing can turn into a certainty.

'Extraordinary!' murmured M. Cauche.

'Quite extraordinary!' echoed M. Dabadie.

Then Roubaud made up his mind:

'What I am still quite sure about is that the express, which goes non-stop from Rouen to Barentin, went at its regulation speed and I noticed nothing unusual . . . I can say this because as we were alone I let down the window so as to smoke a cigarette, and sometimes looked out, so I was well aware of all the train noises. And what's more, at Barentin I saw the station-master, M. Bessière, my successor, hailed him and we exchanged a word or two while he got up on the step and shook hands. Isn't that so, my dear? M. Bessière can be asked and he will say the same.'

Séverine, still pale and motionless, her delicate features disfigured by grief, once more confirmed her husband's declaration:

'Oh yes, he will say the same.'

From that moment any accusation was out of the question, given that the Roubauds had got back into their compartment at Rouen and were spoken to by a friend at Barentin. The shadow of a suspicion that the deputy stationmaster thought he had seen in people's eyes was gone, and the general amazement increased. The mystery was deepening more and more.

'Look here,' said the superintendent, 'are you positive that nobody could have got into that compartment at Rouen after you left M. Grandmorin?'

Obviously Roubaud had not foreseen that question, and for the first time he floundered, presumably caught without a prepared answer. He looked at his wife and hesitated.

'Oh no, I don't think anyone could have ... They were closing the doors and blowing whistles, and we only just had time to get back to our own carriage ... And besides, the coupé was reserved, and nobody could go in, I suppose ...'

But his wife's blue eyes were staring so hard and looked so big that he was afraid of being so positive.

'After all, I don't know ... Yes, perhaps somebody could have got in ... There was a real scrimmage ...'

As he spoke his voice became assured again and this quite new story was taking shape and crystallizing.

'You know, because of the holiday at Le Havre the crowd was enormous. We had to defend our compartment against second- and even third-class passengers ... And besides, that station is very badly lit, you couldn't see anything, and people were shoving and shouting in the stampede of departure ... Yes, of course, it is quite likely that somebody, not knowing where to get in or even taking advantage of the crush, forced himself into the compartment at the last moment.'

He broke off.

'What do you think, dear? That's what must have happened.'

Séverine looked overcome and was holding her handkerchief to her swollen eyes.

'That's what must have happened, certainly.'

That settled the line of inquiry, and without commenting the superintendent and the stationmaster exchanged a look of agreement. There was a prolonged reaction in the crowd, which felt that the inquiry was over and longed to talk about it, and at once theories were bandied about and each one had his story. For a little while the whole business of the station had been suspended, all the staff were there, obsessed by the drama, and it was quite a surprise to see the 9.38 coming into the station. They all rushed as doors opened and streams of passengers poured out. However, all the inquisitive ones had stayed round the superintendent, who, with the conscientiousness of a methodical man, was having a final look at the bloodstained coupé.

At that moment Pecqueux, gesticulating between Mme Lebleu and Philomène, caught sight of his driver, Jacques Lantier, who had just got out of the train and was standing still looking at the crowd. He beckoned frantically, but Jacques did not move. However, eventually he did make up his mind and came slowly over.

'What's up?' he asked his fireman.

He knew perfectly well, and only listened with half an ear to the news of the murder and the conjectures being made. What did surprise him and move him strangely was to land in the middle of this inquiry and find this carriage again which he had glimpsed in the dark, going at full speed. He craned forward and saw the pool of congealed blood on the seat; and the murder scene came back to him, especially the dead body stretched across the line with its throat cut. Then, as he turned his eyes away he noticed the Roubauds, while Pecqueux was going on with the story, telling him how they were mixed up in it, their departure from Paris in the same train, the last words they had exchanged at Rouen. He knew the husband from having passed the time of day with him since he had been working the express, and had just caught sight of the wife occasionally. But he had kept clear of her as he did of other women because of his unhealthy fear. Now, weeping and pale like this, with her soft, frightened blue eyes beneath the heavy black hair, she held his attention. He could not take his eyes off her, and going off into a dream, found himself wondering in a puzzled way how it came about that the Roubauds and he were there, how events had conspired to bring them together in front of this carriage, the scene of the murder, they back from Paris last night and he from Barentin that very minute.

'Oh I know, I know,' he said aloud, interrupting Pecqueux. 'I happened to be there myself last night, just by the end of the tunnel, and I think I saw something just as the train was going past.'

There was a great sensation, and they all crowded round him. And he was the first to shudder in horrified astonishment at what he had just said. Why had he spoken after solemnly promising himself that he would keep his mouth shut? So many good reasons warned him to keep quiet! Yet the words had come out of his mouth unbidden while he was looking at this woman. She had suddenly taken her handkerchief away to fix her tearful eyes on him, and they grew bigger still.

The superintendent came over to him at once.

'What! What did you see?'

With Séverine's eyes fixed on him, Jacques said what he had seen: the brilliantly lit coupé going by in the night at full speed, and the fleeting vision of the profiles of the two men, one on his back, the other holding a knife. Roubaud listened, standing by his wife and studying him with his bulging, alert eyes.

'So,' asked the superintendent, 'you would recognize the murderer?'

'Oh no, I don't think so.'

'Was he wearing an overcoat or a workman's blouse?'

'I couldn't say for sure. Just think, a train that must have been doing eighty kilometres an hour!'

Séverine, in spite of herself, exchanged a glance with Roubaud, who found enough strength to say:

'You'd have to have good eyesight, and that's a fact.'

'All the same,' concluded M. Cauche, 'this is an important piece of evidence. The examining magistrate will help you to see what it adds up to. Monsieur Lantier and Monsieur Roubaud, give me your full names for the summonses.'

That was the end of it, the onlookers gradually drifted away and the normal work of the station was resumed. Roubaud in particular had to run and see to the 9.50 stopping train which was already filling up with passengers. He had given Jacques a much more vigorous handshake than usual, so that he, left alone with Séverine, behind Mme Lebleu, Pecqueux and Philomène, felt he had to take the young woman back into the station as far as the staff staircase, and although he could find nothing to say to her he seemed compelled to stay with her as though some link had been forged between them. By now the day had burst forth in joy and the bright sun was rising triumphantly over the morning mists in the limpid blue vault of heaven, while the sea breeze, springing up with the incoming tide, was bringing in a salty tang. When at last he was taking his leave he once again met those great eyes, whose terrified and supplicating gentleness had stirred him so deeply.

But there was a brief whistle. Roubaud was giving the signal for departure. The engine answered with a long blast and the 9.50 began to move, then accelerated until it disappeared into the golden haze of the sunshine.

[4]

ONE day in the second week of March M. Denizet, the examining magistrate, had summoned for the second time certain important witnesses in the Grandmorin case to his office in the Law Courts at Rouen.

The affair had been an enormous sensation for the past three weeks. It had convulsed Rouen and was the thrill of Paris, and the opposition papers had taken it up as a weapon in the violent campaign they were waging against the Empire. The struggle was embittered by the approaching general election, which dominated the whole political scene. There had been some stormy sessions in the Chamber: one, for instance, in which the ratification of the powers of two deputies attached to the Emperor's person had been bitterly disputed, or another in which there had been a determined attack against the financial administration of the Prefect of the Seine and a demand for the election of a municipal council. And now the Grandmorin affair came just at the right moment for the agitation to be continued, and the most extraordinary tales were being bandied round and every morning the papers spread themselves about new theories harmful to the government. On the one hand they let it be understood that the victim, one of the Tuileries set, an ex-magistrate, Commander of the Legion of Honour, and fabulously rich, was given over to the worst debaucheries; but on the other, the preliminary inquiries having still produced nothing, they were beginning to accuse the police and the legal profession of complacency and were waxing facetious about this mythical murderer, still undiscoverable. The fact that there was a great deal of truth in these allegations made them all the harder to bear.

So M. Denizet was very conscious of the heavy responsibility weighing on him. He was also particularly excited about it because he harboured ambitions and was longing for an affair of this importance which would throw into relief the remarkable

101

qualities of perspicacity and energy he fancied he possessed. Son of a successful Norman stock-breeder, he had read his law at Caen and only entered the magistracy rather late in life, and his peasant origins, aggravated by his father's bankruptcy, had made promotion slow. Deputy prosecutor at Bernay, Dieppe and Le Havre, it had taken him ten years to become public prosecutor at Pont-Audemer. Then he was moved to Rouen as deputy, and now, at over fifty, he had been examining magistrate for eighteen months. Without means of his own and with pressing needs that his meagre emoluments could not cover, he lived in that dependent position of ill-paid magistrate to which only the mediocre resign themselves, and in which the more astute chafe while waiting to be bought. He had a very subtle, alert mind and was actually an honest man, loving his profession, drunk with his own power which made him, in his capacity as a judge, absolute master of the freedom of others. It was self-interest alone that kept his passion under control, and he had such a keen desire to receive a decoration and be transferred to Paris that, having let himself be carried away by his love of truth on the opening day of the inquiry, he was now proceeding with extreme prudence, sensing pitfalls on all sides in which his hopes for the future might be lost.

It should be said that M. Denizet had been influenced, for at the very outset of the inquiry, a friend had advised him to go to the Ministry of Justice in Paris. There he had had a long conversation with the Secretary-General, M. Camy-Lamotte, a very important figure with absolute control over personnel, in charge of appointments and in constant communication with the Tuileries. He was a handsome man who had begun as a deputy public prosecutor like himself, but thanks to his connections and his wife he had become a Deputy and Grand Officer of the Legion of Honour. The case had naturally come to him because the Public Prosecutor of Rouen, worried about this shady story in which a former magistrate was the victim, had taken the precaution of referring it to the Minister, who in his turn had passed it on to his Secretary-General. At this juncture there had been a coincidence, for M. Camy-Lamotte happened to have been a fellow student of President Grandmorin; he was a year or two younger, but had kept up such a close friendship with him that he knew him intimately, even all his vices. So he referred to the tragic death of his friend with deep affliction, and held forth to M. Denizet about nothing but his burning desire to find the guilty party. But he did not hide the fact that the Tuileries were very grieved at this excessive fuss and he had ventured to recommend a great deal of tact. In a word, the examining magistrate had gathered that he would do well not to be in a hurry and not to take any risk without prior approval. In fact he returned to Rouen feeling certain that the Secretary-General had sent his own spies in his anxiety to look into the thing for himself. They wanted to know the truth in order to conceal it better should need arise.

However the days went by and despite his efforts to be patient M. Denizet was getting annoyed by the facetiousness of the press. Then the detective in him reappeared, like a good hound with its nose to the wind. He was inspired by the need to get on the real scent and have the glory of being the first to have nosed it out, but was prepared to abandon it if he were ordered to. So while waiting for some letter, advice, or mere hint from the Ministry, which seemed in no hurry to come, he had actively taken up his inquiry again. Two or three arrests had already been made, but no charge could be sustained. Then suddenly the opening of President Grandmorin's will revived a suspicion that had crossed his mind from the very outset: the possible guilt of the Roubauds. This will, which was a jumble of strange bequests, contained one bequeathing to Séverine the house situated at the place called La Croix-de-Maufras. From that moment the motive for the murder that so far he had looked for in vain was clear: the Roubauds, aware of the legacy, might have murdered their benefactor to gain immediate possession. This stuck all the more firmly in his mind because M. Camy-Lamotte had talked in a peculiar way about Mme Roubaud, saying he had known her at the President's house when she was a young girl. Yet how many unlikely elements and physical and moral impossibilities! Since he had been directing his researches in this direction he had at every step come up against facts which upset his conception of a judicial inquiry pursued in the correct way. Nothing was clear: the great central light, the first cause illuminating everything else, was not there.

There was admittedly another line that M. Denizet had not lost sight of, the hint dropped by Roubaud himself about the man who might have got into the compartment under cover of the confusion of departure. This was the famous mythical murderer that all the opposition papers sneered at. The first concern of the inquiry had been over the description of this man, at Rouen where he got in, and Barentin where he must have got out, but nothing precise had come of this, and some witnesses even said that the coupé could not possibly have been entered by force, while others gave the most contradictory details. This line of inquiry seemed unlikely to lead anywhere until the magistrate, while questioning the level-crossing man Misard, stumbled accidentally across the dramatic story of Cabuche and Louisette, the young girl who was raped by the President and, it was alleged, ran to her sweetheart's home and died there. This was for him the flash of illumination, and the classic murder charge was complete in his mind. It was all there: threats of death made by the drayman against the victim, his deplorable family history, a clumsy alibi that could not be proved. The day before, in a moment of inspired activity, he had had Cabuche removed from the little hut he occupied in the woods like a sort of hidden lair, and there they had discovered a pair of trousers stained with blood. And while still resisting his growing conviction and promising himself not to abandon the Roubaud theory, he exulted in the thought that he alone had had a sharp enough nose to smell out the real murderer. It was in order to be quite certain about this that he had had several of the witnesses, already interviewed immediately after the crime, recalled to his office that day.

The examining magistrate's office was on the rue Jeanne d'Arc side of the old ramshackle building which adjoined and quite disfigured the palace of the Dukes of Normandy, now the Law Courts. This big, gloomy room on the ground floor got such poor daylight that a lamp had to be lit by three o'clock in the winter. Decorated with ancient green wallpaper that had lost all its colour, the only furniture it had was two armchairs and four small ones, the magistrate's desk and a little table for the clerk; and on the shelf over the empty fireplace two bronze urns stood on each side of a black marble clock. Behind the

desk a door led to a second room in which the magistrate sometimes concealed people he wanted to keep available. The other
door opened straight on to the wide corridor which had seats
for waiting witnesses.

Although the appointment was only for two o'clock the Roubauds were there by half past one. They had just arrived from
Le Havre, and had taken hardly any time over lunch in a little
restaurant in the Grande-Rue. They were both dressed in black,
he in a frock-coat and she in a silk dress, like a lady, and they
maintained the rather weary and grieved solemnity of a couple
who had lost a relation. She was sitting on a seat, silent and
motionless, while he walked slowly up and down in front of her,
hands behind back. But each time he turned their eyes met, and
their hidden anxiety passed across their silent faces like a
shadow. Although inheriting La Croix-de-Maufras had filled
them with joy it had also revived their fears, for the President's
family – notably his daughter, who was outraged by the strange
legacies that were so numerous that they amounted to half the
total estate – were talking of disputing the will. And Mme de
Lachesnaye, egged on by her husband, was particularly hostile
to her former friend Séverine, of whom she harboured the
gravest suspicions. Moreover, the thought that there might be a
proof, which had not at first occurred to Roubaud, had now
been haunting him with a continuous fear: that letter he had
made his wife write so as to persuade Grandmorin to leave
Paris. They were going to find that letter if Grandmorin had not
destroyed it, and they might recognize the writing. Fortunately
days had gone by and nothing had happened so far – the letter
must have been torn up. But all the same, each fresh summons
to the examining magistrate's office was enough to bring the
couple out into a cold sweat beneath their correct exterior as
heirs and witnesses. It struck two, and Jacques appeared in his
turn. He had come from Paris. At once Roubaud went forward
with outstretched hand, in a very genial mood.

'Oh, so you've been dragged here too! Isn't it a nuisance, this
miserable business goes on and on!'

Seeing Séverine sitting there motionless, Jacques stood stock
still. For the past three weeks, on his trips to Le Havre every
other day, the deputy stationmaster had lavished kindnesses on

him. Once he had even had to accept an invitation to lunch. And in the presence of the young woman his old trouble had returned and become steadily worse. Was he going to want her too? At the mere sight of the whiteness of her neck at the top of her dress his heart beat faster and his hands began to twitch. He had made a firm resolve to avoid her in future.

Roubaud was still talking: 'And what are they saying about the affair in Paris? Nothing fresh, is there? You see they don't know anything and never will ... Come and say hallo to my wife.'

He dragged him over and Jacques had to go up and greet Séverine, who was embarrassed and smiling like a shy child. Jacques forced himself to chatter about this and that, watched all the time by husband and wife as if they were trying to read beyond even his thoughts, down into vague notions into which he himself hesitated to delve. Why was he so cool? Why did he seem to want to avoid them? Were his recollections getting clearer, had they been recalled for a confrontation with him? He was the one witness they dreaded, and they would have liked to win him over, bind him to themselves with such close ties of friendship that he would never have the heart to speak against them.

It was Roubaud, in his mental anguish, who came back to the affair.

'So you've no idea why we've been summoned? Something new perhaps, do you think?'

Jacques made a gesture of indifference.

'There was a tale going round at the station just now when I got there. Something about an arrest.'

The Roubauds were amazed, and very excited and puzzled. What! An arrest? Nobody had breathed a word to them! An arrest had been made, or was going to be made? They plied him with questions, but that was all he knew.

At that moment footsteps in the corridor made Séverine look up.

'Here come Berthe and her husband,' she murmured.

It was indeed the Lachesnayes. They walked past very stiffly and the wife did not even glance at her old schoolmate. An usher showed them straight into the magistrate's office.

'Ah well, we must be patient,' said Roubaud. 'We're in for a good two hours of it. So you'd better sit down!'

He himself sat down on Séverine's left and with a wave of the hand invited Jacques to sit beside her on the other side. But he remained standing for a moment longer. Then as she was looking at him in her sweet and shy way he made up his mind to sit on the seat. She seemed very fragile between them, and he felt she was tender and submissive, and the slight warmth that came from their proximity all through the long wait gradually cast a spell over him.

In M. Denizet's office the interrogations were about to begin. Already the inquiries had provided the material for a huge dossier, several bundles of papers in blue folders. Great efforts had been made to trace the victim after his departure from Paris. M. Vandorpe, the stationmaster, had testified to the departure of the 6.30 train, with carriage No. 293 added at the last moment, to the few words he had exchanged with Roubaud, who had gone into his compartment shortly before the arrival of President Grandmorin, and finally to his seeing the latter into his compartment, where he was certainly alone. Then the guard of the train, Henri Dauvergne, questioned about what had happened at Rouen during the ten-minute stop, had been unable to make any clear statement. He had seen the Roubauds chatting by the coupé, and he felt pretty sure they had gone back to their own compartment and that an inspector must have shut the door, but it was all a bit muddled, what with the jostling of the crowd and the semi-darkness in the station. As for committing himself that a man, the famous mythical murderer, could have hurled himself into the coupé just as the train was beginning to move, it seemed highly improbable to him, though admittedly possible, for such a thing had happened twice already to his knowledge. Other railwaymen from Rouen, also questioned about the same points, far from throwing any light on the affair had done little more than befog the issue by their contradictory answers. But the one proved fact was the handshake exchanged inside the carriage between Roubaud and the stationmaster at Barentin, who had climbed up on the step. This stationmaster, M. Bessière, had categorically endorsed this as correct, and he had added that his colleague was alone with his wife, who

107

seemed to be fast asleep in a semi-recumbent position. Furthermore, efforts had been made to trace the passengers who had left Paris in the same compartment as the Roubauds. The stout lady and gentleman who had got in at the last moment were worthy people from Petit-Couronne, and they had declared that as they had dozed off at once they could not say anything. As for the dark woman sitting silent in her corner, she had vanished like a shadow and it had proved absolutely impossible to trace her. Lastly there were still more witnesses, the small fry who had been able to identify passengers who had got out at Barentin that night, since the man must have stopped there; the tickets had been checked and all the passengers had been accounted for except one who, naturally, was a big fellow who had his face concealed by a blue muffler, and some said he was wearing an overcoat but others a workman's smock. On this man alone, who had vanished like a dream, there were three hundred and ten items in the dossier, and so muddled that each statement was contradicted by the next.

The dossier was further complicated by legal documents: the affidavit drawn up by the Clerk of the Court, whom the Public Prosecutor and the examining magistrate had brought to the scene of the crime – a voluminous description of the part of the line where the victim was lying, the position of the body, clothing, things found in the pockets which enabled identity to be established; then the report of the doctor also brought to the scene, a document in which the wound in the throat was described at length in scientific terms, the only wound, a terrible gash made by a cutting instrument, presumably a knife; and yet more reports, documents about the removal of the body to the hospital at Rouen and how long it had stayed there before remarkably early decomposition had forced the authorities to return it to the family. But there were only one or two important points in this new mass of papers. First, they had not found in the pockets either his watch or his little wallet in which there should have been ten thousand-franc notes, a sum President Grandmorin owed his sister Mme Bonnehon, which she had been expecting. So it might have seemed that robbery was the motive of the crime, except that a ring with a large stone was still on his finger. Hence a whole new series of hypotheses. Unfortunately they did not have the numbers of the banknotes, but the watch was known, a big keyless watch bearing on the case the President's two initials intertwined, and inside it the maker's number, 2516. Finally the weapon, the knife the murderer had used, had given rise to prolonged searches along the railway track, in the adjoining undergrowth, anywhere it could have been thrown, but these had been fruitless, the murderer must have concealed the knife in the same hiding-place as the banknotes and the watch. The only thing they had picked up was the victim's travelling-rug, a hundred metres before Barentin station, jettisoned there as a compromising object, and it featured among the exhibits.

When the Lachesnayes entered M. Denizet was standing at his desk re-reading the report of one of the first interrogations, which his clerk had just looked out in the dossier. He was a short, rather thickset man, clean shaven and already greying. The heavy jowls, square jaw, flat nose were sallow and expressionless, an effect emphasized by the heavy lids half shut over the big, light-coloured eyes. But all the sagacity and skill he prided himself on had centred itself on his mouth, the mouth of one of those actors who act their own emotions even when off stage, extremely mobile, going to a thin line at moments of great subtlety. This subtlety was most often his undoing, for he was over-perspicacious and played too many tricks with the simple, plain truth out of a sense of professionalism, having envisaged his function as that of a moral anatomist, endowed with second sight and extremely quick-witted. All the same, he was no fool.

At once he was most charming to Mme de Lachesnaye, for he was also something of a fashionable lawyer, moving in the society of Rouen and the country round.

'Please take a seat, Madame.'

He himself moved a chair forward for her. She was a sickly blonde, looking disagreeable and plain in her mourning. But with M. de Lachesnaye, also fair-haired and sickly-looking, he was merely polite and even a bit stand-offish, for in his view this little man, who was a judge of appeal by the age of thirty-six and had been decorated, thanks to the influence of his father-in-law and to services that his own father, also a magistrate, had rendered in somewhat shady affairs, represented the magistracy of privilege and wealth, the mediocrities who got the positions and were assured of a rapid rise because of money and family connections; while he, a poor man and without influence, was reduced to the importunate beggar's task of eternally bending his back to push uphill the constantly slipping boulder of advancement. So he was not averse to making this man realize, here in his office, how all-powerful he was, the absolute power he had over the freedom of all, the power to turn with a single word a witness into a suspect and to have him arrested on the spot if he felt like it.

'Madame,' he went on, 'you will forgive my having to torture you again with this painful story, I know that you are as anxious as we are to see light thrown on it and the guilty party brought to justice.'

He nodded to the clerk, a lanky fair youth with a bony face, and the interrogation began.

But from the very first questions put to his wife, M. de Lachesnaye, who had taken a seat, realizing that he was not being offered one, insisted on taking over from her. He soon began venting all his resentment against his father-in-law's will. It was incomprehensible! Such numerous and considerable legacies that they came to almost half the estate, an estate of 3,700,000 francs! And mostly to quite unknown people, women of all classes! There was even a girl who sold violets in a doorway in the rue du Rocher. It was intolerable, and he was waiting until the criminal investigations were over to see whether there was some way of having this immoral will set aside.

While he was moaning in this way, tight-mouthed and showing what a fool he was, a pig-headed provincial, avaricious to the core, M. Denizet studied him with his big, pale eyes half hidden, and his sensitive mouth expressed jealous contempt for this ineffectual creature, not content with two millions, whom no doubt he would see one day robed in the supreme purple, thanks to all this money.

'I think you would be making a mistake, Monsieur. The will could only be challenged if the sum total of the legacies were greater than half the estate, and that is not the case.'

Then turning to his clerk:

'I say, Laurent, you're not taking all this down, I presume.'

The clerk reassured him with a faint smile, being a man who knew what was what.

'But all the same,' M. de Lachesnaye went on more bitterly, 'you don't imagine, I hope, that I'm going to give up La Croix-de-Maufras to these Roubauds. A gift like that to a servant's daughter! And why? By what right? And besides, if it is proved that they had a hand in the crime . . .'

M. Denizet came back to the matter in hand.

'Really, do you think so?'

'Well of course! If they knew about the will their interest in the death of our poor father is obvious . . . Note also that they were the last to speak to him . . . Anyway, it all looks very fishy.'

Irritated at being thrown off his new theory, the magistrate turned to Berthe.

'And what about you, Madame? Do you think your old friend would be capable of such a crime?'

Before answering she looked at her husband. In the few months of their marriage each one's sourness and pettiness had affected that of the other and increased it. They made each other worse, and it was he who set her against Séverine to such an extent that in order to get the house back she would have had her arrested there and then.

'Oh well, Monsieur,' she said eventually, 'the person you are referring to had some very bad instincts when she was a child.'

'What! Do you accuse her of misconduct at Doinville?'

'Oh no, Monsieur, my father would never have kept her on!'

In this cry was the revolt of a respectable woman's prudery, a woman who herself would never have any stain to reproach herself with, and whose great pride it was to be one of the most indisputably virtuous women in Rouen, respected and welcomed everywhere.

'Only,' she went on, 'where there is habitual frivolity and dissipation . . . Anyhow, Monsieur, things I would never have thought possible strike me as quite certain today.'

Once again M. Denizet made a gesture of impatience. He was no longer on that track at all and anybody who persisted in that

111

direction became his opponent and seemed to him to be challenging the infallibility of his intelligence.

'But come, come, we must be reasonable,' he exclaimed. 'People like the Roubauds don't just kill a man like your father so as to inherit sooner or, if so, there would at any rate be signs of their impatience, and I would find evidence elsewhere of such a passion to possess and enjoy. No, the motive is not adequate, and another would have to be found, and there isn't anything, and you are not providing one yourselves. And then, go over the facts again, don't you appreciate the physical impossibilities? Nobody saw the Roubauds get into the coupé and one railwayman even feels he can assert that they went back into their own compartment. And as they were certainly in it at Barentin you would have to suppose a journey to and fro between their coach and that of the President, with three other coaches in between, and this in the few minutes' journey with the train going at full speed. Is it feasible? I have questioned drivers and guards and they have all said that only long conditioning could give a man enough nerve and strength. In any case the wife would not have been involved and the husband would have taken the risk without her. And for what? To kill a benefactor who had just got them out of a very serious difficulty? No, no, decidedly not, the theory won't hold water and we must look elsewhere. Let's see, a man who had got in at Rouen and out at the next stop, and who had recently threatened the victim with death . . .'

In his enthusiasm he was coming round to his new scheme of things, and was on the point of saying too much when the clerk's head poked round the half-open door. But before the man could say a word a gloved hand opened the door wide and a fair-haired lady came in. She was in elegant mourning, still attractive at fifty and more, the opulent and statuesque beauty of an elderly goddess.

'It's me, my dear Judge. I am late and I hope I am forgiven. You just can't get along the roads, and the three leagues from Doinville to Rouen seemed a good six today!'

M. Denizet rose gallantly to his feet.

'You have been keeping well, Madame, since last Sunday?'

'Very well . . . And you, dear friend? You've got over the

112

fright my coachman gave you? The man told me he nearly overturned taking you back, scarcely two kilometres from the château.'

'Oh, only a shaking, I had already forgotten all about it. Do sit down, and as I was saying just now to Mme de Lachesnaye, forgive my reviving your sorrow with this dreadful business.'

'Oh well, since it has to be . . . Good afternoon, Berthe, good afternoon, Lachesnaye.'

It was Mme Bonnehon, the murdered man's sister. She kissed her niece and shook hands with the husband. Since the age of thirty she had been the widow of a manufacturer who had brought her a large fortune – she was already very well-to-do herself – and having had from the division of property with her brother the Doinville estate, she had had a very pleasant existence there, full of love affairs, it was said, but outward appearances had been so correct and apparently blameless that she had remained arbiter of Rouen society. Because of opportunity as well as her own preference she had chosen her lovers from the legal profession, and had for twenty-five years entertained members of the judiciary at the château. The society of the Law Courts came out from Rouen and returned in her carriages and life was a continual fête. Even now she had not lost her ardour, and she was credited with a maternal attachment to a young deputy prosecutor, son of a judge at the Court of Appeal, M. Chaumette. She worked for the advancement of the son and showered invitations and kind attentions upon the father. And as well she had kept a good friend of earlier days, also a lawyer, M. Desbazeilles, a bachelor and the literary glory of the Rouen courts, whose finely turned sonnets were frequently quoted. For years he had had his own room at Doinville. Now that he was over sixty he dined regularly as an old friend, whose rheumatism would not allow him anything but memories. So Mme Bonnehon kept her regal status through her graciousness, despite the threat of advancing years, and nobody dreamed of challenging her position. She had never been conscious of a rival until this last winter – Mme Leboucq, another lawyer's wife, tall, dark, thirty-four and really very good looking, whom the judiciary was beginning to frequent rather a lot.

This gave a tinge of melancholy to her usually cheerful disposition.

'So, Madame, if I may,' went on M. Denizet, 'I am going to ask you a few questions.'

The questioning of the Lachesnayes was over, but he did not dismiss them. His dreary, cold office was turning into a fashionable drawing-room. The imperturbable clerk got ready to take notes again.

'A witness has mentioned a telegram your brother is alleged to have received, summoning him to Doinville at once. We have found no trace of this telegram. So did you by any chance write to him, Madame?'

Mme Bonnehon, quite at her ease, smilingly began to answer in a friendly, conversational tone.

'I didn't write to my brother, I was expecting him and knew he was coming, but no date had been fixed. He usually just dropped in like that, and almost always by a night train. As he lived in an isolated cottage in the park, with its doors on to a quiet lane, we didn't even hear him come. He would hire a carriage at Barentin and only appear next day, sometimes quite late in the day, like a neighbour who had been living there for some time and was just paying a call. The reason why I was expecting him this time was that he was going to bring a sum of 10,000 francs in settlement of a business deal between us. He certainly had those 10,000 francs on him. That's why I have always believed that he was killed for robbery pure and simple.'

The magistrate let a brief silence reign, then, looking her in the eyes:

'What do you think of Mme Roubaud and her husband?'

This brought forth a strong reaction.

'Oh no, my dear M. Denizet, you're surely not going to get sidetracked once again about those nice people. Séverine was a good little girl, very sweet and even docile, and very pretty as well, which is no drawback. Since you insist on my saying so yet again, I think that she and her husband are incapable of a criminal act.'

He nodded in agreement, and cast a triumphant glance in the direction of Mme de Lachesnaye. Stung, she ventured to intervene:

'Oh Aunt, I think you are very easily pleased.'

Thereupon Mme Bonnehon relieved her feelings with her usual plain speaking.

'That'll do, Berthe, we shall never agree about that. She was gay, fond of laughter, and quite right too ... I know perfectly well what you and your husband are thinking. But really, self-interest must be preventing your thinking straight for you to be so astonished about this bequest of La Croix-de-Maufras your father has made to dear Séverine ... He had brought her up, given her a dowry, and it was quite natural that he should mention her in his will. Didn't he think of her as a sort of daughter, after all? Oh my dear, money has so little to do with happiness!'

And indeed, always having been very rich herself, she displayed complete detachment. Moreover, being a beautiful and much-admired woman, she affected to find beauty and love the sole reasons for living.

'It was Roubaud who mentioned the telegram,' snapped M. de Lachesnaye. 'If there wasn't a wire the President couldn't have told him that he had had one. Why did Roubaud tell a lie?'

'But,' cried M. Denizet, warming up to his theory, 'the President may well have invented the wire himself to explain his sudden departure to the Roubauds. According to their own statement he was not leaving until the following day, and as he was on the same train as they were he had to find some reason if he wanted to hide the real one, which incidentally none of us knows ... This is of no importance, and leads us nowhere.'

There was another silence. When the magistrate went on he spoke very calmly and with infinite caution.

'And now, Madame, I come to a particularly delicate matter, and I beg you to forgive the nature of my questions. Nobody respects your brother's memory more than I do ... There were some rumours, I believe ... he was said to have mistresses.'

Mme Bonnehon resumed her smile of infinite tolerance.

'Oh, my dear sir, at his age! My brother lost his wife when he was very young, and I never took it upon myself to condemn what he himself found good. He lived his own life and I didn't interfere with his existence in any way. But what I do know is

115

that he kept to his own station and remained right to the end of his life a man who moved in the best society.'

Berthe looked at the floor, bursting with rage that people should mention her father's mistresses in front of her, while her husband, equally upset, went and stood at the window with his back to them.

'Please forgive my insisting,' said M. Denizet, 'but wasn't there some story about a young maid of yours?'

'Oh yes, Louisette . . . But my dear sir, she was a vicious little hussy who at fourteen years of age was carrying on with a known criminal. People tried to use her death against my brother. A disgraceful business, I'll tell you about it.'

No doubt she was speaking in good faith. Although she knew all about the President's personal life, and his tragic death had not come as a surprise, she felt the necessity of defending the lofty position of the family. And besides, in this unfortunate business about Louisette, even if she thought her brother quite capable of fancying the girl she was equally convinced that this particular girl was precociously vicious.

'Just picture a little chit of a thing, oh, so tiny and delicate, golden haired and rosy like a little angel, and so sweet as well – the sweetness of a plaster saint – you'd give her the Sacrament without confession! Well, by the time she was fourteen she was the girl-friend of a sort of brute, a drayman called Cabuche who had just done a five-year stretch for killing a man in a public house. This fellow camped out on the edge of the forest of Bécourt, where his father, who had died of shame, left him a hovel made of tree-trunks and mud. There he doggedly worked a bit of the abandoned quarries which I believe once upon a time supplied half the stone Rouen is built of. And it was there, in that den, that the child went to see her savage, who so scared everybody around that he lived absolutely alone like a leper. They could often be seen prowling together in the woods, holding hands, the girl so dainty and he so huge and bestial. In fact such goings-on that you would never credit . . . Of course I only found all this out later. I had taken in Louisette almost out of charity, by way of a good deed. I knew that her family, those Misards, were poor, but they took care not to tell me that they had beaten her black and blue and not been able to stop her

116

from running off to her Cabuche as soon as the door was left open ... And then the accident happened. When he was at Doinville my brother had no servants of his own. Louisette and another woman looked after the lonely cottage he occupied. One morning she went there alone and disappeared. My view is that her flight had been premeditated for a long time, perhaps her lover was waiting to take her off. But the awful thing is that five days later the story was going round about her death, with details about a rape attempted by my brother in such appalling circumstances that the girl had rushed to Cabuche, mad with terror, and died of brain fever. What had really happened? So many versions have been put about that it's hard to say. I think myself that the high fever that she really did die of – indeed a doctor certified that she did – was contracted by some carrying-on at night in the open air in marshy places ... You can't really see my brother torturing that little thing, can you, my dear sir? It's odious, impossible!'

M. Denizet had listened attentively to this narrative, neither approving nor disapproving. Mme Bonnehon was a little worried about how to finish, but then took the plunge:

'Well, after all, I don't say my brother didn't have his bit of fun with her. He was fond of young people and he was very gay, for all his stern exterior. Well, suppose he kissed her.'

This word provoked a shocked reaction from the Lachesnayes.

'Oh, Auntie! Auntie!'

She merely shrugged. Why tell lies to the law?

'He kissed her, or may have tickled her. There's no crime in that. What makes me admit this is that this tale was not concocted by the quarryman. The liar must have been Louisette, the vicious little creature who exaggerated everything, probably to make her lover keep her there. And then of course he, an oaf as I have said, soon decided in all good faith that his mistress had been murdered. He was really mad with rage and went about saying in all the pubs that if the President got into his clutches he would bleed him to death like a pig!'

The magistrate broke his silence and burst in excitedly:

'He said that, can witnesses state this?'

'Oh, dear sir, you can find as many as you like. Well,

anyhow, it's all a very sad business, and we have had a great deal of trouble. Fortunately my brother's position put him above all suspicion.'

Mme Bonnehon had realized that M. Denizet was taking this new tack; it worried her somewhat, and she preferred not to get herself any further involved by questioning him in her turn. He rose and said he did not wish to take advantage any longer of the kindness of the grief-stricken family. On his instruction the clerk read over the statements before they were signed by the witnesses. These statements were wonderfully discreet, so well purged of superfluous or compromising words that Mme Bonnehon, pen in hand, cast a glance of grateful surprise at this Laurent young man, pallid and gangling, whom she had not looked at before.

Then as the magistrate was seeing her and her nephew and niece to the door, she took both his hands.

'You will come again soon, won't you? You know you are always welcome at Doinville ... And thank you, you are one of the last of the faithful.'

Her smile was suffused with melancholy, but the niece, who had stiffly gone out first, had only given a curt nod.

Left alone, M. Denizet took a short breather, standing still, thinking. In his view the thing was becoming clear; there had certainly been some violence on Grandmorin's part, his reputation was known. This made the investigation delicate and he resolved to redouble his prudence until the directives he expected from the Ministry had reached him. All the same, he felt triumphant. At last he had his hand on the criminal.

'Show in M. Jacques Lantier.'

On the seat in the corridor the Roubauds were still waiting with expressionless faces as though they were patiently dozing, but occasionally a nervous tremor ran over them. The voice of the clerk calling Jacques seemed to make them wake up with a little start. They followed him with staring eyes and saw him disappear into the magistrate's room. Then they relapsed into their waiting, a bit paler, and silent.

The whole business had been preying on Jacques's mind and making him uneasy for three weeks, as though it could have turned out badly for him. This was absurd, for he had nothing

118

to reproach himself with, not even with having kept quiet, and yet he was going in to the magistrate with a little shiver of guilt, like a man fearful of seeing his crime exposed. He faced the questions on the defensive, weighing his words for fear of saying too much. He could easily have been a murderer as well, didn't it show in his eyes? Nothing was more unpleasant than being hauled up before the beak in this way, and it made him feel angry and, he said, in a hurry to see the end of being badgered like this over things that were nothing to do with him.

In the event, on that day M. Denizet was only concerned with the description of the killer. Jacques, being the only witness to have caught a glimpse of him, was the only person able to give exact information. But he would not go beyond his first statement, repeating that the scene had only stayed in his mind as a vision of less than one second's duration, such a fleeting picture that it remained in his memory like a formless abstraction. It was just one man killing another, that was all. For half an hour the magistrate, with slow persistence, kept pressing him, putting the same question with every imaginable twist: was he tall? was he short? any beard? long or short hair? what sort of clothes was he wearing? what class of man did he look like? Jacques got bothered and only gave vague answers.

'Well,' M. Denizet suddenly asked, looking him right in the eye, 'if you were shown him would you recognize him?'

Jacques' eyelids flickered a little as he was filled with disquiet by these eyes boring into his skull. His conscience struggled aloud.

'Recognize him . . . yes . . . possibly.'

But at once his strange fear of unwitting complicity threw him back on to his evasive tactics.

'And yet, no, I don't think so. I would never dare to state it as a fact. At a speed of eighty kilometres an hour, think of that!'

With a gesture of despair the magistrate was on the point of sending him into the inner room in case he was wanted, when he changed his mind.

'Stay here, sit down.'

He rang for the clerk again.

'Bring in M. and Mme Roubaud.'

As soon as they came through the door and saw Jacques a

look of worried puzzlement came into their eyes. Had he said anything? Was he being kept for a confrontation with them? At the sight of him all their self-confidence melted away, and they began answering in expressionless voices. But the magistrate merely went over their earlier interrogation, and they simply had to repeat the same phrases in almost the same words while he listened, looking down and not even at them.

Then he suddenly turned to Séverine:

'Madame, you said to the superintendent, whose text I have here, that in your opinion a man jumped into the compartment at Rouen just as the train was starting.'

She was stunned. Why was he bringing that up? Was it a trap? Was he going to compare her statements and make her contradict herself? So she glanced questioningly at her husband, who prudently intervened:

'I don't think, sir, that my wife was so positive.'

'Excuse me, as you were suggesting this fact as a possibility, your wife said: "That is certainly what happened." Well, Madame, I want to know whether you had any special reasons for saying that.'

She really did get worried then, feeling convinced that if she was not very careful indeed he would, from answer to answer, lead her on to admissions. Yet she could not just say nothing.

'Oh no, Monsieur, no special reason. I must have said that just out of common sense, because it really is very difficult to explain the events in any other way.'

'So you didn't see the man, and you can't give us any information about him?'

'No, no, nothing!'

M. Denizet appeared to abandon that line. But he came back to it with Roubaud.

'And what about you, how comes it that you didn't see the man if he really did get into the train, for it appears in your own statement that you were still talking to the victim when the whistle blew for departure.'

This insistence was reducing Roubaud to terror in his anguish as to which line he should take, whether drop the fiction about the man or stick to it. If they had some evidence against him the hypothesis about the unknown murderer was hardly tenable and might even make it worse for him. He answered in lengthy, muddled sentences, playing for time until he could see how the land lay.

'It really is regrettable,' went on M. Denizet, 'that your recollections have remained so hazy, for you might help us to put an end to suspicions that have been put about concerning various people.'

That struck Roubaud as being such a direct hint that he felt an irresistible urge to clear himself. He saw himself being unmasked, and his mind was instantly made up.

'It's so much a matter of conscience! One hesitates, you understand, nothing is more natural. Suppose I did say that I think I saw this man . . .'

The magistrate made a gesture of triumph, feeling convinced that this move towards frankness was the result of his skill. He used to say that experience had taught him how strangely difficult some witnesses find it to admit what they know. And these were the ones he got it out of willy-nilly.

'Well, tell me . . . what was he like? Short, tall, about your sort of height?'

'Oh no, no, much taller . . . Or at any rate I had the impression, because it's only an impression, that I am almost sure I brushed past somebody as I was running back to my own carriage.'

'Just a minute,' said M. Denizet, turning towards Jacques, whom he asked:

'The man you caught sight of, with the knife in his hand, was he taller than M. Roubaud?'

The engine driver, who was getting restive because he was beginning to fear he would miss the 5.00 p.m. train, looked up and examined Roubaud. He felt he had never looked at him before, and was amazed to see how short and powerfully built he was, with a curious profile he had seen somewhere else, or possibly dreamed about.

'No,' he murmured, 'he wasn't taller, about the same height.'

Roubaud protested vigorously:

'Oh, much taller, at least a head taller.'

Jacques stared at him wide-eyed, and beneath that stare, in which he could read growing surprise, Roubaud became more

121

and more agitated, as if trying to dodge his own likeness, and his wife too was frozen with fear as she watched the painful effort to remember that could be seen on the young man's face. It was clear that he had begun by being astonished at certain resemblances between Roubaud and the murderer, and then that he had suddenly known for certain that Roubaud was indeed the murderer, as rumour had said. And now he seemed overcome by this discovery, gaping, and it was impossible to tell what he was going to do next, nor did he know himself. If he spoke their fate was sealed. Roubaud's eyes had met his, and each read into the other's soul. There was a silence.

'So you disagree,' went on M. Denizet. 'If he looked smaller to you it may well be that he was bending over in the struggle with his victim.'

He also was studying the two men. He had not thought of utilizing this confrontation in this way, but his professional instinct made him sense that at that moment the truth was hovering in the air. Even his confidence in the Cabuche line was shaken. Could the Lachesnayes have been right? Could the guilty parties, against all probability, be this respectable employee and this meek young wife of his?

'Had the man got a full beard, like yours?' he asked Roubaud.

The latter found strength to answer without a tremor in his voice:

'Full beard, oh no! No beard at all, I think.'

Jacques realized that he was going to be asked the same question. What should he say? He could have sworn that the man had a full beard. Anyhow, these people meant nothing to him, so why not tell the truth? But as he took his eyes off the husband's they met the wife's, and in her look he read such a desperate supplication, such a complete surrender of her whole being, that he was shattered. His old trouble was coming back – was he in love, was this the woman he could love with real love and without any monstrous lust to destroy her? And at that moment, as a curious side-effect of his malady, his memory seemed to go vague and he now could see no suggestion of the murderer in Roubaud. The vision became misty again, doubt came over him to such an extent that he would have desperately repented of saying anything.

M. Denizet was asking the question:

'Did the man have a full beard like M. Roubaud?'

He answered in all good faith:

'Sir, I really can't say. Once again, it was too quick. I don't know anything and I don't want to swear to anything.'

But M. Denizet would not drop the matter, for he wanted to have done with suspicion of the deputy stationmaster. He pressed Roubaud, he pressed the engine-driver, and from the first man he obtained a complete description of the murderer: tall, big, clean-shaven and wearing a workman's smock – in every respect the opposite of his own characteristics – while all he could get out of the second was non-committal mono-syllables which added strength to the other's affirmations. Which brought the magistrate back to his original conviction: he was on the right track, the portrait the witness was drawing of the murderer was so exact that every new feature added to the certainty. By their overwhelming evidence this couple, un-justly under suspicion, would bring the guilty man to the guillo-tine.

'Go in there,' he said to the Roubauds and Jacques, sending them into the inner room when they had signed their state-ments. 'Wait until I call you back.'

He at once gave the order for the prisoner to be brought in, and he was so pleased with himself that in his good humour he went so far as to say to his clerk:

'Laurent, we've got him!'

But the door had already opened and two police officers ap-peared, escorting a tall fellow of twenty-five to thirty. They disappeared at a sign from M. Denizet, and Cabuche stood alone in the middle of the office, dazed, fiercely on the defensive like an animal at bay. He was a big fellow, with powerful shoul-ders and huge fists, fair and very white of skin, with scarcely any beard, just a slight golden down, curly and silky. The heavy face and low brow suggested the violence of a limited intelli-gence wholly governed by the impulse of the moment, but in the big mouth and square muzzle of a good-natured dog there was a kind of need to be affectionate and submissive. He had been brutally seized very early in the morning in his lair and dragged away from his forest, he was exasperated by accusations he could not understand, and what with his flustered look and torn shirt there was already about him that shifty look of the guilty party, that air of the sly thief that prison stamps on even the most honest man. Night was falling and the room was dark, and he was fading into the gloom by the time the clerk brought in a big lamp without a shade, and the strong light showed up his face. He stood still, bareheaded.

M. Denizet at once fixed him with his big, light-coloured, heavy-lidded eyes. He said nothing, this was the silent opening of the struggle, the first trial of strength before the savage war of ruses, traps and moral torture. This man was guilty, so everything was permissible against him, and the only right he had left was to own up.

The interrogation began very slowly:

'Do you know what crime you are accused of?'

Cabuche growled in a voice thick with impotent rage:

'I've not been told, but I can guess. There's been enough talk about it!'

'Did you know M. Grandmorin?'

'Yes, yes, I knew him all too well!'

'A girl called Louisette, your mistress, went into service with Mme Bonnehon, as a maid.'

The man flew into a furious rage. In his anger he saw red.

'Christ! Anybody who says that is a bleeding liar! Louisette was not my mistress!'

With some interest the magistrate had watched him work himself up. Taking a different tack:

'You are very violent. You have served five years in prison for killing a man in a brawl.'

Cabuche lowered his eyes. This sentence was his shame. He muttered:

'He hit me first ... Anyway, I only did four. Got a year's remission.'

'So,' M. Denizet went on, 'you maintain that Louisette was not your mistress?'

Again he clenched his fists. Then he said in a low, faltering voice:

'Don't you see, she was a kid, not yet fourteen when I came out. At that time everybody gave me a wide berth, they almost threw stones at me. But she, in the woods where I always used to meet her, she would come up to me and talk to me and be nice – oh, she was so nice! So that's how we became friends ... we used to hold hands as we went along. That was so good just then, so good. Of course she was growing up, and I used to think about her in that way, I can't pretend any different, I was half crazy the way I loved her. And she loved me a lot, too, and what you are saying would have happened in the end, but then she was taken away and sent to Doinville, to that lady's house ... Then one evening, coming home from the quarry, I found her on my doorstep, nearly out of her mind, and in such a state that she was burning with a sort of fever. She hadn't dared to go home to her family, but had come to die in my place ... Oh God! That swine! I should have gone and slit him open right away!'

The magistrate pursed his lips, astonished at the ring of truth in this man. Decidedly, he would have to play it cool, he was up against a stronger opponent than he had bargained for.

'Yes, I know the terrible story that you and this girl have cooked up. But note that everything in M. Grandmorin's life put him above your accusations.'

Wild eyed and with shaking hands the quarryman stammered:

'What? What have we cooked up? The others are the liars, and you accuse us of lies!'

'Yes we do, and don't come the innocent. I have already questioned Misard, the man who married your mistress's mother. I will confront you with him if necessary. You'll see what he thinks of your tale ... So mind how you answer, we have witnesses, we know everything, you would do well to tell the truth.'

This was his usual method of intimidation, even when he knew nothing and had no witnesses.

'Will you deny that you said publicly everywhere that you would cut M. Grandmorin's throat?'

125

'Oh yes, of course I did say that. And I meant it, too! My hands were itching like hell!'

M. Denizet was completely taken by surprise because he was expecting some carefully worked out total denial. What! The arrested man admitted uttering threats? What ruse lay behind this? Afraid he had been going too fast, he meditated for a moment, then gave the man a hard look and suddenly asked:

'What did you do on the night of the 14th to 15th of February?'

'I went to bed when it was dark, at about six ... I wasn't feeling very well, and in fact my cousin Louis did me a good turn and delivered a load of stones to Doinville.'

'Yes, your cousin was seen with the cart crossing the line at the level crossing. But when he was questioned all your cousin could answer was that you left him at midday and he didn't see you again ... Prove that you were in bed by six.'

'Look here, that's silly, I can't prove it. I live in a place all alone on the edge of the forest ... I was there, I'm saying so, and that's all.'

Then M. Denizet decided to deal the knock-out blow, the unanswerable statement of fact. He forced his face to remain expressionless while his mouth played the part.

'Now I am going to tell you what you did on the evening of the 14th February. At three in the afternoon you caught the Rouen train at Barentin, the object of this we have not yet been able to ascertain. You were going back on the train from Paris that stops at Rouen at 9.03, and you were in the crowd on the platform when you spotted M. Grandmorin in his reserved compartment. Note that I freely admit that there was no premeditation and that the idea of the crime only came into your head then. You got in, thanks to the crowd, you waited until you were in the Malaunay tunnel, but you didn't get your timing right, for the train was leaving the tunnel when you dealt the fatal blow. And you threw the body out and got out your-self at Barentin, after having got rid of the travelling-rug as well. That's what you did.'

He was closely watching the tiniest movements on Cabuche's pink face, and he was very annoyed when, after being very

126

attentive at first, Cabuche went off into a hearty peal of laughter.

'What on earth are you talking about? If I had done it I should say so.'

Then he went on quite calmly:

'I didn't do it, but I ought to have. By God yes, I wish I had!'

M. Denizet could get nothing more out of him. In vain he went over his questions again and again, coming back ten times to the same points, using different tactics. No, always no, it wasn't him! He shrugged his shoulders to show that he thought that was silly. When Cabuche was arrested they had searched the hut and had found neither the weapon nor the banknotes nor the watch, but they had taken possession of a pair of trousers with some little bloodstains – overwhelming evidence. But once again the man had just laughed – another funny story, that was a rabbit he had taken from a snare, and it had bled down his legs! The magistrate was beginning to lose his advantage because he had a ready-made theory about the crime, and excessive professional finesse, and these had led him to elaborate and go beyond the plain truth. This ignorant man, who was quite incapable of a trial of subtlety but whose strength when he said no and no again was invincible, was gradually throwing him off the track, for he could only consider him as guilty, and each fresh denial outraged him more, like persistence in brutality and lies. He would soon have to force him to give way.

'So you deny it?'

'Of course I do, because it wasn't me. If it was me, well, I should be only too proud and would say so.'

M. Denizet suddenly rose and himself went and opened the door of the little inner room. He called Jacques in.

'Do you recognize this man?'

'Well, I know him of course,' he answered in surprise. 'I've seen him at the Misards.'.

'No, no, do you recognize him as the man in the train, the murderer?'

Jacques suddenly became very wary. In any case he did not recognize him. The other man had looked shorter and darker. He was about to say so when he felt that that would commit him too much. So he remained evasive.

127

'I don't know, I really can't say ... I assure you, sir, I can't say.'

M. Denizet did not press the matter further, but called in the Roubauds and asked them the same question:

'Do you recognize this man?'

Cabuche was still smiling away. He showed no surprise, but nodded at Séverine, whom he had known when she lived at La Croix-de-Maufras as a girl. But she and her husband had had a shock when they saw him, and understood. This was the arrested man Jacques had told them about, the prisoner who explained this second interrogation. Roubaud was overcome with amazement, appalled at the resemblance between this fellow and the imaginary murderer whose description he had invented to be the opposite of his own. It was purely fortuitous, but it affected him so strongly that he did not know how to answer.

'Come along, do you recognize him?'

'Really, sir, I must repeat that it was only a sensation, somebody brushed past me ... Of course this man is tall, like him, and fair, and hasn't got a beard.'

'Well then, do you recognize him?'

Roubaud, in a state of extreme tension, was shaking with a fierce inner struggle. The instinct of self-preservation won.

'I can't say for certain. But there is something in it, yes, there is certainly a great deal in it.'

That made Cabuche begin to swear. All this nonsense was beginning to get him down. It wasn't him, so there, and he wanted to go home. As the blood rose to his head he banged his fists and became so violent that the police officers had to be called in to take him away. But his violence, like the spring of an animal at bay turning on its enemy, made M. Denizet triumphant. Now he was convinced, and he showed it.

'Did you notice his eyes? I can always tell from their eyes .., Ah well, I've put paid to his account, we've got him!'

Quite motionless, the Roubauds glanced at each other. What, was it all over, and they were saved, as the law had got hold of the guilty party? It left them a trifle stunned, with worried consciences about the part that events had just forced them to play. Yet they were flooded with a joy that drowned their scruples, and they smiled at Jacques. And with immense relief and longing for a breath of fresh air they were waiting for the magistrate to dismiss all three of them, when the clerk brought in a letter.

M. Denizet at once sat down again at his desk to study the letter, forgetting the three witnesses. It was the letter from the Ministry, the instructions he should have had the patience to wait for before going any further with his investigations. What he read must be taking the edge off his triumph, for his face gradually froze into its usual expressionless stillness. Once he looked up and cast a sidelong glance at the Roubauds, as though one of the sentences had reminded him of them. They lost their short-lived joy and once again felt uneasy, thinking they were caught again. Why did he look at them like that? Had those three lines, the compromising letter that had haunted them so, been found? Séverine knew M. Camy-Lamotte quite well from having seen him at the President's, and she knew he was responsible for putting the dead man's papers in order. Roubaud was tortured by one bitter regret – he should have thought to send his wife to pay some useful calls in Paris. She would at any rate have secured the protection of the Secretary-General in case the Company got tired of the rumours and sacked him. They both stared at the magistrate and felt their anxiety growing as they watched his expression darken, for he was clearly disconcerted by the letter, which was going to upset all his day's achievements.

At length he put the letter down and sat for a moment looking deeply absorbed, gazing at the Roubauds and Jacques. Then he made up his mind to it and said aloud, as if to himself:

'Ah well, we shall see, we'll come back to it . . . You can go.'

But as the three were leaving he could not resist his need to know, to settle the serious problem which was upsetting his new formula, although he had been instructed to go no further without previous permission.

'No, you stay behind a moment, I've got one more question to ask you.'

Out in the passage the Roubauds stood still. The doors were open, but they could not go, something kept them there, and it was their tormenting curiosity about what was going on in the magistrate's office, a physical inability to go away before hearing from Jacques what fresh question he was being asked. They turned back and walked up and down until their legs were tired. They eventually found themselves sitting side by side on the same seat where they had already spent hours waiting, and there they sat, silent and sour.

When Jacques reappeared Roubaud rose with difficulty.

'We were waiting for you, we'll all go back to the station together ... well?'

But Jacques looked away, feeling awkward as though he were trying to avoid Séverine's eyes that were fixed on him.

'He's not so sure now, he's casting round,' he said at last. 'Now he's been asking me if it wasn't two people doing it. And as I did say something at Le Havre about a dark mass holding down the old man's legs, he questioned me about that ... He seems to think it was only the rug. So he sent for the rug, and I had to say one way or the other. Oh Lord, yes, I suppose it could have been the rug.'

The Roubauds were shuddering. The law was on their track, and a single word from this chap could finish them. He knew for certain, and in the end he would talk. All three, the woman between the two men, left the Law Courts without a word, and then out in the street Roubaud spoke again:

'By the way, mate, my wife's going to have to go to Paris for a day on business. It would be nice if you could go round with her should she need someone.'

[5]

At eleven fifteen, dead on time, the man on duty at the Europe bridge gave the regulation two blasts on the horn to signal the approach of the express from Le Havre as it emerged from the Batignolles tunnel, and soon the turntables clanked as the train entered the station with a short note on the whistle, squealing on the brakes, steaming and running with water from the driving rain that had been pouring down all the way from Rouen.

The porters had not yet released the latches on the doors, but one door opened and Séverine leaped on to the platform before the train had stopped. Her carriage was in the rear, and to reach the engine she had to hurry along through the hordes of passengers tumbling out of the compartments with a clutter of children and luggage. Jacques was there on the footplate, waiting to back out to the sheds, and Pecqueux was polishing the brasses with a rag.

'Right, that's settled, then,' she said, standing on tiptoe. 'I'll be in the rue Cardinet at three, and you will be kind enough to introduce me to your chief so that I can thank him.'

That was the pretext thought up by Roubaud, thanking the supervisor of the Batignolles depot for some unspecified service he had rendered. In this way she would be entrusted to the engine-driver's friendly goodwill and be able to tighten the bonds between them and influence him.

But Jacques, black with coal, soaking wet and exhausted after the struggle with wind and rain, looked at her with hard eyes and made no answer. He had not been able to say no to the husband when they left Le Havre, and this idea of being alone with her was very disquieting, for he now felt sure that he wanted her.

'Is that all right?' she went on, smiling with her sweet, affectionate expression in spite of the surprise and slight repugnance she felt on seeing how dirty and almost unrecognizable he looked. 'Good, I'm counting on you.'

As she was hoisting herself still higher, holding on to an iron handrail with her gloved hand, Pecqueux obligingly warned her:

'Mind, you'll get dirty.'

Then Jacques had to say something, but he did so in a surly tone.

'Yes, rue Cardinet ... unless the blasted rain washes me away altogether.'

She was touched by the pitiful state he was in and added, just as though he had suffered for her alone:

'Oh, you are in a state! And I was so comfortable. You know I was thinking about you, and this deluge made me feel awful! And I was so glad it was you bringing me up this morning and taking me back tonight on the express!'

But this nice, affectionate familiarity only seemed to worry him more. He looked relieved when a voice shouted: 'Back out now!' and promptly pulled the rod of the whistle, while the fireman waved the young woman out of the way.

'Three o'clock!'

'Yes, three o'clock.'

As the engine began moving Séverine left the platform, the last to leave. When she reached the open air in the rue d'Amsterdam and was going to put up her umbrella she was glad to see it had stopped raining. She walked down to the place du Havre, paused a moment to think, and made up her mind that the best thing to do was to have some lunch straight away. It was twenty-five past eleven and she went into a cheap restaurant on the corner of the rue Saint-Lazare, and ordered fried eggs and a chop. Then, taking her time over eating, she relapsed into the reflections that had been haunting her for weeks, and her face became pale and wore a puzzled expression, with no trace of her usual gentle, charming smile.

The day before, that is two days after their interrogation at Rouen, Roubaud, thinking any delay might be dangerous, had made up his mind to send her to see M. Camy-Lamotte, not at the Ministry but at his home in the rue du Rocher, a town house just next door to Grandmorin's. She knew she would find him at home at one o'clock, and she was taking her time, going over what she would say and trying to foresee what he would answer so as not to be flustered about anything. A new cause for worry had arisen the day before and made her journey more urgent: they had learned from gossip going round the station that Mme Lebleu and Philomène were telling everybody that the Company was going to get rid of Roubaud who was considered too compromising. And the worst of it was that M. Dabadie, when asked directly, had not said no, which lent considerable weight to the report. So it at once became urgent for her to go to Paris and plead their cause, and above all ask for the support of this highly placed personage, as they had formerly enjoyed that of the President. But, concealed behind that plea, which at any rate would explain the visit, there was a more pressing motive, a nagging craving to know, the craving that makes a criminal give himself up rather than remain in ignorance. The uncertainty was killing them now that they felt they had been found out, since Jacques had told them that the prosecution now seemed to be suspecting that there was an accomplice. They were wearing themselves out with conjectures – perhaps the letter had been found, the facts reconstructed. They were hourly expecting search warrants or an arrest, and the torment was becoming so agonizing, and the most trivial events round them seemed so fraught with anxiety and threats that they were coming to prefer a catastrophe to these continual alarms. Certainty rather, and an end to suffering.

Séverine finished her chop, and had been so absorbed that she woke up with a start of surprise at being in this public place. Everything was bitter to her, she could not swallow any more and hadn't the heart to have any coffee. But although she had taken her time over eating, it was hardly a quarter past twelve when she left the restaurant. Still three quarters of an hour to kill! Usually she loved Paris, so enjoyed walking in the streets anywhere, on the rare occasions when she came, but this time she felt lost, nervous, impatient to have done with everything and hide away. The pavements were drying already, and a warm breeze was dispersing the last of the clouds. She went down the rue Tronchet and found herself at the Madeleine flower market, a typical March market, all blooming with primroses and azaleas in the pale light of the end of winter. For half an hour she walked round in this premature spring, relapsing into her vague dreams, thinking of Jacques as a foe she had to disarm. It seemed to her that she had already done her call in the rue du Rocher and that everything was going all right in that direction, and that there only remained the job of securing this fellow's silence. And that was a complicated undertaking in which she continually lost the thread, her head spinning with far-fetched schemes. But it was not tiring, nor was it frightening, it was just gently soporific. Then she suddenly caught sight of the time by a clock on a kiosk – ten past one. She had not yet paid her call, and she fell back brutally into harsh reality and hurried up towards the rue du Rocher.

M. Camy-Lamotte's residence was at the corner of this street and the rue de Naples, and Séverine had to go past the Grandmorin house, silent, empty, with shutters all closed. She glanced up and quickened her steps. The memory of her last visit there came back, and the great house rose up, terrifying. A little further on, as she was instinctively turning round and glancing back, like somebody pursued by a hue and cry, she caught sight of the Rouen examining magistrate, M. Denizet, who was also coming along the street on the opposite side. It was a shock to her. Had he seen her looking at the house? But he was walking along quite calmly, and she let him go ahead and followed in a very worried state. She had another shock when she saw him ring the bell at M. Camy-Lamotte's at the corner of the rue de Naples.

She was terror-struck. She would never dare to go in there now. She retraced her steps, through the rue d'Edimbourg and down to the Europe bridge. Only there did she feel safe. In her confused state, not knowing where to go now or what to do, she stood still against a parapet looking down between the girders at the great open space of the station where trains were continually on the move. She watched them with frightened eyes, thinking that for certain the magistrate was there because of the case and that the two men were talking about her and deciding her fate at that very moment. In a fit of despair she suddenly felt a terrible urge to throw herself there and then under a train rather than go back to the rue du Rocher. One was just emerging from under the roof of the main-line station, but she watched it coming and then it passed beneath her, throwing a hot cloud of whirling smoke up into her face. Then the stupid

134

pointlessness of her journey, the awful anguish she would take back with her if she had not the spirit to go and find out for certain, struck her with so much force that she gave herself five minutes to pluck up her courage once again. Engines were whistling, and she watched a little one that was moving out a suburban train on to a siding. As she glanced up to her left she saw, above the parcels yard, the top-floor window of Ma Victoire's room in the house in the rue d'Amsterdam, the top-floor window she saw herself leaning out of before the horrible scene that had caused all their trouble. This reminded her of the peril of her situation in such an acute spasm of suffering that she suddenly felt ready to face anything to get it over. She was deafened by horn blasts and prolonged rumblings of trains, while dense clouds of smoke shut out the horizon as they rose into the clear open sky of Paris. She took the road back to the rue du Rocher, as if going to commit suicide, quickening her step in a sudden panic that she might find nobody at home.

A fresh terror numbed her as soon as she pushed the bell, but already a manservant had taken her name and was asking her to be seated in an anteroom. Then she distinctly heard a heated conversation going on behind some half-closed doors, followed by a deep, absolute silence. She was now only conscious of the dull thumping in her temples, and decided that the magistrate was still in consultation and that perhaps she might be kept waiting a long time; and this wait was becoming intolerable. Then suddenly, to her great surprise, the manservant called her and showed her in. It was clear that the magistrate had not gone. She sensed that he was still there, hidden behind a door.

It was a large study, with dark furniture, heavily curtained doors, thickly carpeted, and all so austere and hermetic that no sound reached it from outside. Yet there were flowers there, pale-coloured roses in a bronze bowl, and they gave a hint of hidden delicacy, a taste for the gracious life behind the severity. The master of the house was standing, very stiff in his frock-coat, looking equally austere with a thin face made slightly wider by greying side-whiskers, but there remained about him the elegance of a former handsome man about town, still slim in body, with a distinction one felt was benevolent beneath the deliberate formality of his official manner. In the half-light of the room he looked very tall.

As she went in Séverine felt overcome by the warmth and the airlessness due to the hangings, and all she could see was M. Camy-Lamotte watching her approach. He made no move to ask her to sit down and made a point of not opening his mouth first, waiting for her to explain the object of her visit. This prolonged the silence, and through some violent reaction she suddenly found complete self-command in this moment of peril and was perfectly calm and circumspect.

'Monsieur,' she said, 'excuse my making so bold as to come and remind you of my case, which I do because you are so kind. You know what an irreparable loss I have sustained, and in my present helplessness I have ventured to think that you might defend us and in some measure carry on the interest shown in us by your friend and my benefactor, whom we both mourn.'

M. Camy-Lamotte could do no less than ask her to sit down, for she had expressed herself with such perfect judgement, without any overdone humility or grief, but with such an instinctive mastery of feminine wiles. But still uttering never a word, he sat down himself and waited. Seeing that something more definite was called for she went on:

'May I refresh your memory by reminding you that I had the honour of seeing you at Doinville. Ah, that was a happy time for me! Now things are going badly, and you, Monsieur, are the only person I have to turn to. I am making a plea in the name of the man we have lost. You were fond of him, continue his good work and take his place in my life.'

As he listened and watched her all his suspicions were shaken, for she seemed so natural and appealing in her grief and supplication. He had decided that the note he had discovered among Grandmorin's papers, the few unsigned lines, could only have come from her, and he knew all about her favours to the President. Then just now the mere announcement of her visit had finally convinced him. He had only interrupted his conference with the magistrate in order to confirm that conviction. But how could he believe her guilty, seeing her so sweet and untroubled as this?

He wanted to get his mind quite clear, and so, keeping his austere manner:

'Please explain, Madame ... I remember you perfectly, and am only too anxious to be of use to you unless there is anything against it.'

So she told him quite simply how her husband was threatened with dismissal. He had very many enemies because of his personal merit and the protection he had enjoyed in high places until then. Now that they thought he was defenceless they hoped to win and were redoubling their efforts. Not that she named any names, she spoke in measured terms in spite of the imminence of the danger. It was because she had been convinced of the necessity for prompt action that she had decided to make the trip to Paris. Perhaps tomorrow would be too late, for her need for help and assistance was urgent. All this was said with such an abundance of logical facts and good reasons that it did indeed seem impossible that she had gone to all this trouble with any other object in view.

M. Camy-Lamotte studied even the tiny, imperceptible movements of her lips, and then he fired the first shot.

'But why should the Company dismiss your husband? It has nothing serious against him.'

She was watching him closely too, examining the smallest lines on his face and wondering whether he had found the letter. Innocent though the question was, she was suddenly quite sure that the letter was there, in some drawer in this room: he knew and was setting a trap so as to see whether she would dare to mention the real reasons for her husband's dismissal. Moreover he had stressed the question too heavily, and she had felt herself being scrutinized to her very soul by the pale eyes of this world-weary man.

She boldly went forth to meet the peril.

'Well you see, it's quite outrageous, but we have been suspected of killing our benefactor because of this unfortunate will. We have had no difficulty in proving our innocence. Only, when such abominable accusations are made, something always sticks, and presumably the Company is afraid of gossip.'

Once again he was amazed and disarmed by the frankness and especially by the sincerity of her tone. Moreover, having

137

thought her face rather ordinary at first glance, he was beginning to think she was extremely attractive, with the gentle
meekness of her blue eyes beneath the black, barbaric hair. He
thought of his friend Grandmorin with admiration and jealousy
— how the hell had that chap, ten years his senior, had such
delicious creatures to the day of his death, while he already had
to deny himself such fun and games so as not to lose what was
left of his energy? She really was most charming, most delicate-
looking, and through the cold grand manner of an official hand-
ling such an unpleasant business he managed to suggest the
smile of a connoisseur, quite impartial, of course, nowadays.

But Séverine, with the recklessness of a woman conscious of
her power, unwisely added:

'People like us don't kill for money. There would have had to
be some other motive, and there wasn't one.'

He watched her and saw a tremor at the corners of her
mouth. Yes, it was she. He was now absolutely convinced. And
by the way he had stopped smiling and by the nervous set of his
chin she immediately realized that she had delivered herself up
to him. It made her feel faint, as though her whole being was
collapsing. Yet she remained sitting upright in her chair and
heard his voice saying the requisite words, still in the same
equable tone. The conversation went on, but henceforth they
had nothing left to learn, and behind the general talk both were
now only speaking of the things they were not putting into
words. He had the letter, and she had written it. This emerged
even from their silences.

'Madame,' he went on eventually, 'I don't refuse to intercede
with the Company if you are really worthy of such interest. I
happen to be seeing the General Manager this evening about
something else. But I shall need certain notes. So now would
you write down the name, age and the stages in your husband's
career, in fact whatever information I may need about your
position.'

He put a little table in front of her and took his eyes off her so
as not to scare her too much. A shudder ran through her: so he
wanted a page of her writing to compare with the letter. For a
moment she was determined not to write, and desperately cast
about for a pretext, but then she asked herself what was the

good, since he knew anyway. They could always get hold of a few lines of her writing. So with no apparent reluctance and in the most natural way in the world she wrote down what he wanted, while he, standing behind her, recognized the writing at once, though it was more upright and less shaky than that of the letter. He came to think that this slim little woman was very brave and, now that she could not see him, once again he smiled the smile of a man no longer susceptible to anything but charm, blasé from having experienced everything. After all, it was not worth the trouble to be just. He was solely concerned with the decorative exterior of the régime he served.

'Very well, Madame, leave that with me and I will make inquiries and do the best I can.'

'I am most grateful, Monsieur ... So you will see that my husband is kept on, and I can consider the business settled?'

'Oh dear no, I can't say that! I can't promise anything ... I shall have to see and think it over.'

He really was hesitating, and did not know what line he was going to take about this couple. She was left with the one great anxiety now that she realized she was at his mercy: this hesitation of his, the alternatives of being saved or ruined by him, and she could not guess at the reasons that would influence him.

'Oh sir, think of the agony we are in. You can't let me go without putting my mind at rest.'

'Oh but I'm afraid I must, Madame. There is nothing I can do. You will have to wait.'

He took her to the door and she was going away in despair, so shattered that in her urgent need to force him to say clearly what he intended to do with them she was on the point of shouting out a complete confession. But, to gain another minute, still hoping to find some way, she exclaimed:

'I nearly forgot. I wanted to ask your advice about this unfortunate will. Do you think we should decline to accept the bequest?'

'The law is on your side,' he answered prudently. 'It is a matter of personal feeling and circumstances.'

In the doorway she made one last bid.

'Monsieur, I beg of you, don't let me go like this, tell me there is some hope.'

139

With a gesture signifying complete confidence in him she seized his hand. He pulled it away. But her beautiful eyes shone with such pleading that he was shaken.

'Very well, come back at five. I may have some news for you then.'

She left the house even more worried than when she had come. The situation had clarified itself, and her fate was still in the balance, with the threat of arrest, possibly at once ... How could she exist until five? The thought of Jacques, whom she had forgotten, suddenly came back – another one who could be her undoing if she were arrested! Although it was not quite half past two, she hurried up the rue du Rocher towards the rue Cardinet.

Left alone, M. Camy-Lamotte stood still by his desk. He was one of the inner circle at the Tuileries, where his position as Secretary-General of the Ministry of Justice took him almost daily, and he was quite as powerful as the Minister himself, and even employed in much more delicate matters. He therefore knew how much annoyance and anxiety the Grandmorin affair was causing in high places. The opposition newspapers were constantly waging a noisy campaign, some accusing the police of being so taken up with political spying that they had no time to arrest murderers, and others digging out the life of the President, hinting that he belonged to the court circle which was given up to the wildest debaucheries, and the campaign was becoming really disastrous as the elections drew near. Hence an urgent desire had been conveyed to the Secretary-General that the matter be closed with all speed, no matter how. As the Minister had handed over responsibility for this delicate affair to him he was the sole arbiter of the decision to be taken – on his own responsibility, of course. So all this had to be thought out carefully, for he had no doubt that he would have to bear the blame for everybody if he bungled it.

Still deep in thought, M. Camy-Lamotte went and opened the door to the adjoining room in which M. Denizet was waiting. He had been listening, and burst in exclaiming:

'There, I told you so, it was wrong to suspect those people ... Obviously this woman is only concerned with saving her husband from possible dismissal. She didn't say a single incriminating word.'

The Secretary-General did not answer at once. He was still preoccupied, studying the magistrate, struck by his heavy, thin-lipped face, and thinking about these law officers, whose fate he held in his hands as unacknowledged head of personnel he was amazed that they were so upright in their poverty and so intelligent in their professional torpor. But really this one, however subtle he thought himself, with his eyes half hidden beneath their heavy lids, was passionately tenacious when he thought he had got hold of the truth.

'So you persist in seeing the killer in this Cabuche?'

Denizet jumped in astonishment.

'Why of course! It's overwhelming! I have gone over the proofs with you and they are, I venture to say, classical, and not one is missing. I have tried hard to find out whether there was an accomplice in the compartment, a woman as you gave me to understand. That seemed to fit in with the statement of an engine-driver who caught a glimpse of the murder actually being done. But in the course of a skilful interrogation by myself the man did not persist in his initial declaration, and he even recognized the travelling-rug as the black shape he had spoken of ... Oh yes, I am quite sure Cabuche is the criminal, especially as if we don't get him we don't get anybody.'

Until that point the Secretary-General had been waiting to tell him about the written proof in his possession. Yet now that his own conviction was firm, he was in even less of a hurry to establish the truth. Why spoil the false trail of the preliminary examination if the right trail was bound to lead to worse troubles? It would all have to be weighed up first.

'Ah well,' he went on with his tired smile, 'I am willing to admit that you may be on the right track. I only asked you to come so as to go over with you certain serious points arising. This is an exceptional case, and now it has become an entirely political one, you do appreciate that, don't you? We are therefore perhaps going to find ourselves forced to act as government officials ... Now tell me frankly, from what you learned from

141

your interrogations, this girl, Cabuche's mistress, really was violated?'

The magistrate pursed his lips to show he was a shrewd man of the world, and his eyes half disappeared beneath their lids.

'Well of course! I think the President had made a nasty mess of her, and that will certainly come out in the trial. What's more, if the defence is entrusted to an opposition lawyer, we can look forward to a nice washing of dirty linen, for there is no lack of stories down in our part of the world!'

This Denizet was no fool when he gave up following his professional routine, sitting enthroned in the majesty of his own perspicacity and omnipotence. He had understood why he had been summoned, not to the Ministry of Justice, but to the home of the Secretary-General.

'In fact,' he concluded, seeing that the latter was not going to be shaken, 'we shall have a pretty kettle of fish!'

M. Camy-Lamotte went no further than a nod. He was busily calculating the results of the alternative case, that of the Roubauds. What was certain was that if the husband were committed for trial he would blurt out everything, how his own wife had also been seduced when she was a young girl, and the subsequent adultery and the jealous rage that must have goaded him to murder, to say nothing of the fact that it was no longer a case of a servant-girl and an old lag, and moreover that this official, married to this pretty wife, would drag in a whole section of the bourgeoisie and people on the railway staff. And besides, with a man like the President, could you ever tell what thin ice you were on? Perhaps they would come upon undreamed-of abominations. No, decidedly, the case of the Roubauds, who were the real guilty ones, was filthier still. He had made up his mind and he rejected it absolutely. If one case had to be followed up, he would be inclined to stick to that of the innocent Cabuche.

'I am won over by your theory,' he finally said to M. Denizet. 'There is indeed heavy circumstantial evidence against this quarryman, especially if he felt obliged to take a legitimate revenge. But dear me, how sordid it all is! And what a lot of mud would have to be stirred up! I know of course that justice must remain indifferent to consequences and that, soaring aloft, above mere sectional interests . . .'

He left off in mid flight, tailing off into a gesture, while the magistrate, now silent, gloomily waited for the orders he felt were coming. Now that his version of the truth, this creation of his intelligence was accepted, he was prepared to sacrifice the concept of justice to governmental necessity. But for all his habitual skill in transactions of this kind, the Secretary was in a bit of a hurry and spoke too fast, like a master accustomed to being obeyed.

'In a word, we want the case dismissed . . . See to it that the thing is shelved.'

'Excuse me, Monsieur,' declared M. Denizet, 'I can no longer do as I like about it, I have my conscience to consider.'

M. Camy-Lamotte at once smiled and took on his official manner again, with the disillusioned, polite air that seemed to be full of mockery.

'Of course, of course. And that is why I am appealing to your conscience. I am leaving you to come to the decision your conscience dictates, in the knowledge that you will weigh the pros and cons equitably with a view to the triumph of healthy doctrines and public morality . . . You know better than I do that it is sometimes heroic to accept one evil so as not to fall into a greater one . . . In short, we are only appealing to the good citizen in you, the civilized man. Nobody would dream of putting pressure on your independence, and that is why I repeat that you are the absolute master of the affair, as indeed the law has laid it down.'

Jealous of his unlimited power, especially when he was by way of misusing it, the magistrate greeted each one of these phrases with a self-satisfied nod.

'Moreover,' the other went on with renewed graciousness, exaggerated to the point of irony, 'we know whom we are dealing with. We have been watching your achievements for a long time now, and I can venture to tell you that we would bring you to Paris at once if there were a vacancy.'

M. Denizet reacted at once. What! If he rendered the service he was being asked to, were they still not going to fulfil his great ambition, his dream of an appointment in Paris? But already

M. Camy-Lamotte had read his thoughts and was going on:

'Your position is settled, it is just a matter of time . . . But, as I have begun to be indiscreet, I am happy to tell you that your name is down for the Legion of Honour next August 15th.'

M. Denizet thought this out for a moment. He would have preferred promotion, for he worked out that it would mean an increase of about 166 francs per month, and in the genteel poverty of his life that meant more comfort, a new outfit and his housekeeper Mélanie better fed and less cantankerous. And yet the cross of the Legion of Honour was worth having. Besides, he had been given a promise. This man, brought up in the traditions of the honest and humdrum magistracy, who would never have let himself be bought, gave way on a mere hope, a vague undertaking by the administration to favour him. The function of magistrate was only a job like any other, and he was fettered by his hopes of promotion, a hungry beggar always ready to bend his back under orders from the powers that be.

'I am deeply grateful,' he murmured, 'please say so to the Minister.'

He rose, sensing that anything else they could say would be embarrassing.

'Very well,' he concluded, with expressionless eyes in a death-mask face, 'I will complete my inquiry bearing your scruples in mind. Naturally, in the absence of clear facts proved against Cabuche, it would be better not to risk the pointless scandal of a trial . . . He will be released, but will remain under observation.'

At the door the Secretary-General now showed himself most charming.

'M. Denizet, we confidently leave everything to your great tact and high principles.'

When he was left alone M. Camy-Lamotte gave in to his now pointless curiosity to compare the page written by Séverine with the unsigned note he had found among President Grandmorin's papers. They tallied exactly. He folded up the letter and put it carefully away, for although he had not breathed a word about it to the examining magistrate he thought that a weapon of this kind might usefully be kept. As the profile of this little woman, who was so fragile and yet so strong in her tough resistance, came back to his mind's eye, he made his indulgent and

144

ironical shrug. Oh, these little bits of stuff, when they are willing!

At twenty to three Séverine found herself ahead of time in the rue Cardinet for the meeting she had arranged with Jacques. He lived there, right at the top of a big building, in a tiny room where he hardly ever went except to sleep at night, and even then he slept away twice a week, the two nights he spent at Le Havre between the evening train and the one next morning. However on this occasion, as he was soaked to the skin and dead tired, he had gone home and flung himself on his bed. And so Séverine might have waited in vain had he not been woken up by a row in the next room where a husband was beating his wife who was screaming. He shaved and dressed in a very bad temper, having seen her down there on the pavement as he looked through his attic window.

'Ah, there you are at last!' she cried, as he emerged from the entry. 'I was afraid I had misunderstood. You did say the corner of the rue Saussure . . .'

Not waiting for an answer, she looked up at the building.

'So this is where you live?'

Without saying so, he had fixed the meeting-place by his own front door because the depot where they were to go together was almost opposite. But he was embarrassed by her question because he imagined she might carry her friendliness to the point of asking to see his room, which was so sparsely furnished and in such a mess that he was ashamed of it.

'Oh, I don't live here, I just roost. Come along, I'm afraid the boss may already have gone.'

And indeed when they asked at the latter's little house behind the depot, on station property, they found he was not there, and they went in vain from shed to shed and everywhere they were told to come back at about half past four if they wanted to be sure of finding him in the repair shops.

'All right, we'll come back,' said Séverine.

When they were outside again and she was alone with Jacques:

'If you aren't busy, do you mind if I stay and wait with you?'

He could not refuse, and besides, for all the awkward feeling he had with her she was exercising a growing charm over him,

145

and it was so strong that as she looked sweetly at him the deliberate surliness behind which he was determined to protect himself was melting away. This woman, with her long face, so tender and timid-looking, must love like a faithful dog you would not even dare to beat.

'Of course I won't leave you,' he answered, and his tone was less brusque. 'Only, we have over an hour to kill ... would you like to go to a café?'

She smiled with happiness as she felt he was being pleasant at last, and protested quite vigorously:

'Oh no, no, I don't want to shut myself in. I'd much rather take your arm and walk in the streets, anywhere you like.'

She took his arm herself, in a very friendly way. Now he was no longer black from the journey she thought he looked quite distinguished in a smart suit suggesting the well-paid employee, but with the bourgeois effect mitigated by a sort of proud independence and a familiarity with rough weather and danger faced every day. She had never realized so clearly that he was a handsome fellow, with his open face and regular features, very dark moustache and white skin. The only thing that still disquieted her was his shifty eyes, eyes flecked with gold that always avoided hers. If he avoided looking straight at her was it because he did not want to commit himself, but remain free to act as he liked, even against her? There and then, given the uncertainty she was still in and the shudder that seized her each time she thought of that study in the rue du Rocher, in which her life was being decided, she kept one single object in view, which was to feel that this man, whose arm she was holding, belonged to her and her alone, and to see to it that when she looked at him he looked back into her eyes, deeply. Then he would belong to her. Not that she loved him at all, that did not even enter her head. She simply wanted to make him her slave so as not to have to fear him.

They walked along for a few minutes without speaking, in the endless stream of people in this very busy district. Sometimes they were forced off the pavement and walked in the roadway among the vehicles. Then they found themselves at the Square des Batignolles, which was almost deserted at that time of year. However, the sky, washed clean by the morning's deluge, was a very soft blue, and the lilacs were budding in the warm March sun.

'Shall we go in there?' she suggested. 'All these crowds make me feel giddy!'

Jacques was going in of his own accord, not realizing his need to have her more to himself, away from the crowd.

'Either here or somewhere else. Let's go in.'

They went on strolling slowly along by the grass between the bare trees. A few women were taking toddlers for a walk and there were people crossing the garden for a short cut, walking fast. They stepped over the brook, climbed up the rock gardens and then, as they were coming back, wondering what to do, they went through some clumps of conifers with their evergreen foliage shining dark green in the sun. There was a seat in this quiet corner, out of sight, and they sat down without even asking each other this time, as if they had been led to this spot by a mutual understanding.

'The weather really is lovely today,' she said, breaking the silence.

'Yes,' he answered, 'the sun's come out again.'

But that was not what they were thinking about. He normally avoided women and was going over the events that had brought him into contact with this one. Here she was, touching him and threatening to encroach upon his life, and he could not get over his surprise. Since the last interrogation at Rouen he had been quite clear in his mind that this woman was an accomplice in the murder at La Croix-de-Maufras. How? Through what circumstances? Because of what passion or interest? He had asked himself these questions and found no clear answer. Eventually, however, he had worked out a story: the husband a covetous and violent man in a hurry to get his hands on the legacy, then perhaps fearing that the will might be altered to their disadvantage, or perhaps calculating that he could keep a hold on his wife by a bond of blood. He was satisfied with this story, which had some exciting and interesting mysteries about it, but he did not attempt to explore them. Moreover he had been haunted by the thought that it was his duty to tell the authorities everything. And indeed it was this thought that had been on his mind ever since he had found himself sitting next to her on this seat, and so close that he could feel the warmth of her thigh against his.

'It's surprising,' he went on, 'to be able to stay in the open air in March. Just like summer.'

'Oh yes,' she said, 'as soon as the sun comes up you can feel it.'

She on her side was reflecting that this chap would have to be very silly not to have guessed that they were guilty. They had made too much of a dead set at him, and even at this moment she was still sitting very close to him. And so during this silence punctuated with banal remarks she was following his thoughts. She caught his glance once and could read in it that he was beginning to wonder whether she was that black shape he had seen holding down the victim's legs with all her strength. What could she do or say to bind him with an unbreakable tie?

'This morning,' she added, 'it was ever so cold in Le Havre.'

'To say nothing of all the rain we've had.'

At that moment Séverine had a sudden inspiration. She did not reason or argue it out; it came to her like an instinctive reflex, from the obscure depths of her mind and heart, and if she had reasoned about it she would have said nothing. But she felt it was all right, and that by speaking she would win him over.

Taking his hand gently she looked at him. The clumps of evergreens concealed them from people walking in the neighbouring streets, and they could only hear a distant rumbling of vehicles, muffled in this sunlit retreat in the garden, and just one child was to be seen at a bend in the path, silently filling a little pail with spadefuls of sand. Without any transition, and from the depths of her soul she murmured:

'You think I'm guilty, don't you?'

He started slightly, then looked steadily into her eyes.

'Yes,' he said, in the same soft, emotional tone.

She had kept his hand in hers, and she squeezed it harder, but did not say any more immediately. She felt that their feverish emotion was drawing them closer.

'You are wrong, I'm not guilty.'

She was saying this not to convince him, but solely to warn him that she had to be innocent in the eyes of the world at large.

148

It was the declaration of a woman saying no and meaning that it must be no, in spite of everything and always.

'I'm not guilty . . . Don't make me unhappy by believing that I am.'

She felt exultant as she saw that he let his eyes go on looking into hers, intently. It might well mean that what she had done was to give herself to him, for she was delivering herself up, and if later he claimed her she could not refuse. But the tie was there between them and it was binding. She could defy him to speak now, he was hers and she was his. They were united by the confession.

'You won't make me unhappy any more, you believe me?'

'Yes, I believe you,' he said, smiling now.

Why should he force her to talk crudely about this horrible thing? She could tell him everything later if she felt the need to. He was deeply touched by this way of finding peace by confessing to him without admitting anything; it was a sign of the deepest affection. She was so confiding, so vulnerable, with her soft, periwinkle-blue eyes! She seemed to him so womanly, belonging entirely to man and always ready to submit to him for the sake of happiness! What thrilled him above all, as their hands stayed clasped and they gazed into each other's eyes, was that this old trouble was not coming back, that terrible malady that came over him when he was with a woman and thought of possessing her. With other women he had not been able to touch their flesh without feeling the urge to dig into it with an abominable lust for slaughter. Could he really love this one and not kill her?

'You can rest assured that I am your friend and you have nothing to fear from me,' he murmured into her ear. 'I don't want to know your business, it shall be as you wish You do understand? You can make any use of me you like.'

He was now so close to her face that he could feel her hot breath on his own. Even that morning it would have made him tremble with the desperate fear of having one of his attacks. What was happening to him? There was hardly a tremor left in him, but only the tired happiness of convalescence. The thought that she had killed, now that it had become a certainty, made her seem different, greater, a creature apart. Perhaps she didn't merely help, but had dealt the blow herself. He was convinced she had, though he had no proof. From then onwards she seemed sacred to him, above all mere reasoning, unaware of the terrified desire she roused in him.

Now they both started chattering gaily, like a couple who had met and were falling in love.

'You should give me your other hand to warm up for you.'

'Oh no, not here, we might be seen.'

'Who could see us? We're alone. And besides, what harm could there be in that? That isn't the way babies are made!'

'I should hope not!'

She laughed away in her joy at being saved. She didn't love this fellow, of that she felt sure, and if she had promised herself she was already working out how not to pay. He looked a nice chap, he wouldn't pester her, and everything would turn out all right.

'That's settled then, we are good friends and nobody, not even my husband, will have any cause for complaint ... And now let go of my hand and don't go on staring at me like that. You'll wear your eyes out!'

But he still kept her delicate fingers between his, and murmured very softly:

'You know I love you.'

She pulled herself free with a little jerk and stood up in front of the seat on which he was still sitting.

'Don't be so silly! Do behave properly, there's somebody coming.'

It was true. A nursemaid was coming along with a baby asleep in her arms. Then a girl went by, looking very busy. The sun was sinking into a purplish haze, and its rays were leaving the grass and dying in gold dust on the green tips of the firs. There was a sort of sudden break in the continuous roar of traffic. Somewhere nearby a clock struck five.

'Good Heavens!' exclaimed Séverine. 'Five, and I have an appointment in the rue du Rocher!'

Her joy vanished as she remembered that she was not yet safe, and once again she felt the anxiety about the unknown which was waiting for her there. She went quite pale and her lips quivered.

'But what about the head of the depot you were supposed to see?' said Jacques, getting up from the seat to take her on his arm again.

'Can't be helped, I'll see him some other time. Look, my dear, I don't need you any more now, so let me get on with my errand. And thanks once again, thanks with all my heart.'

She shook his hand and fled.

'Be seeing you on the train.'

'Yes, be seeing you.'

She was already hurrying away and disappearing between the clumps of trees in the Square, and he slowly made for the rue Cardinet.

M. Camy-Lamotte had been having at his home a long conference with the General Manager of the Western Railway. Ostensibly sent for over some other business, he had eventually admitted how the Grandmorin case was embarrassing the Company. First of all there were the complaints in the papers about the lack of security for passengers in first-class carriages. Then all the staff were involved in the business, several employees being suspected apart from this Roubaud fellow, who was the most compromised and might be arrested at any moment. Finally, the rumours going round about the disgusting morals of the President, who was on the Board of Directors, seemed to reflect on the whole Board. And in this way the supposed crime of some miserable deputy stationmaster, some shady, low, unsavoury business, was spreading upwards through the complicated mechanism and dislocating the vast machine of railway organization, even upsetting the top administration. The upheaval was going even further upwards, affecting the Ministry, threatening the State itself in the unsettled political climate of the time: it was a critical moment for a great social body in which the slightest change of temperature might accelerate decomposition. Hence, when M. Camy-Lamotte had heard from this man that the Company had decided that very morning to dismiss Roubaud, he had reacted strongly against this measure. No, no, nothing could be more ill-timed, it would double the uproar in the press if it decided to represent the stationmaster as a political martyr. Everything would crack more and more from top to bottom, and God knew what unpleasant discoveries would be raked up all round! The scandal had gone on too long as it was, and it must be silenced with all speed. And so the General Manager was convinced and had undertaken to keep Roubaud on and not even move him from Le Havre. It would soon be made clear that there was no blame attached to anybody. It was finished, the matter would be shelved.

When Séverine, out of breath and with beating heart, found herself once again in the austere study in the rue du Rocher, in front of M. Camy-Lamotte, he contemplated her for a minute without a word, interested in the extraordinary effort she was making to appear calm. Yes, decidedly he liked this delicate criminal, with her periwinkle-blue eyes.

'Well, Madame...'

He paused to savour her anxiety for a few more seconds. But she looked at him so intently and he felt that she was imploring him with her whole being, so anxious to know that he took pity on her.

'Well, Madame, I have seen the General Manager and I have persuaded him not to dismiss your husband. The matter is settled.'

She almost collapsed from the wave of excessive joy that washed over her. Her eyes filled with tears, and she said nothing, but just smiled.

He repeated the words, stressing them to give her their full implication:

'The matter is settled ... You can go home to Le Havre in peace.'

She did grasp the full meaning; he meant that they would not be arrested and were pardoned. It was not merely the job safe, but the awful drama forgotten and buried. With an instinctive demonstration of affection, like a pretty domestic pet giving thanks and caressing, she bent over his hands, kissed them and held them to her cheeks. This time he did not pull them away, but was deeply moved himself by the tender charm of her gratitude.

'But,' he went on, trying to recover his dignity, 'don't forget; and behave yourselves properly!'

'Oh, sir!'

But he wanted to keep both man and wife at his mercy. He hinted at the existence of the letter.

'Remember that the file is still here and that at the slightest slip on your part the whole thing can be opened up again . . . In particular, do tell your husband not to meddle any more in politics. In that respect we should be merciless. I know he has already compromised himself – I have been told about an unfortunate dispute with the Sub-Prefect. In fact he is thought to be a republican, and that is detestable . . . So is that clear? Let him be careful or we shall just jettison him.'

She was on her feet and already anxious to be outside so as to find some air, for she was suffocating with joy.

'Monsieur, we shall obey you, we shall be exactly as you want us. No matter when or where, you will only have to give your orders, I am yours to command.'

He was now smiling again with that weary look of his and the touch of disdain of a man who had drunk deep of the vanity of all things.

'Oh, I shan't take advantage, Madame, I never take advantage.'

He opened the study door himself. On the landing she turned back twice, her radiant face still thanking him.

Out in the rue du Rocher Séverine rushed along madly. Realizing that she was going up the street for no reason, she came down the hill again and crossed the road for no reason, at the risk of being run over. She felt she had to move, wave her arms, shout. Already she saw why they were being let off, and caught herself saying:

'Why of course, they're afraid, there's no danger of their stirring all that up, and I was very silly to torture myself. It's obvious . . . Oh, what luck! Saved, saved for good and all this time! All the same, I'll give my husband a fright, that'll keep him quiet . . . Saved, saved, what luck!'

As she came out into the rue Saint-Lazare, she saw by a clock in a jeweller's shop that it was twenty to six.

'Oh well, I'll treat myself to a good dinner, I've got time.'

Opposite the station she chose the most expensive-looking restaurant, installed herself at a little table for one with a spotless white cloth, by the clear glass front window, where she found the activity of the street great fun to watch, and ordered a subtly chosen dinner of oysters, fillets of sole and a wing of roast chicken. The least she could do was make up for her beastly lunch. She tucked in, found the white bread excellent and ordered another delicacy, soufflé fritters. Then she had her coffee and made haste because she only had a few minutes to catch the express.

When he left her, Jacques went home, changed back into his working clothes and went straight to the depot, where usually he arrived only half an hour before his engine was due to leave. He had come to rely on his fireman Pecqueux to check up, although he was drunk two out of three times. But that day, in his emotional, lovesick state, he had unconsciously become full of scruples and wanted to make sure for himself that every part was in perfect running order, particularly as on the way up from Le Havre that morning he thought he had noticed that his engine had been making more effort for less output.

In the huge, coal-black engine-shed, lit by lofty, grimy windows, Jacques's engine, among the others off duty, was already at the head of a line as she was the next to go out. One of the cleaners in the depot had just stoked up the fire, and red clinker was dropping down into the ashpit. It was one of those four-coupled express engines, graceful, elegant and huge with big, light-weight driving wheels and steel coupling-rods, broad-chested with long, powerful haunches, and all the logic and rightness that go to make up the sovereign beauty of metal beings – precision in strength. Like other engines of the Western Railway Company it bore, apart from its own number, the name of a station, Lison in the Cotentin. But in his affection for her Jacques had turned that into a woman's name, Lison, and he called her this with loving tenderness.

It was perfectly true, he had loved his engine with real love for the four years he had been driving her. He had driven others, docile or restive, dauntless or slothful, and he was well aware that each one has her own character, that many of them are not much cop, like some women of flesh and blood. So if he loved this one it was because she had some of the rare qualities of a good woman. She was gentle, obedient, moved off easily, kept up a regular, continuous pace thanks to her good steaming.

154

Some made out that her getting under way so easily was due to the excellent tyres on the wheels and above all the perfect adjustment of the slide valves, and similarly that her good steaming on low fuel consumption could be accounted for by the quality of the copper tubes and the fortunate arrangement of the boiler. But he knew that there was something more, for other engines, identically built, assembled with the same care, showed none of these qualities. There was the soul, the mystery in creation, the something that the chances of hammering bestow on metal, that the knack of the fitter gives to the parts – the personality of the machine, its life.

So he loved Lison with masculine gratitude, for she got away or stopped promptly, like a vigorous and docile mare; he loved her because over and above his regular wages she earned him money, thanks to fuel bonuses. She steamed so well that he saved a great deal of coal. He had only one thing against her, and that was that she needed too much oiling, the cylinders in particular consumed quite unreasonable quantities of oil, an insatiable thirst, a real debauch. He had tried to keep her within bounds, but in vain. She at once got short of breath, she had to have it, it was part of her character. He had resigned himself to overlook this gluttonous passion of hers, just as you shut your eyes to some shortcoming in people otherwise full of good qualities. He just said to his fireman by way of a joke that like beautiful women she needed oiling too often.

As the fire was roaring and Lison was gradually getting up pressure Jacques gave her the once-over, inspecting each one of her parts, trying to find out why that morning she had gobbled down more oil than usual. He could find nothing amiss, she was shining and clean, with the sparkling cleanliness telling of a driver's tender care. He could constantly be seen wiping her, polishing her, particularly at the journey's end, and he rubbed her hard, just as they rub down horses steaming after a long gallop, taking advantage of the fact that she was hot so as to clean off stains and splashes more easily. He never pushed her too hard either, but kept to a regular speed, avoiding delays which necessitate unpleasant spurts to catch up. In fact theirs had always been such a successful marriage that never once in four years had he entered a complaint about her in the depot

155

register in which drivers write down their requirements for repairs, the bad drivers, the lazy or drunken ones, always finding something wrong with their engines. Yet today Jacques really was concerned about her intemperate thirst for oil, and there was something else too, something vague and deep-seated that he had never felt before, a sort of anxiety and mistrust of her, as though he could not quite trust her and would have liked to make sure she was not going to play him up on the journey.

Pecqueux had not yet turned up, however, and Jacques went for him when he did come, with a coated tongue after a meal with a crony. Usually the two men got on very well in this long intimacy that took them from one end of the line to the other, shaken together side by side, taciturn, united in the same job with the same dangers. Although he was over ten years younger, the driver took a fatherly interest in his fireman, covered up his failings, let him take an hour's nap when he was too tight, and the other man acknowledged these indulgences with a dog-like devotion, for he was an excellent workman and highly competent apart from his drinking. Moreover he loved Lison too, and that in itself made for a good understanding. The two of them and the engine made a real threesome, with never a hard word. So Pecqueux was taken aback by such a rough welcome and stared at Jacques, and was even more surprised when he heard him muttering his misgivings about her.

'What's up? But she goes like a bird!'

'No, no, I feel uneasy.'

And still, although each part was in good shape, he went on shaking his head. He tried out levers, made sure the valve was working properly, went up on the footplate, then went and topped up the lubricating cups of the cylinders himself while the fireman wiped the dome where there were slight traces of rust. The rod of the sandbox was all right, in fact everything should have set his mind at rest. The truth was that in his heart Lison was no longer alone, for another love was taking root there, this slim, fragile being he could still see at his side on the seat in the square, with her appealing weakness, so in need of love and protection. Never before, when something out of his control had made him lose time and he had hurled his engine along at eighty kilometres an hour, had he thought about the risks to his

156

passengers. And now the very idea of taking back to Le Havre this woman whom he had almost hated that morning and resented bringing up, was gnawing him with worry and the fear of an accident in which he visualized her injured through his fault and dying in his arms. But now he felt the responsibility of love. He was unsure of Lison, who would do well to behave herself if she wished to keep her reputation for being a good runner.

It struck six. Jacques and Pecqueux climbed up to the little sheet-iron platform between engine and tender, and the fireman having opened the steam-cock at a sign from his chief, a cloud of whirling white vapour filled the black shed. Then, responding to the regulator that her driver slowly turned, Lison moved out of the depot and whistled for her road. Almost at once she could enter the Batignolles tunnel. But she had to wait under the Europe bridge, and only at the scheduled time did the pointsman send her down on to the 6.30 express to which two men coupled her firmly.

They were about to leave, with only five minutes left, and Jacques leaned out, puzzled at not having seen Séverine in the bustling crowd of passengers. He felt sure she would not get into the train without coming up to him first. At last she came, very late and nearly running. And she did come the whole length of the train, not stopping until she reached the engine, with her face aflame and radiating joy.

She stood tiptoe on her little feet, looking up and laughing.

'Don't you worry, here I am!'

He laughed too, overjoyed to see her there.

She pulled herself higher still and went on in a lower voice:

'My dear, I'm happy, so happy ... A wonderful stroke of luck for me ... Everything I wished for!'

He understood perfectly and felt a great joy. Then as she was running off she turned round and added by way of a joke:

'And just you mind you don't smash me up!'

He protested gaily:

'Just as if I would! Never you fear!'

Doors were already banging, and Séverine only just had time to get in. Jacques had the guard's signal, whistled and opened the regulator. They were off. It was the same departure as that

of the tragic train in February, at the same time, amid the same
station activities, the same noises, the same smoke. Only now it
was still daylight, a pale, very soft twilight. Séverine had her
head out of the window, watching.

On Lison Jacques, standing on the right hand side, snugly
dressed in woollen trousers and smock, wearing goggles with
cloth side-pieces tied at the back of his head under his cap,
never took his eyes off the track, leaning out of the cab window
all the time for a clearer view. Shaken roughly by the vibration,
which he didn't even notice, he had his right hand on the reversing-wheel, like a pilot at his wheel, and he moved it imperceptibly but continuously, steadying or increasing the speed,
and with his left hand he kept on pulling the handle of the
whistle because the way out of Paris is awkward and full of
snares. He whistled at level crossings, stations, tunnels and sharp
curves. When he saw a distant red signal in the fading daylight
he asked for the road with a prolonged whistle, then thundered
on. He just glanced from time to time at the pressure gauge,
turning the little wheel of the injector whenever the pressure
reached ten kilograms. But his eye always came back to the line
ahead and he was fully taken up with the smallest details, con-
centrating so hard that he saw nothing else and did not even
notice the wind blowing like a hurricane. The pressure went
down and he opened the firebox door, pulling up the ratchet,
and Pecqueux, knowing the gesture, understood, broke up some
coal with the hammer and spread it evenly with his shovel over
the whole width of the grate. A fierce heat burned their legs,
and then once the door was shut the icy blast blew again.

It was getting dark and Jacques redoubled his caution. He
had seldom known Lison so obedient; he possessed her, rode her
as he willed, with the absolute command of the master, yet he
never relaxed his severity and treated her like a tamed beast
needing constant watching. There behind him in this train hurtling full speed ahead he could see a delicate figure entrusting
herself to his care, confident and smiling. It made him tremble a
little, and he grasped the wheel tighter; his eyes peered through
the deepening night on the alert for red lights. After the
Asnières and Colombes junctions he had breathed more freely.
Everything went well as far as Mantes, the line was dead level

and an easy run for the train. After Mantes he had to push Lison a bit to get her up a rather stiff bank for nearly half a league. Then without slackening he took her down the gentle slope in the Rolleboise tunnel – two and a half kilometres of tunnel that she covered in scarcely three minutes. There was only one more tunnel, Le Roule near Gaillon, before Sotteville, a dreaded station made very perilous by the intricacy of the lines, continual shunting operations and heavy traffic. His whole being was concentrated in his watchful eyes and controlling hand, and Lison, with a whistle and a cloud of smoke, tore through Sotteville at full steam and only stopped at Rouen, whence she set off again in calmer mood, climbing more slowly the bank up to Malaunay.

The moon had risen, very bright and clear, so that Jacques could see the smallest bushes and even the setts in the roads as they rushed past. As they emerged from the Malaunay tunnel he glanced to his right because he was disconcerted by the black shadow of a big tree obscuring the track, and he recognized the lonely spot in a thicket of brushwood from which he had seen the murder. The empty, wild country unfolded with its succession of hills and deep hollows black with small trees, a desolate waste. Then at La Croix-de-Maufras the motionless moon suddenly showed up the house standing obliquely, abandoned and in distress with its shutters permanently closed, horribly dreary. And once again, without knowing why but more strongly than the other times, his heart was gripped with fear as if he were going past his own doom.

Then suddenly his eye was caught and carried away by another picture. By the Misards' house, at the level-crossing gate, Flore was standing. Nowadays he saw her there on each of his trips, waiting and watching for him. She did not move, apart from turning her head to follow him longer in his lightning flight. Her tall silhouette stood out black against the white light, and only her gold-coloured hair caught the pale gold of the moon.

Having pressed Lison hard to get her over the Motteville bank he let her breathe a bit across the Bolbec level, then go all out from Saint-Romain to Harfleur down the steepest incline on the line, three leagues that engines reel off at a gallop like horses rushing madly when they can sniff the stable. He was feeling exhausted by the time they reached Le Havre, when, under the station roof amidst the noise and smoke of arrival, Séverine, before going up to her home, ran up and said in her gay, affectionate voice:

'Thank you, see you tomorrow.'

[6]

A MONTH went by, and a great calm had settled again over the flat occupied by the Roubauds on the first floor of the station buildings, above the waiting-rooms. In their home and those of their neighbours along the corridor, in this little world of employees tied to a clockwork existence by the uniform sequence of regulation hours, life had resumed its monotonous course. It seemed as though nothing violent or abnormal had ever occurred.

The sensational and scandalous Grandmorin affair was being quietly forgotten and was going to be shelved because the law seemed incapable of discovering the criminal. After detaining him for another fortnight Denizet, the examining magistrate, had dismissed the charge against Cabuche on the grounds that there was no case to answer, and a romantic police legend was beginning to take shape: that of an unknown, elusive murderer, a criminal adventurer present everywhere at the same time, made responsible for all murders and who vanished in smoke as soon as the police appeared. The odd joke about the mythical murderer came up only now and again in the opposition press, which was getting worked up about the forthcoming general election. Abuses of power or the violent behaviour of Prefects kept them supplied daily with other material for outraged articles and so, as the newspapers no longer concerned themselves with the case, it had lost its appeal to the passions and curiosity of the mob. Nobody even talked about it any more.

What had really restored calm for the Roubauds was the happy way that the other difficulty had smoothed itself out, the one that President Grandmorin's will threatened to raise. Acting on Mme Bonnehon's advice the Lachesnayes had finally consented not to contest this will for fear of stirring up some scandal, and moreover they were very uncertain about the outcome of a lawsuit. So, in possession of their legacy, the Roubauds had been the owners of La Croix-de Maufras for a week, house and garden, valued at some 40,000 francs. They had at once decided to sell it, for that house of lust and blood haunted them like a nightmare, and they would never have dared to sleep in it for fear of the ghosts of the past. They would sell the whole thing as it stood, with the furniture and without doing any repairs or even wiping off the dust. But as it would have fetched far too little at a public auction because buyers prepared to bury themselves in that solitary place would be few indeed, they had decided to wait for someone really interested, and had merely put a huge board across the front of the house, easy to read from the frequent passing trains. The appeal in large letters, this desolation for sale, added to the dreariness of the closed shutters and garden overgrown with brambles. As Roubaud had refused point blank to go there even for a short visit to take the necessary steps, Séverine had been there one afternoon and left the keys with the Misards, with instructions to show any prospective buyers over if they appeared. Any such could have moved in in a couple of hours, for there was even linen in the cupboards.

So there was nothing left for the Roubauds to worry about, and they let each day go by in peaceful expectation of the morrow. The house would get sold sometime, they would invest the money and everything would be all right. They forgot about it, as a matter of fact, and lived as though they would never leave the three rooms they occupied: the living-cum-dining-room, which opened straight on to the corridor, the quite large bedroom to the right and the kitchen, poky and airless, to the left. Even the sloping zinc of the station roof in front of their windows, which cut off their view like a prison wall, instead of maddening them as it used to, seemed to soothe them by contributing to the atmosphere of total repose and comforting peace which lulled them. At any rate you couldn't be seen by neighbours, you didn't have spying eyes staring at you in your home. So when spring came the only thing they complained about was the stifling heat and the blinding reflection from the zinc roof heated up by the morning sun. After the dreadful shock that had kept them living on tenterhooks for nearly two months they were basking blissfully in this all-pervading torpor. They just asked to stay where they were, happy simply to exist without trembling and suffering. Never had Roubaud shown himself to be a more thorough and conscientious employee: in the week he was on day shift he was down on the platform by five in the morning, did not go up for his meal until ten, came down again at eleven and went on until five in the afternoon, that is to say eleven hours full of duties; in the night-shift week he was on from five p.m. until five a.m. without even the short break of a meal in his own home, for he had his supper in his office. And he bore this harsh servitude with a kind of satisfaction, apparently enjoying it, going into every detail, insisting on seeing everything and doing everything himself as if in the very fatigue he found forgetfulness and a fresh start in a balanced, normal life. On her side Séverine, almost always alone and a widow one week out of two and during the other week only seeing him at early lunch and dinner, seemed to have developed a fever for good housekeeping. Usually she sat about and did needlework, hating housework, which an elderly party, Ma Simon, came and did from nine to twelve. But since she had found peace of mind again at home, she was full of ideas about cleaning and planning. She never sat down before tidying everywhere. What was more, they were both sleeping the sleep of the just. In their rare conversations together over meals or on the nights when they were sleeping together they never mentioned the affair, and they no doubt thought it was dead and buried.

For Séverine especially life became very pleasant again. And her idle fits came back and once again she left the housework to Ma Simon, like a lady who was only brought up to do fine needlework. She had embarked on an endless task, an embroidered eiderdown-cover that threatened to last her lifetime. She rose quite late, enjoying staying in bed alone, gently lulled by the departures and arrivals of trains which for her indicated the exact passage of time like a clock. In the early days of her married life she had been driven crazy by the violent noises from the station, whistles, clanking of turntables, thunderous roarings and sudden crashes like earthquakes that shook her and the furniture alike. Then gradually she had got used to them and the noisy, bustling station had become part of her life; now she liked it, and in the movement and din she found her peace of mind. Until lunchtime she wandered from one room to

163

another, talking to her daily help and doing nothing. Then she spent the long afternoons sitting at the dining-room window, most often with her work lying on her lap, just enjoying doing nothing. The weeks when her husband came in and went to bed in the early hours and could be heard snoring until evening, these had become the good weeks for her, the ones when she lived as she used to before she was married, having all the bed to herself and then amusing herself how she liked, with the whole day free. She hardly ever went out, and all she saw of Le Havre was the smoke from the factories nearby, and the big black clouds dirtied the sky above the zinc roofing which shut off the horizon a few metres from her eyes. The town was there behind that eternal wall, she constantly felt its presence, and her annoyance at not seeing it had at length softened. Half a dozen pots of wallflowers and verbenas which she grew in the valley of the station roofing made a little garden, a flowering solitude for her. Sometimes she talked about herself as though she were a recluse in the depths of a forest. On his own, when taking time off, Roubaud would step over the window-sill and walk up the valley as far as the end, then climb the zinc slope and sit on the top of the gable above the Cours Napoléon, smoking his pipe right up in the sky, dominating the town spread out at his feet, the docks with their tall plantations of masts and the great sea stretching pale green to infinity.

It seemed as though the same somnolence had come over the other couples, their fellow employees. This corridor, along which such a terrible wind of gossip blew as a rule, was now slumbering as well. When Philomène paid her call on Mme Lebleu you scarcely heard the gentle murmur of their voices. Equally surprised at the turn things were taking, they now always referred to the deputy stationmaster with supercilious commiseration: of course, so as to keep him in his job, his wife had been carrying on like mad in Paris. Anyway, he had cooked his goose now, you never cleared yourself of certain suspicions. And as Mme Lebleu was now persuaded that her neighbours were no longer in a position to take her flat away she merely registered great contempt and passed them stiffly without acknowledgement. This in the end put even Philomène off, and she came less and less, finding her too stuck up and so losing interest. All the same, to keep her hand in Mme Lebleu went on watching out for the intrigue between Mlle Guichon and the stationmaster M. Dabadie, though she never caught them. Now there was no sound along the corridor but the imperceptible swish of her felt slippers. As everything had died down, a whole month of blessed peace went by, like the heavy sleep which follows great disasters.

But in the Roubaud home there was still one painful, worrying spot, the spot on the floor of the dining-room on which their eyes could never fall by chance without their feeling the same old uneasiness. It was the oak edging of the parquet that they had lifted and then replaced in order to hide the watch and the ten thousand francs taken from Grandmorin's body, as well as about three hundred francs in gold in a purse. Roubaud had only taken the watch and the money from the pockets so as to make it look like robbery. He was not a thief, and he would have starved to death right by it, as he put it, rather than benefit by a centime or sell the watch. The money of this old man who had defiled his wife, whom he had dealt with as he deserved, this money stained with filth and blood – no, no, it wasn't clean enough money for a decent man to touch. He did not even bother about the house at La Croix-de-Maufras, which he was willing to accept as a gift. No, it was simply the fact of the victim plundered, these banknotes taken in the course of a foul murder, that revolted him and made his conscience recoil in revulsion and fear. And yet he had not found the will-power to burn the notes and then go out one night and throw the watch and wallet into the sea. Although simple prudence advised him to do so, some obscure instinct inside him protested at this destruction. He had a subconscious reverence that would never let him resign himself to destroying such a sum. At the beginning, on the first night, he had hidden it under his pillow, not feeling anywhere else safe enough. During the following days he had used all his ingenuity finding hiding-places and then changing them every morning, fearful of the slightest sound in his terror of a search-warrant. Never had he devoted so much imagination to anything. At length, one day, having run out of ideas, weary of trembling, he had been too sick at heart to take the money and watch out from under the parquet where he had hidden them the day before, and now he would not have delved down there for anything in the world: it was like a charnel-house, a cave of terror and death where ghosts lay in wait for him. He even avoided putting his foot on that strip of floor when he walked, for it felt unpleasant and it seemed to give his legs a slight jolt. When she sat by the window in the afternoon Séverine kept her chair back so as not to be right above the corpse they kept under their floor. They never referred to it between themselves, endeavoured to believe that they would get used to it, and came to be annoyed with it for being there and making itself felt under their feet, more tiresome every hour. And this unease was all the more strange because they were not in the least bit worried by the knife, the beautiful new knife bought by the wife and plunged by the husband into the throat of the lover. It had just been washed and was somewhere in a drawer, and was used sometimes by Ma Simon to cut the bread.

Furthermore, Roubaud had recently brought into this peaceful existence a new source of trouble, and a steadily worsening trouble, by forcing Jacques to come and see them. His schedule of duties took the driver back to Le Havre three times a week: Monday from ten thirty-five in the morning until six twenty in the evening, Thursday and Saturday from eleven five at night until six forty in the morning. On the first Monday after Séverine's trip to Paris the deputy stationmaster had been most insistent.

'Now look here, mate, you can't refuse to have a bite with us. You've been very kind to my wife and, good Lord, I do owe you a bit of thanks!'

Twice in a month Jacques had accepted an invitation to lunch like this. It seemed as though Roubaud, as soon as he could put a guest between them, found relief from the long silences that were now the rule when he ate with his wife alone. He at once found things to talk about again, and chattered and made jokes.

'Come again as often as you can! You can see you aren't putting us out.'

One Thursday evening Jacques, shaved and washed and ready for bed, had met Roubaud having a walk round the engine-sheds, and in spite of the late hour the latter, not wanting to go home alone, had made him go back with him to the station and then forced him to come in. Séverine was still up, reading. They had a drink and even played cards until past midnight.

From then onwards the Monday lunches and the little parties on Thursday and Saturday evenings became a habit. If his friend failed to turn up one day, Roubaud himself would go and hunt him out and reproach him for neglecting them. He was growing increasingly morose and was never cheerful except with his new friend. This fellow who had given him such an awful fright at first, and who should by rights still be an object of execration as the witness and living evocation of the terrible things he wanted to forget, had on the contrary become indispensable, perhaps for the very reason that he knew but had not talked. It remained like the strongest of ties between them, a sort of complicity. Often Roubaud looked at him significantly and shook his hand with a sudden burst of emotion far in excess of a simple expression of their friendship.

But above all Jacques helped them both by taking their minds off things. Séverine, too, welcomed him with joy and exclaimed gaily when he came in, as though the pleasure revived her. She dropped her needlework or book, or whatever, and found relief in talk and laughter from the dreary somnolence in which she spent her days.

'Oh, how nice of you to come! I heard the express and thought about you.'

When he came for a meal it was a celebration. She already knew what he liked, went out herself to get new-laid eggs for him, and it was all done so nicely, like a good housewife welcoming a friend of the family, that he could see nothing more in it, so far, than a desire to be pleasant and the need for something to do.

'Don't forget to come again next Monday. There'll be some cream!'

Yet by the end of a month, when he was a regular visitor, the rift between the Roubauds became more marked. The wife more and more preferred to be in bed alone and contrived to find herself there with her husband as seldom as possible, while he, who had been passionate to the point of brutality in the early days of their marriage, made no move to keep her there.

167

He had made love crudely and she had resigned herself to it with the submissiveness of a compliant wife, supposing that things had to be like that, but finding no pleasure in it. But since the crime, and without her knowing why, this thing had filled her with repugnance. It got on her nerves and frightened her. One night before the candle had been blown out she uttered a shriek, thinking she could once again see the red, convulsed face of the murderer, and after that she trembled every time, and had the horrible sensation that the murder was actually happening, as if he had forced her on to her back at the point of a knife. It was ridiculous, but her heart pounded with fear. As a matter of fact he took advantage of her less and less, feeling her too resistant for his pleasure. Weariness, indifference, such as comes with age, seemed to have been produced between them by the dreadful crisis and spilt blood. On nights when they could not avoid sharing the bed they kept to the two sides. Jacques was certainly contributing to this divorce by dragging them out of their obsession with themselves. He was saving them from each other.

Yet Roubaud felt no remorse. He had only been afraid of the consequences before the case was shelved, and his main worry had been about losing his job. At present he had no regrets. Perhaps, however, had he had to start it all over again he would not have brought his wife into the affair, for women immediately lose their nerve, and now he was losing his wife's affection because he had placed too great a burden upon her shoulders. He would have remained her master if he had not sunk with her into the terrified and acrimonious companionship of crime. But that's how things were, and you had to make the best of them, particularly as he had to make a real effort to get himself back into the frame of mind he was in after his wife's confession, when he had felt that the murder was bound up with his own survival. If he had not killed that man, it seemed then, he could not have gone on living himself. The fire of his jealousy had burnt itself out and he could no longer feel its unbearable heat because a numbness had overtaken him, as though the blood in his own body had been thickened by all the blood shed, and now the necessity of that murder did not look so clear. He was even beginning to wonder whether the killing had really been worth-while. Not that it was even as much as a regret, no more than a disillusionment, the thought that one often does unspeakable things in order to be happy, but gets no nearer to happiness. Usually so loquacious, he now fell into long silences, bouts of muddled thinking whence he emerged in blacker mood than ever. Every day now he would avoid having to stay face to face with his wife after mealtimes by climbing up on the roof and sitting on top of the gable where, in the sea breeze, lulled into vague reveries, he smoked his pipe and looked over the town to the liners as they vanished over the horizon bound for distant seas.

One evening Roubaud had a recurrence of his old fierce jealousy. He had been to find Jacques at the depot and was bringing him back home for a drink when he ran into Henri Dauvergne, the guard, coming down the stairs. The latter looked taken aback and explained that he had just been to see Mme Roubaud about some message from his sisters. The truth was that for some time lately he had been running after Séverine in the hope of a conquest.

As soon as they reached the door Roubaud shouted at his wife:

'What did that fellow come up here for again? You know I can't stand him!'

'But it was only about an embroidery pattern, dear.'

'Embroidery! I'll give him embroidery! Do you think I'm fool enough not to understand what he's after here? Just you watch out!'

He advanced towards her with clenched fists and she backed, went white, and was amazed at this outburst in the middle of their calm indifference to each other. But the fit was over at once, and he said to his friend:

'It's a fact, chaps just drop in to a man's home and seem to think that the wife will at once throw herself at their heads and the husband will be most honoured to keep his eyes shut! It makes my blood boil ... D'you know, if that happened I'd strangle my wife straight away. And don't you let that young fellow-me-lad come back here or I'll settle his hash for him! It makes you sick, doesn't it?'

Jacques was very embarrassed by this scene and didn't know

how he ought to react. Was this overdone anger for his benefit, by way of a warning from the husband? But he was reassured when the latter went on gaily:

'No, silly, of course I know that you would show him the door yourself ... Come on, give us a drink and have one with us.'

He patted Jacques on the shoulder, and Séverine, who had recovered her poise too, smiled at the two men. Then they all had a drink and spent a very pleasant hour.

Thus it was that Roubaud brought his wife and his mate together in the friendliest way, without apparently giving a thought to the possible outcome. This matter of jealousy became the very cause of a closer friendship between Jacques and Séverine, a secret affection made even more intimate by sharing confidences, for when he saw her again two days later Jacques pitied her for having been treated so roughly, while she, with tears in her eyes, admitted, through complaints that escaped her, how little happiness she had found in her married life. From that moment they had a private topic of conversation between themselves, the complicity of close friends who come to understand each other by mere signs. Each time he came he threw her a questioning look which asked whether she had had any fresh reason for being sad. She answered in the same way, with a mere movement of her eyelids. Then their hands would seek each other's behind the husband's back, and as they grew bolder they communicated messages to each other in a long pressure, telling each other with their hot fingers of the growing interest each took in the tiniest events of their existence. They rarely had the good fortune to meet for a moment out of Roubaud's presence. He was always there between them in this depressing dining-room, and they made no effort to escape from him, nor did it even occur to them to arrange a meeting in some quiet part of the station premises. So far it was the genuine affection of two people drawn to each other by strong sympathy, and the husband hardly disturbed that at all, since a glance or a hand-squeeze was all they needed as yet for mutual understanding.

The first time Jacques whispered into her ear that he would be waiting for her the following Thursday behind the depot at midnight, she recoiled and hurriedly withdrew her hand. It was her week of freedom, when Roubaud was on night duty. But she was very scared by the thought of leaving her home and going so far through the darkness of the station to meet this fellow. She felt an embarrassment she had never known before, the apprehension of ignorant virgins whose hearts are beating, and she did not yield at once; he had to beg her for nearly two weeks before she would consent, although she also ardently longed for such a nocturnal excursion. June was beginning, and the nights were getting burning hot, with the sea breeze doing little to cool them. Three times already he had waited for her, always hoping she would come and join him in spite of her refusal. This evening she had said no again, but there was no moon and the sky was overcast without a single star shining through the sultry, heavy clouds. Standing there in the shadows he saw her coming at last, dressed in black and walking without a sound. It was so dark that she might have brushed right by him without noticing him had he not caught her in his arms and kissed her. She jumped and uttered a little cry, then laughed and left her lips on his. But that was all, she would not consent to sit down in one of the sheds that surrounded them. They walked about and talked softly, pressed close to each other. The depot and its buildings occupied a vast area, all the space between the rue Verte and the rue Françoise-Mazeline, each of which has a level crossing over the line: a kind of huge waste land cluttered with sidings, storage tanks and hydrants, all kinds of buildings, the two great engine-sheds, the little house of the Sauvagnats with its pocket-handkerchief vegetable patch, huts with repair oufits, the dormitory block for drivers and firemen, and nothing was easier than to be out of sight and lost in these deserted paths, winding inextricably as in a forest. For a whole hour they enjoyed delightful solitude as they lightened their hearts of the affectionate talk held in for so long, for she would not hear of anything beyond affection, and told him at once that she would never be his, for it would be too nasty to sully this pure friendship she was so proud of, needing self-respect as she did. Then he took her as far as the rue Verte, their lips joined again in a long kiss, and she went home.

At that same time Roubaud was beginning to nod in the

deputy stationmaster's office, in the old leather armchair from which he got up a score of times in the night to stretch his legs. Until nine o'clock there were the incoming and departing night trains to see to. The fish special was his particular concern, with shuntings and couplings and dispatch-sheets to keep a close eye on. Then when the express from Paris had come in and been backed out again he had his lonely supper in the office on a corner of the table, a bit of cold meat between two slices of bread that he had brought down from home. The last train, a slow from Rouen, came in at 12.30 a.m. Then the deserted platforms fell into a deep silence, only a few gas-lamps were left burning, and the whole station slumbered in the eerie semi-darkness. The only staff left were two foremen and four or five workmen, under his orders, and they were snoring away on the dormitory floor while Roubaud, who had to wake them up at the slightest alarm, only dozed with one ear cocked. For fear of being knocked out by sleep before it was light he used to set his alarm clock at five, the hour at which he had to be up in order to see in the first train from Paris. But sometimes, particularly just lately, he could not doze off, and insomnia kept him fidgeting in his chair. At such times he went out and did the rounds and went as far as the pointsman's box and had a word or two with him. The wide black sky and the peace of the night eventually calmed him. Following a struggle with some marauders he had been armed with a revolver, which he kept loaded in his pocket. Often he prowled about like this until dawn, standing still if anything seemed to be stirring in the darkness, and walking on with vague regret at not having to fire, but relieved when the sky lightened and called the great pale ghost of the station out of the shadows. Now that it was getting light by three, he went in and threw himself into his chair, in which he slept like a log until his alarm clock made him jump up in a fright.

Every other week Séverine met Jacques on Thursday and Saturday, and one night when she mentioned the revolver her husband carried, they were scared. Not that Roubaud ever went as far as the depot. All the same, it added a sense of danger to their walks which doubled their charm. They had found one ideal corner in particular, a sort of avenue behind the Sauvagnats' house between enormous stacks of coal which made it

172

look like the main street of a strange city with great square palaces of black marble. There you were quite hidden, and at the end there was a little toolshed in which a heap of empty sacks would have made a soft bed. But one Saturday when a sudden downpour of rain forced them to take shelter there she obstinately remained standing, only giving him her lips in endless kisses. Her modesty did not extend as far as these kisses, for she greedily gave him all her mouth, as if merely in friendship. And when, roused to fever-pitch by this passion, he tried to take her, she defended herself tearfully, every time giving the same reasons. Why did he want to make her unhappy? It seemed so nice just to love each other without all that dirty business of sex! Defiled at sixteen by the lusts of that old man whose bleeding spectre haunted her, violated later by the brutal appetites of her husband, she had kept a childlike purity, a virginity with all the charming modesty of passion unaware of itself. What so appealed to her in Jacques was his gentleness, his obedience in not letting his hands wander all over her as soon as she simply took them in her own hands, weak though they were. She was in love for the first time, and she did not give herself for the very reason that it would have spoiled her love to belong to this man straight away, as she had to the two others. Unconsciously she wanted to prolong indefinitely this delicious sensation, become a young girl again like she was before she was defiled, and have a sweetheart like you have at fifteen, and kiss him shamelessly behind doors. And apart from his moments of arousal he was not at all exacting, and lent himself to this voluptuous deferment of pleasure. Like her he seemed to be going back to boyhood and love's young dream, which until now had always been a matter of horror. If he was docile and withdrew his hands as soon as she moved them away it was because beneath his love there still lurked a nameless dread, a great fear of confusing desire and his old lust for blood. This woman, who had killed a man, was like the dream of his flesh come true. Every day his cure seemed more assured, for he had held her to himself for hours, and his mouth, pressed to hers, had drunk her soul, yet his insane urge to be master by killing her had never awakened. But still he did not dare, and it was so good to wait and leave to love itself the care of uniting them when the time

173

came and their resistance faded away in each other's arms. So the joyful meetings went on, and they never tired of seeing each other just for a moment or walking together in the dark between the great stacks of coal that made the night around them darker still.

One July night, so as to make Le Havre by eleven five, the scheduled time, Jacques had to urge Lison on as though the stifling heat had made her lazy. Since Rouen a storm had been following him on his left, running along the Seine valley with dazzling flashes of lightning, and now and again he turned round anxiously because Séverine was coming to join him that night. His fear was that if the storm broke too soon it would prevent her leaving home. So when he had succeeded in reaching the station ahead of the rain he was impatient with the passengers who seemed to be taking their time to get out of the carriages.

Roubaud was on the platform, kept on duty for the night.

'You're in the hell of a hurry to get off to bed!' he laughed. 'Sleep well.'

'Thanks.'

Jacques backed out the train, then whistled and made for the engine-shed. The sections of the immense door were open and Lison plunged into the covered shed, a sort of gallery with two tracks about seventy metres long, capable of housing six engines. It was very dark inside and four gas-lamps did little to illuminate it, but seemed to deepen the gloom by casting long moving shadows. Only the vivid flashes of lightning momentarily lit up the skylights and lofty windows on each side, when, like a blazing fire, they showed up the cracked walls, sooty beams and all the decrepitude of this old, tumbledown building. There were two engines in already, cold and asleep.

Pecqueux at once began putting out the fire by raking it energetically, and the cinders fell from the ashpan into the pit.

'I'm too hungry for anything, and I'm going to get a bite,' he said. 'You coming?'

Jacques did not answer. Although he was in a hurry, he did not want to leave Lison before the fire was drawn and the boiler drained. It was part of the conscientious routine of a good driver, and he never scamped it. When he had plenty of time he didn't knock off until he had gone over her and rubbed her down with the care one takes over grooming a favourite horse.

The water gushed down into the pit and only then did he say anything:

'Come on, let's get a move on!'

His words were lost in a terrific clap of thunder. This time the high windows stood out so clearly against the flaming sky that you could have counted the broken panes, and there were plenty of them. To the left there was a row of vices used for repair work, and a piece of sheet iron left standing there re-sounded like the continuous vibration of a bell. All the ancient timbering of the roof had cracked.

'Bugger it!' was all the fireman said.

The driver shrugged in despair. This was the end, particularly as a deluge was now lashing the shed. The thundering down-pour threatened to smash the skylights. In any case some of the panes up there must have been broken because heavy drops of rain were falling on Lison in great splashes. A furious wind was blowing in through the open doors and it looked as if the car-case of the ancient building would be blown away.

Pecqueux was getting the engine ready to leave.

'There, we can see properly tomorrow. No need to doll her up more than that now.'

And returning to his first thought:

'Must get something to eat. Raining too hard to get a bit of shut-eye.'

It happened that the canteen was quite handy, next door to the shed, whereas the Company had had to rent a house in the rue François-Mazeline as a dormitory for drivers and firemen sleeping overnight in Le Havre. In a deluge like this they would have been soaked to the skin in the time it took to get there.

Jacques had to resign himself to going with Pecqueux, who had picked up his chief's little food basket to save him the trouble of carrying it. It was really only the knowledge that the basket still contained two slices of cold veal, some bread, and a bottle he had hardly started that made him feel hungry. The rain was heavier than ever, and another thunderclap had shaken the engine-shed. By the time the two men went off through the little door on the left that led to the canteen Lison was already cooling down. She was going to sleep all forlorn in the darkness broken by blinding flashes and with great drops of water soaking her back. Near her a water tap not properly turned off was running and making a pool that drained between the wheels and into the pit.

But before going into the canteen Jacques wanted a clean up. In one room hot water and basins were always available. He took a cake of soap out of his basket and got the dirt off his hands and face that were black after the trip, and as he took care, as drivers are advised, to carry a change of clothing, he could change from head to foot, which he did, as a matter of fact, out of vanity whenever he got to Le Havre on a night they were meeting. Pecqueux was already waiting in the canteen, having just rinsed the end of his nose and his fingertips.

This canteen simply consisted of a little bare room painted yellow in which there was nothing but a stove for heating up food and a table fixed to the floor with a zinc top by way of a cloth. Two benches completed the furnishing. The men had to bring their own food and ate it off a bit of paper by spiking it with a knife. The room was lit by a large window.

'God, what rain!' exclaimed Jacques, standing at the window.

Pecqueux was on a bench at the table.

'Aren't you eating, then?'

'No, mate, you finish off my bread and meat if you feel like it. I'm not hungry.'

Without waiting to be asked twice, Pecqueux attacked the veal and finished off the bottle. He often got windfalls like this because his driver was a small eater, and, in his dog-like devotion, he liked him all the more for all these crumbs he picked up after him. After a pause he went on, his mouth full:

'Oh, the rain! Well, what the hell, now we're bedded down? All the same it's true that if it goes on I shall leave you and go over the way.'

He began to laugh, because he made no secret of it and had had to tell Jacques about his affair with Philomène Sauvagnat so that he shouldn't be surprised at his disappearing so often on the nights when he went to her. In her brother's house she slept in a ground floor room near the kitchen, and so he only had to tap on the shutters, she opened and all he had to do was step over the sill. It was said that every team in the station had made that jump, but now she only had this fireman, who satisfied her, it seemed.

'Bloody hell!' Jacques swore quietly to himself as the deluge came on worse than ever after a lull.

Pecqueux, holding the last mouthful of meat on the point of his knife, again laughed his good-natured laugh.

'I say, did you have something on for tonight? They can hardly accuse us of wearing out those mattresses in the rue François-Mazeline, can they?'

Jacques turned round quickly.

'Why do you say that?'

'Well, because ever since the spring, same as me, you've never got in till two or three in the morning.'

He must know something, perhaps he had come upon them at one of their meetings. In each dormitory the beds went in pairs, the fireman's next to the driver's, for the lives of these two men, whose working understanding had to be so close, were kept as intimate as possible. So it was not surprising that the fireman should have noticed the erratic behaviour of his driver, who hitherto had been so regular.

'Oh, I get headaches,' was the first thing Jacques could think of to say, 'and it does me good to have a walk at night.'

The fireman at once backed down.

'Oh, it's a free country, you know . . . I was only pulling your leg . . . But if ever you're in trouble one of these days, you mustn't mind telling me, because I'm always there for anything you want.'

Without any further explanation he made so bold as to take Jacques's hand and squeeze it to breaking-point, giving himself, body and soul. Then he screwed up the greasy paper that had wrapped the meat and threw it away, put the empty bottle back in Jacques's basket, doing his little chores like a careful servant used to the brush and sponge. As it was still raining hard, although the thunder had stopped, he said:

'Well, I'm off. I'll leave you to your own devices.'

177

'Oh, as it's going on and on I'll go and stretch out on the camp bed.'

He was referring to a room right by the shed which had some mattresses with loose covers over them where men could rest in their clothes when they had a wait of only three or four hours at Le Havre. In fact, as soon as his fireman had disappeared in the rain, making for the Sauvagnats' house, he ventured out himself and ran across to the room by the shed. He did not lie down however, but stopped at the open door, stifled by the stuffy heat inside. Further in a driver was lying on his back, snoring open-mouthed.

A few minutes went by and Jacques still could not make up his mind to give up hope. In his exasperation at this stupid downpour there was growing an absurd desire to go to the meeting-place just the same and at any rate have the joy of being there himself even if he had given up expecting to find Séverine. His whole being pulled him there, and he went out into the storm, reached their favourite corner and went along the black road made by the stacks of coal. Blinded by the heavy rain lashing in his face, he pushed on to the toolshed in which he had taken shelter with her once already. He felt he would be less lonely there.

As he was going into the deep blackness of this retreat two slender arms were thrown round him and hot lips were pressed to his. Séverine was there.

'Good heavens! So you did come!'

'Yes, I saw the storm coming up and ran here before the rain started. What a long time you've been!'

Her voice tailed off into a sigh, he had never known her cling to him with such abandon. She slipped downwards until she was sitting on the empty sacks that took up a whole corner and made a soft couch. He fell beside her, for their arms were still round each other, and he felt his legs across hers. They could not see each other, their breath enveloped them in a kind of intoxication, and all consciousness of their surroundings was lost.

The ardour of their kisses, like a mingling of their life-blood, called up the language of love to their lips.

'My own darling, you were expecting me.'

'Yes, I was waiting, waiting for my beloved.'

At once, within the first minutes and almost without further words, she was the one who pulled him down and forced him to take her. She had not meant to. When she came she had even given up the thought of seeing him, and she had been carried away by the unhoped-for joy of holding him in her arms, in a sudden irresistible urge to be his without any calculation or reasoning. It was because it had to be. The rain lashed down on the roof of the shed, the last train in from Paris went by roaring and whistling, making the earth tremble.

When Jacques got up he was much surprised to hear the noise of the rain. Where was he, then? And as one of his hands touched the handle of a hammer he had noticed on the ground when he sat down, a flood of happiness surged over him. So it had happened – he had possessed Séverine and had not taken the hammer to smash her skull. She was his and there had been no struggle, none of that instinctive desire to throw her on to her back dead, like some trophy snatched from others. No longer did he feel his thirst for revenge on some old, old wrongs he could not clearly recollect, that resentment passed down from male to male ever since the first betrayal in the depths of some cave. No, there was some powerful spell in the possession of this particular woman, she had cured him because to him she appeared different, violent in her weakness, protected by the blood of a man which shielded her like a breastplate of horror. She dominated him because he had never dared. It was with loving gratitude and a desire to be lost in her that he took her again into his arms.

Séverine was also giving herself in joy at being set free from a struggle she now failed to comprehend. Why had she held back so long? She should have given herself as she had promised, for there could be nothing in it but pleasure and sweet caresses. Now she realized that this was what she had always longed for, even when it seemed so pleasant to wait. Her heart and her body only survived because of a need for love, absolute, lasting love, and it had been a horribly cruel thing that these events had thrown her into the horror of such abominations. Until now life had ill-treated her, in filth and blood, with such violence that beneath her tragic crown of black hair her lovely blue eyes,

179

though still innocent-looking, remained dilated with terror. She had remained virgin in spite of everything, and she had just given herself, for the first time, to this young man she worshipped, desiring to lose herself in him and be his slave. She belonged to him, he could do what he liked with her.

'Oh my beloved, take me, keep me, I only want what you want!'

'No, no, dear heart, you are the mistress, and I am only here to love and obey.'

Hours went by. The rain had stopped long since and there was a great silence in the station, only broken by some far-off, indistinct voice coming up from the sea. They were still in each other's arms when a shot brought them to their feet in alarm. Day was almost breaking, and a paler band was lightening the sky over the Seine estuary. What was that shot? They had a sudden vision of what their imprudent folly in dallying like this might mean – the husband pursuing them with a revolver.

'Don't go out! Wait and I'll have a look.'

Jacques had prudently moved to the door, and through the night, for it was still very dark, he heard a number of men running towards them and recognized Roubaud's voice urging on the foremen and shouting that there were three marauders, he had clearly seen them stealing the coal. For the past few weeks in particular, hardly a night had gone by without his having these hallucinations about imaginary thieves. This time, because of some sudden scare, he had fired at random in the dark.

'Quick, quick! We can't stay here,' whispered Jacques. 'They'll search the shed. You get away!'

They seized each other once again, breathlessly, with all the strength of their arms and lips. Then Séverine ran nimbly along the side of the depot, hidden by the high wall, while he quietly hid in the middle of the stacks of coal. And just in time, too, for Roubaud did indeed want to search the toolshed, swearing that the thieves must be in there. The men's lanterns danced along the ground. There was a dispute and eventually they all hurried back towards the station, annoyed at this wild-goose-chase.

As Jacques, now feeling quite reassured, was setting out at last to go and sleep in the rue François-Mazeline, to his surprise he almost bumped into Pecqueux, who was just doing up his clothes, muttering oaths.

'What's up, chum?'

'Oh Christ, don't ask me! Those bloody fools woke Sauvagnat up. He heard me with his sister, came down in his nightshirt and I hopped out of the window as quick as I could. Just you listen to that!'

Screams and sobs could be heard, a woman was being beaten, while a loud male voice was bawling abuse.

'Here we go, he's giving her what for. She's thirty-two, and yet he whips her like a little girl when he catches her at it. Ah well, it's no use, and I keep out of the way, he's her brother after all!'

'But I thought he didn't mind you and was only wild when he caught her with anybody else.'

'Oh, you never know. There are times when he turns a blind eye my way. And then, you see, there are others when he lets her have it. But that doesn't mean that he doesn't love his sister. She is still his sister, and he would rather let everything go than part from her. Only he wants proper behaviour ... Gawd, I think she's getting her packet today!'

The screams were dying down into great moaning sighs, and the two men walked away. Ten minutes later they were sound asleep side by side in the little dormitory painted yellow and furnished with just four beds, four chairs and a table, with one tin wash-basin.

After that, each night they met Jacques and Séverine enjoyed perfect happiness. They did not always have the protection of a storm. Starlit nights and brilliant moons worried them, but when they met on nights like that they crept into strips of shadow or made for dark corners where it was so good to hold each other close. And so all through August and September there were some wonderful nights of such peaceful langour that they might have been surprised by the sun if they had not been torn apart by the morning noises of the station and distant puffings of engines. Even the first chilly nights of October were quite pleasant. She came with warmer clothes, wrapped in a heavy coat into which he also almost disappeared. Then they barricaded themselves in the toolshed, which they had found a way of locking from the inside with the help of an iron bar. There they were quite at home and November's gales and gusts could lift slates off roofs without even blowing on their necks. Yet ever since the first night he had had a desire to possess her in her own home, in that poky flat where she seemed different, more desirable, with the serene smile of the respectable house-wife. But she had always refused, not so much because of the spies in the corridor as because of a last remaining scruple of virtue, keeping the marriage bed a thing apart. But one Monday in broad daylight, as he was there for lunch and her husband was late coming in because the stationmaster was keeping him, he carried her on to the bed for a joke, such a wildly foolhardy thing to do that they both had to laugh, and let themselves go. After that she offered no further resistance, and he went up-stairs to join her after midnight on Thursdays and Saturdays. It was appallingly dangerous – they dared not move because of the neighbours, but that redoubled their passion and heightened their pleasure. Sometimes a sudden whim for an excursion in the night, an urge to rush along like animals let loose, took them out into the black solitude of freezing nights. Once, in a terrible December frost, they made love outside.

Jacques and Séverine had lived like this in growing passion for four months already. They were both genuinely inex-perienced, in the childhood of the heart, that amazed innocence of first love that finds delight in the simplest caresses. They both went on vying with each other in self-sacrifice. He was now convinced that he had found the remedy for his terrible heredi-tary malady, for since he had possessed her the thought of murder had troubled him no more. Was it that physical pos-session satisfied this lust for death? Were possession and killing the same thing in the dark inner recesses of the human brute? He did not reason it out, he was too ignorant, and made no attempt to open the door into horror. Sometimes in her arms he would suddenly recall what she had done, that murder she had only admitted with her eyes on the seat in the Batignolles Square, but he had no desire to know any details. She, on the other hand, seemed to be more and more tormented by the need to tell it all. When she crushed him in an embrace he had a sensation that she was bursting and gasping with her secret and only sought to merge her body with his in order to find relief from the thing that was choking her. A great tremor began in her loins and swelled her breast with passion as confused little cries rose to her lips. Was she about to say something in that dying voice in the midst of a spasm of ecstasy? But on such occasions, seized with panic himself, he hastened to shut her mouth with a kiss and hold down the admission. Why put this unknown element between them? Could they say for sure that it would not alter something in their happiness? He scented danger, and a shudder came over him again at the idea of going over this story of bloodshed with her. Perhaps she guessed as much, for once more she became caressing and yielding at his side, a creature of love destined only to love and be loved. They were carried away by a frenzy of possession that sometimes left them swooning in each other's arms.

Since the summer Roubaud had grown heavier, and as his wife was going back to the gaiety and freshness of a twenty-year-old, so he was ageing and seemed increasingly morose. In four months, as he said himself, he had changed a great deal. He still gave Jacques cordial handshakes and invitations, and was only happy when he had him at his table. The only thing was that this diversion was not enough now, and he often went out as soon as he had swallowed the last mouthful, sometimes leaving his friend with his wife, making out that he felt stiflingly hot and had to get out for some fresh air. The truth was that he was now frequenting a little café in the Cours Napoléon, where he met M. Cauche the superintendent. He didn't drink much, just the odd tot of rum, but he had developed a taste for card-playing that was turning into an obsession. He only ever cheered up and forgot everything when he held the cards in his hand and was involved in endless games of piquet. M. Cauche, who was gambling-mad, had decided that they would put money on it, and they had now reached five francs a *partie*, and Roubaud, amazed that he had only just woken up to his own nature, was consumed by the mania for gain, that burning fever for making money that takes possession of a man to the point where he will stake his job, his livelihood on a throw of the dice. So far his work had not suffered: he escaped as soon as he was free, never coming home until two or three in the morning on nights when he was not on duty. His wife did not complain except about his being even more surly when he did come in, for he had no luck at all and was running into debt.

One evening the first quarrel broke out between Séverine and Roubaud. Though she did not yet hate him, she was finding him difficult to put up with, for she felt he weighed on her, and she might have been so light and gay if he had not burdened her with his presence! Not that she felt the slightest compunction about deceiving him – wasn't it his own fault, and hadn't he almost forced her into it? In their gradual drifting apart each of them sought a remedy for this disorganizing uneasiness in a particular consolation or amusement. As he had gambling, she could perfectly well have a lover. But what did irritate her above all, and she could not accept without rebelling, was the penury resulting from his continual losses. Since the house-keeping five-franc pieces had been disappearing at the café in the Cours Napoléon she was sometimes at her wits' end to pay for the laundry. She was short of all sorts of little comforts or items of clothing. And on this particular evening it happened to be about a pair of shoes she urgently needed that they quarrelled. On the point of going out he could not find a knife on the table to cut himself a piece of bread and so had taken the big knife, the weapon, from its place in a drawer in the sideboard. She looked steadily at him while he refused to find fifteen francs for the shoes, for he hadn't got that sum and couldn't think where to lay his hands on it. She obstinately repeated her demand and forced him to repeat his excuse with increasing vehemence, then suddenly she pointed at the place in the floorboards where the ghosts lay slumbering, said that there was some money there and she wanted some of it. He changed colour and dropped the knife, which fell back into the drawer. For a moment she thought he was going to hit her, for he came up to her muttering that the money could rot there and he would cut his own hand off rather than take it out, and with clenched fists he threatened to knock her down if she took it into her head, when he was out, to lift that floorboard and steal even a single centime. Never, never! It was dead and buried! And she had turned pale, too, feeling just as overcome at the thought of rummaging there. Poverty might well come, but both would die of starvation with the money close by. So it was never mentioned again, even on the lean days. Whenever they set foot on that spot the burning sensation had become so intolerable that finally they always walked round it.

Then other disputes set in about La Croix-de-Maufras. Why wasn't the house being sold? They accused each other of not taking the necessary steps to expedite the sale. He still violently refused to have anything to do with it, and she only got evasive answers to her infrequent letters to Misard: no buyers had appeared, the fruit had not set, the vegetables weren't doing any good for lack of water. Gradually the great calm that had come over the pair since the crisis was being disturbed in this way and looked like being destroyed in another terrible renewal of agitation. Now all the seeds of trouble, the hidden money, the introduction of a lover, had germinated and were thrusting them apart, making each detest the other. In this growing turmoil life was going to be a hell.

Furthermore, as if it were an inevitable repercussion, everything was going wrong round the Roubauds. A new hurricane of gossip and argument was blowing along the corridor. Philomène had just had a violent set-to with Mme Lebleu, following a slanderous statement by the latter, who accused her of having sold her a fowl that was diseased. But the real reason for the break was a reconciliation between Philomène and Séverine. As one night Pecqueux had recognized Séverine on Jacques's arm, the latter had overcome her former scruples and made herself very agreeable to the fireman's mistress; and Philomène, very flattered by this connection with a lady who was unchallenged as the belle and social queen of the station, had turned against the cashier's wife, that old bag, as she called her, who could make mischief anywhere. Philomène now blamed her for everything, proclaiming to all and sundry that the flat on the street side belonged by rights to the Roubauds and that it was disgusting not to let them have it. So things were beginning to turn out very badly for Mme Lebleu, especially as the unrelenting watch she kept on Mlle Guichon in order to catch her with the stationmaster was landing her in serious trouble; she still had not caught them but had been unwise enough to be caught herself with her ear glued to people's doors, with the result that M. Dabadie, furious at being spied on like this, had told the deputy stationmaster Moulin that if Roubaud were to ask for that flat again he was prepared to countersign the letter. And Moulin, not very talkative as a rule, had repeated this, and passions had risen again to such a heat that there had almost been free fights all along the corridor.

Amid all these growing upheavals Séverine had only the one good day, Friday. Since October she had had the cool nerve to invent a pretext, the first thing that had come into her head, some trouble in her knee which necessitated her seeing a specialist, and so every Friday she went off on the 6.40 morning express, driven by Jacques, and spent the whole day with him in Paris, returning on the 6.30 in the evening. At first she felt obliged to give her husband reports about her knee – it was better, it wasn't so good – but then, realizing he wasn't even listening, she had simply stopped talking about it. Sometimes when she looked at him she wondered whether he knew. How could this ferociously jealous man, this man who had killed, seeing nothing but blood in an insane rage, come to accept her having a lover? She could not believe it and simply thought he was going soft.

One bitterly cold night in early December Séverine sat up very late waiting for her husband. On the following day, a Friday, she had to be up before dawn to catch the express, and on those nights she got herself ready most carefully and set out her clothes so as to get dressed in a moment when she got up. At last she did go to bed, and managed to get to sleep at about one. Roubaud was still not in. Twice already he had not shown up until the small hours, being wholly taken up with his growing passion and now quite unable to tear himself away from the café, where a little back room was gradually turning into a real gambling den, and now large sums were being staked on *écarté*. Glad in any case to have the bed to herself, and blissfully looking forward to her good day tomorrow, she slept soundly in the lovely warmth of the bedclothes.

But just before three she was awakened by a strange noise. At first she could not understand, thought she was dreaming and settled down again to sleep. There were heavy thumpings and the cracking of wood as though a door was being forced. A loud noise, a more violent rending sound, made her sit up. Fear seized her, she felt sure someone was forcing the lock of the front door. For a minute she dared not move, but listened through the roaring in her ears. Then she plucked up the courage to get out of bed and look. Walking barefoot without a sound she softly pushed the door open, feeling so frozen that she was white and shrivelled up in her nightdress. The sight she saw in the dining-room rooted her to the spot in amazement and terror.

Roubaud was lying on his stomach on the floor, supported by his elbows, and had prised up the floorboard with the help of a chisel. A candle was standing near him and lit him up, throwing his gigantic shadow up the wall to the ceiling. At that moment his face was over the hole that made a black gap in the floor, and he was staring with goggling eyes. The blood turned his cheeks purple and his face was the face of the murderer. He clumsily thrust his hand down, but in his agitated state found nothing and had to bring over the candle. The purse, banknotes and watch could be seen down in the hole.

An involuntary cry escaped Séverine, and Roubaud turned round in terror. For a moment he did not recognize her and possibly thought he was seeing a ghost, all white with staring eyes.

'What are you doing?' she asked.

Then he understood, but avoided answering by merely grunting. He stared at her, finding her presence a nuisance and anxious to get her back to bed. But he could not find anything sensible to say, just thinking that he ought to hit her, standing there shivering with nothing on.

'So that's it!' she went on. 'You won't let me have any new shoes and then take the money for yourself, because you've lost!'

That made him see red. Was she going to mess up his life still more and stand in the way of his pleasures? He didn't desire this woman any more, and to have her was now only an unpleasant performance. As he was getting his fun elsewhere he didn't need her at all. So he reached down again, but only took out the purse which contained the three hundred francs in cash. Having

187

stamped the floorboard back with his heel he came over and hissed into her face through clenched teeth:

'I'm fed up with you and I'll do what I like. Am I asking you what you are going to do in Paris?'

With a furious shrug of the shoulders he went out and back to the café, leaving the candle on the floor.

Séverine picked it up and went back to bed frozen to the bone, leaving it burning, unable to go to sleep again, waiting more and more impatiently for the time for the train, wide-eyed. Now it was clear, there was a progressive breakdown, as though the crime were eating into this man and rotting him, destroying any link between them. Roubaud knew.

[7]

ON that particular Friday morning passengers intending to catch the 6.40 cursed in surprise when they woke up: it had been snowing since midnight and so steadily and with such big flakes that there were thirty centimetres covering the streets.

Under the station roof Lison was already panting and letting off steam, coupled to a train of seven coaches, three second class and four first. When Jacques and Pecqueux had reached the engine-shed at half past five to get the engine ready they had groaned with anxiety at the sight of the relentless snow coming down from a heavy black sky. Now they were at their post waiting for the whistle, their eyes peering ahead beyond the gaping end of the station roof, looking at the flakes falling silent, continuous and streaking the darkness with quivering whiteness.

The driver murmured:

'Devil take me if I can see a signal!'

'So long as we can get through!' said the fireman.

Roubaud was on the platform with his lantern, having come on to begin his shift at the exact time. Sometimes his swollen lids closed of their own accord with fatigue, but he never relaxed his vigilance. Jacques having asked him if he knew anything about the state of the line, he went up to him, and shaking his hand answered that no report had come in so far. Then as Séverine came down wrapped in a heavy coat he took her along himself and saw her settled into a first-class compartment. He had no doubt noticed the glance of affection and anxiety that passed between the two lovers, but he did not even bother to say to his wife that it was unwise to set off in such weather and she would be well advised to postpone her trip.

Passengers were arriving all wrapped up and carrying bags, quite a rush-hour in the terrible morning cold. The snow on their boots did not even melt, and doors slammed at once as each one barricaded himself in. The platform itself stayed empty and ill lit by the fitful glimmer of a few gas-lamps, while the headlight of the engine, at the base of the chimney, blazed alone like a giant's eye, spreading its sheet of flame far ahead into the darkness.

Roubaud raised his lantern and gave the signal. The guard whistled and Jacques whistled back, having opened the regulator and turned forward the wheel of the reversing-gear. They were moving. For another minute Roubaud calmly watched the train going off into the storm.

'And watch it!' Jacques said to Pecqueux. 'No buggering about today!'

He had noticed that his mate seemed to be dropping with fatigue too, no doubt because of a night on the tiles.

'Oh, no danger of that, no danger!' the fireman muttered thickly.

As soon as they were out of the covered station the two men were in the snow. The wind was blowing from the east, and the engine was caught head-on, lashed in the face by squalls. In the cab they were not too badly off at first in their thick woollies, their eyes protected by goggles. But in the darkness the brilliant light of the headlamp seemed to be soaked up by these falling thicknesses of white. Instead of being lit up for two or three hundred metres ahead, the line appeared out of a sort of milky fog, from which objects only rose at the last moment as from the depths of some dream. And as he had feared, what worried the driver most of all was to realize, from the light at the very first section point, that he would certainly not see the red danger signals at the regulation distance. So from then on he advanced with extreme caution, without however slackening speed because the wind offered enormous resistance and any lateness would become an equally great danger.

As far as Harfleur station Lison kept up a good speed. The depth of the snow was not yet a worry to Jacques, for there were sixty centimetres at the most, and the snowplough could easily clear a metre. He was entirely concerned with keeping up his speed, knowing full well that the real quality of a driver, after temperance and love of his engine, consisted in maintaining a regular speed without jerks and at the highest possible pressure. In fact that was his only fault, his determination never to stop, disobeying signals, thinking he would always have time to check Lison, and sometimes he went too far and ran over detonators, 'corns on the feet' as he called them, which had twice earned him a week's suspension. But this time, in the great danger he felt he was in, the thought that Séverine was there and that he was responsible for her beloved life, multiplied the strength of his will to be on the alert all the way to Paris along this double line of iron fraught with obstacles that he must clear.

Standing on the iron plate between engine and tender, and constantly jolted by the oscillation, Jacques leaned out to the right in spite of the snow to get a better view. He could see nothing through the cab window, smeared with wet, and he stayed there with his face exposed to the squalls of wind, his skin pricked by thousands of needles and so pinched with cold that it felt as if it had been cut with a razor. He came in now and again to recover his breath, took off his goggles to wipe them, then back to his observation post in the full blast, eyes on the lookout for red lights, and he was so absorbed in his effort of will that on two occasions he had the delusion of a sudden spurt of blood-red sparks on the pale, trembling curtain in front of him.

All at once, in the darkness, something warned him that his fireman was no longer with him. The only light was from a tiny lamp to show the water-level so as to save the driver from being dazzled by light, but on the enamel dial of the pressure-gauge, which seemed to gleam on its own, the wavering blue needle was rapidly going down. The fire was burning low. The fireman was sprawled over the chest, knocked out by sleep.

'Bloody skirt-chaser!' Jacques shook him furiously.

Pecqueux got up and grunted some apologetic noises. He could hardly stand, but through force of habit went straight back to his fire, hammer in hand, breaking up the coal and spreading it evenly over the grate, then did a sweep up. While the firebox door remained open a fiery beam stretched back over the train like the blazing tail of a comet and turned the snowflakes falling through it into great drops of gold.

Beyond Harfleur began the great three-league bank up to Saint-Romain, the steepest incline on the line. So the driver got down to skilful management again, expecting a hard pull to get up this slope, difficult enough in fine weather. With his hand on the reversing wheel he watched the telegraph poles go by, trying to calculate the speed. This was rapidly falling, Lison was blowing hard and he could sense the increasing resistance of the snow against the plough. With his toe he opened the door again and the drowsy fireman understood and stoked the fire still more to send up the pressure. By now the door itself was getting red-hot and throwing a purplish gleam on their legs. But they did not feel the blazing heat, enveloped as they were by the icy blast. On a sign from his driver the fireman had also raised the handle of the ashpan, which improved the draught. The needle of the gauge had quickly risen to ten times the pressure of the atmosphere, and Lison was exerting all the effort she was capable of. Once even, seeing the water level sinking, the driver had to give a turn to the little wheel of the injector, even though that diminished the pressure. But it soon recovered, and the engine snorted and spat like a horse being over-driven, jumping and rearing so that you might have thought you could hear her limbs cracking. Jacques gave her a bit of his tongue as if she were an ageing and sickly wife for whom he hadn't the same love as of old.

'She's never going to make it, the lazy old cow!' he muttered through clenched teeth, although usually he never talked while driving.

Pecqueux, half asleep, stared at him in astonishment. What had he got against Lison now? Wasn't she still the same good, obedient engine, so willing to start away that it was a joy to set her going, and such a good steamer that she saved ten per cent of her coal from Paris to Le Havre? When an engine has valve-gear like hers, perfectly adjusted, cutting off steam miraculously, you could allow her a few quirks, like you can a crotchety wife who is a good housekeeper and economical. She might perhaps use too much oil. So what? You just oiled her, that's all!

Jacques happened at that moment to be saying:

'She'll never make it if she isn't oiled.'

So he did what he had not done three times in his life, he took his oilcan to oil her on the road. He stepped over the rail, up on to the frame-plate and went along it the whole length of the boiler. But it was an extremely dangerous thing to do, his feet slipped on the narrow iron plate, wet with snow, he was blinded and the terrible wind threatened to blow him off like a wisp of straw. Lison, with this man clinging to her side, went on her way, panting through the darkness, opening out a deep furrow for herself through the immense white sheet. She shook him, but carried him on. Reaching the head of the engine he crouched over the lubricating-cup of the right-hand cylinder and had all the trouble in the world to fill it, clinging with one hand to the handrail. Then he had to crawl right round like an insect, so as to oil the left-hand cylinder. When he got back he was exhausted and white as a sheet, having felt death pass very close.

'The bloody bitch!' he muttered.

Astonished at this unusual violence about their Lison, Pecqueux couldn't help laughing, and once again ventured his habitual joke:

'Should've let me do it. It's my line, oiling the ladies!'

He was waking up a bit and had gone back to his own post, keeping watch on the left side of the line. Normally he had good eyesight, in fact better than his driver's. But in this blizzard everything had disappeared, and although every kilometre of the route was so familiar to them they could hardly recognize the places they were passing through; the line was submerged beneath the snow, and hedges and even the houses themselves seemed to be engulfed, and all that was left was a bare, endless plain, a chaos of vague whiteness across which Lison seemed to be galloping how she liked, gone crazy. Never had the two men felt so much how tight was the bond of brotherhood that held them together on this racing engine dashing through every peril, where they found themselves more alone, more abandoned by everybody than in a locked room, with the additional and crushing responsibility for the human lives they were hauling behind them.

And so Jacques, though exasperated by Pecqueux's joke, ended by smiling back and bottling up his rising temper. This was not the time to have a row, that was a fact! The snow was heavier, and the curtain obscuring the horizon thicker than ever. They were still climbing when it was the fireman's turn to think he could see a red signal in the distance, and he warned his driver with a word. But already he had lost it again, his eyes had been dreaming, as he sometimes put it. The driver, who had not seen anything, felt his heart thumping with anxiety because of another man's hallucination, and he was losing confidence in himself. What he imagined he could make out beyond the pale whirling flakes were immense black shapes, huge masses like gigantic chunks of night that seemed to be moving and coming head-on at the engine. Were they landslides that had fallen from the hills, mountains blocking the line, into which the train would smash? In a moment of fear he pulled the whistle-rod and whistled long and desperately, and this lamentation tailed off mournfully into the tempest. Then he was quite surprised to find that he had whistled at the right moment, for the train was tearing through Saint-Romain station, which he thought was still two kilometres away.

By now Lison had got over the terrible bank and began to run more easily, and Jacques could breathe for a minute. From Saint-Romain to Bolbec the line climbs imperceptibly, and everything would probably be all right as far as the other end of the plateau. Nevertheless, when he reached Beuzeville, during the three-minute stop he called over the stationmaster whom he saw on the platform, because he was determined to tell him of his misgivings in view of the ever-deepening snow. He would never get to Rouen, and the best thing would be to double-head by adding a pilot engine now that they were at a depot where relief engines were always available. But the stationmaster answered that he had no orders and did not think he ought to take such a step on his own responsibility. The only thing he offered was five or six wooden shovels to clear the rails should need arise. Pecqueux took the shovels and stowed them in a corner of the tender.

In fact on the plateau Lison kept up a good speed without too much difficulty. But she was tiring. Every minute the driver had to make his little movement, open the firebox door so that his fireman could put on some coal, and each time, above the dismal train, black in all this whiteness but covered with a shroud, the dazzling comet's tail shone back and made a gap in the night. It was seven forty-five and day was breaking, but it was hardly possible to make out the lightening sky through the immense, whirling whiteness filling all the space from end to end of the horizon. This deceptive light in which nothing could yet be clearly seen bothered both men still more, for their eyes, full of tears in spite of their goggles, were struggling to see into the distance. Without taking his hand off the reversing-wheel the driver also held on to the whistle-rod, whistling almost all the time out of prudence with a whistle of distress wailing in the wilderness of snow.

They went through Bolbec and Yvetot without any hitch. But at Motteville Jacques once again questioned the deputy station-master, who could not give any precise information about the state of the line. No train had come through yet, and the tele-graph simply said that the down slow from Paris was held up at Rouen as a safety measure. So Lison set off again, going down the gentle gradient to Barentin at her laboured, weary pace. It was now getting light, a dismal light that looked as though it came from the snow itself, for it was snowing more heavily than ever, like a murky, cold dawn falling down and smothering the earth with bits of sky. As it grew lighter the wind increased in violence, the snowflakes whizzed along like bullets, and every minute the fireman had to take his shovel and uncover the coal at the back of the tender between the sides of the water-tanks. On either side the country was so unrecogniz-able that the two men had a sensation of speeding through a dream world: the great flat fields, lush pastures with green hedges, orchards planted with apple trees, were now nothing but a white sea hardly ruffled by a few tiny waves, a pale, quivering immensity where everything lost itself in all this whiteness. The driver, standing still with his face lashed by the wind and hand on the wheel, was beginning to suffer terribly from the cold.

Eventually they pulled up at Barentin, and during the stop M. Bessière, the stationmaster, himself came up to the engine to warn Jacques that considerable quantities of snow were reported near La Croix-de-Maufras.

'I think it's still passable, but you'll have a job.'

At that Jacques lost his temper.

'Oh Christ, that's what I told them at Beuzeville! What difference could it have made to them to double-head? Oh, now we're going to be in a fine old mess!'

The front guard had left his van and he also was angry. He was frozen at his look-out and declared he couldn't tell a signal from a telegraph pole. A proper blind man's holiday in all this white!

'Anyway, you've been warned,' said M. Bessière.

Meanwhile the passengers were already wondering why there was this long stop in the deep silence of a buried station, without a single shout from a porter or bang of a door. A few windows were lowered and heads appeared: a very stout lady with two charming golden-haired girls, no doubt her daughters, all three English for certain, and further along a dark woman, young and very pretty, being forced to go in again by an elderly man, while two men, one young, one old, were carrying on a conversation from one coach to the next with their bodies half out of the windows. But as Jacques glanced backwards he saw only Séverine, leaning out too and looking anxiously in his direction. Oh, how worried his beloved must be, and how his heart ached at the thought of her there, so near and yet so far in this time of peril! He would have given all the blood in his body to be in Paris now and get her there safe and sound.

'Well, you'd better get going,' concluded the stationmaster. 'No point in frightening people.'

He gave the signal himself, the guard back in his van blew his whistle and once again Lison moved off after uttering a long answering wail.

Jacques at once felt that the state of the line was changing. Instead of the plain, the endless expanse of thick snow carpet, through which the engine sailed like a steamer, leaving a wake behind, they were now entering the wild country of hills and valleys whose enormous rise and fall, like a rough sea, went on as far as Malaunay; and here the snow had drifted in irregular ways – sometimes the line was clear while considerable drifts had blocked other places. The wind swept the embankments clean but filled the cuttings. So there was a continual succession of obstacles to get over, stretches of clear line cut off by absolute ramparts. It was now broad daylight, and under its covering of snow the wild country, with its narrow gorges and steep slopes, took on the desolate look of an ocean frozen solid in the middle of a storm.

Never before had Jacques felt the cold go right through him like this. His face, pricked by a thousand needles of snow, felt like bleeding flesh, and he could not feel his hands at all, paralysed with numbness and so insensitive that he realized with panic that he could no longer feel the little reversing-wheel. When he reached up to pull the whistle-rod his arm weighed down his shoulder like a dead limb. With the ceaseless jerk of the shaking engine tearing his guts out he could not have said whether his legs were supporting him or not. The cold and the overwhelming fatigue had engulfed him, and the chill was going up into his head, making him terrified of not being there at all, of not knowing whether he was driving or not, for already he was only turning his little wheel mechanically and listlessly watching the pressure-gauge going down. All the well-known stories about hallucinations were going through his head. Wasn't that a fallen tree across the line? Hadn't he seen a red flag floating over that bush? Weren't there detonators going off every minute in the roar of the wheels? He couldn't have said, but kept on telling himself he ought to stop, yet couldn't summon the will-power. For several minutes he went through this torture, and then suddenly he caught sight of Pecqueux who had gone off to sleep again on the chest, knocked out by the same numbing cold as he was suffering from himself. That made him so mad that it almost warmed him up again.

'Oh you fucking bastard!'

Usually so lenient towards the shortcomings of this drunkard, he now kicked him awake and punched him until he stood up. Pecqueux, only half awake, just grunted as he took up his shovel:

'All right, all right, I'm seeing to it!'

When the fire had been mended the pressure rose again, and it was high time, for Lison had entered a cutting and had more than a metre of snow to plough through. She was moving now with an unparalleled effort that made her shudder from end to end. For a moment she was winded and it looked as though she was grinding to a halt like a ship on a sandbank. What added to her burden was the heavy layer of snow that had gradually accumulated on the carriage roofs. As they went along they made a black line in the white wake of the engine, with this white pall spread over them, but the engine herself only had ermine edges on her dark sides, over which the snowflakes melted and ran down in trickles. Once again, in spite of the weight, she pulled through and got away. Round a wide curve on an embankment the train could still be seen running easily like a ribbon of darkness in a fairyland of dazzling whiteness.

But a little further on the cuttings began again and Jacques and Pecqueux, who had felt Lison touch something, steeled themselves against the cold, standing at the post they could not desert even in the face of death. Yet again the engine was losing speed. She had run between two banks, and the stop came slowly, without any jolt. She seemed to be getting glued up, all her wheels were stuck, she was more and more hemmed in and out of breath. She stopped moving. That was that, the snow had her powerless in its grip.

'Well, that's it,' cursed Jacques. 'Blast it!'

He stuck it out for a few more minutes, hand on wheel, opening everything to see if the obstacle would give. Then hearing Lison puffing and blowing in vain he shut the regulator and cursed harder than ever in his rage.

The front guard leaned out of his van door and when he saw Pecqueux he joined in too:

'That's that, we're stuck!'

He jumped quickly down into the snow, which was up to his knees. He came along and the three men held a council of war.

'The only thing we can do is try and clear a way through,' Jacques concluded. 'Fortunately we've got shovels. Get your guard from the rear and the four of us will manage to get the wheels free.'

They hailed the second guard, who had also got down from his van. He had great difficulty in reaching them, sometimes sinking right into the snow. By now this stop in the open country, in this white solitude, the loud voices discussing what was to be done, the guard hopping along the train with painful strides, had alarmed the passengers. Windows were let down.

People were shouting questions in an ever-swelling chorus of confusion.

'Where are we? What have we stopped for? What's up? Oh dear, is it an accident?'

The guard felt that some reassurance was called for. As he went along, the English lady, whose heavy red face was framed by the two charming faces of her daughters, asked him with a strong accent:

'Monsieur, it's not dangerous, is it?'

'No, no, Madame, just a bit of snow. We shall be off again in a minute.'

The window went up again on the chirruping of the girls, in that music of English syllables that trips so lightly from rosebud lips. They were both laughing, hugely amused.

But further along the elderly gentleman called the guard, while his young wife ventured to poke out her pretty dark head behind him.

'What, didn't they take any precautions? It's disgraceful! I'm on my way back from London, and I have business in Paris this morning, and I warn you I shall hold the Company responsible for any delay!'

'Sir,' was all the employee could answer, 'we shall be off again in three minutes.'

The cold was terrible and the snow was blowing in, so windows went up again. But you could tell by the vague murmur of voices going on inside that people were still agitated and anxious. Only two windows stayed down and, leaning out three compartments away from each other, two passengers were holding a conversation, an American of about forty and a young man who lived in Le Havre, both very interested in the work of clearing.

'In America, sir, everybody gets out and takes a shovel.'

'Oh, this isn't anything, I was snowed up twice last year. My job takes me to Paris once a week.'

'And mine takes me about every three weeks, sir.'

'What! From New York?'

'Yes, sir, from New York.'

Jacques was superintending the job. Having caught sight of Séverine at a window in the first coach, where she always travelled so as to be nearer him, he had entreated her with his eyes, and she had understood and gone in so as not to stay in the icy wind that lashed her face. Thinking of her he now worked with a will. But he noticed that the reason for their being stuck in the snow was nothing to do with the wheels, which could cut through deeper falls than this. It was the ashpan between the wheels that was causing the trouble, pushing the snow along and hardening it into enormous packs. He had an idea.

'We must unscrew the ashpan.'

At first the front guard was against it. The driver was under his orders and he didn't want to authorize him to tamper with the engine. But he let himself be persuaded.

'All right, but it's your responsibility.'

Only it was a hard job. Lying under the engine with their backs in melting snow, Jacques and Pecqueux had to work for nearly half an hour. Fortunately they had some spare screw-drivers in the tool-chest. At last, at the risk of being burned or crushed a score of times, they succeeded in getting the ashpan unscrewed. But they still hadn't got it clear, for it had to be got out from underneath. Enormously heavy, it fouled the wheels and cylinders. However, all four pulled it out and dragged it clear of the line and on to the bank.

'Now let's finish getting the snow away,' said the guard.

The train had been in distress for nearly an hour and the uneasiness of the passengers had grown. Every minute a window went down and a voice asked why they weren't going. Panic was setting in, with shouting, tears and mounting hysteria.

'No, no, we've cleared enough,' declared Jacques. 'Get back in and leave the rest to me.'

He went back once again to his post with Pecqueux and when the two guards had got back to their vans he himself turned on the tap of the steam-cock. The hot, deafening jet of steam melted the last bits of snow sticking to the rails. Then, hand on wheel, he put the engine into reverse. Slowly he backed for about three hundred metres so as to take a good run. Having stoked up a big fire and even exceeded the permitted pressure, he came back at the barrier and hurled Lison at it with all her weight and that of the train behind her. She uttered a grunt like a woodman driving home his axe, and her mighty iron frame seemed to crack. But still she could not get through, and came to a standstill panting and trembling with the shock. He had to go through the operation twice more, reversing, charging at the snow to move it out of the way, and each time Lison braced herself and butted head-on, blowing like a giant. But at last she seemed to get her breath back, tautened her steel muscles with a supreme effort and, followed by the heavy train, got through between the two walls hacked out of the snow. She was free.

'She ain't so bad after all!' growled Pecqueux.

Jacques could not see anything, and took off his goggles and wiped them. His heart was thumping fast and he didn't feel the cold now. But then he suddenly thought of a deep cutting about three hundred metres from La Croix-de-Maufras. The wind would be blowing straight through it and quite a heavy drift must have piled up there; and at once he was sure that that was the reef on which he would be wrecked. He leaned out. In the distance, round a last curve, the cutting came into sight, in a straight line, like a long trench filled with snow. It was broad daylight and the whiteness was unbroken and dazzling, while the flakes were still coming down.

So far Lison was steaming along at a moderate speed, having met no other obstacle. As a precaution the front and rear lights of the train had been kept burning, and the white headlamp at the base of the chimney shone in the daylight like the living eye of a cyclops. She was nearing the cutting, with the eye staring wide. Then she seemed to fetch her breath in little gasps like a nervous horse. She was shaken by violent spasms and reared, only kept going by the firm hand of her driver. He had kicked open the firebox door for the fireman to feed the fire. So now, instead of a comet's tail blazing through the night, she had a plume of thick black smoke, dirtying the cold, pale sky.

Lison went ahead and now had to enter the cutting. On either side the slopes had been blanketed and nothing could be seen of the line in front. It was like the bed of a torrent in which the snow lay right up to the verges. She went in and ran on for some fifty metres, puffing like a mad thing, slower and slower. As she pushed the snow along it made a barrier ahead, piling up in an angry wave that threatened to engulf her. For a moment she seemed overwhelmed and beaten. But with one last heave she freed herself and went on another thirty metres. That was the end, her dying throe. Chunks of snow came down over the wheels, all the moving parts were caught up and bound together with chains of ice. Lison stopped for good, expiring in the intense cold. Her breath had gone, she was motionless and dead.

'So here we are,' said Jacques, 'just as I expected.'

He tried at once to reverse and attempt the same operation again. But this time Lison would not budge, refusing to go back or go ahead, caught on all sides, stuck to the ground, inert, unresponsive. Behind her the train was dead too, buried in the deep drift up to the doors. It was still snowing, thicker than ever, in prolonged squalls. It was like a quicksand into which engine and carriages were disappearing; already they were half submerged in the shivering silence of this white solitude. Nothing moved, and the snow was weaving her shroud.

'Well, are we going to start that all over again?' shouted the front guard, leaning out of his van.

'Buggered!' was Pecqueux's only remark.

This time the position was indeed becoming critical. The rear guard hurried back to lay detonators to protect the train from behind, and the driver whistled desperately in short, sharp blasts, the gasping, mournful whistle of distress. But the snow deadened the sound and the cry was lost and would not even reach Barentin. What was to be done? There were only four of them, and they would never clear such drifts. It would have needed a whole gang. It was essential to go and find help. The worst of it was that panic was again breaking out among the passengers.

A door opened, and the pretty dark lady leaped out in terror, thinking it was an accident. Her husband, the elderly businessman, was shouting:

'I shall write to the Minister, it's outrageous!'

Windows were banged down and sounds of wailing women and furious male voices could be heard coming from the carriages. Only the two English girls thought it was fun, and were calmly smiling. As the front guard was trying to calm people down, the younger girl asked him in French with a slight British accent:

'So we stop here, Monsieur?'

Several men had jumped down in spite of the deep snow which came up to their waists. And so the American found himself with the young man from Le Havre, and both made their way forward to have a look at the engine. They shook their heads.

'We shall be here for four or five hours before they can clear out under there!'

'Quite that, and even then they'll need twenty men.'

Jacques had persuaded the front guard to send the rear guard off to Barentin for help. Neither he nor Pecqueux could leave the engine.

The man moved off and was soon out of sight at the end of the cutting. He had four kilometres to do and might not be back in under two hours. In despair, Jacques left his post for a minute and ran as far as the first carriage, where he saw Séverine who had lowered her window.

'Don't be afraid,' he said quickly, 'you've nothing to fear.'

'I'm not afraid, but I was worrying about you,' she replied in the same tone, for fear of being overheard.

It was said so sweetly that they were both cheered and smiled at each other. But as Jacques turned to go back he was surprised to see Flore and Misard coming along the top of the cutting, followed by two men whom he did not recognize at first. They had heard the distress signal and Misard, who was not on duty, rushed to the scene with two friends to whom he happened to be giving a glass of white wine – the quarryman Cabuche, unable to work because of the snow, and the pointsman Ozil, who had walked through the tunnel from Malaunay to press his suit on Flore, whom he was still running after in spite of discouragement. Out of curiosity she had come along with them, being a strapping girl as strong and brave as a man. For her and her father this was quite an event, an extraordinary adventure, a train actually stopping at their door. During the five years they had lived there, every hour, day and night, rain or shine, how many trains they had seen go by, rushing like the wind! They all seemed to be carried away on this wind that had blown them there, and never had a single one so much as slackened its speed, and before they could know anything about them they were watching them tearing along and losing themselves in the distance. The whole world passed by, the human multitude borne along at full speed without their knowing anything else except faces glimpsed in a flash, faces they would never see again or sometimes faces they got to know through seeing them again on certain days, but for them these faces were nameless. And now here was a train unloading at their door in the snow, the natural order was turned upside down, and they stared at these unknown people tipped out on the line by a mishap, and contemplated them with the goggling eyes of savages collecting on a shore on which some Europeans had been shipwrecked. These open doors revealing ladies wrapped in furs, these men walking about in thick overcoats, all this well-to-do luxury washed up on a sea of ice, rooted them to the spot in amazement.

However, Flore had recognized Séverine. She looked out for Jacques's train every time it passed, and for some weeks she had noted the presence of this woman on the morning express on Fridays, and particularly so because the latter looked out of the window when she was approaching the level crossing to have a glance at her property at La Croix-de-Maufras. Flore's eye darkened as she saw her talking to Jacques in an undertone.

'Ah, Madame Roubaud!' exclaimed Misard, also recognizing her and at once assuming his obsequious manner. 'What an unfortunate thing to happen! But you can't stay here, you must come in to our house.'

Jacques, who had shaken hands with the level-crossing keeper, backed him up.

'Yes, he's right . . . It might go on for hours and you could die of cold.'

Séverine declined, saying she was well wrapped up. And besides, the three hundred metres in the snow scared her a bit. Then Flore, giving her a hard look, came up and said:

'Come along, Madame, I'll carry you.'

And before she had time to accept, Flore had seized her in her strong, manly arms and was lifting her like a child. She put her down on the opposite side of the line where the snow had already been trodden down and your feet didn't sink in. Some of the passengers began to laugh in amazement. What a strapping wench! If they had a dozen more like her it wouldn't need as much as two hours to clear the line!

Meanwhile Misard's proposal – the level-crossing house where they could shelter, find a fire and perhaps food and drink – ran along from carriage to carriage. The panic had died down when they realized that they were in no immediate danger, but still the situation was no less miserable, the foot-warmers were getting cold, it was nine o'clock, and unless help came pretty soon they would be hungry and thirsty. And it might well drag on for ever, who could say whether they might not be there all night? Two rival schools of thought formed: those who were in despair and didn't want to leave the train but wrapped themselves in their rugs and lay down furiously on the seats as though to await death, and those who preferred to risk a trek across the snow, hoping to find something better somewhere yonder, anxious above all to get away from the nightmare of this train, stranded and frozen to death. A sizeable group formed, with the elderly businessman and his young wife, the English lady and her two daughters, the young man from Le Havre, the American and a dozen others, all ready to set forth.

Jacques in an undertone had persuaded Séverine, swearing that he would come and tell her how it was going on if he could get away. And as Flore was still looking at them with her suspicious eyes, he spoke to her nicely like an old friend.

'Right oh, then, you take these ladies and gentlemen ... I'll keep Misard and the others here. We'll start in and do what we can while we're waiting.'

And indeed Cabuche, Ozil, and Misard had seized some shovels to join Pecqueux and the front guard who were already attacking the snow. The little gang was aiming at freeing the engine by digging under the wheels and throwing the shovelfuls up the bank. Nobody said another word and only a silent desperation could be sensed in the breathless dreariness of the white countryside. As the little group of passengers moved off they cast one last look back at the train standing there all forlorn, showing nothing but a thin black line under the thick layer weighing it down. The doors had been shut again and the windows put up. Still the snow was coming down, and slowly but surely was burying the train, silent and inexorable.

Flore had again offered to carry Séverine in her arms, but she had refused, determined to walk like the others. The three hundred metres were very difficult to cover, especially in the cutting, where they sank in up to their waists, and twice there had to be a salvage operation on the stout English lady who was half submerged. Her daughters were still laughing away and enjoying themselves hugely. The young wife of the elderly gentleman, having slipped once, had to accept the hand of the young man from Le Havre, while her husband was holding forth against France to the American. When they were out of the cutting the going was easier, but now they were walking along an embankment and went in single file, buffeted by the wind and taking care to avoid the edges that were ill defined and dangerous under the snow. At last they made it, and Flore got them all into the kitchen, where she could not even give everyone a seat, for there were at least twenty of them crowding into the room which fortunately was fairly big. All she could think of was to go and find planks and fix up two long seats with the help of the chairs she had. She then threw some wood on the fire and made a gesture suggesting that they couldn't expect her to do anything else. She had not uttered a word, and there she stood staring at all these people with her big greenish eyes, looking as fierce and wild as some fair-haired Nordic savage. She only knew two faces, having noticed them at windows for months, those of the American and the young man from Le Havre, and she examined them as one might study a buzzing insect at rest that couldn't be followed when in flight. They struck her as peculiar, and she hadn't thought they were quite like this, not knowing anything about them, of course, except their faces. As for the others, they struck her as belonging to a different race, inhabitants of another planet who had dropped from the sky, bringing into her home, into her very kitchen, clothes, manners and ideas she would never have dreamed of finding there. The English lady was telling the businessman's young wife all about how she was on her way to join her eldest son in India – he was a highly placed civil servant – while the latter was joking about her bad luck on the very first occasion she had taken it into her head to go with her husband to London, where he went twice a year. They were all sorry for themselves, stranded in this godforsaken hole; they would have to eat and sleep here and how on earth would they manage? Flore was listening, motionless, but then she caught the eye of Séverine, who was sitting on a chair in front of the fire, and she made a sign suggesting that she might go through into the living-room.

'Mother,' she said as she went in, 'here's Madame Roubaud ... Haven't you got anything to say to her?'

Phasie was lying down, her face was jaundiced and her eyes swollen, and she was so ill that she had not left her bed for a fortnight, and passed the hours in this miserable room in which an iron stove kept up a stifling heat, turning over in her mind her obstinate obsession, with no other entertainment than to be shaken by trains at full speed.

'Ah, Madame Roubaud,' she murmured, 'oh yes, oh yes.'

Flore told her about the accident and all these people she had brought in and who were through there. But none of that interested her now.

'Oh yes, oh yes,' she repeated in the same weary voice.

But then she recollected and looked up and said to Flore:

'If Madame wants to go and look at her house, you know the keys are on a nail by the cupboard.'

But Séverine declined. A shiver ran through her at the thought of going back to La Croix-de-Maufras in this snow and gloom. No, no, there was nothing she wanted to look at there, she preferred to stay where she was and wait in the warm.

'Sit you down, Madame,' said Flore. 'It's better here than in there anyway. And besides, we shall never find enough bread for all those people, but if you are hungry there'll always be a bit for you.'

She had brought up a chair and went on being attentive, visibly making an effort to curb her usual surliness. But her eyes never left the young woman, as though she were trying to read into her, to make up her mind about a question she had been asking herself for some time; and underneath this con- siderateness there was a need to get near her, look at her closely and touch her, in order to know.

Séverine thanked her and sat by the stove, preferring to be left alone with the sick woman in this room, where she hoped Jacques might find a way of joining her. Two hours went by, and she was giving in to the great heat and drowsing off, after some talk about people round about, when Flore, who was constantly wanted in the kitchen, opened the door again and said in her harsh voice:

'Go in, because she's in there!'

It was Jacques who had run away here to bring good news. The man they had sent to Barentin had brought back quite a team, some thirty soldiers whom the administration had posted to threatened places in case of mishaps, and they were all at work with picks and shovels. But still it would be a long job and they might not get away before nightfall.

'Anyway, you're not too badly off, so be patient. You won't let Madame Roubaud die of hunger, will you, Aunt Phasie?'

Phasie had painfully sat up in bed on seeing her big boy, as she called him, and she was quite revived and happy as she looked at him and heard him talking. When he came over to her in bed:

'Oh no, of course not!' she declared. 'Oh my big boy, so here you are! So you're the one who's got himself stuck in the snow! And that donkey never tells me.'

She turned to her daughter and read her a lecture:

'You may as well be polite, and go and see those ladies and gentlemen and look after them so that they don't tell the management that we're a lot of savages.'

Flore had planted herself between Jacques and Séverine. For a moment she seemed to hesitate, wondering whether she shouldn't stick there in spite of her mother. But she wouldn't see anything because her mother's presence would prevent the two of them from giving themselves away. So she left without a word, staring hard at them.

'What's all this, Aunt Phasie?' Jacques went on, very upset. 'You're in bed altogether now, does that mean it's serious?'

She pulled him, even forced him to sit on the edge of the bed and, without paying any further attention to the young woman who had tactfully moved further away, she relieved her feelings in a very low voice:

'Oh yes, it really is serious! It's a miracle you find me still alive ... I wouldn't write to you because these things can't be put in writing ... I was nearly gone, but now I'm already

208

getting better, and I think I shall get away with it once more.'

Looking at her he was horrified at the progress of her illness, and could see nothing left in her of the fine, healthy woman of former days.

'So you're still getting your cramps and giddy turns, poor Aunt Phasie?'

She squeezed his hand till it cracked, and went on even more softly:

'Just fancy, I caught him at it. You know, I was just giving up trying to find out what he could have put his doses into. I never ate or drank anything he touched, yet every night my insides were on fire. Well, he gave me his doses in the salt! One evening I saw him at it. And to think that I put salt, and lots of it, on everything to make it wholesome!'

Since possessing Séverine seemed to have cured him, Jacques sometimes thought about this tale of slow, steady poisoning as one does about a nightmare, with scepticism. He now took the invalid's hands in his turn, squeezed them affectionately and tried to calm her down.

'But is all that really possible? Before you say things like that you've got to be quite sure. And besides, it's been going on too long. Surely it's more likely to be some complaint the doctors simply don't know anything about.'

She was scornful. 'A complaint he's put into me, if you like! As for the doctors, you're right. Two of them came who couldn't understand anything and couldn't even agree between themselves. I won't let any more of those birds set foot in this house ... You heard what I said, he bunged it in the salt. I swear I saw him. It's for my thousand francs, the thousand Dad left me. He thinks that when he's got rid of me he'll find them all right ... Well, I defy him to, they're in a place where nobody will discover them ever! I can depart and rest in peace, nobody will ever get my thousand francs!'

'But, Aunt Phasie, if I were in your shoes I'd send for the police, if I were as sure as all that.'

She made a gesture of repugnance.

'Oh no, not the police. This is nothing to do with anybody but us, it's between him and me. I know he's out to destroy me, and naturally I don't want to be destroyed. So I've only got to defend myself, haven't I? And not be as silly as I was over his salt. Who would have believed it, an abortion like that, a bit of a man you could put in your pocket, that the creature would end up by getting the better of a strapping woman like me if he were allowed to, him and his rat's teeth!'

She shivered and gasped for breath before going on.

'Never mind, it won't work this time. I'm getting better, and I shall be on my feet in a fortnight . . . And this time he'll have to be very artful to catch me again. Oh yes, I'm quite looking forward to watching it. If he finds a way of giving me his poison again, well, decidedly he's cleverer than I am, and I shall peg out, and that's that . . . It's nobody else's business.'

Jacques thought that it was her illness that was filling her mind with these black fantasies, and he was trying to make jokes to take her mind off it, when she began to shake under the bedclothes.

'Here he comes,' she whispered, 'I can feel when he comes near.'

And indeed Misard came in a few moments later. She had turned deathly pale, seized by the involuntary terror of a colossus at the sight of the insect eating away at it. For in her obstinate determination to defend herself alone she was living in a growing dread of him which she could not admit. Misard had taken the two of them in with a swift glance as he came through the door, and then did not seem to have noticed them side by side, but proceeded, dull-eyed and tight-lipped, looking like a meek little man, to fall over himself in polite attentions to Séverine.

'I thought perhaps Madame might like to take advantage of this chance and have a look at her property . . . So I've got away for a minute . . . If Madame would like me to go with her . . .'

As she declined yet again he went on in whining tones:

'Perhaps Madame has been surprised about the fruit. It had all got the maggot in it and really it wasn't worth sending . . . And besides, there was a gale that did a lot of damage . . . Oh, it is a pity Madame can't find a buyer . . . One gentleman did come, but he wanted repairs done . . . Anyway, I am at Madame's service, and Madame can rest assured that I am acting for her as she would herself.'

Then he insisted on serving some bread and pears – pears from his own garden, and these hadn't got the maggot in. She accepted.

On his way through the kitchen Misard had informed the other travellers that the work of clearing was going on, but that it would last at least another four or five hours. It was just past noon and a fresh lamentation arose because hunger was beginning to pinch. Flore declared that she hadn't enough bread for everybody. She did have wine, and came up from the cellar with ten bottles which she set on the table in a row. Only there weren't enough glasses either, and they had to drink in relays – the English lady and her two daughters, the elderly gentleman and his young wife. The latter, incidentally, was finding in the young man from Le Havre an assiduous attendant, full of ideas, watching over her well-being. He disappeared and returned with some apples and a loaf of bread he had discovered in the depths of the woodshed. Flore was annoyed and said it was bread for her sick mother, but he was already cutting it up and sharing it round among the ladies, beginning with the young wife, who smiled at him, feeling very gratified. Her husband's rage never abated, and he had even given up thinking about her, being engaged with the American in singing the praises of commercial practice in New York. Never had the English girls sunk their teeth into apples with such relish. Their mother was very tired and half asleep. Two ladies were sitting on the floor in front of the fire, knocked out by the long wait. Some of the men, who had gone out for a smoke to kill a quarter of an hour, came back again frozen and shivering. Gradually the uneasiness became more acute, what with unsatisfied hunger, fatigue made worse by discomfort and impatience. The scene was taking on the character of a party of shipwrecked mariners, the misery of a band of civilized people washed up by the sea on to a desert island.

As the comings and goings of Misard left the door open, Aunt Phasie looked at them from her sickbed. So these were the people whom she too had been seeing go by like a flash of lightning for nearly a year now while she had been dragging herself between her bed and her chair. Now she could hardly ever get out by the line, but lived her days and nights alone, tied down here, her eyes fixed on the window, with no other company but these trains tearing past. She had always complained about this outlandish place where nobody ever came to see you and now, lo and behold a real army dropped on them from the unknown. To think that not one of these people in such a hurry to get on with their own business had the slightest suspicion of this thing, this disgusting muck he had put into her salt! She couldn't get over the ingenuity of it, and wondered how in God's name anyone could get away with such a wicked trick without being spotted. And yet a big enough crowd of people went past their house, thousands and thousands of them, but all in such a rush, and none of them could have imagined that in this little squat house one person was killing another with no trouble or fuss at all. Aunt Phasie looked at them one after another, all these folk who had dropped from the skies, and reflected that when you are so busy yourself it is not surprising that you should go through disgusting things and know nothing about them.

'Are you going back?' Misard asked Jacques.

'Yes, yes, I'm just coming.'

Misard went off, shutting the door. Phasie held the young man back and went on whispering into his ear:

'If I peg out, you'll see what he looks like when he doesn't find the nest-egg . . . It makes me laugh to think about it. Never mind, I shall go off quite happy.'

'And so, Aunt Phasie, it will be lost for everybody, and you won't leave it to your daughter?'

'To Flore? So that he can pinch it! I should think not! Not even to you, my boy, because you are too soft as well and he might get something. No, to nobody except the earth, where I shall join it!'

She was tiring herself, and Jacques made her lie down again, and calmed her, kissed her and promised to come and see her again soon. Then as she seemed to be dozing off, he went behind Séverine who was still sitting by the stove, and smilingly raised a finger to warn her to be careful. With a charming quiet movement she threw back her head, offering her lips, and he bent down and put his lips to hers in a deep but restrained kiss. Their eyes were closed and they breathed each other's breath. But

212

when they opened their eyes again they were horrified to see Flore who had opened the door and was standing there watching.

'Madame doesn't require any more bread?' she inquired in a hoarse voice.

Embarrassed and vexed, Séverine muttered some vague words:

'Er, no, no thanks.'

For a moment Jacques glared at Flore with blazing eyes. He hesitated, and his lips moved as though he were going to say something, but with a furious threatening gesture he decided to go. The door slammed hard behind him.

Flore was left standing there, a tall figure like a virgin warrior, with her massive helmet of fair hair. So her terrible misgivings every Friday, on seeing this fine lady in the train he was driving, had not deceived her. She had been watching out for this certainty since she had them there together under her eye, and now at last she was sure, absolutely. The man she loved would never love her; this other woman, this nothing-at-all, was the one he had chosen. Her regret at having refused herself that night when he had brutally tried to take her, now became so bitter and so painful that she could have cried, for, so ran her simple reasoning, she would be the one he was kissing now if she had given herself to him before the other woman. Where could she find him alone now and throw herself into his arms and say: Take me, I was stupid because I didn't know! And in her powerlessness she felt a mounting rage against this puny creature sitting there all ill at ease and stammering. With one grip of her powerful wrestler's arms she could crush her to death like a little bird. Then why didn't she pluck up her courage? All the same she swore she would be revenged, for she knew things about this rival that would have got her clapped into jail, and yet they let her go free like all these whores who sell themselves to influential, rich old men. Tortured by jealousy and bursting with rage, she proceeded to take away the rest of the bread and pears with the fierce movements of a fine, savage wench.

'As you don't want any more, Madame, I'll give this to the others.'

It struck three, then four. The time dragged on endlessly,

with increasing and overwhelming weariness and irritation. Now it was getting dark again, a ghastly gloom over the great white landscape, and every ten minutes the men went out to have a distant look at how the work was getting on, only to come back saying that the engine still didn't seem free. Even the two English girls were crying with sheer nervous exhaustion. In a corner the pretty dark woman had gone to sleep on the shoulder of the young man from Le Havre, and her elderly husband did not even notice in the general lack of restraint that suspended the conventions. The room was getting cold and they were shivering, but it didn't even occur to anybody to put some more wood on the fire, and indeed the American went out, deciding he would be better off lying on the seat in a compartment. That was now everybody's idea and regret – they should have stayed out there, and at any rate they wouldn't have been worried to death not knowing what was going on. They had to dissuade the English lady, who was also talking of getting back to her compartment to lie down. When a candle had been stuck on a corner of the table to give people a bit of light in this pitch-black kitchen an intense depression set in and everything sank into gloomy despair.

Meanwhile out there they were finishing off the work of clearing, and while the team of soldiers who had freed the engine were sweeping the rails in front, the driver and fireman had climbed back to their posts.

Seeing that the snow was at last stopping, Jacques was feeling more confident. Ozil the pointsman had told him that over Malaunay way, beyond the tunnel, far less snow had fallen. He questioned him again:

'You walked through the tunnel. Could you get in and out of it easily?'

'But I'm telling you! You'll get through, believe me.'

Cabuche, who had toiled with the fervour of an amiable giant, was already moving off in his shy, uncouth way, made more marked by his latest encounter with the law, and Jacques had to call him back.

'Look, chum, hand us those shovels that belong to us, over there against the bank. Then we could lay our hands on them if there were trouble.'

214

When the quarryman had done this last service Jacques shook his hand vigorously to show him he still thought highly of him, having seen him at work.

'You're one of the best, you are!'

This token of friendship had an amazing effect on Cabuche.

'Thank you,' was all he said, fighting back his tears.

Misard, who had accused Cabuche before the examining magistrate, had since made it up with him, and he nodded his agreement with a thin-lipped smile. For a long time now he had not been doing any work, but had just been standing with his hands in his pockets, looking at the train with a shifty air as if he was hanging about on the look-out for lost property he might pick up from under the wheels.

At last the front guard had decided with Jacques that they could try to move, when Pecqueux, who had gone down on to the line again, called to the driver:

'Have a look. One of the cylinders has had a knock.'

Jacques went and stooped as well. He had already noted, on looking carefully over Lison, that she was wounded there. As they were clearing they had found that some oak sleepers left alongside by gangers had slipped down the slope and across the rails owing to the action of snow and wind, and even part of the reason for their stoppage must have been this obstacle, for the engine had run into the sleepers. The scratch could be seen along the cylinder casing, and the piston-rod looked slightly out of true. But that was the only perceptible damage and it had at first reassured the driver. Perhaps there were serious things wrong inside, for nothing is more delicate than the complicated mechanism of the slide-valves, the very pulse and living soul of an engine. He went up on the footplate, whistled and opened the regulator to try out Lison's moving parts. She took a long time to get going, like somebody suffering from shock after a fall who can't find her limbs again. Eventually, breathing heavily she moved and did several revolutions of her wheels, but still seemed dazed and sluggish. Never mind, she would manage all right and last out the journey. But all the same he shook his head, for he knew her inside out and had felt something funny about her under his hand, she wasn't the same, but older and struck by some fatal illness. She must have caught it in this

215

snow, some death-blow or mortal chill like one of those healthy young women who are carried off by pneumonia because they come home from a dance one night in the freezing rain.

Once again Jacques whistled, after Pecqueux had opened the steam-cocks. The two guards were at their posts. Misard, Ozil, and Cabuche climbed up on to the step of the front van. The train slowly emerged from the cutting, between the soldiers armed with their shovels who formed a guard of honour on each side along the banks. Then it stopped in front of the level-crossing house to pick up the passengers.

Flore was standing outside, Ozil and Cabuche jumped down and stood by her, while Misard was now all attention, bowing to the ladies and gentlemen and raking in silver coins. Delivered at last! But the wait had been too long, and everybody was shaking with cold, hunger and exhaustion. The English lady bore off her daughters, now half asleep, the young man from Le Havre climbed into the same compartment as the pretty dark woman, now very languishing, and was all at the husband's service. In this mess of trampled snow you would have taken it for the entraining of a routed army, pushing and being pushed, having even lost the instinct to be clean. For a moment there appeared at the window of the living-room, peering through the glass, Aunt Phasie, whose curiosity had got her out of bed and who had dragged herself over to look. The great hollow eyes of the sick woman watched this unknown crowd, the passing world on its way, blown there by the storm and blown away again, never to be seen by her again.

Séverine was the last to leave. She turned and smiled at Jacques, who was leaning out to follow her with his eyes to her compartment. Flore, on the watch, paled once again at their confident acceptance of each other's love. With a sudden instinctive movement she drew closer to Ozil, as if now, in her hatred, she felt the need of a man.

The front guard gave the signal, Lison answered with a doleful whistle, and this time Jacques started and was not to stop again until Rouen. It was six o'clock, and pitch-black night had come down over the white landscape, but a whitish glow, horribly melancholy, hung about at ground level and showed up the desolation of the wild country. There, in this sinister glow,

216

the house at La Croix-de-Maufras stood crookedly, looking more dilapidated than ever and quite black in the middle of the snow, with its FOR SALE notice nailed to its shuttered front.

[8]

THE train did not get into Paris until ten forty that night. There had been a twenty-minute stop at Rouen to give the passengers time to eat something, and Séverine had made a special point of sending her husband a wire to warn him that she would not be returning to Le Havre until the following day, on the evening train. A whole night with Jacques, the first they would spend together in a room on their own, quite free and with no fear of being disturbed!

Just after leaving Mantes, Pecqueux had had an idea. His wife, Ma Victoire, had been in hospital for a week with a badly sprained ankle following a fall, and seeing as how in Paris he had another bed to sleep in, as he put it with a grin, he had thought of offering this room to Mme Roubaud: she would be much more comfortable there than in a hotel room in that district and could stay there until the following evening, just like being in her own home. Jacques at once saw the practical advantages of the arrangement, especially as he didn't know where to take her. In the station, when she came up to the engine in the crowd of passengers at last leaving the train, he advised her to accept, offering her the key the fireman had given him. But she hesitated and refused, embarrassed by the suggestive leer of the latter, who obviously knew how things stood.

'No, no, I've got a cousin who will give me a shakedown on the floor.'

'Why not accept?' Pecqueux said eventually, in his gay, man-about-town manner. The bed's nice and cosy, you know, and ever so big, it would take four!'

Jacques looked at her so pleadingly that she took the key. He leaned over and whispered:

'Wait for me.'

Séverine only had to go up a part of the rue d'Amsterdam and turn into the cul-de-sac, but the snow was so slippery that she had to walk with extreme care. She was lucky enough to find the main door of the building still open, and went up the staircase without even being seen by the concierge, who was engrossed in a game of dominoes with a lady friend, and on the fourth floor she opened and shut the door so softly that none of the neighbours could have any suspicion that she was there. Yet, on the third floor landing, she had distinctly heard laughter and singing coming from the Dauvergnes', presumably one of the sisters' little musical evenings to which they invited friends once a week. After she had shut the door behind her and was in the pitch-dark room she could still hear through the floor the fun and gaiety of all these young things. For a moment the darkness seemed total, and she had a fright when out of the blackness the cuckoo clock began to strike eleven in a low tone, with a voice she recognized. Then as her eye grew accustomed to things the two windows came into view as two pale squares, lighting the ceiling with a reflection from the snow. By now she was already getting her bearings and feeling on the sideboard for the matches in a place where she remembered seeing them. But she had more trouble to find a candle and eventually found an end in a drawer and lit it. The room filled with light, and she glanced round with a quick, worried look as if to make sure she was really alone. Every object came back to her, the round table on which she had had the meal with her husband, the bed with its red cotton hangings on to which he had knocked her down with his fist. Yes, nothing in the room had changed since she had been there ten months ago.

Séverine slowly took off her hat. But as she was about to take off her coat she shivered. This room was freezing cold. In a little box by the stove there was some coal and firewood. At once, before taking anything else off, she thought she would light the fire, and she enjoyed doing it, for it took her mind off the un- comfortable feeling she had had at first. These household prep- arations she was making for a night of love, and the thought that they would both be lovely and warm, brought back the thrill and fun of their escapade – for so long they had dreamed of a night like this with no hope of getting it. When the stove began to roar she thought up other preparations, arranged the chairs how she wanted them, looked out some clean sheets and completely remade the bed, which was a real job, for it was

219

very wide. The trouble was that she couldn't find anything to eat or drink: no doubt, having been on his own for three days, Pecqueux had cleaned up even the crumbs off the floor. It was the same with the light, there was only this one candle-end, but when you're in bed you don't need to see very well! Being quite warm now and excited, she paused in the middle of the room, giving it a look over to make sure nothing was missing.

As she was wondering why Jacques had not yet come, a whistle made her go to one of the windows. It was the 11.20 semi-fast leaving for Le Havre. Down there the huge area of the cutting between the station and the Batignolles tunnel was just a waste of snow on which she could only see the black rails fanning out. Standing engines and carriages were just white heaps slumbering, as it were, beneath ermine. Between the spotless white glass station roof and the laced-edged girders of the Europe bridge, the buildings opposite in the rue de Rome could be made out in spite of the night, dirty and yellow-looking in all this whiteness. The Le Havre train appeared, a dark, crawling mass, with the bright flame of its headlamp cutting a swathe through the darkness, and she watched it disappear under the bridge, its three rear lights staining the snow with blood. When she turned back into the room her slightly uncomfortable sensation came back – was she really alone? She had seemed to feel a hot breath burn her neck, and a brutal hand seemed to have stroked her body through her clothes. She once again looked wide-eyed all round the room. No, nobody.

What was Jacques playing at, to be so long? Ten more minutes went by. She was worried by a faint scratching sound, like fingernails scratching on wood. Then she realized what it was and ran to the door. It was Jacques, with a bottle of Malaga and a cake.

Shaking with laughter, she threw her arms impulsively round his neck.

'Oh, you are a pet! You thought of it!'

But he hurriedly silenced her.

'Sh! Sh!'

So she lowered her voice, thinking the concierge was coming up after him. No, just as he was going to ring the bell he had been lucky enough to see the door opening for a lady and her daughter, just coming from the Dauvergnes' no doubt, and he had been able to slip upstairs without anyone noticing. But he had just seen a door ajar over there on the landing; it was the bookstall woman finishing washing her smalls in a bowl.

'Don't let's make a noise, do you mind? Talk softly.'

By way of an answer she held him in a tight embrace and without a word covered his face with kisses. It was fun to be all mysterious and only whisper very softly.

'Yes, yes, you'll see, we'll be as quiet as two little mice.'

She laid the table with the utmost caution, putting two plates, two glasses, two knives, pausing and wanting to scream with laughter whenever something put down too quickly made a noise.

He watched her working with much amusement and went on in an understone:

'I thought you would be hungry.'

'Yes, I'm dying of hunger! The food was so awful at Rouen!'

'Look, suppose I went down again and got a chicken?'

'Oh no, and then not be able to get up again? No, no, the cake will do.'

They sat down at once side by side and almost on the same chair, and the cake was shared out and eaten with the foolery of a pair of lovers. She complained of being thirsty and drank two glasses of Malaga straight off, which brought still more colour into her cheeks. The stove was getting red-hot behind their backs and they could feel its exciting warmth. But when he was planting kisses on the back of her neck with too much noise, she in her turn stopped him:

'Sh!'

With a sign she made him listen, and once again the silence was broken by a noise coming up from the Dauvergnes', a soft rhythmical sound to music. The young ladies had organized a little hop. The bookshop woman next door was emptying her bowl of soapy water down the sink on the landing. She shut her door, the dancing downstairs stopped for a minute and outside, down below, the snow deadened everything except the soft rumble of a departing train, and its faint whistles sounded like crying.

'Train for Auteuil,' he murmured. 'Ten to twelve.' Then he breathed in a soft, caressing voice:

'To beddy-byes, darling, shall we?'

She did not answer, for in the middle of her ecstatic state she was overtaken by the past, and in spite of herself living once again through the hours she had spent there with her husband. Wasn't this just the continuation of that lunch, with this cake eaten on the same table amid the same sounds? The things in the room worked on her even more powerfully, memories overwhelmed her and never before had she felt such a burning need to tell her lover everything and deliver herself up completely. It was like a physical desire now indistinguishable from her sexual one, and she felt she would belong to him all the more and drain to the depths the joy of being his if she confessed all into his ear in the midst of an embrace. The events came back to her vividly – her husband was there, she looked round thinking she had seen his stubby, hairy hand reach over her shoulder to get the knife.

'Beddy-byes, darling, shall we?' Jacques repeated.

She quivered as she felt his lips crushing hers as though once again he wanted to keep the confession sealed within her. Without a word she stood up, slipped quickly out of her clothes and slid into the bed, without even picking up the petticoats left lying on the floor. Neither did he put anything away, the remains of the meal stayed on the table, while the candle-end was burning out with the flame already flickering. When he too was out of his clothes and in bed, their sudden entwining and wild possession of each other stifled them and left them breathless. In the still air of the room, with the music going on downstairs, there was no exclamation, not a sound, nothing but a thrill of abandonment, a climax deep to the point of losing consciousness.

No longer could Jacques recognize in Séverine the woman of their first meetings, so gentle and passive, with her limpid blue eyes. She seemed, with her mane of black hair, to have grown more passionate every day and gradually in his arms he had felt her waking out of the long, cold virginity from which neither the senile indecencies of Grandmorin nor the brutal 'husband's rights' of Roubaud had succeeded in drawing her. This creature

222

made for love, formerly just docile, now loved actively and held nothing of herself back and displayed a burning gratitude for the pleasure given to her. She had come to feel a violent passion and adoration for the man who had revealed her own senses to her. It was this immense joy of holding him to her, freely, against her breast, bound by her two arms, that had made her tighten her mouth and not give vent to a single sigh.

When they opened their eyes again he was the first to be surprised:

'Oh look, the candle's gone out.'

A little movement on her part suggested that she couldn't care less. Then, with a stifled giggle:

'I was a good girl, wasn't I?'

'Oh yes, nobody heard us . . . Two little mice!'

They lay back again and she again took him in her arms, wriggled close up to him and buried her nose into his neck. Then she sighed with pleasure:

'Oh God, isn't this wonderful?'

No more was said. The room was dark and they could scarcely make out the paler squares of the windows, and on the ceiling there was just one ray of light from the stove, a round, blood-red patch. They both looked at it, wide-eyed. The sounds of music had stopped, doors opened and shut and the whole building was sinking into the heavy peace of sleep. Down there outside the noise of the train from Caen clattering over the turntables hardly reached them and seemed very far away.

Holding Jacques like this soon aroused Séverine anew. With fresh desire there awoke in her the urge to confide in him that had tormented her for so many weeks. The round patch on the ceiling widened and seemed to spread like a bloodstain. As she looked at it her eyes began to see visions and things round the bed began speaking and shouting the story aloud. She felt the words rising to her lips with the mounting wave of sensuality in her flesh. How good it would be to have nothing more to hide, and merge wholly into him!

'Darling, you don't realize . . .'

Jacques had never taken his eyes off the red patch either, and he realized perfectly what she was about to say. In this delicate body entwined with his own he had been following the rising

223

tide of this hidden, unspeakable thing which was in both their minds without ever being put into words. Until then he had prevented her from saying it, fearful of the first warnings of his old disorder, trembling lest it might alter their lives if they talked about blood. But this time there was no strength in him even to move his head over and seal her mouth with a kiss, so deliciously languorous did he feel in this warm bed and this woman's enveloping arms. He thought it was too late now, and that she would say everything. And so he was relieved of his anxiety when she seemed to hesitate in fear, then backed away from it and said:

'Darling, you don't seem to realize that my husband suspects I'm sleeping with you.'

At the last moment, and against her will, it had been the memory of the previous night at Le Havre that had come from her mouth instead of the confession.

'Oh, do you think so?' he murmured incredulously. 'He seems so friendly. Only this morning he shook hands with me.'

'I tell you, he knows everything. At this very moment he must be telling himself that we are like this, part of each other, making love. I can prove it . . .'

She went silent and tightened her hold in an embrace in which the joy of passion was sharpened by resentment. After a tense silence:

'Oh, I hate him! I hate him!'

Jacques was surprised. He personally had nothing against Roubaud. He found him most accommodating.

'Really! Why? He doesn't worry us much.'

She didn't answer him, but repeated:

'I hate him. It's a torture now to feel him near me. Oh, if only I could, I'd run away and stay with you!'

He was moved again by this outburst of passionate love and held her still closer until he had her against his flesh from feet to shoulders, all his. But once again, as she lay snuggled up like this and hardly taking her lips from his neck, she whispered:

'But, my darling, you don't realize . . .'

She was coming round to the confession again, fatally, inevitably. And this time he understood quite clearly that nothing on earth could hold it back, for it was bound up with her frantic

224

desire to be taken again and to be possessed. Not a breath could be heard in the building now, even the bookstall woman must be fast asleep. Out there, Paris was snowbound, without a single rumbling cart, buried, shrouded in silence, and the last train for Le Havre, which had left at 12.20, seemed to have carried off the last bit of life in the station. The stove had stopped roaring and the fire had burned through into red-hot cinders, which made the round patch on the ceiling redder than ever, like an eye staring in terror. It was so hot that a heavy, stifling mist seemed to be weighing down on the bed in which the two lay with limbs entwined in ecstasy.

'Darling, you don't know . . .'

Then he too was compelled to speak.

'Yes, yes, I do know.'

'No, you may have your suspicions, but you can't know!'

'I know he did it for the legacy.'

She started, and laughed nervously in spite of herself.

'Oh yes, the legacy.'

Very softly, so softly that a nocturnal insect buzzing against the window-panes would have made more noise, she told him about her childhood in President Grandmorin's home, wanted to prevaricate and not admit her connection with him, but then gave in to the necessity for frankness and found relief, almost pleasure, in telling everything. Once started, her low, murmuring tale went on like an endless stream.

'Now just think, it was here in this room, last February, you remember, when he had that business with the Sub Prefect . . . We had a nice meal together, just like we have had supper, on that table. Of course he didn't know anything about it, I hadn't gone out of my way to tell him that story! And then all of a sudden, about a ring, a present I had been given long ago, nothing at all, and I don't know how, he saw everything. Oh my dearest, no, no, you can't imagine how he treated me!'

A shudder ran through her and he felt her little hands clawing at his bare skin.

'He knocked me down on the floor with his fist . . . And then dragged me along by the hair. Then he raised his foot over my face as if he wanted to crush it. No, I shall remember it as long as I live . . . And blows, my God! But if I were to tell you all the questions he asked and what he forced me to tell him! You see I'm being honest with you because I'm telling you these things when there's nothing to compel me, is there? I shall never dare to give you even the slightest idea of the disgusting questions I had to answer because I'm sure he would have killed me if I hadn't. I suppose he loved me and must have been terribly upset when he heard all this, and I admit I might have acted a bit more honestly if I had told him before we were married. Only you must realize that it was all long past and forgotten. Only a real savage could go as insane with jealousy as all that . . . And what about you, my dearest, aren't you going to love me any more because you know this now?'

Entwined by a woman's arms tightening round his neck and lower body like coils of a snake, Jacques lay quite still, inert, thinking. He was very surprised, for no suspicion of such a story had ever entered his head. How complicated it was all getting when the legacy would have done as an explanation! Yet he preferred it like this, and the certainty that the couple had not killed for money took away a feeling of contempt which he had sometimes been half conscious of even during Séverine's embraces.

'Not going to love you any more? Me! Why? I couldn't care less about your past. It isn't my business . . . You are Roubaud's wife, but you might just as well have been somebody else's.'

There was a silence. They almost crushed each other to death in an embrace, and he felt her round, hard, swelling breasts against his body.

'So you were the mistress of that old chap! Seems funny, somehow.'

She dragged herself along his body up to his mouth, and whispered while she kissed him:

'You're the only one I love, and I have never loved anyone else but you. As for those others, if you only knew! You see, with them I didn't even know what it could be like, but you, beloved, you make me so happy!'

Her caresses were arousing him as she offered herself, wanting him and drawing him to her with groping hands. So as not to yield at once, though his own passion was as hot as hers, he had to restrain her with all his strength.

226

'No, no, in a minute . . . Well, what about the old chap?'

Very quietly, with a shiver that ran through her whole being, she confessed:

'Yes, we killed him.'

The thrill of desire lost itself in another shudder, that of death which had come back to her. As in the depths of all sensual pleasure, agony came back. For a moment she was overcome by a creeping sensation of vertigo. Then once again burying her nose in her lover's neck, she went on in the same whispering voice:

'He made me write to the President, telling him to leave on the express at the same time as us, and not let himself be seen until Rouen . . . I sat in my corner trembling with fright and thinking about the horror we were going into. And opposite me there was a woman in black who never said a word and frightened me to death. Even without looking at her I imagined that she was reading quite clearly inside our heads and knew perfectly well what we intended to do . . . So the two hours from Paris to Rouen went by, and I did not move, keeping my eyes shut to make her think I was asleep. By my side I could feel him also motionless, and what terrified me was that I knew the dreadful plans he was turning over in his mind, yet couldn't work out exactly what he was resolved to do. Oh, what a journey that was, with all these thoughts going round and round in the whistling, the jolting and the rumbling of the wheels!'

Jacques's mouth was in her thick, perfumed hair, which he kissed regularly with long, absent-minded kisses.

'But if you weren't in the same compartment, how did you manage to kill him?'

'Just a minute, you'll see . . . That was my husband's plan. It's true that his pulling it off was a matter of lucky chance . . . There was a ten-minute stop at Rouen, we got out and he forced me to walk along as far as the President's reserved compartment as though we were stretching our legs. Having got there he pretended to be surprised at seeing him looking out of the window, as though he didn't know he was on the train. On the platform there was a great deal of bustling about, and crowds of people were storming the second-classes because of the holiday at Le Havre the next day. When they began to shut

227

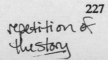
repetition of the story

the doors, the President himself asked us to go in with him. I hesitated and said something about our suitcase, but he wouldn't take no for answer, and said that nobody would steal it for sure, and we could go back to our own compartment at Barentin because he was getting out there. For an instant my husband looked worried as if he wanted to go and fetch it. But at that moment the guard was blowing his whistle, and so he made up his mind, pushed me into the compartment, got in himself and shut the door and the window. How was it that we weren't seen? That's what I still can't make out. Lots of people were running about and the porters were in a flurry, but anyway not a single witness turned up who had seen anything clearly. And so the train steamed slowly out of the station.'

She stopped speaking for a few seconds, living the scene over again. Her limbs were so out of control that, without her realizing it, her left leg developed a tremor that made it rub up and down against one of his knees.

'Oh, that first moment in the coupé, when I realized that the train was moving! I was distracted, and at first the only thing I could think about was our case, and how could we get hold of it? And wasn't it going to give us away if we left it there? The whole thing looked to me stupid and impossible, a nightmare murder thought up by a child which it would be madness to carry out. The very next day we should be arrested and convicted. So I tried to reassure myself with the thought that my husband would never go through with it, that it wouldn't and couldn't happen. But no, just from the way he was talking to the President, I knew that his resolve was fierce and unshakeable. Yet he was still quite calm and was even chatting gaily in his usual way, and it must have been only the look in his eye, sometimes directed at me, that told me that his determination was inflexible. He would kill him a kilometre further on, or perhaps two, at the exact spot he had planned and that I didn't know – that was certain, perfectly obvious from the confident glances he threw at the other man who in a few minutes' time would cease to live. I said nothing, but was struggling to conceal my inner ferment by putting on a smile whenever one of them looked at me. Then why didn't I even dream of preventing it? It was only later, when I tried to sort it all out, that I was

228

amazed that I didn't scream out of the window or pull the alarm signal. At that moment I was paralysed and felt totally power-less. Of course my husband seemed to have right on his side; and to tell you everything, dearest, I must confess this too, that in spite of myself I was wholeheartedly on his side and against the other man because, well, they had both had me, hadn't they? But he was young, while the other – oh, the love-making of that man! Anyway, who can say? You do things you never believed you could. When I think that I wouldn't dare to bleed a chicken! Oh the horror of that night of storm that seemed to be raging inside me!'

This fragile creature, so slender in his arms, now appeared to him impenetrable, a bottomless pit of darkness, as she herself put it. However close he held her, he could not really get to her. This tale of murder, blurted out in their love-making, brought him to fever-pitch.

'Tell me, did you help him kill the old man?'

'I was in a corner,' she went on, without answering his ques-tion, 'my husband was between me and the President, who was in the other corner.* They were chatting about the coming elec-tions. Occasionally I saw my husband lean forward and look out of the window to make sure where we were, as though he were impatient. Each time I followed his glance and so I too knew how far we had got. It was a light night, and the black masses of trees rushed madly by. And the continuous thunder of the wheels – I have never heard a sound like that, an awful tumult of demented, whining voices, the lugubrious wailing of wild beasts howling for slaughter! The train was running at full speed. Suddenly there were lights and the louder noise of the train as it ran between station buildings. We were at Maromme, already two and a half leagues from Rouen. Next Malaunay, and then Barentin. Where was it going to happen? Was it necessary to wait until the last minute! I had lost my sense of time and distance, and was letting myself go, like a falling stone, into the deadening drop through the shadows, when, as we went through Malaunay, I suddenly understood. The thing

---

* A coupé compartment (non-corridor) would have a seat on one side only. Séverine would occupy one window-seat, Grandmorin the other, with Roubaud between.

229

would be done in the tunnel, one kilometre further on. I turned towards my husband and our eyes met – yes, in the tunnel, two minutes more. The train was running fast, the junction for Dieppe had been left behind, and I had noticed the pointsman. There are some hills there, and I thought I could clearly see men standing with raised arms, cursing us. Then the engine gave a long whistle; it was the mouth of the tunnel. As the train plunged in, what a din it made under that low roof! You know, a clanking of iron like the clanging tattoo of hammers on the anvil, and in that instant of panic it sounded to me like peals of thunder.'

She was shivering now, and broke off to say in quite a different voice, almost gaily:

'Isn't it silly, darling, to feel all chilled to the bone even now! And yet I'm lovely and warm with you, and so happy! And besides, you know, there's nothing at all to be afraid of now. The case has been shelved, to say nothing of the fact that all the bigwigs in the government are even less inclined to drag the whole thing up than we are ... Oh, I have seen how things stand, and I'm not bothered.'

Then she laughed outright, and went on:

'Now you're the one who can boast of giving us a real fright! And tell me, I've always wondered about it ... What exactly did you see?'

'What I told the judge, and nothing else. One man stabbing another ... You both behaved in such a funny way with me that I came to have my suspicions in the end ... One moment I even recognized your husband, but it was only later that I was absolutely sure.'

She chipped in gaily:

'Yes, in the Square, when I said no, you remember? The first time we were alone together in Paris ... Isn't it funny? I told you it wasn't us, and knew perfectly well that you realized it was. It was just as if I'd told you all about it, wasn't it? Yes, beloved, I've often thought about that, and I really think it was from that day that I loved you.'

Once again they crushed each other so tightly that they seemed to melt into each other. She took up the tale again:

'The train was rushing through the tunnel. It's a very long

one, and it takes three minutes to go through, but I felt we had been in it for an hour ... The President had stopped talking because of the deafening din of clanking metal. At that last moment my husband's nerve must have failed for a second, for still he did not move. All I did notice in the fitful lamplight was that his ears were going red. Was he going to wait until we were out in open country again? From this point onwards I could see the thing as predestined, so inevitable, that I had only one desire: to get out of this agony of waiting and be finished with it. Why didn't he kill him, then, since he had to? I would have taken the knife myself to get it over, I was in such a state of fear and torture. He looked at me. It must have shown on my face. Then he suddenly threw himself at the President and seized him by the shoulders as he was facing the door. The latter, startled, instinctively jerked himself free and reached for the alarm signal just above his head. He touched it, but was pulled back and thrown on to the seat with such force that he was almost bent double. His mouth was gaping with surprise and panic, and he was uttering inarticulate cries that were drowned by the noise, while I distinctly heard my husband repeating the word: "Swine! Swine! Swine!" in a furious, hissing voice. Then the noise suddenly abated, the train was leaving the tunnel, the dim country-side reappeared with the black trees rushing by. I had stayed in my corner, numbed and pressing against the upholstery as far away as possible. How long did the struggle last? A few seconds at the most, yet it seemed to me that it would never end and that everybody in the train was now listening to the cries and that the trees were watching. My husband had his knife open but could not strike because he was kept at a distance by kicks, and was lurching about on the moving floor of the carriage. He nearly fell on to his knees, and the train was still travelling at full speed, and the engine was whistling as it approached the level crossing at La Croix-de-Maufras ... It was then, and I have never been able to remember since how it happened, that I threw myself on to the legs of the struggling man. Yes, I fell just like a bundle, crushing his legs with all my weight so that he could not move them. And I didn't see anything, but felt it all, the impact of the knife in his neck, the long tremor of the body, and death in three hiccuping gasps, like the spring of a clock

231

breaking ... Oh, I can still feel a sort of echo of his death-struggle in my own limbs!'

Jacques, full of curiosity, wanted to break in with questions, but now she was in a hurry to finish her story.

'No, wait a minute ... As I was getting up again we were passing La Croix-de-Maufras at full speed. I distinctly saw the closed shutters of the house and then the level-crossing hut. Four kilometres to Barentin, five minutes at the outside. The body was bent over on the seat and the blood was running down into a thick puddle. My husband was standing there stupidly, swinging to and fro with the movement of the train, staring while wiping the knife with his handkerchief. All this lasted a minute, and neither of us did anything to help ourselves. If we kept that body with us and stayed there, everything would perhaps be discovered at Barentin ... But then he put the knife back in his pocket and seemed to wake up. I saw him search the body, taking the watch, the money and everything he could find, and then he opened the door and struggled to push it out on the line without taking it into his arms for fear of the blood. "Come on, give us a hand, push with me!" I didn't even try, I felt numb all over. "For Christ's sake, will you give a push with me!" The head, which went out first, was hanging down as far as the footboard while the trunk, which was bent double, wouldn't go through. And still the train went on. In the end a harder shove tipped the body over and it disappeared into the roaring of the wheels. "So much for him, the swine!" Then he picked up the travelling-rug and threw that out as well. So the two of us were left standing there, with the puddle of blood on the seat where we dared not sit down. The open door was still banging to and fro, and at first, in my half-fainting panic-stricken state, I did not understand when I saw my husband get out and disappear down there as well. He came back. "Quick, follow me if you don't want us both to be for the guillotine!" Still I didn't move, and he was losing his temper. "Come on, for God's sake. Our compartment's empty, we'll get back there!" Our compartment empty? Had he been there to see? Was it certain that the woman in black, who said nothing and wasn't noticed, was not still in her corner? "Will you come, or I'll bloody well chuck you out on the line like the other one!" He

232

had climbed up again and was pushing me in a brutal, insane way. I found myself outside, on the footboard clinging with both hands to the brass handrail. He had followed me out and carefully shut the door. "Go on! Go on!" But I daren't, what with being carried along in a headlong course and lashed by the wind blowing like a hurricane. My hair came down, and I thought my stiff fingers were going to let go of the rail. "Go on, for Christ's sake!" He kept pushing me along and I had to go, hand over hand, keeping close to the carriages, and my skirts flying and flapping caught round my legs. Already the lights of Barentin station could be seen in the distance, round a curve. The engine began whistling. "Go on, for God's sake!" What a hellish row and violent shaking I was struggling through! I felt as though a storm had taken me up and was whirling me about like a wisp of straw before smashing me against some wall. Behind my back the country was going by and the trees, pursuing each other in their mad stampede, twisted round on themselves and uttered a little moan as they flashed by. At the end of the carriage, when I had to step across the gap to get to the footboard of the next one and seize the next handrail, I stopped. My nerve had gone, I should never have the strength. "Go on, go on!" He was right behind me and shoving me, and I shut my eyes. I don't know how I went on, except by instinct, like an animal that has dug its claws in so as not to fall. And how came it that we weren't seen? We went along past three carriages, and one of them, a second class, was quite crammed with people. I can remember the rows of heads in the lamplight, and I think I should recognize them if I saw them again some day – there was a fat man with red whiskers, and two girls leaning forward, giggling. "Get on, for Christ's sake, get on!" I don't know anything more, the lights of Barentin were getting closer, the engine was whistling, and the last thing I was conscious of was being dragged along, willy-nilly, by the hair. My husband must have taken hold of me, opened the door above my shoulders and thrown me into the compartment. When we stopped I was there half conscious in a corner, grasping for breath. I did not move, but heard him exchanging a few words with the stationmaster at Barentin. Then as soon as the train started again he fell on to the seat, exhausted as well. We neither of us opened our mouths all the way to Le Havre ... Oh, I hate him! I hate him for all these foul things he has made me go through, can't you see? And I love you, my dearest, you give me so much happiness!'

After the increasing excitement of this long story, her cry marked as it were the full blossoming of her need for joy amid the horror of her memories. But Jacques had been deeply affected by her tale, and was now as tense as she was. He wanted still more from her.

'No, no, just a minute ... You were lying flat across his legs and you actually felt him die?'

Deep within him the mystery was being revealed, and a fierce wave rose from his vitals and flooded his head with a blood-red vision. His curiosity about murder had seized him afresh.

'Well, what about the knife? Did you feel the knife go in?'

'Yes, just a thud.'

'A thud? Not a sudden rending, you're sure?'

'No, nothing except an impact.'

'And then did he have a spasm?'

'Yes, three spasms – oh, from end to end of his body, and they went on so long that I followed them right down to his feet.'

'Spasms that made him go stiff, were they?'

'Yes, the first was very violent and the two others weaker.'

'And then he died, and what effect did it have on you, feeling him die like that of a stab wound?'

'On me! Oh, I don't know.'

'You don't know? Why aren't you telling me the truth? Tell me how it affected you, be honest. Did it upset you?'

'No, no, not exactly upset.'

'Did it give you pleasure?'

'Pleasure? Oh no, not pleasure!'

'Well then, what, my love? Please tell me everything ... If only you knew why ... Tell me what it feels like.'

'Good Lord, how can you say? It's horrible, yet it carries you away, such a long, long way! I lived more in that minute than in the whole of my previous life.'

With clenched teeth and uttering nothing but groans, Jacques took her, and she took him as well. They possessed each other, finding love in death itself with the same agonizing pleasure as

234

beasts disembowelling each other in mating. Only their hoarse gasps could be heard. The bloody light had gone from the ceiling, and now that the stove had gone out the room was getting chilly because of the great frost outside. No sound came up to them from Paris muffled with snow. For a moment snores had come from the woman in the room next door. Then everything had sunk into the black pit of the sleeping building.

Jacques, who had kept Séverine in his arms, felt her give in to invincible sleepiness as though suddenly struck down. The journey, the long wait in the Misards' house and this night of passion had overwhelmed her. She muttered a babyish good-night and was immediately asleep and breathing peacefully. The cuckoo had just struck three.

For nearly another hour Jacques let her lie on his left arm, which was gradually going dead. He could not keep his eyes closed, for an invisible hand seemed to open them again in the darkness. Now he couldn't make anything out in the room full of blackness, in which everything had vanished, stove, furniture, walls, and he had to turn round to find the two lighter squares of window, immobile and faint as a dream. For all his overwhelming fatigue, his mind was prodigiously active and kept him at fever pitch, constantly unravelling the same tangle of ideas. Each time that, by an effort of will-power, he thought he was on the point of dropping off, the same haunting vision came back, the same pictures followed each other and awakened the same sensations. The scene which played itself out with mechanical regularity while his staring eyes saw nothing but blackness was the murder, detail by detail. It always rose up again, identical, obsessive, maddening. The knife went into the throat with a soft thud, the body had three long spasms and life ebbed away in a stream of warm blood, a red stream he thought he could feel running on to his hands. Twenty times, thirty times, the knife went in, the body jerked. The thing was becoming gigantic, stifling him, bursting asunder and dispelling the night. Oh to deliver a stab like that and satisfy this old, old desire to know what it feels like and savour that minute in which you are more alive than in a whole lifetime!

As his stifling feeling grew Jacques thought it was only the weight of Séverine on his arm that was preventing his getting to sleep. Very gently he freed himself and laid her next to him without waking her. Relieved at first, he breathed more freely, thinking that sleep was coming at last. But in spite of his efforts the invisible fingers prised his lids open again, and in the blackness the murder scene reappeared blood-red, the knife went in, the body twitched. A wound streaked through the shadows, the cut in the throat, huge and gaping like a wedge-shaped notch made by an axe. Then he gave up the struggle and stayed on his back, plagued by this persistent vision. He could hear his brain working at high pressure, the grinding of the whole machine. It went right back to his early youth. Yet he had thought he was cured, for this craving had been dead for months, since he had possessed this woman, but he had never known it so intense as it was now, thanks to the tale of this murder that she had been whispering to him, clasped against his flesh and entwined with his limbs. He had moved away, avoiding her touch, seared by the slightest contact with her skin. Unbearable heat ran up his spine as if the mattress under him had turned into live coals. The back of his neck was being pricked with needles like points of fire. For a minute he tried having his hands outside the bed-clothes, but they froze at once and made him shiver. His own hands filled him with panic, so he put them inside again, first clasping them on his stomach, but finally slipping them under his buttocks and holding them crushed and imprisoned there, as if terrified of some horrible outrage on their part, an act he did not mean to do, but did all the same.

Every time the cuckoo struck the hour Jacques counted. Four, five, six. He longed for daylight, hoping that dawn would dispel this nightmare. So he turned and faced the window, looking for the panes. But there was still nothing there but the faint reflection of the snow. At a quarter to five with a delay of only forty minutes, he had heard the semi-fast in from Le Havre, which proved that through running must have been re-established. It was not until after seven that he saw the windows lighten with a milky pallor, very gradually. At last the room grew lighter, with that dim light in which furniture seems to be floating. The stove reappeared, and the cupboard and the sideboard. He still could not close his eyes, but on the contrary they were beginning to hurt with trying to see. All of a sudden, before it was really light enough, he had guessed rather than seen that the knife he had used last night to cut the cake was there on the table, and from that moment onwards all he could see was that knife, a little knife with a pointed blade. The growing daylight, all the white light from the two windows, was now only coming into the room in order to be reflected in that thin blade. Terror of his hands made him thrust them still more firmly under his body, for he could feel them fidgeting, rebelling, stronger than his will. Were they going to act on their own? Hands that must come to him from somebody else, hands passed down by some ancestor from the time when man strangled wild beasts in the forest?

So as not to see the knife, Jacques turned towards Séverine. She was sleeping so peacefully, breathing like a child in her exhaustion. Her thick black hair was loose down to her shoulders, making a dark pillow, and he could see below her chin, through the curls, her breast, delicate, milk-white, scarcely tinged with pink. He studied her as though she were a stranger, yet he still worshipped her, and wherever he went the vision of her was never absent; it was a desire for her that was often agonizing, even when he was driving his engine, and to such a degree that one day he had woken up as from a dream just as he was going through a station at full speed against the signals. But now the sight of this white breast seized his whole attention with a sudden, inexorable fascination and, with a revulsion he still consciously realized, he felt an imperious need rising in him to get the knife from the table and come back and plunge it to the hilt into this woman-flesh. He could hear the soft thud of the blade going in, see the body jerk three times and then stiffen in death, with a gush of red. With every second, as he struggled and tried to tear himself free from this obsession, he was losing a little of his will-power, taken over, as it were, by the fixed idea, the extreme limit beyond which a man is defeated and surrenders to the urges of instinct. Everything became confused, and his rebelling hands, winning over his efforts to keep them hidden, unclasped themselves and escaped. He saw so clearly that from then on he was no longer in control of them and that they would brutally have their way if he went on looking at Séverine, that he used his last bit of strength to leap out of bed, and he rolled on to the floor like a drunken man. He picked himself up, but nearly fell again as he caught his feet in her underclothes left on the floor. He reeled about, desperately looking for his own clothes, the only thought in his mind being to get dressed quickly, take the knife and go and kill some other woman in the street. His desire was now too much of a torment and he had to kill one. He could not find his trousers, touched them three times before being sure he had them. His shoes took him endless trouble to put on. Although it was now broad daylight the room seemed full of a ruddy mist, like dawn on a freezing, foggy day in which everything merged into everything else. Shaking feverishly, he was at last dressed, had taken the knife and concealed it up his sleeve, resolved to kill a woman, the first one he met on the pavement, when a rustling of bedclothes and a prolonged sigh from the bed rooted him there by the table, his face draining of colour.

Séverine was waking up.

'What's up, darling? Going out already?'

He neither answered nor looked at her, hoping she would drop off to sleep again.

'Where are you off to, dear?'

'Oh, nothing,' he muttered, 'just duty ... Go to sleep, I'm coming back.'

Her words became confused as drowsiness overtook her, and her eyes were already closed again.

'Oh, I'm so sleepy, so sleepy. Come and kiss me good-bye, darling.'

But he did not move, knowing full well that if he turned round with the knife in his hand, if he even saw her again, nude and dishevelled yet so dainty and pretty, it was all up with the will-power that was keeping him motionless there beside her. His hand would go up in spite of himself and plunge the knife into her neck.

'Give me a kiss, dearest.'

Her voice tailed off and she went back to sleep, gently, with a loving word. In desperation, he opened the door and fled.

It was eight o'clock when Jacques found himself on the pavement in the rue d'Amsterdam. The snow had not yet been cleared away and the footsteps of the few people about could

238

scarcely be heard. He suddenly caught sight of an elderly woman, but she turned the corner into the rue de Londres and he did not follow her. Various men jostled him, and he went down towards the Place du Havre, gripping the knife with the blade up his sleeve. As a girl of about fourteen came out of a building opposite he crossed the road, but only to see her disappear into a baker's shop next door. Such was his eagerness that he did not wait for her to come out, but went on hunting further down the road. Since he had left the room with the knife it was no longer he himself acting but the other man, the one he had so often felt stirring in the depths of his being, the unknown man from far back, burning with his hereditary lust for blood. He had killed long ago and he wanted to kill again. Things round Jacques now only existed in a dream world, for he saw them through his obsession. His everyday life seemed to be non-existent, and he was moving like a sleepwalker, with no recollection of the past, no concern for the future, wholly given up to his obsessive need. His body moved along, but his personality was not there. Two women who brushed against him as they overtook him made him quicken his pace, and he was catching up with them when a man stopped them. The three of them chatted and laughed. As this man had foiled him he began to follow another woman, a swarthy, miserable-looking woman, poverty-stricken under her thin shawl. She was walking very slowly, probably going to some hated job, hard and badly paid, for she was in no hurry and her face looked desperately sad. Neither was he in a hurry now that he had got one, but waited to choose the right place to strike her down at his ease. She no doubt realized that this fellow was following her, and her eyes turned towards him with indescribable sadness, amazed that anyone should want her. Already she had led him half way along the rue du Havre, and she turned round twice more, each time preventing him from planting the knife, which he had out ready, into her neck. Her poor eyes were so imploring! When she stepped off the pavement, just there, he would strike. But then suddenly he turned round and began to pursue another woman going the opposite way, and this for no reason at all and not because he wanted to, but simply because she was passing at that moment and it was so.

Following her, Jacques came back to the station. She was walking at a brisk pace and her footsteps went tap-tapping along; she was adorably pretty, twenty, if that, with a plump figure already, fair, and her merry eyes laughed with the joy of life. She did not even notice that there was a young man following her, and must have been in a hurry, for she ran nimbly up the flight of steps of the cour du Havre into the main hall and almost ran along it to get to the suburban booking-office. As she asked for a first-class to Auteuil Jacques bought one too and went with her through the waiting rooms, on to the platform and into the same compartment, where he sat by her side. The train left at once.

'I've got plenty of time,' he thought, 'I'll kill her in a tunnel.'

But opposite them was an elderly lady, the only other passenger to get in, and she recognized the young woman.

'Well, fancy, it's you! Where are you off to so early?'

The other burst out laughing, with a gesture of mock despair.

'You just can't do anything without running into somebody! I hope you won't give me away ... It's my husband's birthday tomorrow, and as soon as he had gone off to the office I fled, and am going to Auteuil to a nurseryman's where he has seen an orchid he is mad to have ... A surprise, you understand!'

The elderly party nodded with kindly interest.

'And baby's all right?'

'The little girl? Oh, she's a real joy! You know I weaned her a week ago. You should just see her eating up her soup! We're all bursting with health, it's scandalous.'

She laughed louder still, showing her white teeth between her blood-red lips. Jacques, who had sat on her right, holding the knife hidden behind his thigh, told himself he would be in a perfect position for striking. He only had to raise his arm and do a half-turn to have her just handy! But in the Batignolles tunnel he was stopped by the thought of her bonnet-strings.

'There's a bow,' he thought, 'that's going to get in my way. I want to be certain.'

The two women were still chattering gaily.

'So you're happy, I can see that.'

'Happy, oh yes, if only I could tell you! It's all like a dream ... Two years ago I was nobody. You remember it wasn't very

240

lively living with my aunt, and not a penny for a dowry. When he used to come I was all of a tremble because I had so fallen in love with him. But he was so handsome, so rich ... And now he's mine, he's my husband, and we have our baby to share! I tell you, it's too much!'

Studying the bow Jacques had seen that below it there was a big gold medallion on a black neckband, and he worked it all out.

'I'll take hold of her neck with my left hand and get the medallion out of the way as I pull her head back, and that'll get her throat bare.'

The train was constantly stopping and starting. There had been short tunnels at Courcelles and Neuilly. Any minute now ... it would only take a second.

'Did you go to the seaside this summer?' went on the old lady.

'Yes, six weeks in Brittany, in a remote spot, a real paradise. Then we spent September in Poitou with my father-in-law, who owns a lot of woodland there.'

'Weren't you going to take something in the South for the winter?'

'Oh yes, we shall be at Cannes about the 15th. We've taken the house. A lovely little garden, facing the sea. We've sent someone on ahead to get everything ready for us ... It isn't that either of us is afraid of the cold, but the sun is so nice. Then we shall be back home in March. Next year we shall stay in Paris. In two years' time, when baby is a big girl, we shall travel. I really don't know, it's one long holiday!'

She was so overflowing with happiness that in her expansive mood she turned to Jacques, an unknown man, and smiled. As she moved, the bow changed its position, the medallion went to one side and he could see her neck, rosy pink with a slight hollow in golden shadow.

Jacques's fingers tightened round the handle of the knife as he came to an irrevocable resolve.

'That's the place where I shall strike. Yes, in a moment, in the tunnel before Passy.'

But at the Trocadero station a railwayman got in who knew him and so began talking shop, about a theft of coal for which they had just convicted a driver and his fireman. From that time onwards everything was confused, and later he was never able

241

to piece the facts together properly. The laughter had gone on, such infectious happiness that he was full of it himself and in a daze. Perhaps he went on as far as Auteuil with the two ladies, only he couldn't remember whether they got out there. He had ended up on the banks of the Seine without knowing how. What he did retain a very clear impression of was having thrown the knife away from the top of the bank, for he had kept it held inside his sleeve. After that he knew no more, he had been bewildered and no longer present at all, but neither was the other man; he had gone with the knife. He must have walked about for hours through the streets and squares, wherever his legs took him. People, houses went by, all blurred. He must have gone somewhere and had some food in some room full of people, for he could distinctly recall white plates. He also had a permanent impression of a red poster on an empty shop. Then everything had subsided into a black chasm, a void where neither time nor space counted any more and he lay inert, for centuries, perhaps.

When he came to himself Jacques was in his tiny room in the rue Cardinet, slumped across his bed fully dressed. Instinct had brought him back there like an exhausted dog dragging itself to its kennel. Nor could he recollect coming up the stairs or going to sleep. He came out of a deep sleep with a shock at suddenly finding himself in full possession of his faculties, as one does after a dead faint. He might have slept for three hours or it might have been three days. Suddenly his memory came back: the night with Séverine, the confession of the murder, his rushing out like a beast of prey thirsty for blood. He had taken leave of his own self, and now he was finding himself again, and was stupefied at the things that had been done independently of his own will. Then he remembered that she would be expecting him, and that made him jump to his feet. He looked at his watch, saw it was already four, and with his mind relieved and quite calm as if he had been thoroughly bled, he hurried back to the Impasse d'Amsterdam.

Séverine had slept soundly until noon. When she woke up she was surprised not to see him still there. Then she lit the stove again and finally dressed, and as she was dying of hunger decided at about two o'clock to go down and have something to eat in a nearby restaurant. When Jacques came back she had just done so herself, having done a bit of shopping.

'Oh my dearest, I was getting so worried!'

She hung on his neck and looked him right in the eyes.

'What on earth happened?'

He was exhausted and his flesh numb, and calmly reassured her without a hint of trouble:

'Oh nothing, just a tiresome duty. Once they've got hold of you they never let you go.'

She lowered her voice, and was very humble and caressing.

'You see I imagined . . . oh, a horrible idea that upset me so! I thought that perhaps after what I had confessed you wouldn't want to have anything more to do with me . . . And so I thought you'd gone and wouldn't come back ever, ever!'

Her tears welled up, and she burst into sobs, clinging wildly to him.

'Oh my darling, if only you knew how I need someone to be kind to me! . . . Love me a lot because, you know, only your love can make me forget. Now I've told you all my troubles you mustn't leave me, must you? Oh, I beg of you!'

Jacques was touched by this emotion and gradually he was forced to relax and soften. He murmured:

'No, no, I love you, don't be afraid.'

In his weak state he broke down and cried too in the face of the fatality of this abominable malady that had caught up with him again and of which he would never be cured. Nothing but shame and despair without end.

'Love me, love me too, with all your strength because I need it as much as you!'

That made her start, and she wanted to know why.

'You have your own troubles, you must tell me.'

'No, no, not troubles, things that don't really exist, fits of depression that make me horribly unhappy, and it isn't even possible to talk about them.'

In their embrace they shared the awful sadness of their trouble. It was just suffering without end, and no possibility of forgetting or being forgiven. They wept together, conscious of the blind forces of life weighing down on them, life which consists of struggle and death.

243

'Come along,' said Jacques, breaking free, 'it's time we thought of going. You'll be back in Le Havre tonight.'

Sombre, staring into space, Séverine eventually murmured:

'If only I were free, if my husband weren't there! Oh, how quickly we could forget!'

With a violent gesture he thought aloud:

'But we can't kill him, can we?'

She looked hard at him, and he shuddered, amazed that he had said such a thing, which had never entered his head before. Since he wanted to kill somebody, why not kill this man who was in the way? As he was setting off to hurry to the sheds she took him into her arms again, covered him with kisses and said:

'Oh my beloved, love me a lot. And I'll love you more and more still. We shall be happy, you'll see!'

[9]

IN Le Havre, during the days immediately following, Jacques and Séverine exercised the utmost prudence, for they were uneasy. As Roubaud knew everything, wouldn't he spy on them, catch them by surprise and wreak a terrible vengeance upon them? They recalled his former jealous rages and the brutality of this ex-labourer who smashed out with his fists, and that was why, seeing him so restrained and quiet, with his furtive eyes, they felt he must be meditating some savage trick or setting some trap by which he would have them in his power. So all through the first month they only saw each other with a thousand precautions and were always on the alert.

Meanwhile Roubaud went out more and more. Perhaps he only disappeared like this in order to come back unexpectedly and catch them in each other's arms. But this fear proved groundless. On the contrary, these absences became so prolonged that he was never at home now, but slipped off as soon as he was free, not coming back until the exact minute when he was due to begin his shift. During his weeks on the day-shift he contrived to eat his ten o'clock lunch in five minutes and then not to reappear before eleven-thirty; and at five in the evening, when his colleague went down to replace him, he cleared out, often for the whole night, and only took the minimum of sleep. It was the same with his weeks on night-shift, when he was free from five in the morning, eating and sleeping out presumably, anyhow not coming in until five in the afternoon. For a long time, in spite of this disorganized life, he had remained a model employee for punctuality, and was always present at the exact time, though sometimes so knocked out that he could hardly stand on his feet, yet still keeping up conscientiously with his job. But recently gaps were beginning to open. On two occasions already Moulin, the other deputy stationmaster, had had to wait an hour, and one morning even, after lunch, hearing that he had not shown up, he had gone, decent fellow that he was, and stood in for him to save him from being reprimanded. All Roubaud's work was beginning to show signs of this steady disorganization. In the daytime he was no longer the active man, never dispatching or accepting a train unless he had inspected everything with his own eyes, and entering the smallest details in his report to the stationmaster, equally severe with others as with himself. At night he slept like a log in his big armchair in his office. In his waking hours he still seemed to be asleep, and wandered up and down the platform, hands behind his back, giving orders in an expressionless voice, but not seeing whether they were carried out. But still everything went on all right through force of habit, except for a collision due to negligence on his part, when a passenger train was switched into a siding. His colleagues merely laughed, saying he was sowing his wild oats.

The truth of the matter was that Roubaud was now virtually living on the first floor of the Café du Commerce, in the little private room that had gradually become a gambling den. It was said that women went there every night, but in reality only one woman would have been found there, and she was the mistress of a retired sea captain, was forty at least and herself an inveterate gambler and quite sexless. The only passion Roubaud satisfied there was the dreary one for gambling, which had developed in him immediately after the murder through the sheer chance of a game of piquet, and since then it had grown into a tyrannical habit for the sake of the change and utter oblivion it brought him. It had taken him over to the point of removing all desire for women from this bestial male, and henceforth held him completely in its grip as the only satisfaction through which he could find happiness. It was not that remorse had ever tormented him with a longing for forgetfulness, but in the upheaval that was breaking up his home life, and in the midst of his shattered existence, he had found consolation and forgetfulness in the self-indulgence he could enjoy on his own. And now everything was going to pieces thanks to this passion which was bringing total demoralization. Even drink could not have given him more carefree hours that went by with such swiftness and sense of liberation. He had even ceased caring about life itself, and seemed to be living with extraordinary intensity, and

246

none of the vexations that formerly drove him wild seemed to touch him any more. He was physically very fit and well, apart from getting tired from bad nights, and was even putting on weight, rather lumpy, pasty fat, his heavy lids drooping over lack-lustre eyes. When he did come home with sluggish, sleepy movements, all he brought in was complete indifference to everything.

On the night when Roubaud had come home to get the three hundred gold francs from under the floor, it was because he wanted to pay M. Cauche, the superintendent, after several losses in succession. M. Cauche had the self-possession of a seasoned gambler, which made him formidable. Of course he said he only played for the fun of it, being obliged by his legal status to keep up the appearance of a retired military man. He had never married, and lived at the café as a regular inmate, which did not prevent his playing cards the whole evening and pocketing all the money of the others. Rumours had circulated about him, accusing him also of being so negligent in his duty that there was talk of his being forced to resign. But things dragged on, and as there was so little to do why insist upon greater zeal? And he still contented himself with putting in a momentary appearance on the platforms, where everyone respectfully nodded to him.

Three weeks later Roubaud still owed M. Cauche nearly four hundred francs. He had explained that his wife's legacy had made them comfortably off, but had added jokingly that she held the purse-strings, which excused his tardiness in settling his gambling debts. Then one morning when he was alone and feeling hard pressed he lifted the floor again and took a thousand-franc note out of the hiding-place. He was all of a tremble, and had not felt anything like as upset on the night he took the gold coins. Of course that had only seemed to him like some loose change; but with the note real theft began. He felt on edge when he thought of this sacrosanct money which he had vowed never to touch. Then he had sworn that he would die of hunger rather than do that, and yet now he was touching it, and he couldn't say how his scruples had gone – a little each day, presumably, in the steady decay brought about by murder. Deep down the hole he thought he felt something damp, soft and disgusting which

247

gave him the creeps. He quickly replaced the board once more, swearing he would cut his hand off rather than take it up again. His wife had not seen him, and he breathed again in relief and drank a big glass of water to put himself right. His heart now pounded with joy at the thought of paying off his debt and having all that sum to gamble with.

But when it came to changing the note his agony began again. Formerly he had been a brave man, and he would have given himself up had he not been such a fool as to get his wife involved in it, but now the mere thought of the police brought him out in a cold sweat. He knew perfectly well that the authorities did not have the numbers of the missing banknotes, and that anyhow the case had been shelved and was buried for ever in the files, yet he was seized with panic as soon as he was by way of going somewhere to ask for change. For five days he kept the note on him and developed a constant habit of feeling for it, moving it somewhere else and keeping it on him at night. He worked out highly complicated plans, but always came up against unforeseen reasons for fear. First he had thought of the station, why shouldn't a colleague in the booking-office cash it for him? Then that had struck him as extremely dangerous, and he had hit on the idea of going to the other end of the town, without his uniform cap, and buying something. Only wouldn't they be surprised to see him produce such a large sum for some little thing? And in the end he had settled on producing the note at the tobacconist's in the Cours Napoléon where he went every day – wasn't that the simplest thing? They knew he had had a legacy and the woman behind the counter wouldn't be surprised. He went up to the door, his nerve failed him and he went down to the Vauban dock to screw up his courage. After walking about for half an hour he came back, but still could not make up his mind. That evening at the Café du Commerce, as M. Cauche was there, he took out the note in a sudden fit of bravado and asked the hostess to change it for him. But she had no small change and had to send a waiter with it to the tobacconist's. They even joked about the banknote, which looked brand new although dated ten years earlier. The superintendent had a look at it and turned it over, and said that this one must certainly have been sleeping in some hidey-hole, which started

248

the captain's mistress off on some interminable story about a
hidden fortune that had turned up under the marble top of a
commode.

The weeks went by and this money Roubaud possessed excited his passion to fever-pitch. It was not that he played for
high stakes, but he was dogged by such constant and dire bad
luck that each day's small losses totted up into large sums.
Towards the end of the month he found he hadn't a bean left,
owed several louis, but felt quite ill because he dared not touch
another card. Yet he did put up a fight against it, although he
almost had to take to his bed. The knowledge that nine more
banknotes were slumbering there under the living-room floor
was turning into a continual obsession: he could see them
through the boards and feel them burning his feet. To think that
if he wanted to he could take another! But this time he had
sworn that he would rather put his hand into the fire than feel
down there again. And yet one evening when Séverine had gone
to sleep early, he pulled up the floorboard, so furious at giving
in and distracted with such misery that his eyes filled with tears.
What was the good of fighting it like this? It would only mean
pointless suffering, for he realized that he would now take them
one by one, until the last.

Next morning Séverine happened to notice a new scratch
on one edge of a parquet block. She bent down and saw that it
had been wrenched up. Clearly her husband was still taking
money. She was astonished at the fierceness of her own rage, for
she was not normally interested in money, and besides, she too
thought she was determined to die of starvation rather than
touch those bloodstained notes. But weren't they hers just as
much as his? Why was he spending them stealthily without even
consulting her? Until dinner-time she was tormented by the
need to know for certain, and had she not felt a little cold
breath in her hair at the very thought of looking down there she
might have lifted the block herself to find out. Wouldn't the
dead man himself rise up out of that hole? This childish fear
made the room feel so unpleasant that she took her work into
the bedroom and shut herself in.

That evening as they were finishing up some stew without
saying a word, she was infuriated once again as she caught him

249

casting involuntary glances at the join in the parquet flooring.

'You've had some more, haven't you?' she suddenly asked.

He looked up in surprise.

'More what?'

'Oh, don't come the innocent, you know exactly what I mean ... Now listen, I won't have you taking any more, because it's no more yours than mine, and it makes me sick to know you're dipping into it.'

Usually he avoided scenes. Life together now was only the unavoidable contact of two people tied to each other, spending whole days without exchanging a word, coming and going side by side like strangers now indifferent and solitary. So he merely shrugged his shoulders, declining to offer any explanation.

But she was now very worked up, and meant to settle once and for all the matter of this hidden money, which had been tormenting her ever since the day of the crime.

'I insist on an answer ... I dare you to say you haven't touched it!'

'What's it got to do with you?'

'This is what, it makes my stomach turn over. Even today I have been so afraid that I couldn't stay in this room. Every time you move it I get terrible nightmares for three nights ... We never talk about it. So you be quiet and don't force me to talk about it.'

He stared at her with his big unblinking eyes and repeated sulkily:

'What's it got to do with you if I touch it so long as I don't force you to? It's my business, and mine only.'

She suppressed a violent gesture. Then her emotions got the better of her and her face showed pain and disgust:

'Really, I don't undertand you. And yet you used to be an honest man. Yes, you wouldn't ever have taken a sou from anybody. What you did could be forgiven because you were out of your mind, just as you had driven me crazy too! But that money? That horrible money that shouldn't exist for you at all and you are now stealing sou by sou for your pleasures ... What's happening and how can you have sunk so low?'

In a moment of lucidity, as he was listening to her, he was amazed too that he had come down to stealing. The separate

250

phases of his slow degeneration were blurred, and he could not tie up again what the murder had severed all round him, neither could he now explain to himself how a different way of life, almost a new era, had set in, with his home life destroyed and his wife estranged and hostile. But then in a moment the irreparable regained its hold and he made a gesture as if to push tiresome reflections out of the way.

'When you're fed up with home,' he muttered, 'you go and amuse yourself somewhere else. As you don't love me any more . . .'

'Oh no, I certainly don't.'

He stared at her and banged his fist on the table, his face purple with rage:

'All right then, mind your own fucking business! Am I stopping you having your fun? Am I setting myself up as a judge? There's lots of things a decent man would do if he found himself in my shoes, and I'm not doing them. First of all I ought to kick you out of the door with a boot up your arse. Perhaps then I wouldn't be stealing.'

She went white, for the thought had also often occurred to her that when a man of a jealous nature is eaten up by some inner suffering to the extent of tolerating a lover for his wife, that must be a symptom of a creeping moral gangrene killing all other scruples and disorganizing the whole conscience. But she fought on, refusing to be held responsible, and shouted:

'I forbid you to touch that money.'

He had finished eating. He calmly folded his napkin and stood up, saying in a bantering tone:

'If that's what you're after, we'll go halves.'

And already he was stooping as if to raise the wooden block. She had to rush and plant her foot on it.

'No, no! You know I'd rather die! Don't you open that, no, not in front of me!'

That evening Séverine had an arrangement to meet Jacques behind the goods station. When she got home after midnight the evening's scene came back to her, and she locked herself in her room. Roubaud was on night duty, and so there was not even the fear that he would come home to bed as still happened occasionally. She was snugly tucked under the bedclothes, the lamp was left burning low, and yet she could not get to sleep. Why had she refused to share? Now she no longer felt such a strong revulsion from the thought of benefiting from that money. Had she not accepted the legacy of La Croix-de-Maufras? So she could perfectly well take the money as well. But then her shuddering came back. No, no, never! Just money, she might have taken: what she dared not touch for fear of burning her fingers was this money stolen from a dead man, the abominable wages of murder. But then again she calmed herself by reasoning: she would not have taken it to spend, but on the contrary she would have hidden it somewhere else, buried in a place known to her alone, where it would have slept for all eternity. And besides, even now it would be one half of the money saved from her husband's hands. He would not triumph by keeping the lot, he would not gamble with what belonged to her. By the time the clock struck three she was bitterly re-gretting having refused to share. A thought, still hazy and far away, was beginning to come to her: get up, just put a hand under the floor-boards so that he should have no more. But the thought froze her so much that she refused to entertain it. Take the lot, keep it all, and he couldn't even dare to complain! Yet little by little the project won her over, and a determination stronger than her resistance sprang up from the unconscious depths of her being. She didn't mean to, yet she suddenly jumped out of bed, for she couldn't do anything else. She turned up the wick of the lamp and went into the dining-room.

From that moment Séverine lost all her fear. Her terrors had gone and she proceeded coolly, with the slow, precise move-ments of a sleep-walker. She had to find the poker to lever up the board. When the cavity was open she brought up the lamp because she could not see very well. But she was dumbfounded and struck motionless stooping over the hole: it was empty. Clearly, while she was away making love he had come back, seized even before her with the same desire to take the lot and keep the lot, and he had pocketed the banknotes in one go, for not one was left. She knelt down, but could only see right at the back the watch and chain gleaming gold between the dusty joists. Cold fury held her there a moment, stiff, half-naked, saying a score of times:

'Thief! Thief! Thief!'

With a furious movement she seized the watch and disturbed a big, black spider that ran off along the plaster. She replaced the block with her heel and went back to bed, putting the lamp on the bedside table. When she felt warm again she had a look at the watch that she held in her clenched fist, then turned it over and examined it carefully. The President's two initials, intertwined on the case, interested her. Inside she read the figures 2516, a maker's number. It was an extremely dangerous piece to keep, because the police knew that number. But in her anger at having succeeded in saving nothing but that she lost all fear. She even felt that her nightmares were a thing of the past now that there was no corpse under the floor. At last she would walk where she liked in her own home, without any qualms. She slipped the watch under the bolster, put out the lamp and went off to sleep.

The next day being his day off, Jacques was to wait until Roubaud had gone as usual to camp out in the Café du Commerce and then come for a meal with her. Sometimes, when they felt they dared, they gave themselves this treat. That day she was still in an excited state and so she told him during the meal about the money and how she had found the hiding-place empty. She could not get over her resentment against her husband, and the same cry kept coming back:

'Thief! Thief! Thief!'

Then she fetched the watch and insisted on giving it to Jacques in spite of his obvious distaste.

'You must realize, darling, that nobody will look for it in your possession. If I keep it he will get it away from me again. And don't you see, rather than that I'd let him tear a piece of my flesh out. No, he's had too much. I didn't want anything to do with the money. It gave me the horrors and I wouldn't ever have spent a sou of it. But what right had he to benefit from it? Oh, I loathe him!'

She was now in tears and persisting with such supplications that in the end he put the watch in his waistcoat pocket.

An hour went by and Jacques had kept Séverine on his knee, still only half dressed. She was lying back against his shoulder with one arm round his neck in a drowsy caress, when Roubaud, who had his key, came in. She leapt to her feet, but they had been caught in the act and there was no point in denying it. The husband could not ignore it and just stood still while the lover, appalled, stayed sitting there. But she, not even bothering to embark on any explanation, strode forward and repeated in fury:

'Thief! Thief! Thief!'

For a second Roubaud hesitated. Then with the usual shrug of the shoulders with which he pushed everything aside nowadays, he went through to the other room to get an official notebook he had forgotten. But she followed him, letting him have it:

'You've been down there, you dare deny it! And you've taken everything. Thief! Thief! Thief!'

He crossed the living-room without a word. Only when he reached the door did he turn round, give her a bleak stare and say:

'You shut your fucking jaw, see?'

And he was gone, without even banging the door. He didn't appear to have seen, and had made no allusion to this lover sitting there.

After a long silence Séverine turned to Jacques:

'Well, would you believe it?'

He had not so far said a word, but he now stood up and voiced his opinion.

'He's finished!'

They agreed. Their surprise that he should tolerate a lover after murdering another one was followed by disgust for the complaisant husband. When a man comes down to that he is in the mire and can roll into any gutter.

From that day onwards Séverine and Jacques were absolutely free, and they used their freedom without troubling any more about Roubaud. But now that the husband no longer worried them their great anxiety was the spying of the neighbour Mme Lebleu, who was always on the watch. She certainly had her suspicions. However quietly Jacques crept along the passage, every time he came he saw the door opposite opening almost imperceptibly, and an eye watching him through the crack. It was becoming intolerable, and he dared not go up, for if he did his presence was known and an ear came and glued itself to the keyhole, so that they could no longer embrace or even talk to each other freely. So then it was that in exasperation because of this new obstacle to her passion, Séverine renewed her old campaign against the Lebleus to get their flat. It was an established fact that the deputy stationmaster had always had it. But now she was no longer interested in the splendid view from the windows overlooking the main courtyard and the heights of Ingouville. The sole reason for her desire, which she did not mention, was that that flat had a second entrance, a door opening on to the service stairs. Jacques could come and go that way and Mme Lebleu would not even have a suspicion of his visits. They would at last be free.

The battle was terrible. This question, which had already stirred up the passions of the whole corridor, took on a new life and grew more envenomed hour by hour. Feeling herself threatened, Mme Lebleu defended herself desperately, convinced that she would die if she were imprisoned in the black hole at the back, shut in by the station roofing and as dreary as a prison cell. How could she live in such a hole, accustomed as she was to her lovely light room with an open view over the vast horizon, enlivened by the continual bustling to and fro of travellers? And her legs prevented her from ever going out for a walk, and she would never have anything to look at again except a zinc roof – you might as well kill her straight away. Unfortunately all these reasons were purely sentimental, and she was forced to admit that she only had the flat because the previous deputy stationmaster, Roubaud's predecessor, was a bachelor and had let her have it just to be obliging, and there might even be a letter in existence from her husband undertaking to give it back if it was required by a new man. As the letter had not yet turned up she denied its existence. The more hopeless her cause became, the more violent and aggressive she got. At one stage she had tried to get the wife of Moulin, the other deputy, on her side by compromising her and alleging that she, Mme Moulin, had seen men kissing Mme Roubaud on the stairs. Moulin had been very annoyed, for his wife, a meek, insignificant creature whom nobody ever saw, swore with floods of tears that she had never seen anything nor said a word. For a whole week the gossip blew like a hurricane from end to end of the passage. But Mme Lebleu's great mistake, which was bound to lead to her defeat, was to get on the wrong side of Mlle Guichon, the secretary, by her everlasting nosiness. This obsession of hers was a mania, namely that Mlle Guichon went across every night to the stationmaster; and her desire to catch her had become pathological and all the more inflamed because she had been spying on her for two years and had found out absolutely nothing, not even a whisper. Yet she was sure they were sleeping together, and that drove her mad. So Mlle Guichon, furious at never being able to come or go without being spied on, was now throwing her weight on the side of banishing her to the back. In that way there would be a dwelling between them and at any rate she would no longer have her right opposite or be forced to pass her door. It was becoming clear that M. Dabadie, the stationmaster, who had so far remained neutral in this dispute, was getting more hostile to the Lebleus every day, which was a bad sign.

The situation was further complicated by feuds. Philomène, who now brought her new-laid eggs to Séverine, was extremely saucy every time she met Mme Lebleu, and as the latter deliberately left her door open to annoy everybody, there were continual words between the two women every time she went past. This intimacy between Séverine and Philomène had reached the stage of shared secrets, and now Philomène was bringing messages from Jacques to his mistress when he dared not come up himself. She arrived with her eggs, changed meeting-places and times, said why he had had to be careful the day before, told her what he had said when he had stayed at her place for an hour chatting. Sometimes when something prevented his coming Jacques would spend a short time in the Sauvagnats' little house. He went there with his fireman Pecqueux, as if he had to find something to occupy his mind because he was afraid of a whole evening alone. Even when Pecqueux had disappeared for a binge in some sailors' dive, he would call on Philomène, give her a message to take and then sit down and never go. Gradually, as she became involved in this romance, she grew fond of him herself, for the only lovers she had had so far had been oafs. The delicate hands and polite manners of this melancholy fellow, who looked so gentle, appealed to her as luxuries she had not yet sampled. With Pecqueux it was just like being married, with drunken scenes and more cuffs than caresses, while when she delivered some nice message from the driver to the deputy stationmaster's wife, she herself appreciated its delicate flavour, like forbidden fruit. One day she took him into her confidence and groused about the fireman, who was not to be trusted, she said, for all his jovial appearance, and was quite capable of doing something very ugly when he was drunk. Jacques noticed that she was paying more attention to that lanky, dried-up body of hers – she was desirable all the same with those fine passionate eyes – and that she was drinking less and cleaning the house a bit more. Her brother Sauvagnat, hearing a man's voice one evening, had come in with raised fist intending to give her what for, but seeing who was talking to her had simply brought out a bottle of cider. Jacques, feeling himself welcome and quite free there from this trouble of his, seemed to be enjoying himself. So Philomène displayed more and more friendliness to Séverine and inveighed against Mme Lebleu, dismissing her everywhere as a silly old cow.

One night, when she had come across the lovers behind her little garden, she went with them in the dark as far as the shed where they usually hid.

'You know, you are too kind by half. As that flat is yours by right I should drag her out of it by the hair if I were you ... Why don't you give her what for?'

But Jacques was against making a fuss.

'No, no, M. Dabadie is seeing to it, it's best to wait for things to be done properly.'

'Before the month is out,' declared Séverine, 'I shall be sleeping in her bedroom and we can see each other there at any time.'

In spite of the darkness Philomène had been aware of her giving her lover's arm an affectionate squeeze. She left them and made for home, but some thirty steps away, as she could not be seen in the shadows, she stopped and turned round. She felt deeply moved by their being together, and yet she was not jealous but full of a simple desire to be loved like that.

Day by day Jacques grew more depressed. On two occasions

when he could have seen Séverine he made up excuses, and when he dallied in the Sauvagnats' house it was partly to avoid her. Yet he loved her still, and his desire had grown even stronger through frustration. But now in her arms his horrible malady came over him again, and with such madness that he broke away instantly in cold terror of being no longer his real self and of feeling the wild beast in him ready to bite. He had tried tiring himself out with the fatigue of long journeys, asking for extra duties, spending twelve hours at a stretch standing on the footplate, shaken by the vibration, with lungs seared by the wind. His workmates used to grumble about the hardships of the engine-driver's life and said it finished a man off in twenty years, but he would have liked to be finished off at once. He was never exhausted enough and was only happy when Lison was carrying him along and he stopped thinking and had nothing left but eyes for the signals. At the journey's end he was knocked out by sleep before he had even time to clean himself up. Yet with returning consciousness back came the torment of his obsession. He had also tried to revive his old love-affair with Lison, spending hours again cleaning her and demanding from Pecqueux that the steel parts should shine like silver. Along the line inspectors who climbed up on to his footplate congratulated him. But he shook his head and was still dissatisfied, for he was well aware that since the hold-up in the snow she was no longer the fine, valiant engine of old. In the course of repairs to her pistons she had lost something of her soul, that mysterious harmony of life which results from sheer chance in assembly. This falling off caused him pain, and this turned into fretful peevishness and made him plague his superiors with unreasonable complaints, demanding pointless repairs and thinking up unworkable improvements. These were turned down and he grew more disgruntled, being convinced that Lison was very sick and that nothing would ever go right with her again. His love for her was thus discouraged – what was the point of loving, since he was bound to destroy everything he loved? And so he brought to his mistress this frantic, desperate love that neither suffering nor fatigue could assuage.

Séverine had been very conscious of the change in him and she also was very distressed, thinking that he was getting so gloomy because of her, now that he knew. When she saw him shudder in her arms and suddenly recoil to avoid her kiss, wasn't it because he remembered and she filled him with revulsion? She had never dared to raise these things in conversation again. She was now sorry she had told him and amazed at the way she had poured forth her confession in that strange bed in which they had both burned with passion. She did not even recollect her one-time need to confide, but was satisfied now to have him with her, sharing the secret. And she loved him and wanted him more than ever now that there was nothing hidden from him. Her passion was insatiable, she was at last a woman roused, a creature made for love alone, wholly for loving and not for motherhood. She only found life through Jacques, and she was telling nothing but the truth when she said that in her effort to be lost in him she had but one dream, that he might take her with him and keep her as part of his flesh. Always very gentle and passive, getting her pleasure only from him, she would have liked to curl up and sleep on his lap from morn till night. All she had retained from the terrible drama was amazement at having been mixed up in it, just as from the filth of her young days she seemed to have emerged virgin and pure. It was all a long while ago and she just smiled, and would not even have been angry with her husband had he not stood in her way. But her loathing of this man increased as her passion and her need for the other man grew stronger. Now that the other man knew and had absolved her, he was the master, he was the one she would follow and who could dispose of her like a chattel. She had got him to give her a photo of himself, and she took it to bed with her and went to sleep with her lips touching the picture. She had been very unhappy since she had seen how unhappy he was, but had not succeeded in finding out exactly what was upsetting him so.

Meanwhile they continued to meet out of doors while they waited until they could see each other in peace when the new home had been won. Winter was ending and February was very mild. They prolonged their walks for hours through the open ground adjoining the station, for he avoided stopping, and when she clung to him and he was forced to sit down and make love to her he insisted that it must be in the dark, because of his terror of striking if he saw a bit of her bare skin. As long as he did not see her he could resist, he thought. In Paris, where she went with him every Friday, he carefully pulled the curtains to, saying that strong light took away his pleasure. She now made this weekly trip without even giving her husband any explanation. The old pretext of knee trouble was good enough for the neighbours, and she also said that she went to visit her foster-mother, Ma Victoire, whose convalescence at the hospital was dragging on. They both still enjoyed the break thoroughly, he very concerned that day about his engine's behaviour and she overjoyed to see him less depressed and also finding the journey itself full of interest, although she was beginning to know every little hill and clump of trees on the route. From Le Havre to Motteville it was grassland, flat fields with hedges round and dotted with apple-trees; from there as far as Rouen the country became hilly and empty. After Rouen the Seine opened out. They crossed it at Sotteville, Oissel and Pont-de-l'Arche, and then it kept on reappearing, a broad ribbon across the wide plains. By the time they reached Gaillon they were never away from it, as it flowed to their left, slower now between its low banks lined with poplars and willows. The line ran at the foot of the slopes and only left the river at Bonnières, to find it again on suddenly emerging from the Rolleboise tunnel at Rosny. The river was like a friendly travelling companion. Three more times they crossed it before the journey's end. On past Mantes with its church tower in the trees, Triel with the whitish scars of its chalkpits, Poissy that the line cut right in half, the two green walls of the forest of Saint-Germain, the slopes of Colombes with their profusion of lilacs, and at last the outer suburbs, with Paris hinted at, then glimpsed from the bridge at Asnières, the distant Arc de Triomphe rising above the shabby buildings and factory chimneys. The engine dived under the Batignolles and then you got out into the din of the station. And from then until evening they belonged to each other and were free. On the return journey it was dark, and she shut her eyes and lived through her joy all over again. But, morning or night, every time she went past La Croix-de-Maufras she leaned forward and looked carefully, without letting herself be seen, for she was certain to find Flore standing there at the level-crossing gate, holding her flag in its case and examining the train with blazing eyes.

Since this girl had seen them kiss each other on the day of the blizzard Jacques had warned Séverine to beware of her. He now realized the depth of the wild youthful passion with which she pursued him, and he sensed that her fierce, almost masculine jealousy was uncontrollable and murderous in its resentment. What was more, she must know many things, for he recalled her alluding to the relationship between the President and a young person nobody suspected, whom he had married off. If she knew that she would surely have guessed the truth about the murder, and maybe she was going to talk or write of what she knew, take her revenge by a denunciation. But days and weeks had gone by and nothing was happening, and all he saw of her was that she was always stationed at her post beside the line with her flag, standing at attention. From the far distance when she caught sight of the engine he felt her blazing eyes fixed on him. She saw him through all the smoke, and took in his whole body, followed him through the lightning speed and thunderous roar of the wheels. And at the same time the train was scrutinized, looked right through and searched from the first carriage to the last. And she always found where the other woman was, the rival she now knew was always there on Fridays. This other woman might well only lean her head slightly forward out of an irresistible urge to peep: she was seen, and their glances crossed like swords. Already the train had gone tearing past, and one of the two stood there on the ground, powerless to follow it in her fury at the happiness it was bearing away. She seemed to grow, to Jacques she seemed taller on each trip, and now he was uneasy because she was doing nothing, and wondered what scheme was going to be hatched in the mind of this tall, menacing creature, whose motionless presence he could not avoid.

There was another railway employee too who worried Séverine and Jacques, the guard Henri Dauvergne. He happened to be working the Friday train, and he was pestering her with his attentions. Having noticed her affair with the driver, he told himself that his turn would come too, perhaps. When the train left Le Havre on days when he was on duty, Roubaud laughed about it, so obvious were Henri's attentions becoming — he reserved a whole compartment for her, made her comfortable, tested the foot-warmer. There was even a day when the husband, while quietly chatting to Jacques, had pointed out the young man's tricks with a wink as though asking him whether he would allow that sort of thing. Anyway, when he and his wife had a row he accused her flatly of sleeping with both of them. For a moment the thought had run through her mind that Jacques believed that too, and that that was why he was so distant. In a fit of weeping she had protested her innocence and told him to kill her if she was unfaithful. He had changed colour, but laughed it off with a kiss and answered that he knew she was faithful and certainly hoped he'd never kill anybody.

The first few evenings in March were terrible and they had to suspend their meetings. The trips to Paris and the few hours of much longed-for freedom were no longer enough for Séverine. She was possessed by a growing need to have Jacques to herself and wholly hers, for them to live together day and night and never be parted again. Her loathing for her husband intensified, and the mere presence of the man threw her into unbearable nervous irritation. This affectionate woman, so meek and compliant, lost her temper over anything to do with him and flew into a rage over any obstacle he put in the way of her desires. At such times it seemed as though the shadow of her black hair darkened the limpid blue of her eyes. She turned into a shrew and accused him of poisoning her whole existence, to such an extent that life together became impossible. Wasn't it he who had done it all? And if their marriage lay in ruins and she had taken a lover, wasn't it all his fault? His heavy imperturbability, the unconcerned look with which he met her tantrums, his round shoulders and spreading stomach, all this dreary fat with its appearance of contentment, put the finishing touch to her exasperation when she herself was so unhappy. Oh to break off, go away and begin a new life somewhere else, that was now her constant dream. Oh for a fresh start, above all something to put the past right out of her life, to begin her life again as it was before all these abominations, find herself once again as she was at fifteen, love and be loved and live as she had dreamed of life then! For a whole week she toyed with a plan for flight: she saw herself running off with Jacques, they would disappear in Belgium and set up as a young hard-working couple. But she did not even mention it to him, for at once snags had presented themselves: the irregularity of their situation, the continual state of fear they would be in and especially her vexation at abandoning her fortune, the money, La Croix-de-Maufras, to her husband. They had made wills leaving everything to the one who survived, and she was in his power because the subordination in law of the wife tied her hands. Rather than go away and leave a single sou behind she would have preferred to die there. One day when he came up the stairs livid with rage and told her that as he crossed the line in front of an engine he had felt the buffer touch his elbow, it occurred to her that if he were dead she would be free. She gazed at him with an unblinking stare. Why didn't he die, then, for she didn't love him any more and he was in everybody's way now.

From that day on her dream changed its character. Roubaud had died in an accident and she was sailing away to America with Jacques. But now they were married, had sold la Croix-de-Maufras and had turned everything into cash. Behind them they left nothing to be afraid of. If they emigrated it would be to start a new life hand in hand. Over there none of the things she wanted to forget would exist any more and she could believe that life was new. Having made one mistake she would take up the pursuit of happiness from the beginning. He would easily find a job and she would take on something herself, they would make money and have children, perhaps, in a fresh life of work and happiness. As soon as she was alone, in bed in the morning or doing her needlework during the day, she would slip back into this fantasy, alter it, enlarge upon it, constantly adding delightful details until she saw herself loaded with joy and possessions. Formerly she went out so rarely, but now she had a craze for going and watching the liners sail away. She would go down to the harbour arm and lean on the parapet watching the ship's smoke until it lost itself in the haze of the open sea. And she became two separate persons, seeing herself there on the deck with Jacques, already far from France, outward bound for the paradise of her dreams.

One evening in mid March, when he had ventured to come up and see her in her own home, he told her he had just brought from Paris, in his train, one of his old schoolfriends who was off to New York to promote a new invention, a button-making machine, and needing a partner with mechanical skill he had even offered to take Jacques too. Oh, it was a magnificent venture that would only need about 30,000 francs invested in it, and there were perhaps millions to be made. He was only saying all this by way of conversation, and added that of course he had turned the offer down. And yet he was a bit wistful about it, because all the same it was a bit hard to give up a chance when it was there for the taking.

Séverine stood listening to him with far-away eyes. Wasn't this her dream on the point of becoming true?

'Ah,' she murmured, 'we could go tomorrow.'

He looked up in surprise.

'What do you mean, we could go?'

'Yes, if he were dead.'

She had not mentioned Roubaud by name, but indicated him with a jerk of the head. But he had understood and he made a vague gesture to mean that unfortunately he was not.

'We would sail away,' she went on in her slow, deep voice, 'and we'd be so happy over there! I could have the thirty thousand by selling the property, with a bit over to set ourselves up . . . You could use that to advantage and I could make us a little home where we'd love each other with all our strength . . . Oh, it would be good, it would be so good!'

She added almost in a whisper:

'Far away from any memory, nothing but fresh days before us!'

A great sweetness flowed through his being, their hands met and automatically clasped each other's. Nothing more was said, for both were absorbed in this hope. Then again she was the one to speak.

'Still, you should see your friend again before he sails and ask him not to take a partner without letting you know.'

Once again he was astonished.

'But why?'

'Oh, I don't know, can you ever tell? The other day, with that engine, one second more and I'd have been free. You're here this morning and gone tonight, aren't you?'

She looked hard at him and said yet again:

'Oh, if he were dead!'

'But surely you don't want me to kill him?' he asked, trying to make a joke of it.

Three times she said no, but her eyes said yes, the eyes of a woman in love and wholly dominated by the inexorable cruelty of her passion. As her husband had killed another man, why shouldn't he be killed? The thought had taken root in her quite suddenly as a logical consequence, a necessary conclusion. Kill him and go away, nothing simpler. With him dead everything would be cancelled out and she could start afresh. Already she could envisage no other possible way out and her mind was made up, absolutely; and all the time with a slight shake of the head she was still saying no, not having the courage to put her murderous thoughts into words.

He was leaning against the sideboard, still pretending to joke, but he had caught sight of the knife lying there.

'If you want me to kill him you'd better give me that knife ... I've already got the watch and it'll make quite a little museum.'

He guffawed louder than ever, but she solemnly answered:

'Take the knife!'

When he had put it into his pocket as if to take the joke to its logical end, he kissed her.

'Well, good-bye for now. I'll go and see my friend at once and tell him to wait. Come and meet me behind the Sauvagnats' on Saturday if it isn't raining ... That settled? And don't worry, we shan't kill anybody, it's only a joke.'

Yet, late though it was, Jacques did go down to the harbour and looked up the friend at the hotel where he was staying before sailing the next day. He told him about a possible legacy and asked for two weeks before he need give a definite answer. Then, on his way back to the station along the wide dark avenues, this move of his surprised him. Had he resolved to kill Roubaud, since he was already arranging what to do with his wife and his money? No, of course he had made no such decision, he was only taking these precautions in case he did decide. But the memory of Séverine came back, and the urgent pressure of her hand, her clear gaze saying yes while her lips were saying no. Obviously she did want him to kill the other man. He was plunged into a great perplexity – what was he going to do?

Back in the rue François-Mazeline and lying next to the snoring Pecqueux, Jacques could not get to sleep. In spite of himself his mind kept mulling over this murder plan, the scenario of a drama he was working out, calculating its remotest implications. He went over it and debated the pros and cons. It turned out that when he considered it coolly and without any hysteria, they were all pros. Wasn't Roubaud the sole obstacle to their happiness? With him out of the way he could marry Séverine whom he adored, come out into the open and possess her for ever, all of her. Then there was the money, a fortune. He saw himself leaving his hard job and becoming a boss himself in America, that land he had heard his mates refer to as a land where mechanics could get shovelfuls of gold. His new existence over there passed before him as a dream: a wife passionately in love with him, millions to be made in no time, a full life with no limit to ambition, all he could wish for. To make the dream come true only one act to be done, only a man to destroy, like some creature or weed in your path that you crush. The man wasn't even interesting, he had got bloated and heavy now, bogged down in this stupid craze for gambling that was swallowing up all his former energy. Why spare him? Not a single circumstance, not a single one, argued in his favour. Everything condemned him because, whichever way you looked at it, it was in other people's interests that he should die. To hesitate would be silly and cowardly.

But then Jacques, who had been lying on his stomach because his back was hot, turned over quickly as a thought he had so far only entertained vaguely suddenly hit him so hard that it felt like a spike jabbing into his skull. He had always wanted to kill somebody ever since he was a child, and this obsession had tortured him with horror; then why shouldn't he kill Roubaud? Perhaps he could slake for ever his thirst for murder by choosing this particular victim, and by acting thus not only would he be doing a profitable thing, but he would be cured into the

266

bargain. Cured! Oh God! Be done with this blood-lust and be able to possess Séverine without this brutal awakening of the primitive male carrying off females and ripping them open in an embrace! He broke into a sweat, saw himself with the knife in his hand, plunging it into Roubaud's throat as Roubaud had done to the President, and then satisfied and sated while the wound oozed blood over his hands. He would kill him, his mind was made up, for in this he could find his cure, the woman he loved; and fortune. If somebody had to be killed and he had to kill somebody, this was the one he would kill, for at least he knew what he was doing, rationally, logically and in his own interests.

Having made his decision, and as it had just struck three, Jacques tried to go to sleep. He was already dropping off when he woke up with a violent jerk that left him sitting up in bed, gasping. Good God, what right had he to kill this man? When a fly annoyed him he would squash it. Once a cat had got mixed up in his legs and he had broken its back with a kick, admittedly without meaning to. But this man, a fellow creature! He had to start his reasoning all over again to prove to himself that he had a right to murder, the right of the strong to destroy the weak who get in their way. He was the one whom this other man's wife loved now, and she herself wanted to be free to marry him and bring him her fortune. He was only clearing away the obstacle, that was all. If two wolves come up against each other in the forest when a she-wolf is there, doesn't the stronger get rid of the weaker with a snap of his jaws? And in ancient times when men found shelter like the wolves in the depths of caves, wasn't the desirable woman the property of the member of the tribe who could win her with the blood of his rivals? So as it was the law of life it had to be obeyed, irrespective of scruples invented later in order to make life in society liveable. Little by little his right seemed absolute, and he felt his resolution strengthening: at once, tomorrow, he would select the time and place and get ready. Probably the best way would be to stab Roubaud in the night on the station premises while he was on one of his rounds, so as to suggest that some marauders, caught red-handed, had killed him. He knew of a good spot behind the stacks of coal if Roubaud could be lured there. Although he was trying to sleep he now found himself setting the scene, wondering where he would take up his position, how he would strike so as to knock him out flat, and in a confused, but undeniable way, as he got down to the minutest details, his repugnance came back, protesting inside him and making him feel sick. No, no, he would not do it! He felt it was monstrous, impracticable, impossible. The civilized man in him revolted, with the resistance built up by education and the slowly developed, indestructible fabric of transmitted ideas. Thou shalt not kill – he had sucked that in with the milk of countless generations; his educated fastidious mind, with its collection of scruples, thrust murder aside with horror as soon as it began to reason things out. To kill in self-preservation, when carried along by instinct – yes! But to kill deliberately, with calculated self-interest, no, never would he be able to do that!

It was getting light by the time Jacques managed to doze off, and then his sleep was so light that the horrible debate was still going on in a confused sort of way. The days that followed were the most painful he had ever lived through. He avoided Séverine, having sent her a message not to be at their meeting-place on Saturday, for he could not face her eyes. But he had to see her on the Monday, and as he feared, her great blue eyes, so soft and so deep, filled him with anguish. She made no reference to this thing, made no gesture nor uttered a word to influence him. Yet her eyes spoke of that alone, and questioned him and implored. He didn't know how to avoid their impatience and reproach, he always found them fixed on his and expressing astonishment that he could hesitate to find happiness. When he left her he embraced her with a sudden violence to let her know that his mind was made up. It was indeed, and remained so as far as the bottom of the stairs, and then he relapsed into the struggle with his conscience. When he met her the next day he wore the pasty face and furtive look of a coward running away from doing something that must be done. She said nothing, but burst into tears, weeping on his neck and horribly miserable, and he was deeply moved and filled with self-loathing. The thing had to be settled once and for all.

'Thursday, usual place, will you?' she whispered.

'Yes, Thursday, I'll be waiting.'

That Thursday it was a very dark night with an overcast sky, full of sea-fog hiding everything and deadening all sound. As usual Jacques was there first, standing behind the Sauvagnats' house watching out for Séverine. But the darkness was so thick, and she was skipping along so lightly that he was startled to feel her touch him before he had seen her. At once she was in his arms and upset at feeling him trembling.

'I gave you a fright,' she murmured.

'No, no, I was expecting you ... Come along, nobody can see us.'

They wandered through the railway yards with their arms loosely round each other's waists. On this side of the sheds the gas lamps were few and far between and some dark patches had none, while in the distance nearer the station there were quantities of them, like dancing sparks.

For a long time they walked on like this, without a word. She had her head on his shoulder and sometimes looked up and kissed him on the chin while he leaned over and returned her kiss on the temple, just below her hair. The solemn bells of distant churches had just struck one. They did not speak because in their close embrace they could read each other's thoughts. They were both thinking of nothing else but that, they could never be together now without being haunted by it. The debate was still on, so why say useless words aloud, since what was required was action? When she stretched up for a kiss she could feel the knife in his trouser pocket. Did it mean that he had made up his mind?

But her thoughts did break out and her lips opened as she breathed almost inaudibly:

'Just now he came upstairs again, I didn't know why ... Then I saw him take his revolver which he had forgotten ... That means he's bound to do his rounds.'

Another silence. Only after they had walked on a score of paces did he take up the subject again.

'Last night some thieves pinched some lead from here. He'll come round soon, that's certain.'

She shivered slightly and both fell silent again and slackened their pace. Then she was seized with a doubt – was it really the knife making a bump in his pocket? Twice she kissed him so as

269

to try to make sure. Then, as by just brushing along his leg like this she was still uncertain, she let her hand hang down and felt while giving him yet another kiss. It was the knife all right. He had understood, and he crushed her to his chest and whispered into her ear:

'He's coming and you'll be free.'

The murder was decided. They felt they were no longer walking, but being borne along the ground by some alien force. Their senses had suddenly been extraordinarily sharpened, especially that of touch, for their clasped hands hurt each other, and the slightest brushing of their lips scratched like fingernails. They could also hear sounds that until then had escaped them, engines running and puffing, soft bumping noises, footsteps in the dark. And they could see in the dark too, black shapes of things as if a mist had gone from their eyes. A bat flew by and they could follow its sudden changes of course. At the corner of a stack of coal they stopped motionless, ears and eyes straining, tense in every fibre of their being. Now they were whispering.

'Did you hear somebody calling over there?'

'No, it's a coach being shunted.'

'But someone's walking over there to our left. There was a scrunching of gravel.'

'No, no, rats running in the stack, the coal falling down.'

Minutes went by, and then she suddenly squeezed him harder.

'Here he is.'

'Where? I can't see anything.'

'He has turned the corner of the goods depot and is coming straight at us. Look, that's his shadow going along the white wall.'

'That dark bit, do you think so? Is he alone?'

'Yes, alone, he's alone.'

At that decisive moment she threw herself wildly into his arms and pressed her burning lips to his. It was flesh to flesh, a prolonged kiss in which she would have liked to give him all her blood. How she loved him and loathed that other man! Oh, if she had dared she would have done the job herself a score of

270

times to save him the horror of it, but her hands failed her, she knew she was too soft, it had to be done by a man's hand. This endless kiss was all she could offer him of her courage, and a promise of full possession and identity with her body. An engine whistled somewhere, uttering a plaint of doleful misery in the night, a regular banging could be heard, some huge hammer somewhere, while mists blowing in from the sea crossed the sky like a chaotic procession of rags and tatters and seemed momentarily to put out the bright lights of the gas lamps. When at long last she took her mouth away she felt she had nothing of herself left, but had been drained wholly into him.

He had already snapped the knife open. Then he swore under his breath:

'Blast it! It's no use, he's going away!'

It was true, the moving shadow had come to within fifty steps of them, but then turned left and was walking off at the steady pace of an unruffled night watchman.

She pushed him.

'Go on, go on!'

They both began moving, he leading and she following, and they slipped rapidly along in his tracks, silently stalking him. At the corner of the repair shop they momentarily lost sight of him, then as they took a short cut across a siding they picked him up again, twenty paces off at the most. They had to take advantage of the smallest bits of wall for cover, one false step would have given them away.

'We shan't get him,' Jacques muttered. 'If he gets to the pointsman's box he's safe.'

But she went on whispering behind his ear:

'Go on, go on!'

At that moment, in these wide open spaces, in the darkness, amid the desolation of a big railway depot in the middle of the night, his mind was made up as though he were alone in the friendly shelter of some cut-throat alley. As he furtively quickened his pace he worked himself up, still reasoning it out and finding arguments that would make the murder a wise act, legitimate, logically debated and decided. It really was a right he was exercising, the law of life itself, since the blood of another

271

man was indispensable for his own survival. He merely had to thrust this knife in and his future happiness was assured.

'We shan't get him, we shan't get him,' he furiously repeated, seeing the shadow go past the pointsman's box. 'It's no good, he's going away.'

But then she suddenly gripped his arm with a nervous hand, stopped him and held him close.

'Look, he's coming back!'

He was. He had turned to the right and then come down towards them again. Perhaps he had in some strange way sensed killers on his track. However, he was still walking at the steady pace of a conscientious watchman unwilling to go back before casting an eye everywhere.

Rooted to the spot, Jacques and Séverine stood stock still. Chance had landed them right at the corner of a stack of coal. They backed against it and seemed to be part of it, swallowed up and lost in this inky pool. They hardly breathed.

Jacques watched Roubaud coming straight at them. There were hardly thirty metres between them and each step shortened the distance as regularly and rhythmically as the inexorable pendulum of fate. Twenty more, then ten, and Roubaud would be in front of him, he would raise his arm like this and plant the knife in his neck, jerk it from right to left to muffle a cry. The seconds seemed endless, such a flood of thoughts raced through the blank in his mind that any notion of time was abolished. All the decisive reasons followed each other once again – the murder, its causes and its consequences. Five more steps. His resolution, stretched to breaking-point, was still nevertheless unbreakable. He was determined to kill. He knew why he would kill.

But at two steps, one, there was a collapse. Everything in him crumbled at once. No, no, he wouldn't kill, he couldn't kill a defenceless man like this. A reasoning human being would never commit murder, there had to be the instinct to attack, the leap on to the prey, hunger or passion rending its flesh. If conscience was nothing more than notions transmitted through a long heredity of justice, well, what of it? He didn't feel he had the right to kill and, do what he might, he couldn't persuade himself that he could assume that right.

272

Roubaud quietly walked past. His elbow grazed them both as they stood pressed against the coal. A single breath would have given them away, but they stood there like corpses. The arm did not go up, the knife did not go in. Nothing, not the slightest shudder, disturbed the dense blackness. He was already well away, ten paces, and they were still motionless, backs to the black heap, both still breathless and in terror of this man who alone, defenceless, had brushed past them with such a peaceful step.

Jacques stifled a sob of rage and shame.

'I can't! I can't!'

He wanted to grasp Séverine again and lean on her in his need to be forgiven and comforted. Without a word she eluded him. He had held out his hand and felt nothing but her skirt slipping through his fingers, and only heard her softly running away. He followed her for a moment, but it was useless, and this prompt disappearance utterly cast him down. Was she so angry at his weakness? Did she despise him? Prudence stopped him from going after her, but when he found himself alone in this vast open space, dotted with little yellow lights like tear-drops, he gave in to dreadful despair and rushed to get away from it and bury his head in his pillow and forget the horror of his existence.

Some ten days later, towards the end of March, the Roubauds finally won the war against the Lebleus. The administration had upheld the justice of their cause, and it was supported by M. Dabadie, especially since the vital letter written by Lebleu undertaking to vacate the flat if a new deputy stationmaster asked for it had been unearthed by Mlle Guichon when she was hunting for some old accounts in the station archives. At once Mme Lebleu, exasperated by her defeat, talked of moving – as they wanted her to die she might as well make an end of it all without delay. For three days this world-shaking move was the sensation of the passage. Even little Mme Moulin, so shy that nobody ever saw her come or go, mixed herself up in it by carrying Séverine's work-table from one flat to the other. But it was notably Philomène who fanned the flames of discord. She came at once to help, doing up bundles, shifting furniture, bursting into the front flat before the occupant had left, and it was she who finally kicked her out in the midst of the confusion of the two homes all mixed and muddled up in transport. She was now displaying such an interest in Jacques and in everyone he was fond of, that Pecqueux, amazed and getting suspicious, had asked her, in his nasty, sly tone, the tone of a spiteful drunkard, whether she was now sleeping with his driver, and warned her that he would deal with them both good and proper if he caught them at it. That only made her crush on the young man stronger still, and she became the slave of both him and his mistress in the hope of getting a bit for herself too by putting herself between them. When she had carted out the last chair the doors shut with a bang. Then, seeing a stool Mme Lebleu had forgotten, she opened the door again and hurled it across the passage. That was that.

Life slowly resumed its monotonous routine. While Mme Lebleu was bored to death in the flat at the back, glued to her armchair by the rheumatism, with big tears in her eyes because all she could see now was the zinc roof of the station shutting out the sky, Séverine worked away at her interminable eiderdown-cover by one of the front windows. Below her she had the gaiety and life of the forecourt on the departure side, with pedestrians and vehicles continually on the move. The big trees along the pavements were already bursting into bud in the early spring, and in the background there extended the wooded slopes of the hills of Ingouville dotted with white country villas. But she was surprised to find that she was getting so little pleasure out of this dream come true, being here in this coveted home with space, air and sunshine. And like her help, old Ma Simon, who grumbled and was furious at being thrown off her usual routine, she even lost patience herself and sometimes looked back with regret at her old hole, as she put it, where the dirt didn't show so much. Roubaud had just submitted to it, didn't seem to realize that he had changed his abode, and indeed still often made a mistake and only noticed the error when the new key didn't fit the old lock. In any case he was away more and more and his general disintegration went on. Once, however, he seemed to revive when his political theories became active again, not that they were very clear or violent, but he was still

274

smarting over his affair with the Sub Prefect which had almost cost him his job. Since the General Election had shaken the Empire it had been going through a terrible crisis, and he was triumphant and kept on saying that that gang wouldn't be the masters for ever. However, a friendly warning from M. Dabadie, who had been tipped off by Mlle Guichon in front of whom the revolutionary remarks had been uttered, was enough to calm him down. Since the passage was quiet and everybody lived together harmoniously now that Mme Lebleu was fading away, dying of grief, why have new bothers over things to do with the government? So he just made a gesture to show he couldn't care less about politics or anything else. And putting on weight every day and feeling no remorse, he wandered off with his ponderous gait, turning his back in indifference.

Now that Jacques and Séverine could meet at any time the awkwardness between them had become worse. There was nothing to prevent their being happy now, and he could come up and see her by the other staircase whenever he liked without fear of being spied on. The place belonged to them and he could have stayed all night if he had had the nerve. But it was the act desired and agreed on by them both, the act still not turned into reality, which he still had not accomplished, that made them ill at ease with each other and raised an impassable barrier between them. He carried with him the shame of his weakness, and each time he found her more moody and sick with useless waiting. Even their lips no longer sought each other's, for they had got all they could out of this state of half-possession. What they wanted was complete happiness, departure, marriage far away, the new life.

One evening Jacques found Séverine in tears, and when she saw him she did not stop, but cried more bitterly and clung round his neck. She had cried like this before, but then he had calmed her with an embrace, but this time he could feel her against his heart given up to a despair that became more dreadful the closer he held her. He was shattered, and took her head between his hands and looking at her very close, right into her tear-stained eyes, he took his oath, realizing that the reason for her desperation was that she was a woman whose passive meekness would not let her strike the blow herself.

'Forgive me, wait a little longer . . . I swear it will be soon, as soon as I can.'

At once she glued her lips to his as though to seal this oath, and they had one of those deep kisses in which they mingled one with the other in the communion of their flesh.

AUNT PHASIE had died on a Thursday evening at nine o'clock
in a final seizure, and Misard, waiting at her bedside, had tried to
close her eyes, but in vain; the eyes stayed obstinately open, the
head had stiffened and was leaning slightly over one shoulder as
though it wanted to look into the room, while the retraction of
the lips seemed to turn them up into a teasing grin. A single
candle was burning on a corner of a table near her. Since nine
o'clock trains passing at full speed, unaware of this dead
woman not yet cold, made her shake momentarily in the flickering light of the candle.

Misard at once got rid of Flore by sending her to report the
death at Doinville. She could not be back before eleven, so he
had two hours in front of him. First he calmly cut himself a
hunk of bread, for his stomach felt empty, not having had a
proper meal because of this death-agony that went on and on.
He ate as he walked about tidying up. Fits of coughing made
him stop, bent double and half dead himself, so skinny and
miserable-looking with his dull eyes and colourless hair that he
didn't look likely to enjoy his victory for long. Never mind, he
had finished off this sturdy female, this fine figure of a woman,
as an insect destroys an oak-tree. She was on her back, finished,
reduced to nothing, and he was still there. But a thought came to
him and he knelt down to get from under the bed a basin con-
taining the remains of some bran-water prepared for use with
an enema. Since she had had her suspicions he had been putting
the rat poison into the rectal injections instead of in the salt and,
being so silly and not suspecting anything in that direction, she
had taken some of it, and for good this time. As soon as he had
emptied the basin outside he came back and sponged some
stains off the tiles in the room. So why had she stuck out so
obstinately? She had tried to be clever – well, serve her right!
When a married couple play at which one shall bury the other
without bringing other people into the dispute, well, you keep

Misard was poisoning her – her paranoia justified

your eyes open! He was proud of it, and he sniggered as if it were a funny story – poison innocently drunk in down below when she was watching so carefully everything that went in up above! Just then a passing express shook the little house with such a hurricane that, although he was used to it, he turned towards the window and quailed. Oh yes, that ever-rolling stream, people from all over the place heedless of what they might be killing as they passed, who couldn't care less as they hurried on the devil knew where! In the oppressive silence after the train had gone he met the wide-open eyes of the dead woman, whose fixed pupils seemed to be following his every movement while the corners of her mouth turned up in a smirk.

Misard, usually so phlegmatic, gave in to a little fit of anger. He realized perfectly well that she was saying: 'Go on, look!' But for certain she wasn't taking her thousand francs with her and, now that she wasn't there, he would find them in the end. Shouldn't she have given them to him with a good grace? It would have saved all this trouble. The eyes went on following him everywhere. 'Go on, keep looking!' He glanced round this room that he had not dared to search while she was alive. The cupboard first: he took the keys from under the bolster, ransacked the shelves of linen, emptied both drawers and even took them out to see if there was a hiding-place. No, nothing. Then he thought of the bedside table. He pulled off the marble top and turned it over – no good. Behind the mirror over the mantel-piece, one of those thin pieces of looking-glass sold at a fair, which was hanging on two nails, he did some exploring by slipping in a flat ruler, but all he got out was black fluff. 'Go on, keep looking!' Then, so as to avoid those great open eyes that he felt were on him, he went down on his hands and knees, tapping the floor gently with his knuckles to hear whether any resonance might reveal a hollow place. Several tiles were loose, and he took them up. Nothing, still nothing! When he stood up again the eyes were still upon him, and he turned and tried to stare into the fixed eyes of the dead woman, but with the curled up corners of her mouth she seemed to broaden her horrible grin. He was now certain she was laughing at him and saying 'Go on, keep looking!' In a frenzy he went over to her with a dawning suspicion and a sacrilegious idea that made his pasty face go

278

looking for
1000 francs

paler still. Why had he been so sure that she wouldn't take the thousand francs away with her? Perhaps she really had. He found the nerve to uncover her, strip off her clothes and search her, going over all the crannies of her body, since she kept on challenging him to search. He searched underneath her, behind her neck, under her haunches. The bed was turned inside out and he thrust his arm into the mattress right up to his shoulder. He found nothing. 'Go on, have a look!' And the head, which had fallen back on to the rumpled pillow, still looked at him with its mocking eyes.

While Misard, trembling with rage, was trying to put the bed to rights, Flore came back from Doinville.

'It's fixed for the day after tomorrow, Saturday at eleven,' she said.

She was referring to the funeral. But a glance was enough to tell her what the job was that Misard had been working so hard at in her absence. She made a gesture indicating scornful indifference.

'Give over, you won't find it.'

He thought she was defying him too. He went up to her and muttered between clenched teeth:

'She gave the money to you, you know where it is.'

The idea that her mother might have given her thousand francs to anybody, even to her, her own daughter, made her shrug her shoulders.

'Given it to me? You bet! Given it to the ground, more like. That's where it is, you can look!'

With a wave of the arm she indicated the whole house, the garden with its well, the railway line and the great wide countryside. Yes, there, in some hole where nobody would ever find it again. Then while he, out of his mind with frustration, went back to turning over the furniture, tapping on walls without bothering about her presence, she stood at the window and went on to herself:

'Oh, it's so mild out of doors, a lovely night! I walked fast, the stars make it as light as day. How lovely it will be tomorrow at sunrise!'

She stayed for a minute at the window looking at this serene countryside, her mood softened by the first warm April days, but this left her pensive and suffering still more from the re-opened wound of her own torment. However, when she heard Misard go out of the room and begin attacking the other rooms, she in her turn went over to the bed and sat down and looked at her mother. The candle on the corner of the table continued to burn with its still, upright flame. A train went by, shaking the house.

Flore had resolved to stay there all night, and she fell to thinking. At first the sight of the dead woman took her mind off the obsession that was pursuing her and that she had been going over with herself under the stars in the peaceful night all along the road from Doinville. Yet now a surprising thought softened her suffering – why hadn't she felt more sorrow at her mother's death? Why, even now, wasn't she weeping? For she was very fond of her, in spite of the undemonstrative ways of a girl running wild in the fields as soon as she went off duty. During this last attack, which had proved to be fatal, she had come a score of times and sat there, begging her mother to send for a doctor, for she suspected Misard's game and hoped that fright would make him stop. But all she had ever got out of the sick woman was a furious 'No!', as if the honour of war forbade her accepting help from anybody, for she was certain in any case that she would win because she would take the money with her. And so Flore did not intervene, but got caught up again by her own suffering, running wild in order not to think about it. It must be this that was closing up her heart: when you have a sorrow that is too great it leaves no room for any other. Her mother had gone, and she saw her there, white and lifeless, yet could not feel any sadder for all her efforts. What was the point of calling in the police and denouncing Misard, since her whole world was about to collapse? Gradually, and in spite of all she could do, although her eyes looked steadily at the dead woman, she ceased to see her and went back to her inner vision, wholly taken up again by the idea that had driven its nail into her head, and only aware of the thunder of the passing trains which sounded the hours for her.

An approaching slow from Paris had been roaring in the distance for a minute, and when at last it passed the window its headlight lit up the room like a flash of lightning.

'One-eighteen,' she thought. 'Seven more hours. This morning at eight-sixteen they'll be going past!'

Every week for months past this wait had oppressed her. She knew that on Friday mornings the express, driven by Jacques, also took Séverine to Paris, and in a torment of jealousy she lived for nothing else but to look out for them, see them, telling herself that they were going to possess each other there in freedom. Oh, that speeding train, that abominable feeling that she couldn't cling on to the last coach and be taken there too! All those wheels seemed to be cutting through her heart. She had suffered so bitterly that one evening she had shut herself in to write to the police, for there would be an end to it if she could get this woman arrested. She had once caught her at her filthy tricks with President Grandmorin, and it seemed to her that by informing the authorities she could hand her over to justice. But once the pen was in her hand she could never manage to express it properly. And anyhow, would justice take any notice of her? All these grand people were bound to be hand in glove. Maybe she would be the one they would put in prison, as they had Cabuche. No, she wanted revenge and she would do it herself, without the help of anyone else. It wasn't even the thought of vengeance as she heard others define it – the idea of causing suffering to heal one's own suffering – it was a desire to have done with it all, wreck the lot as if a storm had swept them all away. She was very proud, stronger and better looking than that other woman, convinced of her right to be loved, and on her lonely walks along the tracks of this savage country, with her mass of golden hair always uncovered, she would have liked to have that woman in her clutches and settle their differences in the depths of some forest, like two warring Amazons. No man had ever touched her yet, she could beat all the males, and that was her invincible strength. She would win.

A week before, the sudden thought had planted itself in her and been driven in by some hammer, how or where from she didn't know: to kill them both and stop them from going by and ever being together in Paris again. She did not reason it out, but obeyed the primitive instinct to destroy. When a thorn got stuck in her flesh she pulled it out, even if it meant cutting her own finger. Kill them, kill them the first time they went by, and to

281

that end wreck the train, drag a baulk of timber on to the line, take up a rail, in fact smash everything and send it to perdition. He at any rate would stay on his engine, his limbs crushed, and the woman, who was always in the leading coach so as to be nearer him, couldn't escape. As to the rest, the ever-rolling stream of passengers, they didn't even enter her thoughts. They weren't anybody, did she even know who they were? And so this smashing of a train and sacrifice of so many lives became the obsession of her every hour, the sole catastrophe big enough and full enough of human blood and suffering for her to bathe her swollen heart in, her heart swollen with tears.

But on Friday morning she had weakened, not having yet decided where and how she would take up a rail. But in the evening, being by then off duty, she had an idea, and went through the tunnel to explore as far as the Dieppe junction. The underground road, this straight, vaulted avenue a good league and a half long, was one of her favourite walks where she had the thrill of having trains coming straight at her with their blinding headlights. She was nearly run over every time, and it must have been the peril that attracted her and challenged her craving for bravado. On this particular night, having dodged the watchman's eye and walked as far as the middle of the tunnel, keeping to the left so as to be sure that any train coming towards her would pass on her right, she had been unwise enough to turn round, just to look at the tail-lights of a down train; and when she set off again she had stumbled and spun round, and then not known which way the red lights had gone. Still bewildered by the roar of the train she had been unable to move, and for all her courage her hands had gone cold and her hair had stood on end in terror. She imagined that when the next train passed she would not know whether it was an up or a down, and would throw herself to right or left and be cut to pieces. She had struggled to hold on to her reason, remember, think it out. Then suddenly her panic had driven her headlong, straight on, anywhere, in a frantic gallop. No, no, she was determined not to be killed before killing those other two! Her feet stumbled over the rails, she slipped and fell, then ran faster than ever. It was tunnel madness, the walls seemed to be caving in to crush her, the vault re-echoed with imaginary noises, threat-

282

ening voices, formidable rumblings. Every second she glanced backwards, thinking she could feel the burning breath of an engine on her neck. Twice, suddenly sure she was wrong and would be killed by going in that direction, she had jumped round and gone the other way. She was still rushing on and on when a star had appeared far ahead, then a round and blazing eye that grew bigger. But she had nerved herself to fight the irresistible urge to retrace her steps yet again. The eye became a brazier, the mouth of a fiery furnace. She had blindly leaped to her left, not knowing what she was doing, and the train had thundered by, only hitting her with its rush of wind. Five minutes later she was out at the Malaunay end, safe and sound.

It was nine o'clock, and in a few minutes the express from Paris would be there. She had gone on at once at a normal walking pace for the two hundred metres to the junction for Dieppe, examining the track to see if some circumstance might be useful to her. And it so happened that a ballast train was standing on the Dieppe line in connection with some repairs; her friend Ozil had just switched it there. In a flash of inspiration she found what she wanted and hit on a plan: merely prevent the pointsman from putting the points back to the Le Havre line, and then the express would crash into the ballast train. Now ever since he had leaped on her in a frenzy of lust and she had half cracked his skull with a stick, she had kept on friendly terms with this Ozil, and she enjoyed going through the tunnel, like a goat running down from the mountain, and paying him unexpected visits. He was an ex-soldier, gaunt and taciturn, wrapped up in his job, and had never been guilty of any negligence, keeping on the watch day and night. Nevertheless this wild girl, strong as a young man, who had beaten him off, could arouse his flesh by simply lifting her little finger. Although he was fourteen years older than she was, he desired her and had sworn to get her, biding his time and being pleasant, since force had not succeeded. And so on this dark night when she had gone up to his box and called him out he had joined her, forgetting everything. She bemused him and led him away into the country, spinning complicated yarns about her mother being ill and her not being able to stay at La Croix-de-Maufras if she lost her. All the time she had one ear listening for the distant sound of the express leaving Malaunay and approaching at full speed. When she felt it was coming she turned round to look, but she had not thought of the new system of interlocking: by entering the Dieppe line the engine had automatically set the signal at danger and the driver had had time to bring it to a standstill a few metres short of the ballast train. Ozil, yelling like a man waking up to find the house collapsing on top of him, rushed back to his post while she, stiff and motionless in the dark, watched the backing necessitated by the mishap. Two days later Ozil had been sacked and had come in all innocence to say good-bye and beg her to come to him as soon as she lost her mother. Oh well, her plot had misfired and she would have to think of something else.

Now, as she called this incident to mind, the dreamy mists that had obscured her vision dispersed, and Flore once again saw the dead woman in the yellow light of the candle. Her mother was dead, should she go off and marry Ozil, who wanted her and might make her happy? The thought made her heave. No, no, if she was coward enough to let those two live and live herself, she would prefer to tramp the roads, work as a servant rather than belong to a man she didn't love. An unusual noise caught her attention and she realized that Misard was digging into the earthen floor of the kitchen with a pick; he was so determined to find the nest-egg that he would have torn the very guts out of the house. Yet she didn't want to stay with that man either. What could she do? A hurricane sprang up, the walls shook, the glare from a firebox passed across the white, dead face, turning the staring eyes and the ironical grin a blood red. It was the last stopping train from Paris, with its slow, heavy engine.

Flore turned and looked at the stars twinkling in the serene spring night.

'Three ten. Five more hours and they'll be going past.'

She would have another try, for her suffering was too great. Just to see them like this, going off every week to make love, was beyond her endurance. Now she was certain she would never possess Jacques for herself alone, she preferred that he and everything else should cease to exist. This mournful room in which she was keeping watch filled her with a sense of loss and a growing desire to be done with everything. As there was nobody left who loved her, the rest might as well go with her mother. There would be more dead, and yet more, and they would all be carted off at once. Her sister was dead, her mother dead, her love dead, what could she do – be alone here or elsewhere, always alone while they would be two? No, no, rather let the whole lot come crashing down, let death, who was present in this dismal room, breathe on the railway line and blow them all away!

So now, her mind made up after the long debate, she went over the best way of putting her project into execution. She came back to the idea of taking up a rail. It was the most certain and the most practical way and easy to carry out: you only had to knock the wedges out of the chairs with a hammer and take up the rail from the sleepers. She had the tools and nobody would see her in this lonely spot. The best place was certainly beyond the cutting towards Barentin, where the curve crosses a valley on an embankment seven or eight metres high. At that point there would certainly be a derailment and the headlong plunge would be terrible. But the timetable which she then worked out left her in some anxiety. On the up line the only thing before the express from Le Havre, which passed at 8.16, was a slow train at 7.55. So that left her twenty minutes for the job, which was ample. The only thing was that between the regular trains they often sent along unscheduled goods trains, especially at times when a lot of cargo was landed. What a pointless risk in that case! How could she know in advance if it really would be the express that would crash there? She turned the probabilities over in her mind for a long time. It was still dark, a candle was still guttering with a long charred wick that she had given up snuffing.

Just as a goods train from Rouen was coming Misard returned. His hands were covered with dirt because he had been hunting in the woodpile, and he was puffed and furious after his fruitless search, and so frantic with impotent rage that he began hunting under the furniture again, in the chimney, everywhere. The endless train went on and on, with the regular bang-bang of its heavy wheels, each thud of which jolted the corpse in the bed. As he was stretching up to unhook a little picture off the wall, he once again met the staring eyes following him round while the grinning lips moved.

He went green and shook himself, muttering in mingled anger and fright:

'Yes, yes, hunt, go on hunting! Never you mind, I'll bloody well find it if I have to turn over every stone in the house and every clod of earth all round here!'

The black train had gone past, lumbering slowly through the night, and the dead woman, now still again, went on looking at her husband with such mockery, such certainty of winning, that he disappeared again, leaving the door open.

Flore, disturbed in her reflections, got up and shut the door again to stop that man from coming back and upsetting her mother. She was amazed to catch herself saying aloud:

'If it's ten minutes before it'll do all right.'

Yes, ten minutes would be time enough. If no train was signalled ten minutes before the express she could begin on the job. Now that the matter was decided on, her anxiety went away and she was quite calm.

Day dawned at about five, a fresh dawn, beautifully clear. Although it was chilly she threw the window wide open and the lovely morning came into the melancholy room, full of the miasma and smell of death. The sun was still below the horizon, a hill crowned with trees. Then it appeared, fiery red, flooding down the slopes, filling the sunken paths with the blithe gaiety of the earth at each recurring springtime. She had made no mistake about it yesterday, it would be a fine morning, one of those days when the weather is full of youth and radiant health and you are glad to be alive. How lovely it would be to wander off at her own sweet will along the goat-tracks through this wild country, among the endless hills and narrow dales! When she turned back into the room she was surprised to see that the candle was as good as out and only glimmering in the broad daylight like a pale tear. The dead woman now seemed to be gazing at the line along which trains went on passing in both directions without even noticing this dim candle-light beside the corpse.

It was not until daylight that Flore went on duty again. She only left the room for the Paris slow at 6.12. By six o'clock

Misard had also relieved his colleague who did the night turn, and it was when he sounded his horn that she went and took up her position by the gate, flag in hand. She paused and watched the train go by.

'Two hours to go,' she thought aloud.

Her mother had no further need of anybody, and from now on the thought of going back into that room filled Flore with unconquerable repugnance. It was all over, she had kissed her and now she could settle her own existence and that of others. Usually she went off and made herself scarce between trains, but this morning a sort of fascination seemed to be keeping her at her post near the gate, on a bench, just a simple plank beside the line. The sun was coming up, a warm shower of gold rained down through the pure air, and she never moved, but let herself be bathed in this warmth, surrounded by the vast countryside all quickening with the mounting sap of April. For a moment her attention had been caught by Misard in his wooden hut across the line, for he was clearly worked up and not in his usual somnolent state, darting in and out and working his apparatus with nervous hands, glancing continually towards the house, as if his mind were still there and still hunting. But then she had forgotten him and did not even know he was there. She was wholly absorbed by her wait, her face stonily rigid, her eyes fixed on the end of the line in the Barentin direction. You could tell by the unremitting stare of her fierce eyes upon that point in the gay sunshine that some vision was rising before her.

The minutes ticked away and she never moved. Finally, at seven fifty-five, when Misard warned of the slow from Le Havre on the up line with his two horn blasts, she rose to her feet, shut the gate and stood in front of it, flag in hand. Almost at once, after making the ground tremble, the train was disappearing again; it could be heard plunging into the tunnel and the noise suddenly stopped. She did not go back to her seat, but stayed standing there, once again counting the minutes. If no goods train was signalled within ten minutes she would run along in that direction, beyond the cutting, and take up a rail. She was quite cool and only felt a certain tightening in the chest as though it were pressed down by the enormous weight of the act. But in any case at this last moment the knowledge that Jacques and

287

Séverine were approaching and, unless she stopped them, would go past again on their way to make love was sufficient to stiffen her and make her blind and deaf in her determination, without even calling the matter into question again. It was irrevocable, like the blow of a she-wolf as she smashes her victim with her paw. In her single-minded vengeance she could see nothing but the two mutilated bodies, and did not bother her head about the crowd, the stream of unknown people who had been passing in front of her for years. Corpses, blood, let them shut out the light of the sun, perhaps, for the gentle gaiety of the sun got on her nerves.

Two minutes more, one minute and she would set off. She actually was setting off when she was pulled up by heavy bumpings along the Bécourt road. A vehicle, a quarry dray no doubt. The man would ask her to let him through and she would have to open the gate, talk to him and stay there: it would be out of the question to do anything and the thing would go by default. With a furious gesture denoting that she couldn't care less she ran off, deserting her post, abandoning the waggon and its driver to fend for themselves. But a whip cracked in the morning air and a voice shouted gaily:

'Hi, Flore!'

It was Cabuche. She stood rooted to the spot, stopped at the very beginning of her flight, just in front of the gate.

'What's up?' he went on. 'Still asleep in this lovely sunshine? Come along quick, so that I can get through before the express.'

For her everything crumbled. The thing had misfired, those two would go on to their happiness and she could find no way of putting an end to it. As she slowly pushed open the half-rotten old gate and the rusty iron hinges squeaked, she madly tried to think of some obstacle, something she could throw across the line, and so set was she on it that she might have lain down there herself had she believed her bones were hard enough to make the engine jump the rails. But then her eye was caught by the dray, this heavy, low vehicle laden with two blocks of stone that five strong horses could hardly haul along. These huge, high, wide blocks, so enormous that they filled the roadway, were there for her to use, and the sight of them kindled in her a sudden desire, a mad lust to take them and place them there.

The gate was now wide open and the steaming, puffing horses were waiting.

'What's up with you this morning?' went on Cabuche. 'You look quite funny.'

At last Flore spoke:

'My mother died last night.'

He exclaimed in friendly sympathy. Putting down his whip, he squeezed her hands in his.

'Oh, poor Flore! It's only to be expected and has been for a long time, but it's very hard all the same. Well, she's in there and I would like to see her because we should have come to an understanding in the end if that terrible business hadn't happened.'

He walked slowly with her towards the house. But on the doorstep he glanced back at his horses. She reassured him with a word:

'There's no fear they'll move. And besides, the express is still a long way off.'

She was lying. Through the sounds of nature on this warm day her practised ear had just heard the express leaving Barentin station. Five more minutes and it would be emerging from the cutting, a hundred metres from the level crossing. While the quarryman, standing at the door of the dead woman's room, was lost in thought, dreaming of Louisette and deeply moved, she stayed outside in front of the window, listening to the regular beat of the engine still some distance away but getting nearer all the time. Suddenly she thought of Misard: he would be able to see her and he would stop her. But it was like a blow in the chest when she looked round and saw he wasn't at his post. She discovered him at the other side of the house, turning over the soil under the masonry round the well, unable to resist his mania for hunting, perhaps suddenly struck with a certainty that the nest-egg was there. Wholly engrossed by his passion, blind and deaf, he was digging, digging. It was the final spur she needed. Even inanimate objects willed it. One of the horses began to whinny as beyond the cutting the engine could be heard puffing very hard, like somebody running up in a hurry.

'I'll go and keep them quiet,' Flore said to Cabuche, 'never you fear!'

She leaped across, seized the leading horse by the bit and pulled with all the superhuman strength of a wrestler. The horses stiffened to the job, and for a minute the heavy dray with its enormous load rocked but did not move forward. But as though she had harnessed herself as an extra horse, it did begin to move and cross the line. And there it was, right across the rails, when the express emerged from the cutting, a hundred metres away. Then, to hold the dray for fear of its getting right across, she held back the team with a sudden jerk, her limbs cracking with the superhuman effort. This girl who was a legend, whose extraordinary feats of strength were fabled – a runaway truck stopped on a slope, a cart pushed out of the way of a train – was now performing the act of holding back with her iron grip five horses rearing and whinnying with instinctive fear.

What seemed an eternity of terror really lasted scarcely ten seconds. The two huge blocks of stone seemed to shut out the horizon. The engine was gliding along on its smooth, murderous way, with its shining brass and polished steel gleaming in the golden sunshine of this lovely morning. It was the inevitable, nothing on earth could now prevent the crash. Yet the wait went on.

Misard rushed screaming back to his post, waving his arms and shaking his fists in a crazy effort to warn and stop the train. Cabuche had come out of the house when he heard grinding wheels and whinnyings, and rushed screaming too, in order to make the horses go forward. But Flore, who had jumped clear, held on to him, which saved his life. He thought she had not been strong enough to master the horses and that they had dragged her along. He thought it was all his fault, and burst into sobs of hopeless terror while she, towering motionless, with wide, blazing eyes, stood and watched. At the very moment when the front of the engine was about to hit the blocks with not more than a metre left to go, in this split second, she clearly saw Jacques with his hand on the reverse. He turned and their eyes met in a look she found immeasurably long.

That morning Jacques had given Séverine a smile when she came down to the platform at Le Havre to catch the express as she did every week. Why spoil life with a lot of bugaboos? Why

290

not take advantage of happy days when they came? Everything would sort itself out in the end, perhaps. And he was determined to make the most of this day, anyway, making plans, thinking about having a meal with her in a restaurant. And so, when she made a despairing face at him because there was no first-class coach in front, and had to go a long way from him in the rear of the train, he had tried to cheer her up with a gay smile. Anyway, they would get there together and make up for having been separated. Moreover, after leaning out to see her get into a compartment right at the back, he had even taken his good humour to the point of chipping the guard, Henri Dauvergne, who he knew was sweet on her. The previous week he had had the impression that the latter was getting a bit bolder and that she was encouraging him as if she needed to take her mind off the life of torment she had made for herself. Roubaud said as much, that she would end up by sleeping with that young man, not for the pleasure but simply because she wanted to begin on something different. And Jacques had asked Henri who it was he had been blowing kisses to on the previous day when he was hiding behind one of the elms in the station forecourt; which had made Pecqueux roar with laughter as he was shovelling coal into Lison's grate while she was blowing off at high pressure, waiting to start.

From Le Havre to Barentin the express had gone at its regulation speed with no untoward incident, and as they emerged from the cutting Henri was the first to give the warning about the quarryman's dray across the line, which he saw from his perch in the look-out. The leading van was crammed with baggage, for the train was packed, carrying a whole shipload of travellers who had disembarked the night before. The vibration of the train kept the piles of trunks and cases jigging about, and hemmed in the midst of them the front guard was standing at his desk going through dispatch sheets, while his little bottle of ink hanging on a hook was continually on the swing too. After each station where he put down luggage he had four or five minutes' writing to do. As two passengers had got out at Barentin he had just put his papers in order and gone up to sit in his look-out and give his usual glance up and down the line. He stayed sitting on the watch in his glass box during all his free time. The tender hid the driver from him, but thanks to his high position he could often see further and quicker than the driver. And indeed the train was still rounding the curve in the cutting when he saw the obstacle ahead. He was so thunderstruck that for a moment he could not believe it and was paralysed with horror. Several seconds were lost and the train was already leaving the cutting and a great cry was going up from the engine by the time he made up his mind to pull the cord of the alarm bell dangling in front of him.

At this crucial second Jacques, with his hand on the reversing-wheel, was looking out with unseeing eyes in an absent-minded moment. He was dreaming about vague, far-off things from which even the vision of Séverine was absent. He was jerked out of it by the frantic jangling of the bell and a shriek from Pecqueux behind him. Pecqueux had lifted the firebox door because he didn't think the fire was drawing properly, and had just seen it as he leaned over to check the speed. Jacques, pale as death, saw everything, understood everything – the dray across the line, the engine at full speed, the frightful collision – and with such sharp clarity that he could even make out the grain of the two blocks of stone, while already in his bones he could feel the shock of the impact. It was inevitable. He violently turned the reversing-wheel, shut off steam, applied the brakes. He had put her into reverse and instinctively hung on to the whistle in a powerless yet frantic desire to give a warning and get that huge obstacle moved out of the way. But in spite of all this awful whistling of distress rending the air Lison was not responding, but still going on with scarcely slackening speed. She was no longer the docile creature of former days; since she had lost her good steaming in the blizzard, and her quickness off the mark, she had got crotchety and cantankerous, like a woman showing her age and gone all chesty with the cold. She puffed and blew, jibbed against the brake but still went on and on with the uncheckable obstinacy of her weight. Mad with fear, Pecqueux jumped for it. Jacques, frozen at his post, his right hand clinging to the reversing-wheel and the other unconsciously pulling at the whistle, waited. And Lison, steaming and blowing, with the high-pitched scream going on all the time, hit the dray with the enormous weight of the thirteen coaches she was hauling.

Twenty metres away, where they were paralysed with terror, Misard and Cabuche with arms in the air, Flore with eyes staring out of her head, saw this monstrous thing: the train rising up, seven coaches rearing on top of each other and then falling with a sickening crash into a shapeless mass of wreckage. The three leading ones were reduced to matchwood and the four others were just a mountain of jumbled of smashed-in roofs, broken wheels, chains, buffers and bits of glass. Above all they had heard the crunching of the engine against the blocks of stone, a dull crunching sound ending in a cry of agony. Lison, disembowled, had overturned to the left, on top of the dray, and the stones had split and flown in splinters as though blasted in a quarry, while four of the five horses had been rolled and dragged along, killed instantly. The six remaining coaches at the tail of the train were still intact and had stopped without even being derailed.

Shouts went up, calls for help, but the words tailed off into inarticulate animal yells.

'Save me! Help! Oh God, I'm dying! Help! Help!'

But all consciousness of sounds and sights had gone. Lison had heeled right over and was losing steam through her open belly, through taps ripped off and broken tubes, in roaring blasts like the desperate gasps of a dying giant. A continuous mass of white vapour billowed forth from her in dense clouds along the ground, while the red-hot coals falling like the life-blood from her vitals added their black smoke. In the violence of the impact the chimney had been forced into the ground; at the point where it had taken the weight the frame was broken and both frame-plates were bent. Like some monstrous steed ripped open by a gigantic horn, Lison lay with her wheels in the air, displaying her twisted coupling-rods, broken cylinders, smashed valve-gear with its eccentrics in one fearful wound gaping to the sky, through which her life was still issuing with a hiss of rage and despair. And by her side the one horse not killed outright was lying with its two fore-legs gone and, like her, was losing its entrails through a rent in its belly. By the look of its head, stiff and straight in a spasm of atrocious pain, it could be seen to be screaming in a last terrible whinny, though nothing could be heard above the noise from the expiring machine.

Strangled cries passed unnoticed, drowned, carried away.

'Save me! Finish me off! The agony's too much, kill me, go on, kill me!'

Amid all this deafening tumult and blinding smoke the doors of the carriages still intact had flown open and the passengers had poured out in a raging mob. They fell on to the line, picked themselves up again, fought, kicked and punched. Then as soon as they felt they were on solid ground, with nothing before them but the open country, they tore off at a gallop, leaping over the hedge, cutting across fields, giving in to the one instinct to get as far as possible from the danger. Men and women disappeared shrieking into the woods.

Séverine, trampled on, her hair down and her dress in shreds, had at last got free, but she did not run away. She was running towards the hissing engine when she found herself face to face with Pecqueux.

'Jacques, Jacques! He's safe, isn't he?'

By a miracle the fireman had not even suffered a sprain, and he was now rushing back, full of remorse at the thought that his driver was now under all that. The two of them had travelled so far and toiled so hard together, lashed to exhaustion by the continual tempests! And their engine, their poor engine, the beloved mistress in their threesome, was lying there on her back, giving up the ghost through her pierced lungs!

'I jumped,' he faltered, 'I don't know anything, nothing at all. Come on, let's make haste!'

By the side of the line they ran into Flore, who was watching them come. Dazed by the accomplished fact of the slaughter she had brought about, she still had not moved. It was over and it was all right, her only feeling was of a necessity accomplished – no pity for the suffering of others, that never even occurred to her. But when she saw Séverine her eyes dilated and a shadow of dreadful pain darkened her pale face. What! This woman was alive when he was certainly dead? In the intense pain of her murdered love, of the knife wound she had inflicted on her own heart, she had suddenly realized the full horror of her crime. She had done this, she had killed him, she had killed all these people! She uttered a piercing shriek, wrung her hands and rushed frenziedly to and fro.

'Jacques, oh Jacques! He's under there, he was thrown back-wards, I saw him. Jacques, Jacques!'

Lison's gasping was not so loud, a hoarse moan, weakening so that now the clamour of the injured could be heard through it, growing louder and more heartrending. But the smoke was still thick and the huge pile of wreckage, out of which came ago-nized and terrified voices, seemed to be cloaked in a black dust that the sun could not shift. What was to be done? Where to begin? How could those poor wretches be reached?

'Jacques!' Flore went on shouting. 'I tell you, he looked at me and then he was thrown down there underneath the tender ... Come on, give me a hand!'

Cabuche and Misard had already helped up Henri, the guard, who had also jumped for it at the last moment. He had dis-located one foot, and they sat him down on the ground with his back to the hedge, and from there he watched the rescue work, dazed and silent but apparently not in pain.

'Cabuche, why don't you come and help me, Jacques is under there, I tell you!'

But he did not hear, for he was running to help other injured, carrying off a young woman, both of whose legs were dangling, the thighs broken.

It was Séverine who ran up in answer to Flore's call.

'Jacques! Where? I'll help you!'

'That's right, you help me.'

Their hands met and they pulled together at a broken wheel. But the one's delicate fingers could do nothing, whereas the other's strong arm cleared away the obstacles.

'Look out!' cried Pecqueux, who was also starting on the job with them.

With a quick movement he stopped Séverine as she was about to tread on an arm, torn away at the shoulder and still wearing a blue sleeve. She recoiled in horror. But she did not recognize the sleeve; it was an unknown arm that had rolled there from a body that would no doubt be found somewhere else. It left her in such a shaky state that she was virtually paralysed, standing there whimpering, looking at other people working, incapable of even picking out splinters of glass that cut her hands.

By now the rescue of the dying and the search for the dead

were full of worry and danger because the fire from the engine had spread to some of the pieces of timber, and in order to check this potential blaze they had to throw on shovelfuls of earth. While somebody was running to Barentin to ask for help and a telegram was sent off to Rouen, the work of clearing was getting organized as actively as possible, and all hands were courageously getting on with it. Many of those who had run away had slunk back again, ashamed of their panic. But they proceeded with infinite caution as every bit of wreckage required care for fear of finishing off the buried victims if it became dislodged. Some of the injured were sticking out from the heap, buried there chest-deep, crushed as in a vice and screaming. It needed a quarter of an hour's work to release one of them, who was not complaining, but said there was nothing the matter with him and he couldn't feel anything, although he was as white as a sheet. When they had got him out he had lost both legs and died at once, never having known or felt this terrible mutilation because of his intense fear. A whole family was moved from a second-class carriage that had caught fire, the father and mother had injuries in the knees, the grandmother had a broken arm, but they could not feel their own pain either, for they were sobbing and calling for their little girl who had vanished in the crash, a little Goldilocks not yet three, who turned up under a bit of roofing safe and sound, gay and smiling. But another little girl who was covered in blood, with her poor little hands crushed, had been moved to one side until her parents could be discovered, and there she stayed, forlorn and unknown and so cowed that she could not utter a sound, but her face was contorted into an expression of unspeakable terror if anyone went near her. Doors could not be opened because the impact had twisted the metal locks, and compartments could only be entered by going down through broken windows. Four bodies had already been laid in a row by the side of the line. Ten or so injured were stretched out on the ground near the dead, waiting, but there was no doctor to dress their wounds and no help available. The work of clearing had hardly begun, for a new victim was being pulled out from under each piece of wreckage. The pile of human flesh, palpitating and running with blood, never seemed to get any smaller.

296

'But Jacques is under there, I tell you!' Flore kept repeating, finding some relief in this obstinate cry she was shouting quite irrationally, like the moaning of her despair. 'He's calling, look, look, listen!'

The tender was pinned underneath the carriages that had piled on to each other and then collapsed on top of it. And it was true that now that the noise from the engine was dying down a strong male voice could be heard yelling from beneath the pile of wreckage. As they approached, this agonized clamour got louder still, expressing such frightful pain that the toilers could not bear it and began crying and shouting themselves. When at last they freed the man's legs and caught hold of them and pulled, the scream of pain stopped. He was dead.

'No, no, it isn't him,' said Flore, 'he's lower down, underneath.'

With her amazon's arms she lifted wheels and hurled them out of the way, bent zinc roofing, broke doors, tore off lengths of chain. As soon as she came upon a dead or injured person she would give a shout for somebody to come and take them away, not wanting to relax for a single second from her own frantic hunt.

Behind her Cabuche and Misard were working away, while Séverine, exhausted by standing there without doing anything, had sunk down on to a broken carriage-seat. Misard, however, had soon recovered his stolid, passive indifference and was avoiding the more tiring jobs and mainly helping to transport the bodies. Like Flore, he examined the corpses as though hoping to identify them out of the multitudinous thousands of faces that for ten years had been passing them at full speed, leaving only the blurred impression of a crowd, here and gone like a flash of lightning. No, still nothing more than the unknown stream of people on the move: death, brutal and accidental, was still as anonymous as the hurrying life that tore past on its way to the future. They could not attach any name or precise bit of information to the horror-struck faces of these poor creatures, cut down on their travels, trampled on and crushed like soldiers whose bodies fill holes in the ground before the charge of an attacking enemy. Yet Flore did think she found someone she had spoken to on the day when the train was snowbound, that

American whose profile she had got to know so well without knowing his name or anything about him or his. Misard carried him as he did the rest of the dead who had come from the unknown and had been stopped here on the way to the unknown.

There was yet another heartrending sigh. In a first-class compartment turned upside down they had just found a young couple, probably newly married, who had been thrown against each other in such an awkward position that the woman was crushing the man underneath her but could not make any movement to take the weight off him. He was already suffocating and gasping his life away while she, who had her mouth free, was desperately pleading for someone to make haste, horrified, heartbroken, realizing she was killing him. When they had both been set free she was the one to expire at once, for a buffer had torn her body open. The man recovered consciousness and wailed with grief on his knees beside her. Her eyes were still wet with tears.

The dead now numbered twelve and there were over thirty injured. But they had managed to shift the tender and Flore kept stopping to thrust her head down between shattered timbers and twisted metal, feverishly searching for any glimpse of the driver. Suddenly she uttered a loud cry:

'I can see him, he's underneath. Look, there's his arm in his blue woollen jacket . . . He's not moving, he's not breathing . . .'

She straightened up and swore like a man:

'Come on, for Christ's sake! Stir your bloody stumps! Get him out from under there!'

With both hands she tried to break off the flooring of a carriage that other wreckage prevented her pulling to one side. So she ran off and came back with the axe which they used at home for splitting logs, and whirling it through the air like a woodcutter in an oak forest she attacked the piece of floor with furious energy. The others got out of the way and let her get on with it, shouting to her to be careful. But the driver was the only injured person there, protected underneath a twisted mass of axles and wheels. Not that she paid any attention to anybody, being carried along in a self-confident and irresistible burst of energy. She hacked away the timber, each blow cutting through

298

an obstacle. With her fair hair flying, her blouse torn off exposing her bare arms, she looked like some terrible harvester scything a way through this destruction she had caused. One final blow on an axle broke her iron axe-head in two. So, with the others' help, she moved away the wheels that had protected the young man from being crushed to certain death, and she was the first to seize him and bear him off in her arms.

'Jacques, Jacques! He's still breathing, he's alive. Oh God, he's still alive! I knew I had seen him fall and he would be there.'

Séverine ran frantically after her. Between them they set him down by the hedge next to Henri, who was still gazing in front of him in a daze, apparently not realizing where he was or what was going on round him. Pecqueux had come over, and there he stood in front of his driver, shattered at seeing him in such a dreadful state. The two women were now kneeling, one on each side, supporting the poor man's head and desperately watching for the slightest tremors on his face.

At last Jacques opened his eyes. His troubled gaze fell on each of them in turn, but without seeming to recognize them. They meant nothing to him. But when his eyes saw the dying engine a few metres away they were startled at first and then stared with increasing emotion. This loved one, Lison, he did recognize, and she brought everything back to his mind, the two blocks of stone across the line, the dreadful impact, the grinding sensation he had felt both in her and himself, from which he was recovering but she was surely going to die. It was no fault of hers if she had been tiresome, for since she had caught her illness in the snow she could not be blamed for not being so alert, apart from the fact that old age comes and makes your limbs clumsy and your joints stiff. And so he forgave her with all his heart and was filled with deep horror, seeing her mortally wounded and in her death-throes. Poor Lison couldn't last more than a few minutes. She was cooling, her live coals were falling out as cinders, the breath that had hissed so violently out of her pierced side was petering out into the soft whimpering of a crying child. Always so bright and shining, she was now soiled with dirt and dribble, lying on her back in a black sea of coal; it was like the tragic end of a thoroughbred steed knocked down

299

in a street accident. For a little while it had been possible to see her organs still working in her torn-open body, her pistons still beating like twin hearts, the steam circulating through her slide-valves like the blood in her veins; but as though they were arms in convulsion her driving rods were now only quivering in the last struggles for life, and her soul was departing along with the strength which had kept her alive, that powerful breath she still could not completely expel. The disembowelled giant quietened down still more, then gradually dozed off into a gentle sleep and final silence. She was dead. The heap of iron, steel and brass that this smashed colossus left behind, with split boiler, dis-jointed limbs, internal organs broken and exposed to the light of day, took on the gruesome misery of a vast human corpse, a whole organism that had been alive but whose life had been wrenched away in agony.

Realizing that Lison was no more, Jacques shut his eyes again, wishing to die as well, and being in any case so weak that he thought the last little breath of the engine was carrying him off too. Tears welled slowly from under his closed lids and ran down his cheeks. This was too much for Pecqueux, who was still standing there motionless, with a lump in his throat. Their dear sweetheart was dying, and now his driver wanted to follow her. So this was the end of their threesome? All over, those journeys when they did hundreds of leagues together on her back, with never a word exchanged because all three of them knew each other so well that they didn't even need a sign in order to understand! Oh, poor Lison, so gentle in all her strength, so lovely when she gleamed in the sunshine! Although he wasn't the worse for drink Pecqueux burst into violent sobs, with gasps that shook his great frame and would not be held back.

Séverine and Flore were equally shattered with anxiety when Jacques fell back into unconsciousness. Flore rushed off home and came back with some camphorated spirit which she rubbed him with for the sake of doing something. But the anguish of the two women was made even more unendurable by the inter-minable death-agonies of the only surviving horse of the team of five, both of whose fore-legs had been severed. It lay near them and its continual whinnying cry was almost human, and so

300

loud and expressing such excruciating pain that two of the injured caught the infection and began howling too, like animals. Never had a death-cry rent the air with a plaint like this, deep, unforgettable, blood-curdling. The torment became atrocious, voices quivering with pity and rage grew more insistent and begged somebody to finish off this wretched horse in its suffering, for its endless death-cry, now that the engine was dead, was going on like the final lament for the disaster. So then Pecqueux, still sobbing, picked up the axe with the broken head and put the horse down with a single blow on the skull. Silence fell over the scene of slaughter.

Help came at last, after two hours of waiting. The shock of the collision had thrown all the coaches to the left, and so the work of clearing the down line would only take a few hours. A train of three coaches, drawn by a pilot engine, had brought from Rouen the Prefect's chief assistant, the Public Prosecutor, the Company's engineers and doctors, quite a crowd of worried, busy people, while M. Bessière, stationmaster of Barentin, was there already with a gang of men dealing with the wreckage. This remote country spot, normally so deserted and silent, was full of extraordinary bustle and frayed nerves, the frenzied panic of the passengers who had escaped safe and sound had left them with a need for feverish activity; some were terrified at the thought of going back into the train and were trying to find horse-drawn vehicles, others, seeing that there was not even a wheelbarrow to be found, were already worrying about where they could get something to eat and somewhere to sleep. And everybody was anxious to find a telegraph office, and some set off on foot for Barentin, taking messages to be telegraphed. While the authorities, helped by the Company's staff, were beginning an inquiry, doctors were hastening to attend to the injured, many of whom had fainted and were lying in pools of blood. Others were quietly whimpering because of the pain from tweezers and needles. Altogether there were fifteen passengers dead and thirty-two seriously injured. The dead were laid out in a row on the ground alongside the hedge, with their faces turned to the sky, waiting to be identified. There was only a deputy prosecutor, a fair, pink young man, fussing about over them, going through their pockets for any papers, cards or letters that might help him to label each body with a name and address. Meanwhile a circle of gapers was forming round him, for although there was not a single house for nearly a league around, the onlookers had arrived from somewhere, about thirty men, women, and children who got in the way and did nothing to help. Now that the black dust and enveloping cloud of smoke and steam had blown away, the brilliant April morning triumphed over the field of carnage, pouring down its gay, bright sunshine like gentle rain upon the dead and dying, on Lison lying disembowelled and the horror of the piled-up wreckage which was being cleared by the gang of workmen, like ants toiling to repair their anthill kicked by someone walking heedlessly by.

Jacques was still unconscious and Séverine had begged a passing doctor to stop. He examined the young man and found no obvious wound, but he was afraid of internal injuries, for thin trickles of blood were coming through his lips. Unable to diagnose yet, he advised that the injured man be moved at once and put to bed, but he must not be jolted.

Feeling hands going over him Jacques had once again opened his eyes and uttered a little cry of pain. But this time he recognized Séverine, and in his panic he muttered:

'Take me away, take me away!'

Flore leaned over. Having turned his head he recognized her too. His eyes took on the scared look of a frightened child, he recoiled with hatred and horror and turned back to Séverine.

'Take me away, my dearest, quick, quick!'

She asked him in the same loving terms, alone with him, for this girl did not count:

'Would you like to go to La Croix-de-Maufras, my darling? If you don't mind that . . . It's right opposite, and we shall be in our own home!'

He accepted, still trembling, for his eyes caught sight of the other woman.

'Wherever you like, but quick!'

Flore stood there, deathly pale at his look of terrified execration. So in this slaughter of unknown, innocent people, she had not managed to kill either of them! The woman had come out of it without a scratch and he would probably get over it

302

too. All she had succeeded in doing was to bring them closer together, alone with each other in this lonely house. She could see them installed there, the lover cured and convalescent and his mistress busily looking after him, rewarded for her watchful care by continual caresses, and both, in absolute freedom, far from the madding crowd, prolonging this honeymoon vouch-safed them by the disaster. She felt icy cold as she looked at the dead whom she had killed to no purpose.

At that moment, as she was looking at the slaughter, Flore saw Misard and Cabuche being questioned by some gentlemen who were bound to be the police. And indeed the prosecutor and the Prefect's chief of staff were trying to make out how this quarryman's dray had got stuck across the line like that. Misard maintained that he had never left his post, he really didn't know anything, he made out that he had his back turned, he was busy with his instruments. As for Cabuche, who was still dazed, he was telling a long, rambling tale about why he had done wrong to leave his horses – how he was anxious to see the dead woman, how the horses had started off on their own, how the girl hadn't been able to stop them. He got into a muddle and began again, but could not manage to make anything clear.

Flore's frozen blood began flowing faster again as a mad desire for freedom took possession of her. She wanted to be a free agent, free to think and decide for herself, never having needed anyone else to set her on the right path. Why should she wait to be pestered with questions or perhaps even arrested? For apart from the crime itself there had been a neglect of duty, and she would be held responsible. And yet she stayed there, unable to move as long as Jacques were there.

Séverine had begged Pecqueux so hard that he had at last managed to get a stretcher, and he came back with another man to carry the patient away. The doctor had also made Séverine consent to take the guard, Henri, into her home as well. He only seemed to be suffering from shock, and didn't know where he was. He could be moved after Jacques.

As Séverine leaned over to unbutton Jacques's collar, which was choking him, she openly kissed his eyes, wanting to give him courage to face the move.

'There's nothing to be afraid of, we shall be happy together.'

303

He smiled and returned her kiss, and for Flore that was the supreme wrench which tore her from him for ever. She felt that her own life-blood was now ebbing away from an incurable wound. When they carried him away she took to flight. But as she passed the little, squat house she caught sight, through the window of the death chamber, the pale flame of the candle burning in broad daylight beside her mother's body. All through the disaster the dead woman had been there alone with her head half turned, her eyes staring and her mouth twisted, as though she had been watching all these unknown people being crushed to death.

But Flore rushed on, then immediately turned at the bend in the Doinville road and plunged to her left through the thicket. She knew every corner of this country and could defy any police to catch her if they were sent after her. So she stopped running and sauntered slowly on, making for a hiding-place where she loved to bury herself on her days of depression, an excavation above the tunnel. She looked up at the sky and could tell by the sun that it was midday. Once in her retreat she lay stretched out on the hard rock and stayed motionless, with her hands clasped behind her head, thinking. Only then did she become conscious of an aching void within her, a sensation of being already dead gradually numbed her limbs. It was not remorse at having killed all these people to no purpose, and she had to make an effort to remind herself of any regret or horror. But she was now certain that Jacques had seen her holding back the horses, for she had just realized from the way he had recoiled that she filled him with the terrified revulsion one feels for monstrosities. He would never forget. What was more, you may fail with other people, but you must not fail with yourself. Therefore she would kill herself. She had no other hope left, and she realized the absolute necessity of this now that she was here, recovering her calm and thinking reasonably. The only thing preventing her from getting up and looking for some means of finishing herself off was exhaustion, an emptying-out of all her being. And yet, from somewhere deep down in the invincible sleepiness taking possession of her, there rose once more the love of life, the instinct for happiness, a last dream of being happy herself as well, since she was leaving those two the happiness of living together in freedom. Why not wait for nightfall and go and find Ozil, who worshipped her and would be able to defend her? Her thoughts became pleasant and confused and she fell into a deep, dreamless sleep.

When she woke up night had already fallen, pitch dark. Not realizing where she was, she felt round her and suddenly recollected as she touched the bare rock on which she was lying. In a flash the absolute necessity came back to her: she must die. The cowardly sense of well-being, the attack of weakness in the face of the possibility of a new life, had apparently vanished with her fatigue. No, no, only death would do. She could not live in the midst of all this blood, with her heart torn from her body, execrated by the only man she had wanted, and who belonged to another. Now she was strong enough and she had to die.

Flore stood up and left her hiding-place in the rocks. She hadn't a moment's hesitation, for she had found instinctively where she had to go. Another glance skywards at the stars told her it was getting on for nine. As she was nearing the railway a train went by at full speed on the down line, which seemed to please her; everything would be all right and they had obviously cleared that line, but the other must still be blocked, for the traffic did not seem to be moving on it yet. From there she followed a hedge through the deep silence of this wild country. There was no hurry, there wouldn't be another train before the express from Paris which would not pass until 9.25, and she kept steadily on by the hedge in the thick darkness, as calm as if she were taking one of her usual walks along the lonely paths. But before she reached the tunnel she climbed over the hedge and walked on along the line itself, just strolling along as usual, to meet the express. She had to be a bit artful so as not to be seen by the watchman, but she did that in any case every time she went to see Ozil at the other end. Once inside the tunnel she walked steadily on. But this time was not like the time before, she was no longer afraid of losing her sense of direction if she turned round. Her head was not pounding now with tunnel madness, that attack of panic in which everything, time and space, gets confused in the thunderous noise and the sensation that the roof is falling in. What did she care? She did not reason why, or even think at all, but had the one fixed resolve: keep on

305

walking, straight ahead so long as there was no train, then still walk on, straight at its headlamp when she saw it shining through the darkness.

She was surprised because she seemed to have been going on like this for hours. How far off it was, this longed-for death! For a moment her courage failed her when she thought she might journey on for leagues and leagues and never meet that death. Her feet grew tired. Would she have to sit down and wait for it, lying across the rails? But that struck her as a shameful thing to do, she must march on to the end and die on her feet like a fighting Amazon. When she saw the headlamp of the train far away, like a little lone star twinkling in the black sky, her energy revived and she resumed her onward march. The train had not yet entered the tunnel, no sound could yet be heard and there was nothing but this bright, cheerful light gradually getting larger. Drawn up to her full height like a graceful statue, swinging along on her athlete's legs, she advanced with long but unhurried strides, as though she were going to meet a friend whom she wanted to spare a bit of the journey. But now the train had entered the tunnel and the terrifying rumbling was coming nearer, like a hurricane making the earth tremble, while the star was now a huge eye and still growing, bursting forth from its inky socket. Then, through some unexplained compulsion, possibly so as to be the only thing to be destroyed, and without slackening her determined, heroic march, she emptied her pockets and placed quite a little collection beside the line – a handkerchief, keys, some string, two knives – and even took off the scarf round her neck and opened her blouse until it was half off. The eye was turning into a blaze, an open furnace door vomiting forth fire, the monster's breath could already be felt, steamy and hot, and the rumble of thunder was ever more deafening. Still she strode on, making straight for this blaze so as not to miss the engine, fascinated like a moth drawn by a flame. Even at the moment of the terrible impact, the very embrace, she drew herself up again as though, rising in a final urge to fight, she meant to seize the colossus and strike it down.

More than an hour passed before they came to pick up her body. The driver had of course seen the tall white figure walking straight at the engine, a strange and frightening apparition in

306

the shaft of brilliant light shining upon it, and when the lamp suddenly went out and the train thundered on in utter darkness, he had shuddered, feeling death pass by. On leaving the tunnel he had tried to shout the news of the accident to the watchman. But it was only at Barentin that he had been able to report that somebody had got herself hacked to pieces back there—a woman for sure – some of whose hair, with bits of scalp, was still sticking to the broken glass of the lamp. When the men of the search party found the body, they were amazed to see how white it was, as white as marble. It lay on the up line where it had been flung by the violent collision, the head was a horrible mess, but the rest of the body was without a scratch, half naked, admirable in its pure, strong beauty. The men silently covered the body. They had recognized her. Of course she must have sought death in a mad attempt to escape from the awful responsibility weighing on her.

By midnight Flore's body was lying in the little house, next to her mother's. A mattress had been put on the floor and a new candle had been lit between the two. Phasie's head was still turned to one side, her mouth still twisted in a horrible grin, and she now seemed to be watching her daughter with her big, staring eyes. And all the time through the deep silence in this lonely place could be heard the heavy breathing of Misard at his dogged labour, still searching. The trains went by at their regular times, passing each other on both lines as normal running was now completely restored. On they went, inexorable, all powerful machines, unperturbed and unaware of these dramas and crimes. What did it matter that some unknown people had met their death on the journey, crushed beneath the wheels? The dead had been carried away, the blood cleaned up, and people were on the move again towards the future.

[11]

It was in the best bedroom at La Croix-de-Maufras, the room, hung with red damask, which had two tall windows looking out on to the railway line only a few metres away. From the old four-poster bed opposite the windows you could see the trains go by. For years and years nothing had been taken out of that room or any furniture moved.

Séverine had had Jacques brought up to this room injured and still unconscious, while Henri Dauvergne had been left in a smaller room on the ground floor. She reserved for herself a room near Jacques's, with only a landing between them. They were all reasonably well installed within two hours, for the house had remained fully furnished and there was even linen in the cupboards. With an apron over her dress Séverine had turned into a nurse, having simply wired to tell Roubaud not to expect her because she would probably stay there several days to look after some of the injured she had taken into the house.

By the following day the doctor thought he could answer for Jacques, and even expected to have him on his feet in a week's time – it was really miraculous, only very minor internal injuries. But he stipulated the utmost care and that he be kept absolutely still. So when Jacques opened his eyes again Séverine, who was watching over him like a child, begged him to be good and obey her in everything. He was still very weak and just promised with a nod. His mind was perfectly clear and he recognized this room she had described on the night of the confession: the red room in which at only sixteen and a half she had submitted to President Grandmorin's lusts. It was in this very bed where he was now, and those were the very windows through which, without even raising his head, he could see the trains go by shaking the whole house. He could feel this house round him, just as he had so often seen it when he himself had rushed past on his engine. He could visualize it standing slantwise beside the line, looking distressed and forlorn with its closed shutters, made even more miserable and dubious-looking, since it had been put up for sale, by the huge board which added to the melancholy of the garden overgrown with brambles. He recalled the awful sadness that came over him every time with a haunting dread, as though this house stood there as a menace to his existence. Now, lying in this room in such a weak state, he thought he understood. It could only be because he was doomed to die here.

As soon as she saw that he was in a fit state to understand, Séverine had hastened to reassure him by whispering in his ear as she was pulling up the bedclothes:

'Don't worry, darling, I've emptied your pockets and taken the watch away.'

He stared at her wide-eyed, making an effort to remember.

'The watch . . . oh yes, the watch.'

'You might have been searched. So I've hidden it with some things of mine. There's nothing to fear.'

He thanked her with a squeeze of the hand. Turning his head he caught sight of the knife on the table, also found in one of his pockets. But there was no need to hide that, it was just a knife like any other.

But already by the following day Jacques was gaining strength and beginning to hope he would not die there. He was really glad to see Cabuche busying himself round him, clumping heavily about on the floor with his great feet, for ever since the accident the quarryman had been haunting Séverine, caught up like everyone else in an ardent need to devote himself. He neglected his work and every morning he came and helped her with the heavy jobs in the house, doing things for her like a faithful dog with his eyes looking into hers. As he expressed it, she was a tough woman in spite of her delicate appearance. He might at any rate do something for her as she was doing so much for other people. The lovers got used to him and went in for love-talk and even kissed each other without bothering, when he crossed the room very tactfully, keeping his lumbering body as much out of the way as possible.

Yet Jacques was surprised how often Séverine was away. The first day, on doctor's orders, she had kept from him the fact that

Henri was downstairs, realizing how soothing it would be for him to think they were absolutely alone.

'We are on our own, aren't we?'

'Yes, my darling, quite, quite alone . . . Just sleep peacefully.'

But all the same she was disappearing at every moment, and the very next day he heard footsteps and whisperings downstairs. Then the day after that there was quite a lot of subdued merriment, high-pitched laughter and two young girls' voices prattling away incessantly.

'What's up? Who is it? So we aren't alone?'

'Well, no, we aren't, dear, there's another injured man down there just below your room. It's another one I had to take in.'

'Oh! Who?'

'Henri, you know, the guard.'

'Henri . . . Oh, I see!'

'And this morning his sisters have turned up. It's them you can hear, they giggle about everything. As he's much improved, they'll go back this evening because of their father who can't get on without them. Henri will stay on two or three days longer until he's quite better. Just fancy, he leaped off the train, and no bones broken. The only thing was he'd lost his memory, but that's come back now.'

Jacques said nothing, but looked so hard at her that she went on:

'You do understand, don't you? If he wasn't there people might talk about us. So long as I'm not alone with you there's nothing my husband can say and I've a good excuse for staying here . . . You do understand?'

'Oh yes, it's quite all right.'

And until the evening he listened to the laughter of the Dauvergne girls, which he remembered hearing in Paris coming up from the floor below that room in which Séverine, in his arms, had told him everything. Then quiet was restored and he could only hear Séverine's light step as she went from him to the other patient. The door of the downstairs room shut again and the house fell into deep silence. Twice, when he was very thirsty, he had to bang on the floor with the leg of a chair to make her come up. And when she reappeared she was all smiles and very

310

attentive, explaining that her jobs were never done because she had to keep changing cold compresses on Henri's head.

By the fourth day Jacques was able to get out of bed and sit for two hours in an armchair by the window. If he leaned forward a little he could see the narrow garden, cut in two by the railway, with its low wall overgrown with pale pink wild roses. That reminded him of the night when he had hoisted himself up to look over that wall, and then he thought of the fair-sized piece of land which had only a hedge round it that he had gone through and behind which he had come upon Flore, sitting on the doorstep of the little ruined greenhouse, untangling some stolen rope with the help of scissors. Oh, what an awful night that was, full of panic because of his affliction! Since his memory had been clearing, that vision of Flore standing tall and lithe like a fair Amazon, with her blazing eyes staring into his, had been haunting him. At first he had never opened his mouth about the disaster and nobody round him said a word about it out of prudence. But every detail was coming back clearer and clearer, and he was reconstructing the whole thing and thinking only of that with such concentration that now, sitting at the window, his sole occupation consisted of searching for clues and trying to identify the actors in the tragedy. So why didn't he now see her standing at her post by the level crossing, flag in hand? He dared not ask that question, but it added to the uneasiness inspired in him by this grim house which seemed to him full of ghosts.

But one morning, when Cabuche was there helping Séverine, he made up his mind.

'And what about Flore, is she ill?'

In the shock of the moment Cabuche misinterpreted a sign from Séverine and thought she was telling him to speak.

'Poor Flore, she's dead!'

Jacques looked at them both, horror-struck, and they had to tell him the whole story. Between them they told him about the girl's suicide and how she had thrown herself under the train in the tunnel. Her mother's burial had been put off until the evening so that the daughter could be taken away as well, and they were laid to rest side by side in the little cemetery at Doinville, where they had joined the first to go, the younger girl, sweet, unhappy Louisette, who had been carried off by violence as well, soiled with blood and mire. Three poor wretches of the kind who fall by the wayside and are crushed and disappear, swept aside, as it were, by the terrible hurricane of these passing trains.

'Dead, oh God!' muttered Jacques. 'Poor Aunt Phasie, and Flore, and Louisette!'

At this last name Cabuche, who was helping Séverine to move the bed, instinctively looked up at her, embarrassed by the memory of his old love just at this moment when he felt himself being conquered by a new passion, vulnerable, affectionate and simple soul that he was, like a good dog who devotes himself as soon as you fondle him. But Séverine, well aware of his tragic love-story, remained serious and looked at him with eyes full of sympathy; he was deeply touched, and as his hand had inadvertently brushed hers as he gave her the pillows, he was quite overcome when Jacques asked him whether she had been accused of causing the accident, and stammered out:

'Oh no, no . . . Only it was her fault, don't you see.'

He came out with what he knew, in faltering sentences. He himself hadn't seen anything because he was inside the house when the horses had started off, pulling the dray across the line. That was the cause of his own nagging remorse, and the gentlemen had given him a severe reprimand about it. You mustn't leave your horses, and the awful thing wouldn't have happened if he had stayed with them. So the inquiry had concluded that it was simple negligence on Flore's part, and as she had punished herself in an appalling way there the matter rested, and they weren't even going to remove Misard, who had got out of it in his usual humble and subservient manner by laying the blame on the dead girl: she always went her own way and he constantly had to leave his post to shut the gate. Moreover, the Company had had to admit that that morning he had been meticulous in carrying out his duties. So until such time as he remarried they had authorized him to take on as gate-keeper an elderly party who lived nearby, Ma Ducloux, an ex-barmaid who was living on savings of dubious origin.

When Cabuche left the room Jacques held Séverine back with a look. He was very pale.

'You do realize, don't you, that it was Flore who dragged the horses across and blocked the line with the stones?'

It was Séverine's turn to go pale.

'My dearest, what are you talking about? You've got a temperature, and you must get back to bed!'

'No, no, this isn't a nightmare ... Can't you understand? I saw her as plain as I see you. She held on to the horses and prevented that dray from going right across, with that strong arm of hers.'

Unable to hold up, she sank on to a chair opposite him.

'Oh my God, it's terrifying! It's unthinkable, and I shan't ever be able to sleep again.'

'Good heavens, it's perfectly clear, she tried to kill us both in a general massacre. She had been after me for years, and she was jealous. And besides, she was quite cracked, with the weirdest ideas ... So many murders in one go, a whole crowd in one bloodbath! What a woman!'

His eyes were staring and his lips twitching. He fell silent, and they went on looking at each other for a full minute. Then he forced himself to turn away from the abominable vision rising between them, and said softly:

'So she's dead, and that's why her ghost is haunting me. Ever since I came round I have been feeling she is here. Only this morning I turned round thinking she was at my bedside ... She's dead and we're alive. Let's hope she won't take her revenge now!'

Séverine shivered.

'Stop it! Stop it! You'll drive me mad!'

She went out. Jacques heard her go down to the other invalid. He stayed by the window and again lost himself studying the line, the little level-crossing house with its big well, and the section-post, the little wooden shack in which Misard seemed to be dozing at his regular, monotonous job. These things now absorbed him for hours, like a problem he worried at and could not solve, but the solution to which was essential for his salvation.

He never grew tired of watching this man Misard, so puny,

meek and colourless, continually racked by a nasty little cough, this man who had poisoned his wife, wearing down that fine strapping woman like some insect nibbling away in obstinate determination. It was certain that for years he had had no other thought in his head, day and night, all through the twelve interminable hours of his stretch of duty. Each time the electric bell rings to offer a train, blow the horn; then after the train has passed and the section is blocked, press a button to offer it to the next section-post, then press another button to give the line clear to the preceding post – these were purely automatic movements that ended by being like reflexes in a vegetable life. Uneducated, obtuse, he never read anything, but sat there with his arms dangling down and his eyes looking vaguely into space, between the tinklings of his apparatus. Almost always sitting in his shelter, the only pastime he had was making his lunch last as long as possible. Then he relapsed into his normal stupidity, empty-headed, without a single thought, but tormented by terrible drowsiness and sometimes going to sleep with his eyes open. At night, so as not to give in to this irresistible sleepiness, he had to stand up and walk about on unsteady legs like a drunken man. And so it was that the struggle with his wife, the secret fight for the hidden thousand francs – who should have them after the death of the other – must have been the sole subject of reflection in this lonely man's sluggish brain for months on end. As he blew his horn or worked his signals, automatically watching over the safety of so many lives, he was thinking about poison, and during the waits, as he sat there with dangling arms and eyes closing with sleep, he was still thinking about it. Beyond that, nothing; he would kill her, hunt for the money and he'd be the one to get it.

Today Jacques was amazed to see him looking just the same. So you could kill, be quite unconcerned and life went on. And indeed, after the first frenzy of hunting, Misard was falling back into the stolid, shifty gentleness of a feeble creature who dislikes upheavals. In reality he had destroyed his wife to no purpose, for she was still the winner and he was still the loser, still turning the house upside down and finding nothing, not a single centime. In his pasty face only the eyes, the worrying, ferrety eyes, betrayed his obsession. He continually saw the

314

dead woman's great staring eyes and the terrible grin on her lips as she repeated: 'Hunt, hunt!' And hunt he did, unable now to give his brain a moment's peace, it was working and working away without respite in search of the place where the nest-egg was concealed, going on with the examination of possible hiding-places, rejecting those he had already gone through, getting feverishly worked up whenever he thought of a new one, and then he dropped everything else in hot haste in order to rush there, but to no avail. This at length was becoming a relentless, avenging torture, a kind of cerebral activity that kept him awake, torpid yet still thinking in spite of himself, as the obsession ticked on like a clock. When he blew his horn, once for down trains, twice for up, he was searching, when he answered the bells, when he pressed the buttons to block or clear the line, he was still searching, he was searching ceaselessly, madly, in the daytime during his long periods of waiting in lumpish inactivity, at night fighting against drowsiness in the silence of the vast, black countryside where he might as well be exiled to the end of the world. And Ma Ducloux, the woman now working the gate, desperate to find a husband, was full of little attentions and worried because he never seemed to close his eyes nowadays.

One night when Jacques, who was now beginning to take a few steps in his room, got up and went to the window, he saw a lantern moving to and fro at Misard's – he must be on the prowl. But the following night, as he was looking out of the window again, he was surprised to realize that a big, dark shape standing in the road under the window of the next room, the one in which Séverine slept, was Cabuche. But instead of annoying him this filled him for some reason or other with sympathy and sadness: another poor devil, that great oaf stuck there like some faithful, demented animal. So Séverine, who was so slight and not beautiful when you came to look at her features, really had such powerful charm with her ink-black hair and pale periwinkle-blue eyes that even brutes, great brainless giants, were so aroused that they could spend whole nights just standing outside her door like nervous little boys! Things came back to his mind such as the quarryman's eagerness to do jobs for her and the slavish looks he gave her when he offered to do anything. Yes, certainly Cabuche was in love with her and desired her. The following day he watched him attentively and saw him furtively pick up a hairpin that had dropped while she was making the bed, and keep it inside his fist so as not to have to give it back. Jacques recalled his own tortures and all he had gone through because of his own sexual desires, and he thought of the confusion and fear coming back with his returning health.

Two more days went by, the week was coming to an end and, as the doctor had said, the patients would soon be able to go back to their jobs. One morning, standing at the window, Jacques saw a brand new engine go by with his fireman, Pecquex, on it, waving at him as though he were beckoning. But he was in no hurry because he was being kept there now by reviving passion, a kind of anxious expectation of what was bound to happen. That very day he once again heard young, fresh peals of laughter downstairs, and girlish merriment filling the gloomy house with the noise of a school during break. It was the Dauvergne girls, he knew. He did not mention it to Séverine, who incidentally was missing for most of the day, and never could stay with him for five minutes together. Then in the evening the house relapsed into a deathly silence. And as she now stayed in his room, looking serious and a bit pale, he looked hard at her and asked:

'So he's gone, his sisters have taken him?'

'Yes,' she answered curtly.

'And we are alone, really alone?'

'Yes, quite alone ... Tomorrow we have to part and I go back to Le Havre. This is the end of camping out in the wilderness.'

He still gazed at her, smiling but embarrassed. Then he made up his mind:

'You're sorry he's gone, aren't you?'

As she started and wanted to protest he cut her short.

'I'm not trying to pick a quarrel. You can see I'm not jealous. You told me one day to kill you if you were unfaithful, didn't you? I don't look like a lover out to kill his mistress ... But really, you never moved from down there. I couldn't have you to myself for a single minute. In the end I remembered what your husband said to me once. He said that one of these nights you would sleep with that chap, not for the pleasure, but simply for the sake of something new.'

She stopped protesting, but slowly said twice:

'Something new, something new.'

Then in a burst of irresistible frankness:

'All right then, it's true. You and I can tell each other everything. There are enough ties binding us together. For months that man had been running after me. He knew I had given myself to you, and he thought it wouldn't make any difference to me if I went with him too. And when he turned up downstairs he said so again, and repeated that he was dying for love of me, and looked so overcome with gratitude for all the care I was taking of him, and was so gentle and affectionate that it's true it did cross my mind to love him too and start something new, something better and very gentle ... Yes, there might not have been any thrill in it, but it would have calmed me.'

She broke off, hesitating to go on.

'Because, you see, there's no road ahead for us, there's no future ... Our dreams of going away and hopes of being rich and happy over there in America, all that happiness depended on you, and it is impossible because you couldn't do it ... Oh, I'm not blaming you, and perhaps it's even all to the good that the thing wasn't done, but I do want to make it clear that there's nothing more I can hope for from you. Tomorrow will be the same as yesterday, same troubles, same torments.'

He let her run on, and only put his question when he saw that she had finished.

'So that's why you slept with the other chap?'

She had begun to walk across the room, but came back, shrugging her shoulders.

'No I didn't, and I'm saying that quite simply, and I'm sure you believe me because there's no point now in our lying to each other. No, I couldn't do it, any more than you could do that other thing. Does it surprise you that a woman can't give herself to a man when she thinks it out and decides that it would have been to her interest to do so? I didn't go into it to that extent, neither had it ever cost me very much to be nice – I mean, to give that pleasure to my husband or to you when you wanted

317

me so much. Well, anyway, this time I couldn't. He did kiss my hands, but not even my lips, I swear to you. He will be expecting me in Paris some time later because I saw how miserable he was and didn't want to leave him with no hope.'

She was right, and Jacques believed her because he could see she wasn't lying and then his panic began to return, the horrible madness of his desire was growing with the realization that he was now imprisoned alone with her, far from everybody, and the flame of their passion was reviving. Seeking a way out he said:

'But still there's the other one, Cabuche!'

Again she turned quickly back.

'Oh, so you've noticed, you know that too ... Yes, it's true that there's that one as well. I wonder what's the matter with them all ... But that one has never said a word. Yet I can see him writhe every time you and I kiss. He hears me talk lovingly to you and goes away and cries. And besides he steals everything I possess, things of mine like gloves, even hankies – they vanish and he carries them off to his lair as treasures ... But surely you aren't going to suppose I could give in to that savage! He's too big, he'd frighten me. Anyway, he doesn't ask for anything. No, no, when hulking creatures like that are shy, they die of love without asking for anything. You could entrust me to him for a month and he wouldn't touch me with his finger-tips, any more than he did Louisette. I can guarantee that now.'

This memory made them look into each other's eyes in silence. The events of the past came back to them, their meeting before the examining magistrate in Rouen, then their first journey to Paris and how blissful it had been, their love-making at Le Havre and all that had followed, both good and terrible. She drew closer to him, so close that he could feel her warm breath.

'No, no, even less so with him than with the other one. Not with anybody, don't you see, because I couldn't. And do you want to know why? Believe me, I realize it now and I'm sure I'm right, it's because you have taken me, the whole of me. Yes, taken, there's no other word, like something you take with both hands and carry away and use every minute as one of your

318

belongings. Before you I never was anybody's. I am yours and yours I shall remain even if it is against your wishes and against my own. I can't explain it. Our paths have crossed like this. With the others it frightens and disgusts me, but with you it is a wonderful joy, truly heavenly bliss. Ah, I only love you and can't ever love anyone else but you!'

She made as if to hold out her arms to take him to herself in an embrace and rest her head on his shoulder with her lips to his. But he seized her hands and held her at a distance, panic-stricken at feeling the old trouble stirring in his limbs as the blood beat through his head. It was the old familiar singing in the ears, the hammer-blows and multitudinous clamourings of his old, terrible attacks. For some time already he had been unable to possess her in the daylight or even by candle-light for fear of losing his head if he could see her. And now there was a lamp throwing a strong light on them both and the reason for his trembling and for the oncoming attack of madness must be that he could see the white mounds of her breasts down the open front of her dressing-gown.

But she went on, imploring him in her own passion:

'I don't care if our future life is hopeless. Even if I can't expect anything else from you and know that tomorrow will bring us the same troubles and torments, I don't care. I've nothing else to do except drag my existence on and suffer with you. We'll go back to Le Havre and things can go on as they like so long as I can have you like this for an hour now and again. I haven't slept for three nights, I've been suffering tortures in my room across the landing because of my longing to come and join you. You had been so ill and looked so depressed that I didn't dare ... But keep me with you tonight, won't you? You'll see how lovely it will be, and I'll take up no room at all so as not to be a nuisance. And besides, don't forget it's the last night. We're at the world's end here in this house. Listen, there's not a breath, not a living soul. Nobody can come, we're alone, so completely alone that nobody would know if we died in each other's arms.'

In the frenzy of his desire, excited by her caresses, Jacques, having no weapon to hand, was already stretching out his fingers to strangle her when she, out of force of habit, turned and

319

put out the lamp. Then he carried her in his arms and they lay down together. It was one of their most passionate nights of love, the best of all, the only one in which they felt as one, lost in each other. Yet, utterly exhausted by their pleasure, numbed to the point of losing the feel of their own bodies, they did not go off to sleep, but stayed locked in an embrace. And just as on the night of her confession in Ma Victoire's room, he listened in silence while she, with her mouth close to his ear, softly whispered on and on. Possibly she had felt death brush past her that evening before she put out the lamp. Until that day she had always been smiling and unconcerned in spite of the continual threat of murder in her lover's arms. But she had now felt the little cold shudder of death, and it was this unexplained terror which bound her so closely to him now in her need for protection. Her gentle breathing was like the very gift of herself.

'Oh my dearest, if you had been able to do it, how happy we should have been over there! No, no, I'm not asking you again to do what you can't do, and yet I do so wish our dream had come off! Just now I felt frightened. I don't know, but it seems as though there is something threatening me. It's childish no doubt, but I keep looking over my shoulder every minute as if there were somebody there waiting to strike. And I've only got you, my darling, to defend me. All my joy depends on you, you are now my only reason for living.'

He did not answer, but held her closer still, putting into this pressure what he could not say: his emotion, his sincere desire to be kind to her and the violent love she had never ceased to inspire in him. And yet once again he had wanted to kill her that very evening, for had she not turned away to put out the lamp he would certainly have strangled her. He would never be cured, the attacks came on as the turn of events dictated, and he couldn't even discover the causes, let alone reason them out. Why, for example, that particular evening, when he found out how faithful she was and how all-embracing and trusting her love was? Was it that the more she loved him the more the frightening depths of male domination in him wanted to possess her to the point of destroying her? To have her like the earth, a dead body!

320

'Tell me, my beloved, why am I afraid like this? Do you know of any threat hanging over me?'

'No, no, set your mind at rest, there's nothing threatening you.'

'There are moments when my body is all of a tremble. There's some danger always lurking behind me that I can't see, but can feel quite distinctly ... Why ever should I be afraid?'

'No, don't be afraid ... I love you and I won't let anybody hurt you ... Now look how lovely it is to be one with each other like this!'

There was a silence full of wonder.

'Oh dearest,' she went on in her caressing whisper, 'oh for nights and still more nights just like this one, never-ending nights when we could be like this together as one body ... You know, we could sell this house, take the money away with us and join your friend who's still waiting for you in America. There isn't a single time I go to bed without working out our life over there ... Every night would be like this one, you would take me and I would be yours and we should end by going off to sleep in each other's arms ... But you can't do it, I realize that. If I keep talking about it it's not because I want to upset you, but it comes out of my heart whatever I do.'

A sudden decision took over Jacques's mind. He had already made it so often before: <u>kill Roubaud, so as not to kill her.</u> This time, as before, he thought his determination was absolute and unshakeable.

'I wasn't able to then,' he whispered back, 'but I shall be. Haven't I promised?'

She protested, but not very strongly.

'No, don't promise, please ... It makes us feel so bad afterwards when your nerve lets you down ... And besides, it's horrible, no, no, you mustn't!'

'But I must, you know, I must. It's because I must do it that I shall find the strength. I wanted to talk to you about it, and now we're going to, as we are here alone and so quiet that we can't even hear our own thoughts.'

She was already beginning to resign herself, but sighing and with her heart thumping so hard that he could feel it beating against his own.

'Oh Lord, so long as it was not going to come off I wanted it to happen. But now it's getting serious I can't bear it.'

They stopped talking and a fresh silence fell, pregnant with this resolve. They were conscious of the empty desolation of the wild country round them. They were very hot, and their damp entwined limbs seemed to be melting into each other.

Then in his wandering caresses he planted his lips on her neck, below the chin, and she took up her soft murmuring again.

'He would have to be got here ... Yes, I could find some pretext or other and send for him. I don't know what, but we'll think of that later. Then you could be waiting for him, couldn't you? You could hide somewhere and it would go off quite simply because you're certain not to be disturbed here. Don't you think that's what's got to be done?'

As his lips went down from her neck to her breast he answered obediently:

'Yes, yes.'

But she was coolly planning every detail, and as the plan developed in her head she thought it over and improved upon it.

'Only, dearest, it would be too silly not to take our precautions. If it meant getting arrested the next day, I'd rather stay as we are. Look here, I read somewhere, it must have been in a novel, that the best thing to do is to make it look like suicide ... He has been very peculiar lately, so nervy and depressed that nobody would be surprised if they suddenly heard he had come here to make an end of himself. But there you are, we should have to find the means and arrange things so that the theory of suicide is plausible, shouldn't we?'

'Yes, I suppose so.'

She went on puzzling, gasping a little because he was gathering her up in his arms so as to cover her bosom with kisses.

'Something to leave no trace ... I say, this is an idea! Suppose he had that knife in his neck, all we should have to do is pick him up and carry him between us and put him across the line. Do you see, we could put his neck on a rail so that the first train cut his head off. After that they could hunt as much as they liked. With all that part squashed, there would be no wound, nothing left! Isn't that all right?'

322

'Oh yes, quite all right.'

They both grew quite excited, and she was almost merry and proud of having such an imagination. As his caresses became more insistent she stiffened and said:

'No, leave me alone, wait a bit. Because, darling, now I come to think of it, it's not quite right yet. If you stay here with me suicide will look a bit fishy. You must go away, don't you think, and openly, in front of Cabuche and Misard so that your departure is clearly witnessed. You'll take the train at Barentin, find some reason for getting off at Rouen, and then as soon as it's dark come back and I'll let you in by the back door. It's only four leagues, and you can be back here in under three hours. This time it's all settled. If you are willing it's on.'

'Yes, I am willing and it's on.'

He was musing as well now, and had stopped caressing her. There was another long silence while they stayed like that, motionless in each other's arms as though frozen in the future deed, now settled and certain. Then consciousness of their bodies slowly came back, and they were crushing each other in an increasingly urgent embrace when she stopped and loosened her hold.

'Well, and what's to be the excuse for bringing him here? In any case he can only catch the eight o'clock in the evening, after his duty, and can't be here before ten, which is all to the good ... Ah yes, of course, that buyer for the house Misard mentioned who is coming to look over it the day after tomorrow, in the morning. So there you are, I'll send a wire to my husband as soon as I get up, saying that his presence is absolutely necessary. He'll be here tomorrow night. You'll go off in the afternoon and can get back before he arrives. It will be dark, there's no moon, nothing to prevent. It all fits in perfectly.'

'Yes, perfectly.'

This time they did make love to the point of exhaustion. When at last they went off to sleep in deep silence, still in each other's arms, it was not quite daylight, but the first greyness of dawn was beginning to lighten the shadows that had hidden them from each other like a black cloak. He slept like a log until ten, in a dreamless sleep, and when he opened his eyes he was alone, she was dressing in her own room across the landing. A ray of brilliant sunshine came in through the window and turned the red hangings of the bed, the red wallpaper, all this red in the room into flames of fire while the house was shaking with the thunder of a passing train. It must have been the train that woke him up. He was dazzled by the sun and this flood of red in which he found himself. Then it came back to him, it was settled, and this coming night, when the bright sun had gone again, he would kill a man.

Things passed off that day just as Jacques and Séverine had planned. Before breakfast she asked Misard to take the telegram for her husband to Doinville, and at about three, as Cabuche was there, Jacques openly got ready to leave. And indeed as he was setting off to catch the 4.14 at Barentin, Cabuche came with him, partly for the sake of something to do, but also because he was drawn to Jacques by his own secret passion and was happy to find in the lover something of the woman he desired. Jacques reached Rouen at 4.40 and found a room near the station at a pub run by a woman who came from his part of the world. He talked to her about seeing some friends of his next day before going on to Paris to start work again. But he said he was very tired from having overtaxed his strength, and at six o'clock he went to get some sleep in the room he had taken on the ground floor with a window opening on to a quiet back street. Ten minutes later he was on his way to La Croix-de-Maufras, having stepped over the window-sill without being seen, and taken care to push back the shutters so as to be able to get in again unperceived.

It was not until a quarter past nine that Jacques was back in front of the lonely house standing slantwise by the railway, dreary and forlorn. It was a very dark night and not a glimmer of light could be seen coming from the hermetically closed front of the house. Once again he experienced a stab of pain, a fit of dreadful distress like a sort of presentiment of the inevitable doom waiting for him in this place. As he had arranged with Séverine, he threw three pebbles at the shutters of the red room, then went round to the back of the house, where in due course a door opened noiselessly. Having shut it behind him he followed the soft steps up the stairs, groping his way. But upstairs, in the light of the big lamp on the corner of the table, he stood amazed to see the bed already disturbed, her clothes over the back of a chair and Séverine herself in her nightdress, with bare legs and her heavy hair tied up for the night on top of her head, exposing her neck.

'What! You're gone to bed?'

'Yes of course, it's much better . . . I've had an idea. You see, when he comes and I go down like this to let him in, he will be even less suspicious. I shall say I've got a headache. Misard already thinks I'm not very well. That will enable me to say that I've never been out of this room when they find him tomorrow out there on the line.'

A shiver ran through Jacques and he lost his temper.

'No, put some clothes on . . . You must be up and about. You can't stay like that.'

She smiled in astonishment.

'Why not, dear? Don't fuss, I assure you I'm not in the least cold. See how warm I am!'

She cuddled up to him meaning to throw her arms round his neck, displaying her round breasts, uncovered because her nightdress had slipped down over one shoulder. As he recoiled with growing irritation she went all gentle and obedient.

'Don't be angry, I'll get back into bed and then you won't be afraid I shall catch cold!'

After she was back in bed with the sheet up to her chin he did seem a little calmer. And she went on talking quite unruffled, explaining how she had thought things out.

'As soon as he knocks I shall go down and open the door. At first I thought of letting him come up here where you could be waiting for him. But that would have made it more complicated for getting him down again, and besides, this room has got a wooden floor and the hall downstairs is tiled, which will be easier for me to wash if there are any bloodstains . . . As a matter of fact, while I was undressing just now I remembered a novel in which a man who was planning to kill another stripped himself naked. You see it's easy to wash yourself afterwards and not have a single stain on your clothes . . . Suppose you stripped too and we both took everything off?'

He looked at her, appalled. But she had her mild expression

and the innocent eyes of a little girl and was only concerned with doing the thing properly so as to be sure of success. All that was going through her head. But in him this vision of their two naked bodies splashed with blood revived his malady in a horrible shaking of his whole body.

'No, no! What, like savages? Why not make a meal of his heart and have done with it? You really do loathe him, don't you?'

Her face suddenly darkened. This question transported her from the preparations of a careful housewife back to the horror of the deed. Her eyes filled with tears.

'I've had too much to put up with these last months to be able to have much love for him. I've told you a hundred times – anything, rather than stay with that man one more week. But you're right, it's awful that it should come to this, we really must want to be happy together ... Well, anyway, we'll go downstairs in the dark. You'll stand behind the door, and when I've opened it and he has come in you can do as you think fit. I'm only concerned to help you, so that you don't have all the bother alone. I'm doing the best I can.'

He had paused by the table, looking at the knife, the weapon the husband himself had already used and that obviously she had put there for Jacques to stab him with in his turn. It was open and gleaming in the lamplight. He picked it up and examined it. She said nothing, but looked at it too. As he had it in his hand there was no point in talking about it. She only went on when he had put it down again on the table.

'I'm not forcing you, am I, dearest? There's still time to go away if you can't do it.'

With a violent gesture he insisted:

'Do you think I'm funking it? This time it's settled, I swear!'

Just then the house was shaken by the thunder of a train tearing past, so close to the room that it seemed to be roaring through it. He went on:

'That's his train, the Paris semi-fast. He has got off at Barentin and will be here in half an hour.'

Neither of them said any more and there was a long silence. They could visualize that man coming along the narrow path in the dark night. Jacques had automatically begun walking up

326

and down in the room as if he were counting the steps of the other man whom every stride was bringing nearer. One more, one more, and at the last one he would be lying in wait behind the hall door and would thrust the knife into his neck as soon as he entered. She, with the bedclothes still up to her chin, lying on her back, followed him up and down with her big, staring eyes, hypnotized by the rhythm of his steps which struck her like an echo of the other distant steps out there. Always one more and one more, and now nothing would stop them. When there were enough of them she would jump out of bed and go down barefoot to open the door in the dark. 'Here you are, dear, come in, I've gone to bed.' But he wouldn't even answer, he would fall in the darkness with his throat slit.

Another train went by, a down train, the slow which passed La Croix-de Maufras in the opposite direction within five minutes of the semi-fast. Jacques stopped in surprise. Only five minutes! What a long wait half an hour would be! He felt he must keep moving and began pacing up and down the room again. He was already having doubts about himself, like those men whose nerves affect their virility – would he be able to do it? He knew so well how the phenomenon worked itself out in him because he had gone through it more than ten times; first, certainty, an absolute resolve to kill, then a tightness in the chest, cold feet and hands, then finally a sudden collapse, with his will-power unable to act on muscles that had gone flabby. In an attempt to work himself up by reasoning he repeated what he had told himself many times, the advantage to him of doing away with this man, the fortune waiting in America and the possession of the woman he loved. The worst of it was that when he had found her half naked just now he had thought that the thing was going wrong again, for he lost control of himself as soon as the old trouble reappeared. For a moment he had wavered in the face of too powerful a temptation, with her offering herself and the open knife lying there. But now he felt strong and braced up for the effort. He could do it. So, pacing the room from door to window but trying not to look each time he passed the bed, he went on waiting for the man.

In the bed, where they had loved each other through the passionate dark hours of the previous night. Séverine still did not move. Her head motionless on the pillow, she followed him up and down with her eyes, keyed up herself and worried by the fear that tonight his courage would fail him again. To make an end of it and then start afresh was all she wanted, being a woman made for love and unconcerned with anything else, submissive to man, wholly belonging to the man who possessed her and heartless towards the other whom she had never wanted. As he was in the way he was being got rid of, nothing was more natural. It was only when she thought about it that she felt upset by the abominable nature of the crime, and as soon as the vision of blood and the horrible complications faded once again, she fell back into her smiling calm, with her expression of affectionate docile innocence. And yet, well though she thought she knew Jacques, she was amazed. He had the same round, good-looking face, curly hair, very black moustache and brown eyes flecked with gold, but his lower jaw was thrust so far forward, like that of a ravening beast, that it quite disfigured him. As he passed her he looked at her but against his will, it seemed, his bright eyes were filmed over with a ruddy mist and he jumped back, his whole body recoiling from her. What was he trying to avoid? Was it that his nerve was failing him once again? For some time now, unaware of the continual danger threatening her in her relationship with him, she put down the motiveless, instinctive fear she felt to a presentiment of an impending break. She suddenly felt convinced that if he failed to strike in a few minutes' time he would run away and never return. So she made up her mind that he would go through with the killing, and she would give him the strength, if necessary. At that moment another train was going by, an interminable goods train whose tail of trucks seemed to have been rumbling by for ever in the oppressive silence of that room. Propped up on one elbow she waited for this storm to fade away in the distance into the sleeping countryside.

'Another quarter of an hour,' Jacques said aloud. 'He's got past the Bécourt wood by now, half way. Oh what a long time it is!'

But on his way back to the window he ran into Séverine, standing in her nightdress by the bed.

'Suppose we go down with the lamp,' she suggested. 'You

could have a look round and put yourself in the right position, and I could show you how I will open the door and how you can do it.'

He recoiled, trembling.

'No, no! Not with the lamp!'

'Look, we can hide it afterwards, but we must see the lie of the land.'

'No, no! Get back to bed!'

She took no notice, but advanced towards him with the invincible, imperious smile of the woman who knows she is all-powerful through the lust she inspires. When she had him in her arms he would yield to her flesh and do what she wanted. So she went on talking in caressing tones, to subdue him.

'Really, darling, what's got into you? Anyone would think you're afraid of me. As soon as I come near you seem to avoid me. If you knew how much I need your support at this moment, and to feel you're there and that we are of the same mind for ever and ever, don't you see!'

She had managed to push him back against the table and he could not retreat any further, but looked at her in the bright lamplight. He had never seen her like this, with her nightdress all open and her hair tied up so high that she was quite naked, neck and breasts bare. He felt stifled, struggling but already losing, carried away by the rush of blood to his head and his horrible desire. He remembered that the knife was there behind him on the table, he could feel it and only had to put out his hand.

Once again with an effort he managed to stammer:

'Get back into bed, for God's sake!'

But she was sure she knew that he was trembling because of his overmastering desire for her. It filled her with a sort of pride. Why should she obey him, for she wanted to be loved that night to the limit of his powers, to the point of madness. So with wheedling affection she drew still nearer until she was pressing him close.

'Give me a kiss, my beloved ... Kiss me with all your might as you love mc. It'll give us both courage. Yes, we could do with some. We must love each other in a different way from other people and more than them, more than all of them, so as to do

329

what we are going to do. Kiss me with all your heart and soul!'

He no longer dared to breathe, he was choking. There was a howling mob in his skull that deafened him, and teeth like fire were biting into his head behind the ears, then reached his arms and legs, driving him out of his own body as the other creature, the invading brute, advanced. Soon his hands would no longer belong to him in the frenzy inspired by this naked woman. Her bare breasts were crushed against his clothes, her bare neck was offering itself, so white, so delicate, an irresistible temptation, and her sharp, warm, all-powerful scent drove him into a frenzied dizziness, endless swaying to and fro, in which his will-power, torn away from him and destroyed, was sinking without trace.

'Kiss me, darling, while we still have a minute. You know he'll be here any moment. If he has walked fast he may knock any second now. As you don't want us to go down, keep this in your mind. I'll open the door and you'll be behind it; and don't waste a second, do it at once, at once to get it over ... I love you so much and we'll be so happy together! He is just a wicked man who has made me suffer, and is the only obstacle in the way of our happiness. Kiss me, go on, hard, hard! As though you were eating me up so that there's nothing of me left apart from you.'

Without turning round Jacques had groped behind him with his right hand and taken hold of the knife. He stayed like that for a second, clutching it. Could this be his thirst coming back, the thirst to avenge ancient wrongs no longer clear in his memory, that resentment that had grown as it had come down from male to male ever since the first one had been betrayed in some cavern? He stared at Séverine wild-eyed, conscious of only one urge, to throw her on her back dead, like some prey snatched from other men. The door of terror opened over the black chasm of sex, love even unto death, destruction for fuller possession.

'Kiss me, kiss me!'

She threw back her head in readiness, full of imploring tenderness, exposing her bare neck where it left the voluptuous curve of her bosom. Seeing this white flesh as in a flash of fire he raised the fist which held the knife. She saw the gleam of the

330

blade and leaped backwards, gasping with surprise and terror.

'Jacques, Jacques! My God, why me? Why?'

Clenching his teeth, he pursued her without a word. There was a brief struggle and she was back by the bed. She shrank away, desperate, defenceless, her nightdress torn off.

'Why, oh God, why?'

He brought down his fist and the knife nailed the question in her throat. As he struck he turned the knife round, through some gruesome desire of his hand which was having its own way – the same kind of stab as for President Grandmorin, in the same place, with the same savagery. Had she cried out? He never knew. At that moment the Paris express dashed past, so noisy and fast that the floor shook, and she was dead as if this storm had struck her down.

Jacques stood motionless staring down at her, lying at his feet beside the bed. The noise of the train was dying away, and he contemplated her in the deep silence of the red room. Surrounded by these red walls and red curtains, she was lying there, bleeding profusely in a red stream running down between her breasts spreading over her stomach and down to the thigh, from which it was dripping in great drops on to the floor. Her nightdress, half torn off, was soaked in it. Never would he have believed there was so much blood in her. He was held there spellbound by the expression of unspeakable terror which this pretty woman's face, so meek and gentle, had taken on in death. Her black hair, standing on end, looked like a helmet of horror, dark as night. The periwinkle-blue eyes, unnaturally dilated, were still questioning, frantic and terror-struck by the mystery of it all. Why, why had he murdered her? She had been crushed and thrown away by the inexorable laws of murder, uncomprehending, swept along by life from the mire into blood, and yet tender and innocent in spite of all, never having understood.

But Jacques was astounded. He could hear the sniffing of an animal, the snorting of a wild boar, the roaring of a lion, but then he was reassured – it was only his own heavy breathing. At last, at last! He had satisfied himself, he had killed! Yes, he had done it. Boundless joy and an awful exultation bore him aloft in the complete contentment of his eternal desire. He felt a surprising pride, an enhanced sense of his male sovereignty.

Woman – he had killed her, and now, as he had so long desired, he possessed her completely to the point of destroying her. She was no more and never would be anybody else's. An intensely vivid memory came back to him of the other murdered body, that of President Grandmorin, which he had seen on that terrible night only five hundred metres from there. This delicate body, so white and streaked with red, was the same human lump, the broken puppet, the limp rag that a knife-thrust makes out of a living creature. Yes, that was it. He had killed, and the thing was there on the ground. She had been chucked down like the other one, but on her back, with legs outspread and the left arm doubled back under the body and the right twisted and half wrenched from the shoulder. Wasn't it that very night that he had sworn with beating heart to dare in his turn, as the sight of a slaughtered man had turned his itch for murder into a lust? Oh, to have the nerve, satisfy himself and thrust the knife in! And it had mysteriously germinated within him and grown, and there had not been a single hour this last year when he had not moved a stage towards the inevitable; even in this woman's arms and during her kisses the hidden leaven had gone on working. The two murders were coupled together. Was not one the logical outcome of the other?

Jacques was jerked away from his gaping contemplation of the dead woman by the din of a collapsing building and shaking floor. Were the doors being shattered into splinters? Were they coming to arrest him? But looking round he found nothing but solitude, deaf and mute. Oh of course, yet another train. And then there was that man about to knock downstairs, the man he wanted to kill! He had forgotten all about him. He had no regrets, but already he knew he had been idiotic. What had happened? The woman he loved and by whom he was passionately loved lay on the floor with her throat slit, while her husband, the obstacle in the way of his happiness, was still alive and coming nearer, step by step, through the darkness. He had been unable to wait for this man, whom he had spared for months because of the scruples of his upbringing and the humanitarian ideas slowly acquired and passed on. And now, against his own interests, he had been carried away by inherited violence, the instinct for murder that in the primeval forests

332

hurled one beast on to another. Does anyone kill as the result of reasoning? No, men only kill when driven on by their blood and nerves as a legacy of ancient struggles for survival and the joy of being strong. All he felt now was sated weariness. He was frightened and tried to understand, but could find nothing else deep down in his satisfied passion except the shock and bitter distress of the irreparable. The sight of the wretched creature still gazing at him in terrified questioning became unbearable. He tried to look away, and suddenly had the impression that another bloodless face was rising up at the foot of the bed. Was it the dead woman's ghost? Then he saw it was Flore. She had already come back once in his delirium after the accident. No doubt she was triumphant now, enjoying her revenge. He went cold with horror, wondering what he was up to, wasting time in this room. He had killed, he was gorged, satiated, drunk with the dreadful wine of crime. He tripped over the knife on the floor and fled, almost tumbling down the stairs, flung open the front door on to the main steps, as though the little back door wasn't wide enough, and rushed out into the inky blackness and galloped wildly away. He never turned round. That evil house, standing slantwise by the line, he left wide open and desolate behind him in the solitude of death.

On that night, as on the others, Cabuche had come through the boundary hedge and was prowling under Séverine's window. Knowing that Roubaud was expected, he was not surprised at the light filtering through a gap in a shutter. But he had been stupefied to see a man leaping down the steps and making off like a stampeding animal. It was too late to run after him, and he stood there bewildered, worried and hesitating at the open door and gaping into the big black hole of the passage. What was going on? Ought he to go in? The heavy silence and absolute stillness, with the light still burning up there, gripped his heart with increasing anxiety.

At last he made up his mind and groped his way upstairs. He stopped again outside the door, which was left open too. In the soft lamplight he thought he saw some clothing lying in a heap by the bed. She must be undressed. He called softly, suddenly scared, with the blood pumping through his veins. Then he saw the blood, understood and leapt forward with a terrible cry that came from his breaking heart. Oh God, it was Séverine, murdered, thrown down there in her pitiful nakedness! He thought she was still gasping for breath, and felt such terrible despair and such agonizing shame at seeing her dying in her nakedness, that he threw his arms round her like a brother, lifted her up and placed her on the bed, pulling up the sheet to cover her. But in this embrace, the only sign of love between them, he had covered himself with blood on his chest and both hands. He was streaming with her blood. At that moment he realized that Roubaud and Misard were there. They too, finding all the doors open, had decided to go upstairs. The husband was late because he had stopped to talk to the level-crossing keeper, who had come along with him to finish the conversation. Appalled, they both stared at Cabuche, whose hands were bloody like a butcher's.

'Same way as the President,' said Misard at last, examining the wound.

Roubaud nodded in silence, unable to take his eyes off Séverine, with her face of unspeakable horror, black hair standing on end and blue eyes monstrously dilated, asking why.

[12]

THREE months later, one warm June night, Jacques was driving the 6.30 express from Paris to Le Havre. His new engine, No. 608, brand new, whose maidenhead he possessed, as he put it, and whom he was beginning to know, was awkward, restive, moody, like young fillies who have to be broken in by hard work before they will yield to the harness. He often swore at her and missed Lison; he had to keep a close eye on this one and always have his hand on the reversing-wheel. But on this particular night the sky was so lovely and calm that he felt in an indulgent mood and let her run on as she felt inclined, glad himself to be filling his lungs with air. He had never felt better, had no remorse and seemed relieved of a burden, happy and at peace.

Although usually he never talked on the job, he teased Pecqueux whom they had left as his fireman.

'What's up with you? You're as wide awake as a chap who's drunk nothing but water.'

And indeed Pecqueux, unlike his usual self, looked stone-cold sober and very gloomy. He answered in a harsh tone:

'You've got to keep your eyes open if you want to see.'

Jacques glanced at him with some misgiving, like a man with something on his conscience. A week before he had let himself go in the arms of his mate's mistress, that terror Philomène, who for a long time had been rubbing round him like a skinny cat on heat. There had not been a single moment of sexual interest about this. He had been mainly concerned with trying out an experiment – was he definitely cured now that he had satisfied his terrible craving? Could he have this woman without sticking a knife into her breast? He had already had her twice, and nothing had happened to him, not even any untoward feeling or thrill. His great joy, his air of happy contentment, must be due, even if he didn't realize it, to his now being just a man like the others.

335

Pecqueux opened the firebox door to throw in some coal, but Jacques stopped him.

'No, no, don't push her too hard, she's all right!'

The fireman muttered a few vindictive remarks.

'All right is she? Blimey! A nice tart she is, a regular bitch! When I think how you used to go for the old one, and she was so easy! This here cow isn't worth a kick up the arse!'

Jacques made no answer, wanting to keep his temper. But he realized that the old threesome was a thing of the past, the good companionship between him, his mate and the engine had gone with Lison's death. Now there were squabbles over the slightest thing, a nut turned too tight, a shovelful of coal put on wrong. He resolved to be careful about Philomène, not wanting to come to open warfare on this narrow footplate carrying him and his fireman along. So long as Pecqueux, out of gratitude for not being hustled, being allowed to take forty winks now and again and finish off lunch-baskets, had been like a faithful dog, ready to go for anyone else in his defence, they had got on together like brothers, silent in daily peril, needing no words to understand each other. But it would be hell if they couldn't get on any more, what with always being cheek by jowl and shaken up together, while bent on destroying each other. Only the week before the Company had had to separate the driver and fireman of the Cherbourg express because, over a woman who had come between them, the driver had rough-handled the other because he no longer obeyed orders; there had been blows and real fights on the journey, without a thought for the trainload of passengers following behind at full speed.

Twice more Pecqueux opened the firebox door and threw in some coal, deliberately disobeying and presumably looking for a quarrel, and Jacques pretended not to see and to be taken up with driving, but each time taking the precaution of turning the wheel of the injector to bring down the pressure. It was so warm, and the fresh breeze caused by their speed was so welcome on a hot July night!* When the express reached Le Havre

* *Translator's note:* At the beginning of the chapter this journey is said to have happened in June. The discrepancy is Zola's.

at 11.05 the two men cleaned up the engine together, apparently in perfect harmony as of old.

But as they were leaving the shed to go and sleep in the rue François-Mazeline a voice hailed them:

'Are you in such a hurry? Come in for a minute!'

It was Philomène on her brother's doorstep, who must have been looking out for Jacques. She looked very put out when she saw Pecqueux, and only made up her mind to call to them both for the pleasure of talking to her new lover, even if it did mean putting up with the old one.

'Bugger off!' snarled Pecqueux. 'You're a nuisance, we want to get some sleep!'

'Isn't he sweet!' Philomène went on gaily. 'But Monsieur Jacques isn't like you, he'll have a little drink all the same. Won't you, Monsieur Jacques?'

Jacques was on the point of prudently declining, but Pecqueux quickly accepted, as it occurred to him that he might watch them and make sure. So they went into the kitchen and sat down at the table on which she had put some glasses and a bottle of brandy, and she went on very softly:

'We must try not to make too much noise because my brother's asleep upstairs and he's not keen on my having visitors.'

While pouring out she went on quickly:

'By the way, did you know that old Mother Lebleu pegged out this morning? Oh, I always said it would kill her if she was put in that flat at the back. It's a real prison. She managed to last four months, eating her heart out and looking at nothing but a zinc roof. And what finished her off when she couldn't get out of her chair any more, was certainly the fact that she couldn't spy on Mademoiselle Guichon and Monsieur Dabadie. It was a habit she had got into. Yes, she got so wild at never coming across anything between them that it killed her.'

Philomène paused for a nip of brandy, then went on with a laugh:

'Of course they sleep together. Only they're so artful! What the eye don't see ...! All the same, I think Mme Moulin saw

337

them one night ... But no risk of her talking, she's such a ninny, and then her husband, the deputy stationmaster ...'

But then again she broke off and said:

'Oh, and by the way, it's coming up next week at Rouen, the Roubaud case.'

Until then Jacques and Pecqueux had listened without uttering a word. The latter simply thought she was in a very chatty mood. She never spread herself so much in conversations with him, and he kept his eyes on her and gradually grew more jealous as he saw how animated she was with his driver.

'Yes,' Jacques answered, looking perfectly composed. 'I've had the summons.'

Philomène came over, enjoying being able to touch him with her elbow.

'So have I, I'm a witness ... Oh, Monsieur Jacques, when they questioned me about you – you know, they wanted to know the real truth about your connection with the poor lady – yes, when they questioned me I told the magistrate: "But he worshipped her, sir, it's impossible that he could have done her any harm!" That's a fact, isn't it? I've seen you together, and I'm in a position to speak.'

'Oh,' answered Jacques with a gesture of indifference, 'I wasn't worried, I could give an account of my movements hour by hour ... If the Company have kept me on, it's because there isn't the slightest blame they can attach to me.'

There was a pause while all three took a sip.

'It gives you the horrors,' went on Philomène. 'That wild beast Cabuche they arrested, still covered with the poor lady's blood! Some men must be fools! Fancy killing a woman because they want her, as though that got them anywhere when the woman's gone! And you know, what I shall never forget all my life is when M. Cauche came and arrested M. Roubaud too, down on the platform. I was there. You know it happened only a week later, when M. Roubaud had calmly gone back to his job after his wife's funeral. Well then, M. Cauche tapped him on the shoulder and said he had orders to take him away to prison. Think of that! And those two were inseparable and played cards together whole nights through! Still, when you're a policeman you'd take your own mother and father to the guillotine, wouldn't you? It's your job. Not that M. Cauche cares! I saw him again the other day at the Café du Commerce, shuffling the cards with no more thought about his friend than the Grand Turk!'

Pecqueux, tight-lipped, banged his fist on the table.

'God Almighty! If I were in that cuckold Roubaud's shoes ... You're the one who went with his wife. And some other bloke kills her. And he's the one sent for trial. No, really, it's enough to make you go berserk!'

'But you great silly,' said Philomène, 'can't you see he's accused of making the other chap get rid of his wife for him, yes, something to do with money, or something. It seems they have found President Grandmorin's watch at Cabuche's place – you know, that's the gent who was murdered in the train eighteen months ago. They have connected this crime with the other one, quite a long story, a real rigmarole. I can't explain it all to you, but it was in the paper, a good two columns of it.'

Jacques's mind was on something else and he hardly seemed to be taking it in. He murmured:

'What's the good of worrying yourself silly about it? What's it got to do with us? If the law itself doesn't know what it's doing, we shan't be able to.'

Then he went on, with a far-away look and changing colour:

'The only thing that matters is that poor woman. Oh poor thing, poor woman!'

'Well, as far as I'm concerned,' Pecqueux burst out. 'I've got a woman of my own, and if someone took it into his head to mess about with her I'd start by throttling the pair of them. After that they could cut my head off, I wouldn't care.'

There was another silence. Philomène, refilling the glasses, made a point of shrugging her shoulders in scorn. But really she was very upset, and studied him out of the corner of her eye. He didn't look after himself at all, he was dirty and his clothes were in rags now that Ma Victoire, crippled as the result of her fracture, had had to give up her job in the lavatories and go into an institution. No longer was she at hand to make allowances and mother him, slip him the odd silver coin and do his mending, not wanting the other woman at Le Havre to accuse her of not looking after their man properly. Now Philomène, entranced by the spruce and dapper look of Jacques, put on a disgusted air.

'You mean you'd strangle your wife in Paris?' she said out of bravado. 'Not much risk of anyone taking her away from you!'

'Either her or somebody else!' he growled.

But already she was laughing away and clinking glasses.

'Anyway, here's to you! And just bring me your smalls to wash and mend, because really you aren't much credit to either of us ... Cheers, Monsieur Jacques!'

Jacques shivered as though he were coming out of a dream. Sometimes it happened like this that in spite of the total absence of remorse and the sense of relief and physical well-being in which he had lived since the murder, Séverine passed through his mind and touched the kindly man inside him to the point of tears. So he joined in the drink and to cover up his emotion said hastily:

'You know there's going to be a war?'

'You don't say!' exclaimed Philomène. 'Who against?'

'The Prussians of course. Yes, all because some prince of theirs wants to be king of Spain. Yesterday they talked of nothing else in the Chamber.'

This made her lament:

'Well, that'll be a nice thing! We've had about enough of this lot already, what with their elections, their plebiscite and their riots in Paris! If it comes to fighting do you mean they'll take all the men?'

'Oh, we're reserved, they can't disorganize the railways ... But what a do it would be for us, with moving the troops and supplies! Still, if it comes to it we shall have to do our duty.'

Thereupon he stood up, realizing that she had managed to slip one of her legs under his and that Pecqueux had noticed it, was going red in the face and clenching his fists.

'Let's go to bed, it's time we went.'

'Yes, it'd be better,' muttered his fireman.

He had gripped Philomène's arm and was squeezing it to breaking-point. She held back a scream of pain, and managed to whisper to Jacques while the other man was furiously gulping down his drink:

'Mind how you go, he's a real brute when he's been drinking.'

But then a heavy footstep could be heard coming down the stairs, and she took fright.

'My brother! Get out, quick, quick!'

The two men had not gone twenty paces away from the house before they heard blows followed by yells. She was taking a terrible punishment, like a little girl caught with her nose in a pot of jam. Jacques stopped and was for going back and helping her. But he was stopped by Pecqueux.

'What's it got to do with you, eh? The bitch! I wish he would finish her off!'

In the rue François-Mazeline Jacques and Pecqueux went to bed without exchanging a word. Their two beds almost touched in the narrow room, and they stayed awake a long time, listening to each other's breathing.

The hearings in the Roubaud case were due to start on Monday. It was a triumph for Denizet, the examining magistrate, for in legal circles there was unstinted praise for the way he had brought this complex and obscure affair to a triumphant conclusion. It was a masterpiece of analysis, it was said, a logical reconstruction of the truth, in a word a genuine act of creation.

As soon as he had betaken himself to the scene of the crime at La Croix-de-Maufras, a few hours after Séverine's murder, the first thing he did was to have Cabuche arrested. Everything clearly pointed to him, the blood all over him, the damning evidence of Roubaud and Misard who told how they had come upon him with the body, alone and distraught. When questioned and pressed to say how and why he was alone in that room, he mumbled some tale that the magistrate heard with a shrug of the shoulders, it seemed so foolish and stereotyped. The story was just what he was expecting, always the same – the imaginary murderer, the fictitious criminal whose flight through the dark countryside the real criminal alleged he had heard. This bogeyman would have gone a long way by now, wouldn't he, if he was still running! Moreover, when asked what he was doing in that house at such an hour, Cabuche got flustered, wouldn't answer, but eventually said he was just out for a walk. It was childish, how could anyone believe in the mysterious stranger, murdering, running off, leaving all the doors open without having looked inside a single piece of furniture or taken so much as a handkerchief? Where was he supposed to have come from? Why kill anybody? All the same, as the magistrate knew from the outset of his inquiry all about the affair between the victim and Jacques, he was anxious to check the latter's movements, but apart from the accused man's acknowledging that he had walked with Jacques when he caught the 4.14 from Barentin, the innkeeper at Rouen swore by all the gods that the young man went to bed at once after his evening meal and only left his room the next morning at about seven. And besides, a lover doesn't kill for no reason at all a mistress he idolizes and with whom he has never had the faintest shadow of a disagreement. It would be preposterous. No, no, there was only one possible, obvious murderer, the ex-convict who had been caught there red-handed, with the knife on the floor, this wild brute who was telling fairy-tales to a court of law.

But at this stage, for all his own conviction and the intuition that, he said, was more reliable than proof, M. Denizet did have a moment of embarrassment. A first search in the accused's hut in the depths of the Bécourt woods had revealed nothing. Theft not having been proved, some other motive had to be found. Suddenly, by sheer chance in an interrogation, Misard put him on the track by saying that one night he had seen Cabuche scale the garden wall so as to peep into Mme Roubaud's bedroom as she was going to bed. When questioned in his turn Jacques calmly said what he knew, which was the quarryman's silent adoration, the ardent desire to do little jobs for her which made him run round after her, always tied to her apron-strings. So now there could be no doubt whatever, he had been motivated by nothing but a bestial passion, and from that point onwards everything fitted together perfectly – the man coming in by the door of which he could have had a key, leaving it open in his excitement, then the struggle which had culminated in the murder, and finally the act of rape interrupted only by the arrival of the husband. Nevertheless there was one final objection, for it was strange that the man, knowing that the husband might arrive at any moment, should have chosen exactly the time when the latter could catch him. But when you came to think it over, that worked against the prisoner and finally damned him by establishing that he had acted in a supreme crisis of lust, maddened by the thought that if he did not take advantage of the moment while Séverine was still alone in this empty house, he would never get her again because she was leaving the next day. From that minute the magistrate's conviction was absolute and unshakeable.

Tormented by interrogations, caught over and over again in the skilful web of questions, unaware of the traps set for him, Cabuche stuck to his original version. He was walking along the road, taking a breather in the cool night air, when an individual had brushed past him, running at such a speed in the dark that he couldn't even say which way he went. So, feeling worried, he had glanced at the house and noticed that the door was wide open. And he had eventually made up his mind to go upstairs and had found the dead woman still warm and staring at him with her big eyes; thinking she was still alive he had got himself all over blood through moving her on to the bed. That was all he knew, and that was all he kept on repeating, and he never changed a single detail, apparently determined not to be moved from a prearranged story. When they tried to make him budge he took fright and kept his mouth shut as though his intelligence was limited and he couldn't understand anything else. The first time M. Denizet asked him about his passion for the dead woman, he went very red, like a young boy being scolded for his first love-affair, and denied it, denied ever having dreamed of having relations with this woman as if it were a dreadful, unspeakable thing, a delicate and mysterious thing too, buried in the most secret place of his heart and never to be admitted to a soul. No, no, he didn't love her, he didn't lust after her, and he would never be induced to speak about what he felt to be a profanation now she was dead. But this persistence in not admitting a fact that several witnesses asserted, also told against him. Naturally, according to the version of the prosecution, he had an interest in hiding the insane lust he harboured for the unhappy woman whom he was to slaughter in order to satisfy himself. When the examining magistrate, gathering all the proofs together and seeking to force the truth out of him by dealing a knock-out blow, made a point-blank accusation of the murder and rape, Cabuche protested in a furious outburst. What, him? Kill her so as to have her? He respected her like a saint! Policemen had to be called in to hold him down while he talked of throttling the whole bloody lot of them. In a word, the most dangerous type of scoundrel and artful too, yet his violence burst out and gave away the crimes he was denying.

The hearings had reached that point, and each time the question of murder came up the prisoner went into a rage and screamed that it was the other man, the mystery man who ran away; and then M. Denizet made a sudden discovery which transformed the whole affair and gave it ten times more importance. As he put it, he had a nose for the truth, and therefore a kind of presentiment made him determined to carry out another search in Cabuche's hovel. And there he found, simply behind a beam, a hiding-place in which there were a woman's handkerchiefs and gloves, and under them a gold watch which he recognized at once, and his heart leaped with joy. It was President Grandmorin's watch for which he had hunted so long the previous time, a big watch with two initials intertwined, bearing on the inside of the case the maker's number 2516. Everything was lit up by a flash of inspiration, the past was connected to the present, and the facts he linked together delighted him by their logic. But the consequences were going to be so far-reaching that he did not mention the watch at first, but interrogated Cabuche about the gloves and the handkerchiefs. For a moment the latter was on the point of an admission: yes, he did love her, yes, he desired her to the point of kissing dresses she had worn or picking up and stealing behind her back anything she dropped, bits of stay-lace, hooks and eyes, pins. Then a sense of shame and unconquerable shyness closed his mouth. When the magistrate decided to make him look at the watch he stared at it in horror. He recollected perfectly: he had been surprised to find that watch tied up in a handkerchief he had taken from under a pillow and borne off home as a prize, then it had stayed there while he racked his brains to think of some way of returning it. Only what was the use of telling them that? It would mean having to own up to his other pilferings – clothes and underwear that smelt so nice and that he was so ashamed of. Already they didn't believe a word he said. In any case he was beginning to lose a clear notion of things that were all jumbled

344

up in his simple mind. He was entering a nightmare world. He even stopped flying into a rage when accused of murder, but stood dazed and to every question just answered that he didn't know. As to the gloves and handkerchiefs, he didn't know. As to the watch, he didn't know. They were all getting him down, why not leave him alone and guillotine him straight away.

The following day M. Denizet had Roubaud arrested. Drunk with power, he had issued the warrant in one of those inspired moments when he believed in the genius of his own perspicacity, and even before he had an adequate case against the deputy stationmaster. Although there were still many obscure points, he had a hunch that this man was the pivot, the source of the double murder, and this was triumphantly borne out when he put his hands on the deed of gift to the survivor which Roubaud and Séverine had executed before Maître Colin, a lawyer in Le Havre, a week after gaining possession of La Croix-de-Maufras. From that point the whole story fitted together in his head with an infallible logic and overwhelming obviousness that gave the edifice of his indictment such indestructible strength that truth itself would have seemed less true and flawed with more fantastic and inconsistent elements. Roubaud was a coward who on two occasions, not daring to strike himself, had used the arm of this violent brute Cabuche. The first time, knowing the nature of President Grandmorin's will, impatient to inherit his money, and moreover aware of the quarryman's grudge against him, he had pushed Cabuche into the compartment at Rouen after putting the knife into his hand. Then, having shared out the ten thousand francs, the accomplices might never have seen each other again had not murder led on to murder. And it was here that Denizet displayed that profound insight into criminal psychology that was so much admired, for he now declared that he had never ceased keeping an eye on Cabuche, being convinced that the first murder would lead mathematically to a second. Eighteen months had sufficed for the Roubaud marriage to go on the rocks, the husband to gamble away his five thousand francs and the wife to take a lover for the sake of something to do. No doubt she refused to sell La Croix-de-Maufras for fear he would squander the money, and perhaps in their perpetual bickering she threatened to hand him over to the police. In any case there were plenty of witnesses to testify to the total breakdown of the marriage and this led finally to the long-term consequence of the first crime: Cabuche reappeared on the scene with his brutal appetites, the husband in the background had thrust the knife into his hand again so as to make sure once and for all of the ownership of that accursed property that had already cost one human life. Such was the truth, the blinding truth to which everything led, the watch found at the quarryman's hut and above all the two bodies stabbed in the throat in the same way, by the same hand, by the same weapon, the knife picked up in that room. On this last point, however, the prosecution did express a doubt, for the President's wound seemed to have been caused by a smaller and sharper blade.

Roubaud began by answering yes or no in the sleepy, heavy manner now habitual to him. He did not seem surprised at being arrested, for he was now indifferent to everything in the steady break-up of his personality. To make him talk he had been put in the charge of a warder who never left him, and he played cards with this man from morning till night and was perfectly happy. In any case he was still convinced of Cabuche's guilt, for he alone could be the murderer. When questioned about Jacques he had laughed it off with a shrug, which showed that he knew all about the affair between the engine-driver and Séverine. But when M. Denizet, after carefully feeling his way, set out his theory and pressed him hard, confounding him with his complicity and attempting to extract a confession from him in the shock of realizing that he had been found out, Roubaud became extremely circumspect. What sort of a tale was this? It wasn't him, it seemed, but the quarryman who had killed the President, just as he had killed Séverine; and both times he was supposed to be the guilty party because the other was doing it in his interests and instead of him! This involved story staggered him and made him extremely cautious: clearly they were setting a trap for him and were lying in order to force him to admit his own part in the murders, namely the first crime. From the moment of his arrest he had suspected that the earlier story was coming up again. When confronted with Cabuche he swore he did not know him. But as he kept on declaring that he had found him covered with blood and on the point of raping his victim, the latter flew into a rage and a violent and extremely complicated scene ensued that confused things even more. Three days went by, the magistrate stepped up his interrogation, feeling certain that the two accomplices were in league to put on this act of hostility so as to take him in. Roubaud, tired out, had made up his mind to answer no more questions, but then suddenly, in a moment of exasperation, wanting to make an end of the whole thing, he gave in to an urge that had been quietly developing inside him for months, and came out with the truth, the whole truth and nothing but the truth.

It happened that that day M. Denizet was deploying all his art, seated at his desk with his eyes veiled by their heavy lids, while his mobile lips were pursed to express sagacity. For a whole hour he had been wearing himself out with cunning ruses on this stolid prisoner who had run to unhealthy yellow fat, for he thought that beneath this lumpy exterior the man had an astute, crafty mind. And so he thought he had tracked him down step by step, thrown a net all round him and really caught him in a trap when Roubaud, with the gesture of a man who could stand no more, shouted that he had had enough and preferred to come clean so as not to be tormented any more. As they were determined to find him guilty in any case, he might as well be guilty of the things he really had done. But as he told the story of how his wife had been perverted as a young girl by Grandmorin, his own mad jealousy when he found out about these disgusting things, how he had killed him and why he had taken the ten thousand francs, the magistrate's eyelids reopened in an expression of doubt, and an irresistible scepticism, professional scepticism, made him poke out his lips in a mocking pout. By the time the accused finished speaking he was smiling outright. This fellow was even sharper than he thought, for to take the first murder upon himself and represent it as simply a crime of passion, and thus clear himself of any premeditated theft and above all of any complicity in the killing of Séverine, was certainly a master-stroke indicating quite unusual intelligence and strength of character. Only, of course, the thing didn't hold water.

'Come, come, Roubaud, it's no use taking us for children ...

So you are making out you were jealous and you killed in a fit of jealousy?'

'Yes I am!'

'And if we accept your tale, you married your wife without knowing anything about her relationship with the President. Does that seem likely? On the contrary, everything in your case might prove that this was a deal offered, discussed and accepted. You are given a girl brought up to be a lady and with a dowry, her protector becomes yours as well, you are perfectly aware that he is leaving her a country house in his will, and you make out that you had no suspicions, absolutely none at all! Now look here, you knew all about it, otherwise your marriage would be incomprehensible. Moreover, we need only establish one simple fact to prove you wrong. You are not a jealous man, just you dare to say again that you are.'

'I am telling the truth, I killed him when I was mad with jealousy.'

'So, having killed the President because of some vague, long-past affair (which, incidentally, is an invention of yours), will you explain to me how you have managed to wink at your wife's having a lover? Yes, this Jacques Lantier, and a fine young man he is, too! Everybody has told me about this affair, and you yourself have not denied that you knew all about it . . . You left them free to get on with it together – why?'

Slumped in a heap, wild-eyed, Roubaud stared into space and could find no explanation. Eventually he mumbled:

'I don't know . . . I killed the one but didn't kill the other.'

'Then stop telling me you are a jealous man taking his revenge, and I don't advise you to repeat that fairy-tale to the gentlemen of the jury, for they would laugh at you. Take my advice and change your tune. Only the truth can save you.'

From then onwards, the more Roubaud obstinately told the truth, the more he was palpably lying. Everything worked against him, and even his earlier testimony at the first inquiry, which should have endorsed his new version since in that he had accused Cabuche, became a proof of an extraordinarily clever collusion between the two of them. The magistrate savoured the psychology of the affair with true professional enjoyment. Never, he said, had he delved so deep into the recesses of

348

human nature. And it was inspiration rather than observation, for he flattered himself that he belonged to the school of perceptive and disconcerting judges who can break a man down with a single glance. Besides, there was an abundance of proofs, altogether overwhelming. Henceforward the prosecution was on a solid foundation, and certainty shone forth as blinding as the light of the sun.

What added still more to the glory of M. Denizet was that he brought the two cases together into one whole, after having patiently pieced it together in the most profound secrecy. Since the noisy success of the plebiscite the country had been in a continual state of hysteria, like the unstable condition which precedes any catastrophe. Society, in this closing phase of the Empire, was pervaded in politics and above all in the press by a continual restlessness, a highly-strung condition in which even joy took on an unhealthy violence. And so, when a woman had been murdered in this lonely house at La Croix-de-Maufras and it was learned by what a stroke of genius the examining magistrate at Rouen had resurrected the old Grandmorin case and established the link between it and this new crime, there was a burst of triumph in the government-inspired papers. It still occasionally happened, as a matter of fact, that the old jokes appeared in the opposition press about the mythical, untraceable murderer thought up by the police and trotted out to hide the immoral goings-on of certain highly placed persons who were involved. And now the answer would be decisive, the murderer and his accomplice had been arrested and the good name of President Grandmorin would emerge from the story untarnished. The controversies started again, and excitement grew from day to day in Rouen and Paris. Apart altogether from the gruesome story that haunted the imagination, tempers rose as if the stability of the state depended upon the truth being irrefutably established at last. For a whole week the press splashed details.

M. Denizet was sent for and presented himself at the rue du Rocher, the Paris home of the Secretary-General, M. Camy-Lamotte. He found him standing in the middle of his plainly furnished study, looking more drawn in the face and more tired, for his star was on the wane and he was filled with sadness even

349

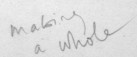

in his scepticism, as though he could foresee beyond this burst of triumph the coming crash of the régime he served. For two days he had been in the throes of an inner struggle, still not sure what use he would make of Séverine's letter, which he had kept. This letter would have destroyed the whole case for the prosecution by supporting Roubaud's version with irrefutable evidence. Nobody in the world knew of its existence, and he could destroy it. But only the day before the Emperor had said to him that this time he insisted that justice should run its course independent of any influence, even if it should damage his own government: a simple cry from the heart, possibly the superstition that a single unjust act, after this nationwide acclaim, might change the course of destiny. And although the Secretary-General did not suffer from scruples of conscience, having reduced the affairs of this world to a simple matter of mathematics, yet he was upset by an order received, and wondered whether he ought to love his master to the point of disobeying him.

M. Denizet at once exclaimed in triumph:

'There you are, my hunch hadn't deceived me, it was indeed this Cabuche who stabbed the President ... All the same I admit that the other line of argument did have an element of truth in it, and I myself felt that the case against Roubaud was still a bit fishy ... Anyway, we've got both of them.'

M. Camy-Lamotte looked hard at him with his pale-coloured eyes.

'So all the facts in the dossier sent to me have been verified, and you are absolutely convinced?'

'Absolutely, no possible hesitation ... Everything hangs together, and I can't recollect any case in which, in spite of some complications, the crime followed a more logical course and one easier to see clearly in advance.'

'But Roubaud is protesting, admitting responsibility for the first murder, and telling a story about his wife being violated as a girl and how he, mad with jealousy, killed in a blind fit of rage. All the opposition press is full of it.'

'Oh, but only as a bit of tittle-tattle, and they don't dare believe it themselves. This Roubaud jealous, a man who facilitated his wife's meetings with a lover! Let him repeat that yarn at the Assizes – he won't succeed in stirring up the hoped-for scandal! If he produced some proof ... well perhaps; but he can't. Of course he talks about the letter he makes out he forced his wife to write, and which should have been found among the victim's papers. In that case you, sir, who went through those papers, would have found it, wouldn't you?'

M. Camy-Lamotte did not answer. It was true, the scandal was going to be buried at last, thanks to the theory of the magistrate: nobody would believe Roubaud, and the President's reputation would be cleared of foul suspicions, the Empire would benefit from this much-publicized rehabilitation of one of its pillars. And besides, since this Roubaud man confessed his guilt, how did it affect the principle of justice if he were convicted of one version or of the other? Of course there was Cabuche, but even if he had nothing to do with the first murder, he really did seem to be responsible for the second. And then, good Lord, justice ... the crowning illusion! The desire to be just was a snare, surely, when the truth is so tangled with brambles? It was better to play for safety and once again support this dying society threatening to collapse in ruins.

'That is so, isn't it?' M. Denizet persisted, 'you didn't find that letter?'

Once again M. Camy-Lamotte looked up at him, and as sole master of the situation, taking upon his own conscience the scruples that had disturbed the Emperor, he calmly replied:

'I found nothing whatsoever.'

Then, smiling most affably, he heaped flattery upon the magistrate, and only his slightly pursed lips betrayed his invincible irony. Never had a case been prepared with so much insight, and it was now definitely decided in the highest quarters that he would be summoned to Paris as counsellor after the vacation. In this manner he saw him out to the hall.

'You are the only one who has really understood it all, it is truly admirable ... And once the truth speaks out nothing can stop it, either private pressures or even reasons of state ... Carry on, let the case follow its course whatever the consequences.'

'That is where the whole duty of the judiciary lies,' concluded M. Denizet, bowing his way out, radiant.

Left alone, M. Camy-Lamotte lit a candle, then went and took Séverine's letter out of the drawer where it had been filed. The flame lengthened, he unfolded the letter, feeling a desire to read the few lines over again, and they brought back the memory of that frail-looking criminal with the periwinkle-blue eyes who had aroused such tender emotions in him all that while ago. Now she was dead, and he saw her as a tragic figure. Who could tell what secret she must have taken with her? Yes, truth and justice where certainly an illusion. Of this unknown and charming woman all that remained for him was a momentary desire she had aroused in passing, and which he had not satisfied. As he held the letter to the flame, and it was burning, a great sadness came over him and a presentiment of woe. What was the point of destroying this document and taking this deed upon his conscience if fate decreed that the Empire should be swept away, like the pinch of black ash from between his fingers?

M. Denizet concluded his investigation in less than a week. He found the Western Railway Company extremely co-operative in supplying all the documents he wanted and all useful evidence, for the Company was also very anxious to see the end of this deplorable story of one of its employees, which had gone up and up through the complicated machinery of its hierarchy until it had nearly wrecked even its board of directors. The gangrened limb must be amputated with all speed. So once again there paraded through the magistrate's office the staff of the station at Le Havre, M. Dabadie, Moulin, and the others, who supplied damning details about the conduct of Roubaud; then the stationmaster at Barentin, M. Bessière, and various employees from Rouen, whose testimonies were of vital importance in connection with the first murder; next M. Vandorpe, the Paris stationmaster, Misard the man at the section-post, and the guard Henri Dauvergne, the last two very positive about the complaisance of the accused as a husband. And Henri, whom Séverine had nursed at La Croix-de-Maufras, even alleged that one night, while he was still very ill, he thought he heard the voices of Roubaud and Cabuche conspiring together outside his window, which explained many things and upset the plan of the two accused, who pretended not to know each other. From the whole staff of the Company there arose a howl of condemnation and expressions of sympathy for the unhappy victims, this poor young woman whose misconduct had so much justification and this most honourable old man whose name was now cleared of the ugly stories circulated about him.

But above all the fresh case had revived the strong passions in the Grandmorin family, and although M. Denizet derived considerable help from this quarter, he also had to fight to safeguard his case in its entirety. The Lachesnayes were singing songs of victory, for, in their exasperation about the bequest of La Croix-de-Maufras, which made their hearts bleed with avarice, they had always maintained that Roubaud was guilty. So when the case came up again the one thing they could see in it was a chance to challenge the will, and as there was only one way of getting the legacy set aside, namely to expose Séverine's ingratitude, they partially accepted Roubaud's version of his wife's complicity, helping him with the murder, not in revenge for an imaginary infamy but for robbery. Hence the magistrate was at odds with them, and with Berthe in particular. She was very bitter about the murdered woman, her former friend, whom she maligned abominably, but he defended her, becoming very excited and angry as soon as anyone laid a finger on his masterpiece, this edifice of pure reason, so beautifully constructed (as he proudly declared) that if a single piece were dislodged the whole thing would tumble down. In this connection there was a very heated scene in his office between the Lachesnayes and Mme Bonnehon. The latter, formerly well disposed towards the Roubauds, had had to give up supporting the husband, but she still defended the wife through a sort of sentimental complicity, being very tolerant towards charm and love, and terribly upset by this tragic, blood-stained romance. She was very explicit in her scorn for money. Wasn't her niece ashamed to rake up this matter of the legacy again? If Séverine was guilty didn't it mean accepting all the alleged confessions of Roubaud and therefore besmirching the President's memory all over again? Had the truth not been so ingeniously established by the magistrate's case they would have had to invent it for the honour of the family. She also referred with some bitterness to all the gossip going on in the society of Rouen, the society over which her reign had ended now that old age was approaching and she was losing even that majestic blonde beauty of an eld-erly goddess. Yes, only the day before at the house of the coun-sellor's wife, that tall, elegant brunette Mme Leboucq who was ousting her, some spicy anecdotes had been whispered round, like the Louisette story, anything public spite could think up. When M. Denizet interrupted to remind her that M. Leboucq would be sitting as an assessor at the forthcoming Assizes, the Lachesnayes fell silent, apparently yielding through anxiety. But Mme Bonnehon reassured them, being sure that justice would do its duty, for the Assizes would be presided over by her old friend M. Desbazeilles (whose rheumatism now only al-lowed him to live on memories), and the second assessor was to be M. Chaumette, father of the young deputy prosecutor who was under her wing. So she was not worried, although a wistful smile flitted over her lips as she mentioned the last named, whose son had been seen for some time at Mme Leboucq's where she herself sent him so as not to hinder his prospects.

When the famous trial opened at last, the rumours of a coming war and the uneasiness spreading all over France stole much of the thunder from the court proceedings. Nevertheless Rouen went through three days of feverish excitement; there were crowds fighting at the doors and the reserved seats were taken over by fashionable ladies. Never had the ancient palace of the Dukes of Normandy seen such an influx of people since it had been converted into a court of law. It was towards the end of June, with hot, sunny afternoons, and the strong light came through the ten leaded windows, bathing with light the oak panels, the white stone crucifix standing out at once end from its background of red hangings embroidered with Napoleonic bees, the celebrated Louis XII ceiling with its coffered com-partments of carved wood gilded with the softest old gold. It was already stifling before the hearing opened, women stood on tiptoe to look at the prosecution exhibits set out on the table: Grandmorin's watch, Séverine's bloodstained nightdress and the knife that had been used for both murders. Cabuche's defender, a lawyer from Paris, was also very much stared at. Twelve citizens of Rouen sat in line in the jury seats, stiff in their black frock-coats, pompous and solemn. When the court entered there was so much jostling among the standing audience that the President of the Court was obliged to threaten to clear the hall at once.

At last the case began, the jury were sworn, and again a thrill of curiosity ran through the crowd as the witnesses were summoned: heads swung round at the names of Mme Bonnehon and M. de Lachesnaye. But it was Jacques above all who excited the ladies; their eyes never left him. Moreover, once the prisoners were there, each between two police officers, eyes were constantly upon them and opinions were being exchanged. They struck people as ferocious and vile, two obvious criminal types, Roubaud, in his dark-coloured jacket with a tie carelessly knotted like a gentleman run to seed, looked surprisingly old, with his listless, bloated-looking face. As to Cabuche, of course he was just what they had imagined, in a long blue working smock, looking every inch the murderer, with huge fists and the jaws of a ravening beast – in fact not at all the sort of chap you'd want to meet in a lonely wood. The examinations confirmed this bad impression, and some of his answers gave rise to loud murmurs. Cabuche replied to every question from the President by saying he didn't know: he didn't know why he had let the real murderer get away, and clung to his tale of the mysterious stranger whom he heard rushing off into the night. Questioned about his bestial passion for the unhappy victim he became incoherent with such sudden and violent anger that the two officers seized his arms. No, no, he didn't love her, he didn't desire her, it was a pack of lies, even to want her would have seemed like sacrilege, she was a lady, while he had served a stretch and lived like a savage! Then he calmed down and relapsed into gloomy silence, uttering nothing but monosyllables, indifferent to the condemnation that might follow. Similarly Roubaud stuck to what the prosecution called his plan, describing how and why he had killed Grandmorin and denying having any hand in the murder of his wife. However, he did so in disconnected and almost incoherent phrases, with sudden lapses of memory and eyes so vague and voice so indistinct that at times it looked as if he were thinking up and inventing details. As the President persisted, pointing out the absurdities of his story, he finally shrugged his shoulders and refused to

355

Casts doubt on criminal type[n]

answer. What was the use of telling the truth since only lies seemed to make sense? This attitude of aggressive scorn for justice did him the greatest disservice. Moreover the indifference the two prisoners showed to each other was noted as a proof of a long-standing arrangement between them, a clever plan carried out with remarkable tenacity. They pretended not to know each other and even made charges against each other solely to deceive the court. By the time the examinations were over the verdict was clear, such was the skill with which the President had manœuvred them, so that Roubaud and Cabuche, by falling into all the traps he set, appeared to have condemned themselves. On that day a few more unimportant witnesses were heard. By five o'clock the heat was so intolerable that two ladies fainted.

But the next day's great sensation was the examination of certain witnesses. Mme Bonnehon scored a real success by her refinement and tact. The testimony of the Company employees was listened to with great interest: M. Vandorpe, M. Bessière, M. Dabadie and especially M. Cauche, very prolix this one, who told how well he knew Roubaud from having often played cards with him at the Café du Commerce. Henri Dauvergne repeated his damning evidence about his almost certain recollection of having heard, while feverish and drowsy, the voices of the two accused plotting in undertones, and when questioned about Séverine he became very discreet, giving the impression that he loved her, but that as he knew she had given her heart to another he had loyally stood aside. And so when this other man, Jacques Lantier, was at length called, a buzz went up from the crowd, people stood up for a better view of him and there was even a display of passionate attentiveness from the jury. Jacques was perfectly controlled, leaning with both hands on the rail of the witness-box in the same professional position he stood in when he was driving his engine. This appearance, which should have disturbed him very deeply, left him with a completely lucid mind, as though nothing in the case concerned him personally. He was about to give evidence as a stranger and an innocent party, for he had not felt the slightest emotion ever since the crime, and had not even given these things a thought,

356

his memory of them had been wiped out and his body was in a state of equilibrium, perfectly healthy. And again now, standing at that rail, he felt neither remorse nor scruples, as though quite unconcerned with the whole thing. He at once looked at Roubaud and Cabuche with candid eyes. He knew the former was guilty, and he gave him a slight nod by way of discreet recognition, not reflecting that today everybody knew he was his wife's lover. Then he smiled at the latter, the innocent one, in whose place, seated in the dock, he should have been himself – he was a decent creature really, for all his outlandish appearance, a chap he had seen at work and had exchanged the time of day with. So he was quite composed as he gave his evidence, answering the President's questions in short, clear sentences. The latter took him at inordinate length through his relationship with the victim, made him tell how he had left La Croix-de-Maufras some hours before the murder, taken the train at Barentin and slept in Rouen. Cabuche and Roubaud listened and confirmed these replies by their attitude, and at that moment there hovered between these three men an inexpressible sadness. A deathly silence had fallen on the court, the throats of the jurymen tightened with some emotion they could not have explained: it was the truth passing by in silence. When the President asked him what he thought about the quarryman's story of the unknown man vanishing into the night, Jacques merely shook his head as if to say he didn't want to pile on the agony for an accused man. And then something happened which put the finishing touch to the onlookers' emotion. Jacques's eyes filled with tears, which then ran down his cheeks. The vision of Séverine came back to him, as he had already seen her once before, the ghastly murdered woman with enormously dilated blue eyes and dark hair standing on end like a helmet of horror, whose picture he had carried away in his mind. He still worshipped her, a great pity had overwhelmed him, and he wept bitterly for her, still unaware of his own crime and forgetting where he was in the midst of this crowd. Ladies were touched by this emotion and sobbed. Everybody was deeply moved by the lover's grief while the husband remained dry-eyed. The President asked the defence whether they had any

357

questions to put to the witness, the lawyers declined with thanks and the dazed prisoners watched Jacques go back to his seat amid general sympathy.

The third session was wholly taken up by the speech of the Public Prosecutor and those of various counsel. First the President gave a summing-up in which, beneath a veneer of absolute impartiality, the charges of the prosecution were stressed. The Public Prosecutor, who followed, did not appear to be in his best form – usually he showed more conviction and his eloquence was less empty. This was put down to the heat, which really was exhausting. On the contrary, Cabuche's defender, the lawyer from Paris, was most entertaining but unconvincing. Roubaud's defender, a distinguished member of the Rouen Bar, also made the most of his weak case. The Public Prosecutor was tired and did not even reply. When the jury retired to consider its verdict it was only six, broad daylight was still coming through the ten windows and the last rays of the sun lit up the arms of the towns of Normandy decorating the piers. A loud babble of voices went up under the low gilded ceiling, and impatient movements shook the iron grille separating the reserved seats from the standing public. But as the jury and the court reappeared a religious hush fell once again. The verdict took account of extenuating circumstances, and the tribunal sentenced both men to hard labour for life. This was a great surprise, the crowd broke into a tumult and a few whistlings were heard, as though it were a theatre.

All over Rouen that evening the sentence was mulled over and endlessly commented upon. The consensus of opinion was that it was also a slap in the face for Mme Bonnehon and the Lachesnayes. It was thought that nothing short of the death sentence would have satisfied the family, and it seemed certain that hostile influences had been at work. The name of Mme Leboucq was already being whispered, for three or four of the jury were numbered among her intimates. There had no doubt been nothing irregular about her husband's attitude as one of the assessors, and yet people thought they had noticed that neither the other assessor, M Chaumette, nor even the President, M. Desbazeilles, had felt themselves really as fully in control of the proceedings as they would have liked. Perhaps it

358

was simply that the jury had felt some scruples and, by admitting extenuating circumstances, had been affected by the uncomfortable feeling of doubt that had momentarily run
through the court when the melancholy truth had silently
passed by. All in all, the case remained a triumph for the examining magistrate, M. Denizet, for nothing had succeeded in
blemishing his masterpiece. Even the family lost many people's
sympathy when it was rumoured that in order to recover la
Croix-de-Maufras, M. de Lachesnaye, contrary to legal pre-
cedent, was talking of bringing an action for revocation in spite
of the death of the donee, an astonishing thing coming from a
lawyer.

Outside the Courts Jacques was joined by Philomène, who
had stayed as a witness, and she held on to him, determined to
spend the night with him in Rouen. He did not have to report
for work until the following day, and was quite willing to keep
her for a meal at the inn near the station where he was supposed
to have slept on the night of the crime, but he was not going to
spend the night there, for he was absolutely obliged to go back
to Paris by the 12.50 a.m. train.

'Do you know,' she said as she was making for the inn on his
arm. 'I could swear that just now I saw somebody we know . . .
Yes, Pecqueux, and he was saying again only the other day that
he wouldn't show a leg in Rouen over this business. I turned
round for a second and a man slipped off into the crowd, and I
only saw his back . . .'

He stopped her and shrugged it off.

'Pecqueux is in Paris, living it up, only too glad of the holiday
he's getting because of my time off.'

'That may be . . . All the same, we must be on the look-out
for he's a very ugly customer when he gets wild.'

She clung closer to him and went on, glancing behind again:

'And do you know who's following us now?'

'Yes, don't you worry . . . I suppose there's something he
wants to ask me.'

It was Misard, who had indeed been keeping some distance
behind them all the way from the rue des Juifs. He had given
evidence too, looking half asleep, and he had hung round
Jacques without making up his mind to ask him a question he

obviously had on the tip of his tongue. When the couple disappeared into the inn he went in too, and asked for a glass of wine.

'Well fancy, it's you, Misard!' exclaimed Jacques. 'And how's it going with your new wife?'

'Oh, so-so!' growled Misard. 'Oh, the miserable old geezer! She's taken me in proper. I told you all about that, didn't I, last time I came here.'

Jacques was very tickled at this story. Old Mother Ducloux, the ex-barmaid with the shady past whom Misard had taken on to mind the level crossing, had been quick to see from the way he grubbed about in corners that he must be hunting for a nest-egg hidden by his late wife, and to get him to marry her had had the bright idea of giving him to understand, by little reticences and giggles, that she had found it herself. To begin with he had nearly strangled her, then, thinking that the thousand francs would escape him yet again if he did away with her before he'd got them as he did the other one, he had come over very wheedling and nice. But she repulsed him, refusing to let him even touch her: no, no, when she was his wife he would have everything, her and the money thrown in. So he had married her, and she had laughed at him and told him he was a great booby if he believed everything people said. The beauty of it was that now she was wise to it she caught the fever herself, and began hunting with him just as furiously. Oh, they'd run them to earth one day, those thousand undiscoverable francs, now there were two of them at it! So they hunted and hunted.

'Still nothing doing?' teased Jacques. 'Isn't Mother Ducloux helping you, then?'

Misard looked hard at him and then it came out.

'You know where the money is, tell me.'

That made Jacques angry.

'I know nothing at all! Aunt Phasie didn't give me anything, and you aren't accusing me of stealing, I hope!'

'Oh, she didn't give you anything, that's for sure ... Look here, you can see it's making me ill. If you know where it is, tell me.'

'Oh, bugger off! And mind I don't talk too much. Have a look in the salt-box, it might be there.'

360

Misard went on staring at him, his eyes blazing in his pasty face. He had a sudden flash of illumination.

'The salt-box, gosh, that's true! There's a place under the drawer I've not looked in!'

He hurriedly paid for his drink and rushed off to the station to see if he could still catch the 7.10. And there, in the little squat house, he would go on hunting for ever and ever.

After their meal and before the 12.50 train Philomène insisted on taking Jacques along dark back streets and out into the country. It was a very sultry July night, hot and with no moon, and her bosom swelled with heavy sighs as she almost hung round his neck. Twice she thought she heard footsteps behind them and looked round, but the night was so dark that she couldn't see anybody. He was finding the thundery night very trying. Although ever since the murder he had felt calm and balanced and had enjoyed perfect health, yet just now at table he had felt a vague unease coming back every time this woman's groping hands had touched him. Must be tiredness, no doubt, or jumpiness due to the oppressive weather. Now his agonizing lust was reviving, stronger, and filling him with inexpressible dread as he held her like this against his body. And yet he really was cured, surely, since he had tried the experiment and had had her in cold blood, just to find out. His agitation became so great that in his dread of having an attack he would have freed himself from her arms had not the darkness hiding her reassured him. For never, even in the worst days of his malady, would he have struck without seeing. And then, as they were passing a grassy bank in a quiet lane and she dragged him down and offered herself, the monstrous urge suddenly came back, and he flew into a frenzy and felt round in the grass for some weapon, a stone to bash her head in. He forced himself to jump up and was already rushing madly away when he heard a man's voice, a lot of swearing and a real scrimmage.

'You whore! I waited until the end just to make sure!'

'It isn't true, let me go!'

'Oh, so it isn't true? That chap can run as fast as he likes, I know who he is and I'll get even with him! Now you bitch, just you tell me again it isn't true!'

Jacques was rushing off into the night, not from Pecqueux,

whom he had recognized, but from himself, crazy with grief.

What! One murder hadn't been enough, so he wasn't satisfied with Séverine's blood, as he still believed only this morning? Here he was at it again. Another and then another, and always another! As soon as he was glutted, and after a few weeks of torpor, this horrible hunger would come back and he would have to go on having woman's flesh to appease it. And now he didn't even have to see the flesh that tempted him – even to feel it warm in his arms was enough to make him give in to his murderous lust, like a fierce male beast ripping females open. Life was over, and all he had left before him was this utter darkness, endless despair in which he went on running away.

A few days later Jacques had gone back to his job, avoiding his comrades and relapsing into his old touchy surliness. After some stormy sessions in the Chamber war had just been declared, and there had already been a skirmish between outposts, successful, it was alleged. For a week the mobilization of troops had been exhausting the railwaymen. Regular services were disorganized and continual unscheduled trains were causing long delays, on top of which the best drivers had been commandeered to speed up the concentration of army corps. Thus it came about that one evening at Le Havre, instead of driving his usual express, Jacques was put on to an enormous train of eighteen vehicles crammed with soldiers.

That evening Pecqueux was very drunk when he turned up at the sheds. The day after he had caught Philomène and Jacques he had returned to engine No. 608 as Jacques's fireman, and since then he had never referred to the matter, but had been morose and seemed as if he dared not look his driver in the face. But the latter sensed that he was getting more and more truculent, refusing to obey and responding to every order with a low growl. In the end they stopped speaking to each other altogether. This shaking bit of sheet-iron, this little bridge on which they used to travel along in such harmony, had now become nothing but the narrow and perilous stage on which their rivalry was playing itself out. Hatred was growing between them, and they had reached the point of open war as they hurtled along at full speed on these few square feet from which the least jerk could have sent them flying. So this evening, seeing

Pecqueux drunk, Jacques was nervous, for he knew he was too crafty to make trouble when he was sober; only drink unleashed the beast in him.

The train, due to leave at about six, was held up. It was already dark by the time the soldiers were loaded like sheep into the cattle-trucks. Some planks had been nailed across by way of seats, and the men were piled in by squads, stuffing the trucks beyond the limit, some sitting on each other and some standing so tightly pressed that they couldn't move an arm. There was another train waiting in Paris to take them on at once towards the Rhine. They were already dropping with fatigue and dazed with all the fuss of departure. But as they had been issued with brandy, and many of them had been frequenting the pubs in the locality, they were in a state of tipsy, coarse gaiety, very red in the face, with eyes popping out of their heads. As soon as the train moved they burst into song.

Jacques glanced up at the sky, where the stars were hidden by storm-clouds. It was going to be a very dark night, and not a breath stirred the stifling air. The very wind made by the speed, usually so refreshing, seemed hot. No other lights on the black horizon than the twinkling lamps of signals. He raised the pressure so as to climb the steep bank from Harfleur to Saint-Romain. Although he had been studying her for weeks he still had not mastered No. 608; she was too young, and her moods and growing-pains constantly caught him out. That night in particular she seemed restive and temperamental, and ready to tear off if she got a few extra lumps of coal. So with his hand on the reversing-wheel he kept an eye on the fire, feeling more and more uneasy about the look of his fireman. The little lamp lighting the water gauge left the footplate in semi-darkness, tinged mauve by the red-hot firebox door. He could not see Pecqueux clearly, but twice he had felt something touching his legs, as though fingers were trying to get hold of them. But it was probably only the clumsiness of a drunken man, for above the noise of the train he could hear his very loud sneering laugh as he was breaking up his coal with exaggerated blows of the hammer and sparring about with the shovel. He opened the door every minute and threw absurd amounts of fuel on to the grate.

'That'll do!' shouted Jacques.

The other pretended not to understand and went on throwing in one shovelful after another. When the driver caught hold of his arm he wheeled round menacingly, at last finding the pretext for a showdown he had been seeking as his drunken rage increased.

'Take your hands off me or I'll bash you one! I like going fast, I do!'

The train was now running at full speed along the level from Bolbec to Motteville. It was to go non-stop to Paris except for scheduled halts for water. The huge mass, eighteen trucks chock full of human cattle, was careering across the black countryside with a ceaseless roar. These men being carted off to the slaughter were singing, singing their heads off, making such a din that it drowned the noise of the wheels.

Jacques kicked the firebox door to and then, operating the injector and still keeping his temper, he said:

'Too much fire . . . Go to sleep if you're tight!'

Pecqueux promptly opened it again, determined to put some more coal in as though he wanted to blow up the engine. This was open defiance, orders disregarded in an outburst of rage now quite heedless of all these human lives. When Jacques leaned forward to lower the rod of the ashpan himself so as at any rate to lessen the draught, his fireman suddenly caught him round the body and tried to push him backwards and with a violent heave throw him on to the line.

'You swine, so that was it? You'd say I fell off, wouldn't you, you artful bastard!'

He had saved himself by catching hold of one side of the tender, and they slipped down together and the struggle continued on the little sheet-iron bridge which was violently dancing about. With clenched teeth and never a word they each wrestled to pitch the other one out through the narrow opening which had only one rail across. But it was extremely awkward. The engine was rushing on, eating up the distance, Barentin was passed, the train plunged into the Malaunay tunnel and still they were in a clinch, rolling about in the coal, banging their heads against the water-tank and avoiding the red-hot firebox door, which burned their legs each time they stretched them out.

For a moment Jacques thought that if he could get up he would shut off steam and whistle for help to get rid of this lunatic, crazy with drink and jealousy. But being the smaller of the two he was getting weaker and felt he would never find strength to throw him; for he was already beaten, and terror of the fall seemed to be blowing through his hair. As he was making one desperate effort, groping with his hand, the other man understood, and stiffening his back pulled himself up and lifted Jacques like a child.

'Oh, so you want to stop, do you ... You've taken my woman ... Well, now you're for it!'

The engine tore on and on and the train thundered out of the tunnel, racing on across the empty, black country. Malaunay station was rushed through at such a whirlwind speed that the deputy stationmaster, who was standing on the platform, did not even see the two men fighting to the death as they hurtled past.

With a final heave Pecqueux threw Jacques; and he, feeling nothing behind him, frantically clung to his neck, and so tightly that he dragged Pecqueux with him. Two terrible screams mingled and faded away. The two men, who for so long had lived together like brothers, fell together and were sucked under the wheels by the very speed and hacked to pieces, locked together in that frightful embrace. They were found headless and without feet, two bloody trunks still crushing each other to death.

Now out of control, the engine tore on and on. At last the restive, temperamental creature could give full rein to her youthful high spirits, like a still-untamed steed that had escaped from its trainer's hands and was galloping off across country. The boiler was full of water, the newly stoked furnace was white-hot, and for the first half-hour pressure went up wildly and the speed became terrifying. The front guard had presumably succumbed to exhaustion and gone to sleep. The soldiers, whose drunkenness was getting worse through their being so tightly packed, suddenly saw the funny side of this mad race and sang louder than ever. They went through Maromme like a rocket. No more whistling before signals or through stations, just the all-out gallop of an animal charging head

365

down and silent between obstacles. The engine ran on and on as though lashed to madness by the strident sound of her own breath.

They should have taken water at Rouen, and the station was transfixed with horror when this mad train rushed past in a whirlwind of smoke and flame, the engine without driver or fireman and cattle-trucks full of troops yelling patriotic songs. They were off to war and this was to get them sooner to the banks of the Rhine. Railwaymen gasped and waved their arms. Suddenly there was one general cry: that driverless train would never get clear through Sotteville station, which was always blocked by shunting operations and cluttered up with vehicles and engines like all large depots. They rushed to send a warning by telegraph. A goods train standing on the line there could, as it happened, be backed into a shed just in time, for the roar of the escaping monster could already be heard in the distance. It had charged through the two tunnels on either side of Rouen and was approaching at a furious pace, like some prodigious, irresistible force that nothing could now stop. It scorched through the station at Sotteville, finding its way unscathed through the obstacles, and plunged into the night again, where its roar gradually died away.

By now all the telegraph bells along the line were ringing and hearts were beating fast as the news came through about the ghost train seen going through Rouen and Sotteville. It made you shake with fright; an express running ahead was bound to be caught up with. But the train, like a wild boar in the forest, held to its course, heedless of red lights and detonators. At Oissel it almost smashed into a light engine, it terrified Pont-de-l'Arche, for its speed showed no sign of slackening. Yet again it vanished, on and on into the darkness, whither no one knew.

What did the victims matter that the machine destroyed on its way? Wasn't it bound for the future, heedless of spilt blood? With no human hand to guide it through the night, it roared on and on, a blind and deaf beast let loose amid death and destruction, laden with cannon-fodder, these soldiers already silly with fatigue, drunk and bawling.

THE PENGUIN CLASSICS

A Selection

Lautréamont
MALDOROR
Translated by Paul Knight

Aristophanes
THE KNIGHTS, PEACE, THE BIRDS, THE ASSEMBLY WOMEN, WEALTH
Translated by David Barrett and Alan H. Sommerstein

Cicero
LETTERS TO ATTICUS
Translated by D. R. Shackleton Bailey

Daudet
LETTERS FROM MY WINDMILL
Translated by Frederick Davies and illustrated by Edward Ardizzone

Cicero
LETTERS TO HIS FRIENDS
(in two volumes)
Translated by D. R. Shackleton Bailey

FIVE ITALIAN RENAISSANCE COMEDIES
Edited by Bruce Penman

Martial
THE EPIGRAMS
Translated by James Michie